THE DEMON AND
THE PHOENIX
- I -

I0665722

THE
DEMON LORD
OF
CALIFORNIA

BENNU BRIGHT

Book cover & phoenix bird logo branding by Get Covers
Triple wing spiral clock illustration by Lara Yokoshima
Breese & Dasheel phoenix bird illustrations by APHOTICMOTH
Calico's family tree chart by Deranged Doctor Design

Bennu Bright: Romantic Fantasy Branding Logos.

Content Placard

- Robbery and assault, brief mention of guns / gun violence

- Mentioned sexual harassment / assault

- Mental abuse from a parent

- Fire, burning, burning alive (phoenix and fire elementals)

- Possibly implied prostitution, and suicide (by fire from phoenix)

- Some sexual innuendos

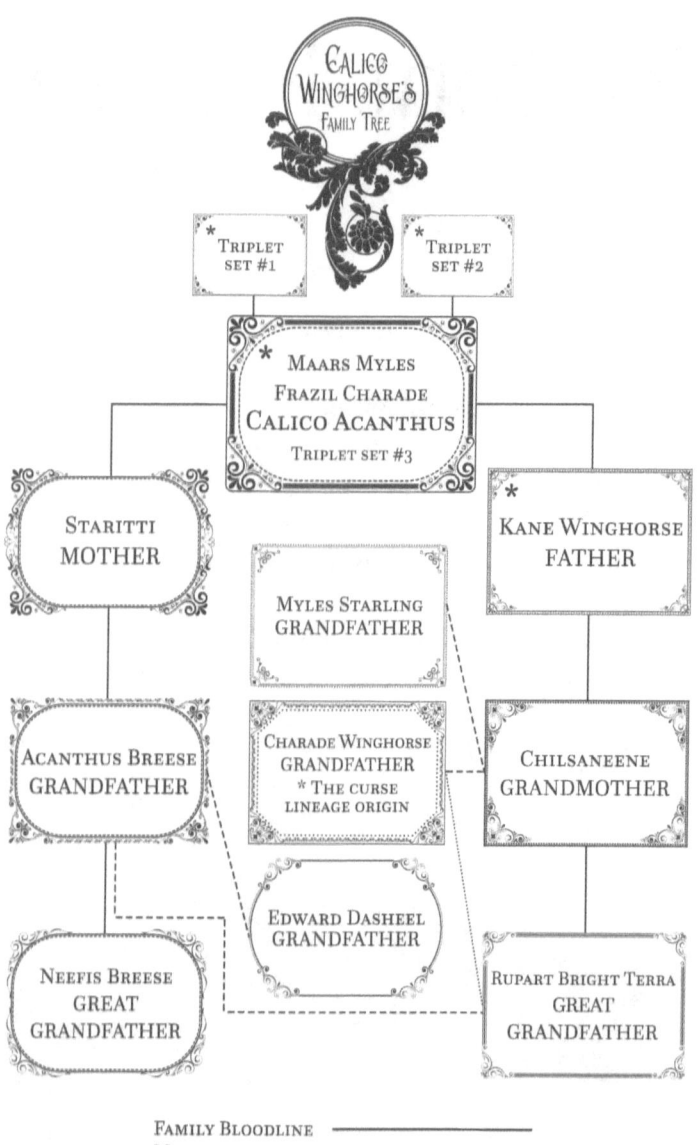

CALICO WINGHORSE'S FAMILY TREE

TRIPLET SET #1

TRIPLET SET #2

* MAARS MYLES
FRAZIL CHARADE
CALICO ACANTHUS
TRIPLET SET #3

STARITTI
MOTHER

* KANE WINGHORSE
FATHER

MYLES STARLING
GRANDFATHER

ACANTHUS BREESE
GRANDFATHER

CHARADE WINGHORSE
GRANDFATHER
* THE CURSE
LINEAGE ORIGIN

CHILSANEENE
GRANDMOTHER

EDWARD DASHEEL
GRANDFATHER

NEEFIS BREESE
GREAT
GRANDFATHER

RUPART BRIGHT TERRA
GREAT
GRANDFATHER

FAMILY BLOODLINE ————————
MARRIAGES — — — — — — — — —
ESTRANGED RELATIONSHIP ················

Chapter 1

Agustin Chavez de la Cruz

He was the Demon Lord of California, dammit. His California citizens counted on him for guidance and protection. But here he sat in a stuffy, dark, and empty theater. With peeling wallpaper. Watching the most god-awful vaudeville try outs.

The matinee had been half-price due to the open casting call, so he'd ducked inside to seek some relative quiet. Agustin had needed a place to think. To reflect upon the life choices he'd made—as well as ponder future obligations to the angelic-run Infinity Corporation.

Obligations he never wanted to begin with.

And of a more immediate concern, to digest that questionable lunch from an even more questionable eatery. Holding a fist against the fading heartburn, he quietly belched. Thankfully, at his earlier distress, the mundane human waitress had taken pity on him by offering water with a sprinkle of baking soda. He'd tipped her generously.

Fidgeting in a chair too small for his height, Agustin didn't want to dwell on why the floor was sticky beneath his polished oxfords. He really didn't, for the theater was vaudeville by day, and burlesque shows by night. He made a mental note to burn his shoes before entering his home.

He'd chosen front row seating at stage left because it was the only place suitable for his long legs. Here in the brighter shadows, he stood out like a peacock amongst plucked chickens. His towering height and perfectly pressed nobleman's attire were to blame for that. His black braids, brown skin, upside-down golden triangle earrings, and heterochromatic eyes didn't help matters.

The mundane humans—those who were unaware of the clandestine paranormal world around them—lined up at the stairs of stage right, waiting for their turn to perform. They speared him with nervous glances. Unfortunately, Agustin had wrecked two acts already; they couldn't handle his scrutiny. While he felt guilty over that, he reminded himself actors couldn't let distractions ruin a show.

The exact reason why he was at this matinee had to do with Etney. His Infinity Corporation second-in-command did her job too well. She'd rallied their Infinity 8 team, as well as his entire household staff.

They'd insisted he'd been working himself too hard when that wasn't the case at all. They'd informed him it'd be too much of a temptation to think of work if he visited his usual haunts. So he'd been temporarily barred from seeking paranormal places to loiter.

He'd been mob-escorted—with Etney in the lead—out to the motorcar. They'd ordered him to telepathically shut out the chaotic minds of every San Francisco resident for six hours and relax. Then, he was chauffeured into the heart of the city and abandoned.

He'd been kicked out of his own damn mansion before he'd realized it.

Agustin grumbled.

Corporation duties always caused his beloved California work to suffer. There were inter-state trade agreements and various contracts stacked on his desk, waiting for approval. Laws to enforce to safeguard his California citizens. Meetings to attend that would enhance their well-being and quality of life. Reports to read.

Not to mention he was still working to merge his offices with the court of the Demon Queen of the United States—with permission from the Demon Queen of Mexico, of course. The mundane humans only made California a state fifty years ago. And it'd taken this long to convince Her Mexico Majesty the unification would be a smart move for their paranormal kind.

However, those duties paled in comparison to what Harper expected out of him. Infinity Corporation was more than another duty of his dual birthright. It was a prison. One that demanded his soul.

Agustin grimaced.

Protect the humans from the Amaranth Empire's harvests at all costs.

At all costs...

That was Harper's motto. The Corporation's motto. And the pledge of all earthbound angels employed by IC. It was a maxim drummed into Agustin's head since he'd been a small boy. One he'd been ordered to verbally recite, three times in a row, at the start and end of his daily lessons.

Damnation, Agustin, Harper would berate during his daily childhood lectures. *The Lady California was too lenient with you. I knew I should've removed you from her care sooner. If you love me, if you love humanity, do as you're told. Why can't you do as you're told?*

It was suddenly difficult to breathe. His heart was pounding too fast and double vision cascaded. Agustin felt like he was coming out of his own skin, then running away from it. The numbness swallowed him whole, and cold sweat gathered.

His angelic birthright had molded him into nothing but a brainless automaton, bent this way and that at Harper's whim. An object without a will or voice.

Think about something else, dammit. Anything but Harper.

In the low, shadowed light of the electric wall sconces, Agustin hurried to consult his fancy new wristwatch on a shaking wrist. It was a gift from his son away at university.

His son. *His son his son his son.* Agustin was finally able to take a single, even breath.

It was 3 p.m. The day was half over. He might survive his forced recess after all. But he had to get out. He had to move. Had to keep moving and get Harper out of his head. He clenched his fists to quell his upset.

His feet wouldn't yet obey.

He winced when the miniature dogs on stage all started barking on command. As much as he loved dogs, the constant, high-pitched cries echoing off the gilded, high ceiling had him shrinking down in his squeaking chair.

Vaudeville was too pedestrian for his taste. It reminded him of what Harper forbade him to have. Happiness. Joy. A family of his own. *A life of his own.*

A jarring sensation blossomed in his heart. It had him doubling over. Not in pain, more like...a brilliant flash of such crystal clear clarity, he was dumbfounded at its presence.

Why? Why *couldn't* he have the life he wanted?

Where this instant realization originated from, he didn't know. His powers didn't work this way. Whatever it was, from where ever it had emerged, it had liberated his mind from the dark loop of an endless burden. Allowed him to break free of Harper's subjugation.

Agustin had put in his time to the Corporation. He'd given up everything. His dignity. His self-respect. His life. The woman he loved. As well as the woman who'd willingly bore him the heir Harper demanded.

No woman or man Agustin had chosen had ever been good enough for Harper.

Agustin swallowed a cry, and trembled.

He'd been brainwashed into giving up his son.

His son, who was now a young man. He'd missed out on Ganymede's life. Decades he would never get back. Agustin clutched at his wristwatch.

Harper had always demanded more of him, even when there was nothing left. And Agustin had dutifully obeyed.

How? How had he been so blind until now?

There were other angels among Harper's ranks who were staunchly dedicated to IC's unwavering cause. They were just as capable of running the business and keeping the humans safe—and ever willing to be Harper's shiny new puppet-in-command.

Heart pounding in his chest, Agustin took a moment to let that sink in. Perspiration dampened the fine leather of his gloves.

What Harper thought, of him, suddenly, strangely, didn't matter anymore.

He was going to quit the Corporation.

Quit Harper.

And finally live.

Chapter 2

Observing Joy

AGUSTIN LET OUT A little laugh. Of joy. Of relief. The emotions flooded outward, their soothing tendrils sluicing through his soul. He felt lighter. More at ease and eager to explore this newfound revelation of freedom.

What he would say in his resignation letter formed in his mind. His hands shook with excitement now at the thought of putting pen to paper. Of handing it to Harper personally.

From the other side of the theater, sharp, disruptive movement caught Agustin's attention. A man, vibrant with paranormal—nym—energies, emerged from the right side stage door. This man was engaged in animated conversation with the human beside him.

Agustin reeled. His paranormal vision had never seen such wonderful, although chaotic energies. Slowly swirling about its host, yet also so fractured and jagged in beautiful shades of white, ivory, and beige with faint hints of blue.

While still so very beautiful, there was something wrong with that energy signature. Like it was broken or disrupted somehow.

Agustin's telepathic abilities hungrily soaked up discarded thought-threads from the pair. But the remnants from this exchange weren't in English. Or any other language his hyper-polyglot brain could interpret.

Yes, there were root words of other languages he could identify. But those words were cut in half. Stitched together with another word from a completely different language he did, or did not know. Some of these cleaved words blended better than others, but it still made an all new comprehensive language he didn't understand.

Both men appeared to be of the working class. Although the nym's suit was of better quality, the human wore the more contemporary style. The nym clutched at his top hat along with a flimsy-looking box.

The noise and barking onstage blotted out their voices. But Agustin continued to savor the happy thought-threads pouring out of them both. Sampling another's contentment—a fellow paranormal's contentment—temporarily consoled his own that was forever limping along.

Agustin was breaking his promise to Etney and his household staff. But when attraction and feelings were involved, it wasn't as easy to mute psychic abilities that had been switched on during his time in the womb.

Attraction? Agustin acknowledged the heated flush that invaded his body. His fellow nym was adorable. Wholesome in a sense, although he wasn't sure where that observation came from.

Maybe it was the way the paranormal man moved. Proper, yet bubbly. Carrying himself somewhat stiff. Maybe a little awkward, with his arms up and elbows out. The tailcoat of his jacket brushing that trim backside with each step. As if he wasn't quite comfortable in his overly thin human disguise, but embraced it all the same.

Nyms were often in human spaces, although hidden from the mundane world. Many, like himself, wore spells to conceal their most frightening and fantastic attributes. Or could shape-shift. Agustin wondered what ability allowed his fellow nym to hide himself.

Besides sporting a nice black jacket, the nym man wore a matching silk scarf tied neatly around his head. A modest bun of dark hair hid beneath the knot at the nape of his neck. He continued to balance that thin box he carried along with his top hat.

The two men parted, and the human retreated backstage. The nym smiled and waved at the theater management seated in front of center stage. They exchanged brief pleasantries, as well as the box of...Agustin craned his head to see. Cupcakes topped with brightly colored frosting. The treats were gladly accepted.

Gifts given, the nym moved on. Agustin chuckled at the endearing quality of this man's gait—slightly march-bouncing up the middle aisle. He chose a row far away from the managers, and the performer's queue, and sat down.

Agustin wanted to go over. But as usual, would his height and heterochromatic eyes be too intimidating? Even to a nym? Especially to a nym who seemed so adorably wholesome? Agustin suddenly wished that in weaving his own concealment spells, he'd added the guise of matching-colored eyes.

When the dogs stopped barking and scurried off the stage, the nym man jumped up into a standing ovation and clapped wildly in support. Then did the same for the next two acts.

Agustin found himself smiling at the carefree nature of the moment itself. Of this fellow nym finding joy in the smallest of things. It shocked Agustin to realize he was still sitting here, in the theater. Not watching the tryouts, but the nym who was the only other spectator in the audience. One who was being sincerely supportive and kind to complete strangers—to these mundane humans, at that.

Agustin felt lured. Sunk. Captured. Thoroughly intrigued.

By this time, romantic piano and flute tunes echoed throughout the auditorium. A quick glance at the owner and managers showed they had handkerchiefs at teary eyes with one hand, and half-eaten cupcakes in the other.

Agustin hadn't realized he'd gotten up and strolled over to the nym. In his eagerness, he realized he'd been looming a little too close, and backed up a bit.

"Hello," Agustin said, getting his voice to work. "Is this seat taken?" That was a good start. He wasn't so rusty in a courting attempt after all. He stopped. Courting? Was that what he was doing?

Sky-blue eyes blinked up at him in question. Then widened in surprise. The genuine smile melted Agustin's heart.

"Gus!" the man exclaimed in shockingly deep, guttural tones. "Where have you been?"

Chapter 3

The One Who Got Away

"Alas, I am all out of cupcakes," the man told Agustin. "If I had known you would be here, I would have reserved you one. With sprinkles. And butterscotch syrup. Please, sit. Join me."

Agustin sunk down into the adjacent seat. Barely realizing he did so. Because butterscotch. Because that...that voice.

There was a lot to comprehend in those vocal notes. First, a British accent. The Queen's English, or at least of the upper class. Every note articulated into something so excitingly deep and guttural for such a delicate and adorable package. Such deliciously earthy inflections. So husky—no—sensuously smoky.

What could this nym be? Another demon? An incubus or imp maybe? Perhaps, from that grating vocal inflection. Although, he'd never heard of incubi or imps having such unique voices.

"Do you come here often?" As soon as the words were out of Agustin's mouth, he wanted to face-palm himself. What a stupid and cheap opening. That tawdry suggestion was not what he'd intended.

"I make weekly deliveries here."

Agustin didn't mind being crowded into these small theater seats. Especially if he could sit here with this man. This spontaneity was something he would've done in his university days.

Now, it was so out of his character. He was too mature and too sophisticated for this avenue of simple joy. Too busy. He had work to do—it was going to take a lot of nerve to finally tell Harper to stay out of his life, once and for all.

"Gus?"

Agustin was captivated by those incredibly blue eyes. Like a warm and cozy spotlight in the dim auditorium.

Agustin's half-smile twisted. "So you do know who I am."

"Of course I do!"

"And here I was hoping I'd go unrecognized. But that's forward, don't you think? Addressing me in such a familiar manner? You're cute, so I'll allow it."

Agustin figured this was Etney's doing. She was always trying to introduce him to new sweethearts. He was always dodging them—until now.

"Even after all this time," that incredibly unusual voice said. "I must work on my social skills. I do wish to make this work between us."

Etney had set this up. Agustin grinned. "What did you have in mind?"

"Well," the man placed a finger to his cheek in thought. "A picnic in the park. A trip to the Conservatory of Flowers. We have not been there in over a hundred years."

The faint scents of fresh baked bread, sugar, vanilla, and traces of smoke drifted as the man gestured with the excitement of planning. This cupcake man. Such amazing eyes of summer sky blue. He wondered where Etney had found him.

Agustin bit his cheek and narrowed his eyes with acute curiosity and amusement. The Conservatory only opened some twenty years ago. However, a picnic in the park sounded like perfection.

"How much did Etney pay you to pretend to know me?" She'd changed her tactics, for sure.

There was a gasp. And a confused glare. That was an unusual reaction.

Agustin tried again. "I'll double it if you have dinner with me. Tonight, if you don't have plans."

That brought a fierce glare and razor-sharp indignation. "Gus, have you misplaced your marbles?"

"My what marbles? Uh, no. The question was a serious one."

"You insult me, then?"

"I'd pay your estimated worth—"

The man gasped again and jumped to his feet. He sputtered. Choked. Speared him with more outrage. "Surrender your glove, sir!"

"W-what?"

"Your glove. Now."

Confused, Agustin pulled the covering off his right hand, revealing the rings on each finger. He was curious when the rent boy didn't even pause to marvel at the glitter. Handing the glove over, Agustin sucked in a breath and realized he'd been resoundingly slapped with it.

"Now," the rent boy said, hands on his hips. "Are you going to apologize for this most bizarre and offensive behavior, or do I need to slap you again to save my honor?"

Was this really happening?

There was a loud bang from the stage. Agustin glanced towards the disturbance. When his attention returned to the man before him, Agustin startled.

There was a massive shift in the man's expression and manner. High doses of horror stepped down into curiosity. And finally, timid bashfulness diluted some of that horror.

Agustin found the cascade of emotions intriguing. Especially since the nym's interactions with the human staff had been verbal and robust.

Agustin was stared at. In question. In surprise. The man opened his mouth to speak, but silenced himself with a palm-slap.

Yet another curious change of events.

Composed, the man's fingers steepled, then fluttered with obvious nerves before pointing to the adjacent chair.

Agustin furrowed his brows. "Of course you may sit." He figured the man had come to his senses over his odd behavior, and was too embarrassed to speak.

The man stuck out a hand. When Agustin took it, it was pumped vigorously and with great enthusiasm. Parting, the man now hesitated. He poised to speak with a friendly vigor before going silent again. He bit his lip and flushed.

The blush was too cute. Much to Agustin's surprise, the man spoke now, but this time it was by use of his hands. With fingers folded and his thumb sticking out, he made small, circular motions at his jawline a few times in quick succession, then pointed toward the uniqueness of Agustin's eyes.

Sign Language.

This was getting more interesting by the moment. He wished Sign was among the many languages he already knew. It just went to show that no matter how much he learned or prepared himself, there would always be something he didn't know. And suddenly, he wished to know it.

While not understanding the first gesture, the inquiry over his one gold eye and one blue eye was clear.

"Yes," Agustin replied, although he wasn't sure why he spoke in hushed tones. There was enough noise in the hall to blot out any conversation. "My eyes are quite unique. You're not put off by them?"

The man shook his head indicating a no. It was another bashful response. "H-hello," came the timid reply, his fingers drumming nervously on his knees. "I-I am Mr. Scrivens."

Scrivens. The rent boy—no, the cupcake man had a name. Agustin hadn't realized how much he'd missed that grating, earthy voice.

Another loud bang from the stage. Irritated, Agustin glanced over. When he turned back, there was only an empty seat. He searched further along the row. Make that rows. His new acquaintance was hot-footing it to the main exit doors.

Damn, Scrivens was fast. And nimble.

"Wait!" Agustin called, his voice drowned out among the performers. "Please." He stumbled through the bulky-seated row, hitting his knees against the open seats every few steps before pausing to flip them up out of his way.

By the time he made it to the lobby, the cupcake man was gone. With the imported leather glove Etney had given him for his birthday last year.

Chapter 4

The Demotion

AGUSTIN CONSIDERED TURNING AROUND and asking the management about their mysterious cupcake man. Even if just to get that glove back. Grease a few palms with cash if need be. But that would be awkward. He wasn't Lord California for nothing. He had his own resources.

He gripped his top hat and exited the theater, all the while keeping an eye out for his sweet baker.

The sun's rays peeked through scattered rain clouds. Top hat brought low over mismatched eyes, Agustin squared his shoulders and hoped he wouldn't be waylaid by any of his paranormal citizens. Except for Mr. Scrivens.

Agustin stepped off the curb, narrowly missing a fresh pile of horse dung. He pressed a handkerchief to his nose, cursing the stench. The odors of horse, oil, and gas followed, bleeding right through the expensive linen fibers.

He tolerated the vivacious pace San Francisco offered, with its views of the sea, the bay, and its steep hills. Though the noise, hustle—and smells—grated on his temper. He hoped the city's stink wasn't a permanent cling. His valet would accuse him of wallowing in the gutters as revenge for being nagged to take time off.

Dodging equine taxis and motorcars alongside the humans, he ignored their open-mouthed gawking. While magic concealed the frightening brilliance of his true demonic-angelic self, he refused to hide his eye color or height.

Agustin knew he better concentrate on where he was going. He didn't want to trip and end up crushed under wheel or hoof. Or both. His son would be very upset at having to embrace the mantle of California before he could even graduate university. So Agustin braced himself and dodged some more, wincing at the repetitive clang of trolley bells.

The tight grip on his telepathy, and his forced intermission was taking a toll. He tried to recapture the excitement and joy he'd experienced in the theater. But it escaped his grasp. Agustin lowered the linen square and tucked it away. The visible puff of his melancholy drifted to join the intermediate bands of rolling fog.

He deliberately ignored the plain gold band on his pinky. Instead, glancing at the communication ring on his right index finger—the one with the oval cut ruby. The one assigned to Etney. The tension strangling him wasn't so tight now.

Agustin was so tempted to call her. Tell her he finally fell for one of her match-making schemes. Maybe gloat over his newfound decision to quit IC and start a new life. Inform her she was promoted to head their Infinity 8 team.

His feet slowed.

She'd laugh in his face at the job offer, and congratulate him at the same time.

Agustin felt a smirk creep onto his lips.

He'd threaten to dock her pay.

She'd quip that he was no longer her boss, but she still had unlimited access to his check book.

And the banter with his best friend would go on.

Gods love her. Etney was his rock, his grounding sanity in all things Infinity Corporation. Even if she drove him batty and often overstepped her bounds.

Agustin paused on the sidewalk. He glanced at his wristwatch again, then did a double take. 3:19? Oh, gods and demons, would this day never end? There were three more hours of scheduled merriment before the motorcar arrived to collect him. He was fooling himself. He wouldn't survive after all.

But that was the old Agustin. What could the new Agustin marvel over until Ramirez picked him up? A leisurely carriage ride through Golden Gate Park to admire the gardens. That was it.

A presence invaded his personal space, yanking him back into the mundane cacophony of Market Street. "My pardon, Lord California. Please, I must have a word with you."

California. His birthright spoken aloud revealed that whoever addressed him was of paranormal origin. And they dared to pull on his coat sleeve.

Like they were family.

"Yes," Agustin answered. "I am California." He withdrew his arm and held himself rigid. Even with the jarring distraction, he was too well practiced to let this disrupt his telepathic closure. He also noted his wallet's weight still tucked into his inner vest pocket.

Beneath a wide-brimmed rattan hat, the man who addressed him wore a gauzy black hood that completely concealed his face. Layers of white translucent scarves anchored into the hat brim billowed from the bustle of traffic, and further hid his face. The sharp, cream-colored suit with matching shoes had not picked up a trace of grime.

Paranormal indeed. Perhaps a spell kept him tidy. Agustin scanned the passing crowd of mundanes. As suspected, all eyes remained upon his height.

Some sort of magic concealed his visitor. This nym man was about six feet; Agustin took the advantage of being at least six inches taller, so he loomed a little as he stared.

He often alarmed even the most hardened of demons, but this man's body language conveyed no alarm whatsoever. Just like Mr. Scrivens, the cupcake man. Curious. Was he losing his aura of intimidation?

A whinny. The clip-clop of hooves and the rattle of a wagon. Agustin knew the sounds were as mundane as the humans that surrounded them. Still, he felt compelled to look up.

It was him. The cupcake cutie bundled up in rain gear. Driving a pony cart. The glittering gold lettering painted on the side of the wooden walls read *Scrivens Bakery, Redwood City, California.* An answer wrapped joyously in pastry paper. Agustin lunged forward, ready to run in pursuit.

The stranger in white blocked his chase. A gentle laugh arose. "You'll see Mr. Scrivens again. Soon."

Agustin frowned. The candidates Etney sent his way were mostly of the upper class—that was their deal when he realized he couldn't stop the match-making. Sometimes, not very often, they were rent folk.

Was this the cupcake man's pimp? Here to shake him down for money? As much disgust and offense as he felt right now, he could understand why someone as sweet and attractive as Mr. Scrivens would be closely guarded.

A distressed chuckle, followed by a fake cough. "Good afternoon." The stranger bowed slightly. "I'm *not* a pimp. And no, Mr. Scrivens is *not* a rent boy."

Horrified and furious, Agustin further closed off his mind. He rarely bothered to lock off his own thoughts. The other telepaths in this region weren't strong enough to get through the basic blocks of someone of his caliber.

"My name is Mr. Triptych. I'm IC's new regional manager for the San Francisco Peninsula. HQ said you'd be around here today."

Infin—? Ugh. He had to get his mind back on business. Mr. Scrivens forgotten, Agustin's jaw tightened and his eyes narrowed into lines thinner than his valet's sewing threads. Had Etney been going behind his back? Reporting to headquarters with her ridiculous concerns that he was overworking himself?

"My pardon, Mr. Triptych," Agustin corrected in a polite, steely tone. "*I* am the peninsula's regional manager." No, he had been. Just like he was resigning as heir to the Corporation. He still needed to inform Harper of his decision before alerting various employees, though.

Triptych opened his carry case and offered an envelope. "Here. This'll explain things."

Flipping it over, Agustin inspected the wax seal. It was Harper's official crest as head of Infinity Corporation: white wings above the glowing blue infinity symbol.

Agustin studied Triptych's tall grace. And dismissed the instincts screaming at him. Triptych shouldn't feel familiar. He didn't know this man. He'd never seen him before, until now. Well, seen was merely an expression, as the veils concealed even the faintest view.

Agustin broke the wax seal and removed the missive. There was no proper form of address beneath the glittering, magical letterhead. Just Harper's familiar hurried scrawl and smeared ink, as usual. The letterhead only glowed and came to life like that when the script was penned, or dictated, directly from Harper, so he had to accept this as legit. He skimmed the words:

A—

Mr. Pascal Triptych is Infinity Corporation's newest liaison. He is now the district overseer on the Peninsula.

You and your Infinity 8 team now report to <u>him</u>. He will present your new assignment. <u>Do not put up a fuss</u>.

—H

Demoted.

He'd been demoted through a dammed intermediary.

Agustin's jaw clenched further as he pocketed the letter. The slashes beneath the words were another long-suffered and familiar touch.

Harper had always provided his duties directly. It was the one courtesy, the only courtesy the head of Infinity Corporation had ever bothered to extend to his son and heir. Apparently, Harper couldn't even bother to do that anymore.

Agustin took that second to clear the dark, fuzzy anger. He wasn't surprised it had gone down this way. Why did this constant hurt still have such fresh venom? Especially since he'd stopped caring.

Okay. He'd play along. No sense alerting Harper before he could personally hand in his resignation. Striving for calm, Agustin asked, "What qualifies you to relieve me of my liaison position?"

Triptych pointed to the envelope. "You were advised not to put up a fuss."

"You read a letter addressed to me?"

The hat shook a too easy no. "I was present when Mr. Harper scripted it. He's assigned you a most important task. One that'll take up all your time, so he's cleared your calendar, so to speak."

Agustin steeled the anger that further threatened to seep inside.

Triptych wiggled the cream-colored satchel in his possession. "Is there someplace where we can go and talk? I'll spring for a cup of coffee. A glass of port? Some fancy cheese? Nooo. Chocolate cake or butterscotch pudding, right?"

Agustin glared, studying the man who now possessed one of his many jobs—ex-jobs. And knew his weakness for sweets. Chocolate cake and butterscotch pudding were his favorites. Damn Harper for leaking personal information.

Agustin tempered most of the rage out of his question. "Is this your first time working for IC?" Triptych wasn't a green recruit. Harper wouldn't place the inexperienced in such an important position. Still, Agustin was compelled to dig for some clues of his own.

"I'm no bright-eyed newbie, if that's what you're asking." Beneath the heavy layers of gauzy veils, Agustin knew Triptych smiled wide. It was in the tone.

Agustin tapped a finger against his crossed arms. He'd traveled abroad for several decades after graduating from The Royal and Pontifical University of Mexico, and he couldn't place Triptych's strange slang and dialect. It took alien liberties with the English language, felt lazy and too intimate, and matched nothing currently spoken.

As if it didn't even exist.

More humans passed by in their working-class clothing. The garments were like rags compared to Triptych's glowing, magicked finery. Even the handful of middle and upper-class humans in their colorful, modern attire hurrying past fail to shine. This mundane crowd looked right through Triptych, but Agustin suffered their stares for talking to himself.

"Where are you from?" Agustin asked before nodding to a pair of ladies sporting ostrich-feathered hats. The women grasped each other's forearms, and their long skirts rustled as they rushed past. "I haven't seen you at ICHQ before."

Triptych made a noise, seeming to mash his lips together to keep from a raucous laugh. "You don't trust me. Mr. Harper's magical, and tamper-proof letterhead should be trust enough."

Triptych's annoying reminder was correct. Straightening his shoulders, he addressed his new supervisor. "Raynard's."

"Pardon?" Triptych tilted his head, his big, floppy hat following the motion. It made him look like a rather large white bird in flight, lazily changing direction.

"You wanted a place to talk," Agustin clarified. "Raynard's is a private club that does not permit the mundanes."

The hat tilted back the other way in question.

Agustin's eyelid twitched. "The mundanes. Humans without powers. Humans who don't know about us. Raynard's is a haven for our kind."

"Oh? Is it far from here?"

"It's within the city."

Agustin didn't like the suspected unseen grin, and the restrained excitement of that voice beneath those veils. Triptych was playing with him. Everyone knew of Raynard's.

Triptych let out a high pitch whistle, and waved his arm. A horse-drawn taxi rolled to a stop. The driver stared at them both with bored, impatient eyes.

Yes, magic of some sort was afoot from the feel of it. Triptych was indeed talented to cast multiple illusions in so many directions at once.

Triptych's white-gloved hand opened the carriage door for him. "Well? Are you coming? The surprise I planned won't keep forever, you know."

Surprises weren't Agustin's favorite thing. He'd been on the receiving end of them too much in his dealings with Harper. But work was work, no matter the trivial annoyances. He leveled Triptych with a no-nonsense stare before climbing into the horse-drawn taxi.

Agustin prayed he wasn't making a huge mistake by allowing this administrative change to go unchallenged. Now Harper would think he was throwing a tantrum and resigning because of the demotion. So he would follow through with this mission briefing until he could see his father in person in the morning. Harper didn't accept no for an answer. Even from his own son.

It was a battle Agustin wagered to win. Because at stake was his happiness, with a yet unknown someone, who was somewhere, who could be his happily ever after.

Chapter 5

Chocolate and Manipulations

THEIR DRIVER NAVIGATED AROUND the afternoon cacophony of trolley bells and automobile horn honks. Being a fire elemental atop his demonic heritage, Agustin was grateful the cab's sturdy frame and leather-bound walls muted the noise and shielded him from the damp weather.

Triptych seemed in agreement. The new district manager drew the thin curtains shut against the rolling fog before giving his arms a quick rub for warmth.

When they arrived at their destination, they were greeted at the door, both by name, with gushing compliments. The maître d' acted as if he'd known Triptych awhile, asking him of his travels. It proved that the man had been messing with him, and Agustin did his best to keep his temper to a minimum.

They were escorted into one of several private dining suites at the back of the club. In fact, it was the most expensive, boasting access to a private outdoor garden. Agustin tsked. Harper wouldn't pay for such extravagance, so the new liaison had to be buttering him up.

Truer words were never thought. Before they reached the table, Agustin noticed, on the fine linen tablecloth, was an intricately decorated, and expensive chocolate cake. His brows flattened. Oh. Of course.

"Surprise!" Triptych's exclamation was airy and bright. His new boss added to the drama by waving his gloved hands.

Sparing Triptych an exasperated glance, Agustin clenched his jaw as he tried to defuse the anger at Harper's manipulations.

At least there was chocolate.

Manipulations.

Chocolate.

Manipulations.

To heck with it. He had no choice but to accept Harper's third party bribe.

Taking his seat, Agustin tried to ignore what was in front of him. He looked out the windowed walls into the garden instead. Glass French doors opened up to a stone path snaking over green grass. It led to a gazebo covered with flowering vines. Scattered cigarette stands encouraged clients to loiter and smoke. He could still detect a trace of cigar stench from the last patrons. But the scent of chocolate was overpowering, and he grudgingly redirected his attention.

He forgot himself as his eyebrows rose. It was a cake unlike any he had ever seen in his life. It wasn't just the paper-thin chocolate garnishes molded into jagged, dramatic trees that caught the eye. It was the three-dimensional miniature dragon basking atop the cake's surface.

Agustin stared at it. Baffled. At first, he thought it was a cake topper. But it appeared edible, so it had to be made of fondant? Marzipan? Sugar work?

Decorated pastries were always in high demand among the elite, but the artistry of this beast was astonishing. It looked real with textures and faux scales painstakingly scratched into the figure. Whoever created it had a firestorm of imagination and talent. Again, the Corporation wouldn't have paid for this extravagance, so his new supervisor must be swimming in coin.

Triptych's chuckles were small at first, then candid. It jarred Agustin from his musings. So he snapped out the serviette artfully folded into the form of a swan, and spread it over his lap. When he looked up, Triptych was staring at his own plate and the swan serviette on it.

"I'm sorry," the man said. "It's just that this," he pointed to the cloth swan. "is unplanned. But a lovely coincidence backdropping your assignment. Do you like birds? Of course you do."

"The assignment is?" Agustin prompted with impatience. He wanted to go home so he could get started on his resignation letter while it was still fresh in memory, and before it got too late in the evening. There was still Lord California business to address.

California wasn't just a job. It was his beloved heritage. A love willingly given, by caring for the welfare of his citizens. The honor of being California would no longer be doled out in half-measures because of the Corporation.

Before Triptych could answer, a waiter arrived with coffee and cut two large wedges of the cake. Agustin watched the knife slice through the head of the dragon with a bit of effort. The chocolate sponge dipped from the light pressure. The scent of almonds drifted. Marzipan, then? The plated delight set before him displayed the beast's head. Triptych got half the body.

Their server bowed to him, then nodded at Triptych. Triptych handed over a generous wad of bills, and the waiter exited with a grin on his face.

Triptych cleared his throat. Elbows on the table and hands lightly clasped. "My lord, have you heard the rumors?"

Considering his reply, Agustin picked at his dessert. Spearing the sugary snout with his fork, he shoved it into his mouth. Then let it melt around his tongue. Oh gods, did he need this. As the cake and frosting made its way through his system, his mood elevated. Just a little.

Sifting through all the gossip that passed by his breakfast table, Agustin settled on the one most bantered about. "So I'm to bring in the mongrel triplets who recently moved to the area."

Triptych lifted his palm to signal a correction. "Where I'm from, we prefer the term mixed-bloods now. Well, mixed-race. Terminology changes so quickly." From his satchel, Triptych plunked down a bundle of file folders. "Now," his new ex-boss said. "The brothers we're dealing with are phoenix."

Agustin shoveled in more cake to avoid a surly response. Phoenix were a secretive, unfriendly bunch and their united forges had no love for the Corporation. This assignment should be of high interest to Etney though, since she was of the Dasheel Forge line. But more likely, she'd be no help at all.

"Lord Chavez?" Triptych asked, trying to gain his attention.

"Lord California," Agustin corrected, gathering up a double scoop of cake. "I'm listening."

Triptych's hat tilted again, and this time he appeared taken aback. "Oh, my apologies."

Agustin waved his empty fork in dismissal, not giving it a second thought.

"Um, uh." Triptych sorted through the files. "The brothers are a smattering of other races as well, but they are primarily phoenix. Our focus is on the youngest triplet calling himself Acanthus Scrivens. His real name is Calico Winghorse."

Agustin's fork clattered. *Scrivens.* Could he hope...? Well, he did have a one in three chance.

Winghorse. Hmm. The surname was vaguely familiar, but he couldn't place it right now. He'd try to remember to consult the books in his private library—if he had a moment to do so.

Triptych reached for his coffee; Agustin broke from his thoughts to watch. But the man only partially lifted the veils of his wide-brimmed rattan hat, and sipped from behind them. Not even showing his chin as he pulled at that gauzy black hood that shielded his face. It made Agustin all the more curious.

He ruled out vampire. Harper banned vampires from IC, even in a liaison capacity. Angels did not tolerate humans being a food source.

He sensed Triptych was still smiling behind those veils, as if this were all a game to him. Defying the wishes of his household, and because it was official business, Agustin summoned up a tentative telepathic ear in the man's direction. That proved a dead end. Which meant Triptych had extensive training to block someone of his caliber. Or maybe it was because of his headache. Chocolate was a near cure-all.

"Go on." Agustin finished his slice and helped himself to a second piece, even though he knew he shouldn't. The cake was spongy and moist; the chocolate wasn't overpowering or heavy like bricks in his belly.

Raynard must have hired new confectioners since his last visit. He'd have to send his chef here to purchase cakes or collect the recipe. His diet would be consisting of a lot of this treat in the next several weeks.

Triptych took another sip of his coffee before arranging his veils and hood back into place. "Calico controls a portal—"

"Portals are a dime a dozen," Agustin said dismissively.

"This isn't any portal," Triptych stressed. "Calico's godhood gives him absolute control over space and time—well, because he is the God of Space and Time."

The fork stopped halfway to Agustin's mouth. "Triplet deities? Absolute control? Without any lengthy preparations or meditations? Are we talking about wayfaring gods here? Oh hell, they're phoenix gods?"

Agustin considered ordering a port to go along with his dessert. Chocolate was a barrier against bad news and dashed dreams. Was Harper preparing to stick his nose into phoenix business? Merely being related to Harper would cause him centuries of turmoil, no matter if he cut ties with IC or not.

His stomach soured. Would he ever escape IC's leash?

"No, they're not phoenix gods," Triptych corrected. "Although they are descended from a line of gods. Only Calico's a god. Luck of the birthright lottery, that one. And yes. Calico can open and close his portal at will."

Agustin mashed a bit of the cake under his fork. Trying to find joy in the little block of frosting and the dark, spongy mass that stuck to the tines. "So what am I supposed to do with this god?"

"You're to take full control, and ownership, of Calico's inter-dimensional gate. For the Corporation."

Of course. No wonder Harper was so focused on this portal. IC's sole mission was to guard Earth. Specifically from the otherworldly Amaranth Empire—

That captured Agustin's attention. "Have the Amaranth broken through any of the protection wards?"

"There's been tampering with the protective shields over England," Triptych replied. "But our Infinity teams report the barriers are holding strong."

"So Winghorse is the reason why the Amaranth have been so interested in England."

Triptych nodded. "Calico's portal would allow them access to Earth, yes. You're also expected to serve as Calico's bodyguard in case the Amaranth do show up. But I doubt they will. We are secured from them."

Agustin believed that. He let the chocolate pool on his tongue. Harper had a lot of faith in him if he was expected to handle a god. This assignment should've brought him some sort of pride. Maybe it would have, several hundred years ago. Now, it only instilled an indifferent numbness. If that.

Knowing Harper, this new duty raised suspicions. "You said to acquire full control of the gateway?" Agustin asked. "Steal it out from under Winghorse is what Harper means."

Triptych hunched his shoulders. "I've come here to try and prevent that from ever happening. With your help, of course. Mr. Harper is a lot more...unyielding than I expected."

Agustin had no sympathy and no patience. "You've taken my job. You'll have to handle Harper on your own now. So why me?" he pushed. "Infinity 1 is composed entirely of angels. Most of them full-bloods. What better group than that to deal with a god? Especially when this god finds out he's been duped?"

"There'll be no duping if you appeal to Calico's morality."

Agustin pushed aside his empty plate. He was tempted to pull the remaining cake, stand and all, in front of him and dig in. "On what grounds am I best suited for this task?" he demanded.

"Your compassion for one. Being half angel also permits you the celestial power should you need it."

To hell with appearances and propriety. Agustin yanked the cake stand closer and helped himself to thirds. "Compassion and being half angel doesn't ensure his cooperation."

"Then does it help that you're both fire elementals?"

"No." Agustin was being ornery. Although, being a fire elemental had opened up the dialog between him and a trauma-ridden Etney when she'd first joined his Infinity 8 team.

Triptych crumpled up his serviette. "Mr. Harper wants Calico folded into the Corporation, and he wants that portal. He has full faith in your plans to do so."

"Offering me complete control of the reins?" Agustin sneered. "That doesn't sound like Harper. *At all.*"

Triptych found more interest in slowly folding his serviette into thirds.

"Well..." Agustin continued, highly suspicious of this odd behavior. "I-8's roster's been empty in the last decade. I'm not sure Winghorse would wish to join. Not many want to be on a team geared toward rehabilitating burnouts and screw-ups."

The large hat nodded. "That's why I'm now in charge of this sector—to help re-brand Infinity 8's image."

Agustin raised an eyebrow at the insult toward his prior accomplishments, but let it pass. "Where can I find these Winghorse triplets?"

Triptych slid the files toward him, then motioned to the cake with a formal grace. "That new bakery everyone's raving about? The one that opened in Redwood City? Calico owns it."

Agustin wondered why he didn't put two and two together sooner. Headache, that's why. The cupcake man had to be Calico. Everything was falling into place too easily. He was afraid to hope. Agustin glanced at the dessert, then to the stacked files. "Who's been doing the recon-naissance?"

There was another chuckle behind the veils. "Me."

"You? And this Calico baked that?" He'd have to stop and buy out anything chocolate left on the shelves. He was going to need it.

"I special ordered it for our late afternoon tea. I'm also the one who greeted the triplets when they first came to this world. Well, that hap-pened before I joined IC."

Agustin eyed the report. "If you have firsthand knowledge, why me?"

"Because Harper wishes it," Triptych said. "I'll throw you a helpful tip. Calico's the brains behind their magic. His brothers are more like his keepers, and they stick close to him. He doesn't function well without them, so have patience."

Hmmm. That behavior could describe his cupcake man. "Are we talking about a single collective mindset?"

"Ah...n-no. Their gestalt can operate on an individual ba-sis—uh...mostly."

"Their what?" Even though Agustin was a hyper-polyglot, he scrab-bled at the strange word. Triptych's native tongue, most likely.

"Ah, uh, uh, never mind the term—it's a much more modern word. They are individuals, to put it plainly, but are...well, more whole, stronger as a group. Calico is...uh...how do I say this? Chaotic and a chaotic thinker. Whimsical. Flighty."

That definitely did sound like the delightful cupcake man. Agustin opened the first mission folder Triptych had slid across the table. And braced himself. Here was the detailed colored sketch of the most unusual man he had ever seen, despite being overly thin.

Brilliant blue eyes the shade of a summer sky did convey a...unique, yet troubled nature. But the most strange and distinctive features were

Calico's hairstyle and the odd barrette he wore. A half-shaved scalp with long black hair rippled over his shoulder. Upon closer study, Agustin saw that the tiny piece of jewelry looked like a rat. The rodent's extra-long tail twisted around the man's hair queue.

Hmm. A kerchief had covered the cupcake man's head, obscuring his identity. Could he be patient enough to learn who was who? He'd have to brace himself for possible disappointment. Sure, he would be meeting Calico, eventually. But was the cupcake man the brother he was to work with for the portal inquiry?

"Oh," Triptych said. "Calico's not just running a bakery. He's been poking around in the less than favorable paranormal neighborhoods, asking questions about where to confer with other wizards and sorcerers. Mr. Harper wants that stopped. You can handle that, correct? You still dabble in magic, right?"

Agustin frowned. Still? He'd always practiced a bit of magic, ever since he was a small boy. He remained at an apprentice-level, for sure, because he never wanted to pursue the higher craft. He'd had other responsibilities and ambitions to keep himself busy. "You've read my file since you took my job," Agustin countered briskly.

Magic was yet another reason Harper wanted these triplets reined in. If Calico was frequenting the disreputable magic neighborhoods, then joined an angelic organization, Harper would be automatically responsible for any under-the-table behavior. That would damage IC's reputation.

"I'll look into the magic situation, but I don't promise anything." He'd actually said that? Yes, he did. Maybe his resignation could be put off for a couple of more days. At least until he looked into this unusual assignment.

Agustin reached over and claimed the cream-colored satchel. He tucked the dossier inside and placed the bag at his feet. When he straightened up, Triptych was gone.

Irritated at the rudeness, Agustin slipped one last bite of that marvelous cake. Hopefully made by who he was thinking about. He closed his eyes, letting the sweet flavors provide the smallest of reprieves. To shift his focus and mindset upon what needed to be accomplished.

Leisure time was thankfully over. Retrieving the carry case, he yanked off his remaining glove, and tapped the black onyx band on his left index finger. It was time to stage his own reconnaissance and learn the truth. His stomach knotted with excited nerves.

"Ramirez," he called, looking into the ring. The black onyx band glowed when his hail was acknowledged on the other end.

"I'm here, señor California."

"We've been assigned a mission. I'll be waiting for you at Raynard's."

"Sí señor. I'm on my way."

Chapter 6

A Flame That Was Not His Own

CALICO SLID THE CUPCAKE tin into one of the six wood-burning Acme Regal Steel Ranges that lined the wall. He immediately closed the heavy, cast iron door. The wave of warmth caressing his face ended much too soon. The part of him that was phoenix was disappointed he could not leave it open to bask in the fading embers. But he would not sacrifice the delicious treats for a few moments of comfort, nor waste the last vestiges of the fuel.

Being primarily of phoenix heritage, he could easily bake his treats with a thought or a motion of his hand. Or light the ovens each morning like that.

Or, he used to.

Before the death god's curse upon Great-Grandfather Rupart traveled its way onto him. Infecting and corrupting more than his psychic powers. It had shut down and damaged parts of his mind. Trapping him within this humanesque form. Calico bit his lip. He was at fault that this grief had ever happened.

He shook the memories out of his head.

Meditation and effort had allowed him to achieve a precarious acceptance at the loss of those powers. But his heart remained heavy with grief, and often frustration.

On a brighter note, Calico found he enjoyed using matches to bring forth a flame. It was far more satisfying to create in this slow, primal fashion. The expected, but always renewed surprise of the match strike's result. The anticipation of greeting and studying a brand new spark each day. To train himself in patience. To honor the element itself. To sit in the cozy company of a flame that was not his own.

His breath staggered. *A flame that was not his own.*

Calico stared at the bright, flickering light through the stove slats. He folded his arms, thin fingers cradling his elbows. It was not just melancholy stemming from the near-fatal psychic wounds caused by his great-grandfather.

With a heavy heart, he pondered this need for something more.

The solitude had pressed down upon him since their departure from England. He'd silently suffered through his combined ills until this last week, where he finally felt that his business was stable enough to indulge. To assuage the loss of his psychic powers, and his anxiety-ridden isolation. With treats. Every day after closing.

Because he was lonely.

The gentleman patron from the theater popped up in his thoughts. The one with the bi-colored eyes that reminded him of Aunt Ysannee. The surprise of encountering the unusual eye trait triggered a bout of homesickness so severe, he had fled. He did not want to make a blubbering fool out of himself, and in front of his best customers! Especially with his guttural voice.

That elegant gentleman had been a barely banked personification of elemental fire. The thought of it crackling, snapping in its power.

The demon's personal scent of ash and smoke. Calico caught himself murmuring in excitement at the memory. He wanted to wrap those bold elements around himself and sob and try to feel whole again. But it was impossible as he was.

Calico drew another ragged breath and pinched his cheeks to admonish himself. Did he regret racing out of the theater? Leaving behind someone that might have understood him? Unfortunately, he'd thrown away his chance to find out.

Dabbing teary eyes with a clean handkerchief, he declared himself a silly pumpkin. He was not alone. He had his brothers to look after. Therefore, he should not be lonely.

The telephone box ringing from its place on the far wall jarred him. "Frazil, Maars," he called out in his wince-inducing guttural voice. "The telephone rings. Please attend to it."

His ugly tones grated like sandpaper and falling rocks, and made him even more self-conscious. Yet another reason he'd run from that gentleman's attention; he had been too cowardly to witness the repulsed reaction after introducing himself. But it was his voice, and he had had it since coming into his magic as a child.

No rushing footfalls nor voice replied from the storefront. He wiped his hands on his apron, then turned over the small hourglass that counted out ten minutes. It would be minus the two-ish minutes his treats had already started baking while he'd been lamenting. He should not require such a crude device, as he was the embodiment of Time Incarnate, but that was another matter he would rather not dwell upon.

The shrieking telephone bells continued to pierce his eardrums.

"Frazil, Maars!" he called again, nervous hands waving about at waist level. "The telephone is ringing! A customer beckons! We cannot lose the business!"

There was still no answer from the front room. The late afternoon rush had subsided, and Maars had returned hours ago from his rounds of selling in the neighborhood. Calico poked his head through the curtain, only to be greeted by the storefront's meager display cases. His brothers had not started sweeping up and sorting the stock into the day-old receptacles.

Glancing out the large picture windows, Frazil was not outside smoking. Maars was also not in sight. Odd that he had not heard the jingling bells over the door when they departed. He must have been too absorbed in his cupcake creation. Muttering, Calico hurried over to the wall, where he stared at the boxy, wooden device.

His fingers quivered in a panic over the receiver. In desperation, he glanced over his shoulder to check for his brothers one last time. The curtain separating the kitchen from the storefront did not stir.

With a croaky distressed whine, he cleared his throat as best he could and squared his shoulders. He picked up the receiver, brought it to his ear, and leaned forward to speak into the protruding mouthpiece.

"Scrivens Bakery, how may I serve you?" His pitch rose and fell and cracked as he tried to temper his voice into something acceptable and utterly failed.

Calico winced, his free hand gripping the pencil tied to the small sloping shelf at the bottom of the telephone box. The notepaper there crinkled as he fussed with it. He prayed this potential customer would follow through with an order.

"Calico!" the man on the other end greeted. "Good afternoon. I'm surprised to reach you right away. How are you?"

A familiar voice. Calico slumped against the wall in relief before consulting the large clock above his sink. He doubled checked the time via his pocket watch. His spirits lifted. It was almost time to go home for the day.

"Hello, Mr. Triptych. It is good to hear from you. I am doing as well as can be expected."

"Oh?" Concern arrived through the mild static. "Is there anything I can do?"

"I have misplaced my brothers." Calico let go of the pencil and stuck a thumbnail between his teeth before looking back at the curtain. "They assisted with the morning and afternoon customers, but now I cannot find them anywhere."

There was a sympathetic hum. "I'm sure Frazil's only around the corner in the little park on a smoke break. He most likely won't be more than a few feet from the front door. If it's Maars's turn to make dinner, he probably went home early."

"Smoke? Break? The smoke is broken? I-I apologize. I do not understand."

"Sorry. I meant he's most likely outside smoking his cigarettes."

Calico pinched the bridge of his nose and sighed. "Ah, yes, yes, you are correct. He knows I cannot stand the overly processed stench."

"You're still having trouble with English?"

"Yes. It is quite disheartening. Frazil and Maars have taken to the language so easily."

Another grunt of sympathy. "Don't fret. You'll get the hang of it, someday," Triptych said. "Anyway, thanks for rushing my special order through and delivering it at the last minute. My guest loved it, and it's his favorite dessert."

Calico glanced at the kitchen timer before mentally reviewing the state of his chocolate supply. "That is wonderful news. You have been a most generous benefactor, Mr. Triptych, and you have already done so much for us."

There was a carefree laugh. "Nonsense. Persuading all of you to leave England and come to America was selfish on my part. I was worried about leaving you behind. How're you getting along in your new life?"

"Oh, I am most pleased." Calico bounced once, twice, on the tips of his toes. "My brothers are delighted as well. Ah, how do you say it? Paranormal?"

"Nym's the slang you're looking for," Triptych offered.

"Ah, right. It is a younger generation of nym in America, and we're all focused upon making a living. The magical energies here are still fresh. Slightly untamed, yet they have direction. I do enjoy working them without so many muddy bootprints to wade through. It will be quite easy to re-anchor my portal here because of that."

Calico paused, putting a finger to his chin. "Although, I'm still searching for the best spot, and other factors are in play before that. I am also switching from British Sign Language to the American style. It is quite different, and most challenging to learn how to spell alphabetically with one hand instead of two."

"Wow, you have been busy. Why the Sign swapping?"

"I have concluded it will save time in the bakery when my magic steals my voice."

"How do you figure that?"

"If I spell with one hand, I will have the other free to keep kneading or rolling the dough. That way, I may still communicate with my brothers. Especially since my telepathy is out of commission."

Triptych laughed. And laughed. Until, "Then they're learning the new Sign, too. That's...clever. Maybe you've been keeping too busy. Have you met any of your neighbors or enjoyed a community social yet?"

"Oh, well," Calico hedged. "Ah, no. Bakery hours, you see."

"That's too bad. How is the bakery doing?"

Now this was a subject of ease. "Business has been lovely." Calico looked up to find the hourglass timer had run out. "Oh," he cried. "My cupcakes!"

Calico waved his hand, summoning up his magic. Drawing upon the essence of the natural world itself. As he did so, two things happened. First, the oven's heavy cast-iron door flipped open. Then he grimaced and spasmed.

That pain was the internal psychic energy within him. His psychic power took note of that magical draw, and had attempted to snap back on, but failed. The curse had deprived him of being able to use his mental abilities. Sometimes, if he was not focused, his magic could often get caught up in the curse as well.

So with another careful motion, and concentrating harder upon the external forces swimming around him instead of any internal ones, the cupcake tray slid out of the baking apparatus. With a flick of his fingers, the goods floated over to rest on a cooling rack.

The bells above the shop door jingled. His tray of delicious bakes clattered as his concentration faltered. Another rebound of what seemed to be his telekinetic power this time lanced through his system in a backlash of pain. Calico pulled a handkerchief from his apron pocket and dabbed his forehead from the strain.

"Cal?" Mr. Triptych inquired. "Cal, are you okay?"

"I-I am ecstatic to have had a chin-wag with you, Mr. Triptych, but a customer beckons." Calico winced at the slight alteration of his vocal tone. It had become more guttural than normal. Hopefully, it wouldn't last too long, as it had been just a little magic. A small price to pay for the craft. "And I must get these cooled and frosted before closing."

Static cut through Triptych's warm good-bye. "I...I understand. Cal? Please, take it easy. Enjoy your treats. We'll chat later."

"I will. Cheery-bye." Calico placed the earpiece back into its cradle. It had been a good thing he'd had a proper lunch this afternoon. With the brisk exercise of delivering goods to the playhouse, and Raynard's club. He had to stay in shape or else he'd lose further control.

Taking a deep breath, Calico smoothed his apron and turned around. Now, to attend to his customer.

Chapter 7

The Winghorse Triplets

A SUBTLE BILLOW OF chilly air rose. His middle brother was near. Calico shivered, giving his arms a quick rub for heat. A conventional phoenix his brother was not.

Frazil parted the curtain and walked in. "I heard you talking to someone and rushed to your rescue—" His blue eyes were wide with surprise. "You answered the telephone?"

"Because you were not here." Calico put his hands on his hips. "We were fortunate this time, for it was Mr. Triptych."

Frazil pulled off his baker's cap and ran a hand through his short-cropped white-blond hair. The air around them got a tad cooler. "I'm really sorry, Cal, but I haven't had a smoke all day. I snapped at Maars and nearly yelled at a customer."

Triptych's soothing words had been true. Calico hesitated, sympathetic to his sibling, and embarrassed over his own silly panic.

"I am sorry as well. From now on, I will make certain you get the proper recess for your broken smoking."

"Smoke breaks," Frazil corrected. "So, uh, how's Trippy?"

"He is doing well. He thanks us for our rush order and delivery. Where is Maars?"

"I sent him home to make dinner. Because I, uh, wanted to talk to you alone. About the bakery."

Astounding. Triptych was correct again. Calico walked over to stare at his cupcakes, still trapped in the muffin tin—perfectly baked, as expected. If Triptych was a clairvoyant, then perhaps he should inquire if they would ever be permitted to return home.

Oh. Dear mother goddess. *Home.* Not England. Not their little rental house here in America procured for them by Mr. Triptych, but their birth realm. A place so far away, separated from them by the twists and folds of time and space. In another dimension, so similar yet also so different from this one. How long had it been?

He tried to calculate. A year in England? A few months in America? And how many more would they have to endure away from loved ones after that? The acute blades of isolation cleaved ever deeper into his heart.

Calico's thin frame shuddered, and the sudden brimming tears turned into a hitching sob. He leaned against the workbench. No. He would not cry. Having another—even his brothers—hear him grunt and roar like a wounded grizzly bear with his offensive, guttural voice was unacceptable.

Frazil came over and stood close. "Cal?" He gestured toward the tin. "Oh. You've made those cupcakes again."

Calico looked away, unable to keep his lip from quivering. Just as his middle triplet had taken up a smelly habit in order to cope, he could not stop making and consuming cinnamon vanilla cupcakes. They had been Grandfather Acanthus's favorite.

A whoosh of the curtain had them both turning. The scent of peppermint drifted in, along with a slight rise of warmth within the air. It was Maars.

Calico sniffed, brushing away tears. "I thought you went home to prepare dinner."

"Sibling empathy," Maars said. "I turned my bicycle around. Now what's going on with my little brothers?"

Frazil grimaced before swinging an arm over Calico's shoulders. "Uh, I know this isn't a good time to bring up bakery finances—"

Maars pinned Frazil with a visual warning. "Then don't. This is about Cal, not the account ledgers."

Calico winced. His moping about had been noticed, yet ignored since arriving in America. He had had his chance to wallow and grieve about their misfortune while in England. He knew he had to move on.

While his siblings bickered, all Calico wanted to do was forget the agonies that haunted him. To lose himself in the sugary sweets and delicate flavors their family had once enjoyed, when life was simpler, happier.

Maars put arms around them, offering a small squeeze. "Cal. Frazil and I are worried about your urge to flame up and ash out—"

"Don't." Frazil said, breaking away from the brotherly embrace. "You know he's not ready to talk about a Burn." Frazil turned to Calico. "Cal, the bakery? Customers are bored. They're starting to complain. Our livelihood's at stake."

The mention of his customers got Calico's attention. "Oh?"

"The novelty of a new shop with fun and strange desserts has worn off," Frazil reported. "Not everyone can afford fancy cakes, cookies, and doughnuts. They want normal staples they can consistently put on the table. We have to cut back to keep the customers happy."

Cut back? Calico looked around. Along the wall, ovens awaited all manners of dough concoctions. At the corner was another Acme Regal Steel Range reserved for fried goods. At the kitchen center, there were five workstation benches prepped for tomorrow morning. The number of sugar canisters matched the number of flour canisters.

"But my cupcakes are a best seller," Calico defended.

"They were best sellers when we opened two months ago," Frazil reminded.

Calico drew back in surprise, mumbling about the increments of time. "Has it been that long?"

"It's not been long at all." Frazil exchanged troubled glances with Maars. "You've just been absorbed in your tasks."

"Mentally running away is more like it." Maars pulled a cupcake from the tin and took a bite. "Nice and warm, and still the best, even without frosting."

Calico worried at his apron. Why had he not realized all this? He had informed Mr. Triptych all was peachy. "How is the financial ledger?"

Frazil gave him a steady look. "In the last week, sales have been down by an average of twenty dollars."

Twenty dollars was more than the cost of just one of his Acme Regal Steel Ranges! "That much? What of our shop rent? Our home lease, our supplies?" Calico fluttered his fingers against his lips in dismay. Frazil was correct. He had been too self-absorbed, and he had risked his siblings' well-being.

"Easy, I've been tracking it all," Frazil assured. "We have enough to keep paying bills on time, if we act now. Reduce the sweets. Increase production on breads."

"Indeed," Calico said unhappily. "I will reassign the workstations. Two for cake, pastry, and special orders. Three for mundane staples?"

His brothers conferred with a glance. "It's for the best," Maars agreed. They swapped the canisters and tins among the tables.

"Now then," Maars said when that was finished. "We have to talk about this urge to Burn. Cal, you've been so moody lately. You know what happens to us if our kind gets too stressed and traumatized—"

"Y-yes," Calico admitted, scared and shaking at the reminder. Burns almost destroyed both of their phoenix grandparents, mentally and physically.

"Then you should know better," Maars pressed. "Especially since the Breese are more prone to illness and decay. The parlor is so full of your chosen spices—"

"As well as all the other spices, florals, and herbs you've hoarded like a dragon," Frazil cut in. "It's giving even us a headache. Cal, are you feeling a draw to a new foundational scent? Is that why you're chaotically hoarding so many? If so, you know you need to tell us."

"No, no," Calico reassured. "It is nothing like that."

"Then why?"

Calico shrugged, unable to answer.

"Maybe it is time to talk to us," Frazil pressed. "Maybe we can head off this Burn and keep it from happening. Maars and I made peace with our forced exodus after we landed in England. We so desperately want that for you, too."

"We should've insisted on it." Maars tilted Calico's chin upward. "Cal. Baby brother. If you Burn, he," Maars pointed to Frazil, "can't do anything to help you during it, and I can't handle you all by myself." Maars took his other hand. "Please, talk to us."

Calico drifted free of the brotherly embraces, and paced a little. He massaged the back of his neck. Once, he and his brothers did not even need to talk to each other. Only think. Or feel via their empathy to be wholly understood. But the psychic bond they shared as triplets had been obliterated. It was a horror caused by an angry god's curse.

His brothers had always been able to function individually. But for him, having that gestalt ripped away nearly spiraled him into madness.

The truths hurt. Facing these deep-rooted facts were even more brutal. How could he let go of baking the only confections that made him feel better?

How could he convey he felt nothing but death and suffocation without their minds wrapped about him? Trapped within this human casing and unable to morph back into his true phoenix-self? Or being unable to sense all the unending threads of the universes through his space-time abilities? This lingering demise was unbearable, especially to a child of the Goddess of Life.

He sighed. None of that mattered. He had to start listening to their customers, or they would be living on the street. A tragedy that could have befallen them if his portal had not opened up right atop Mr. Triptych. Calico was still highly embarrassed about landing on the poor fellow and giving him a bloody nose and ruining the fine craftsmanship of all those veils.

Calico rubbed his eyes. "Perhaps I can work up to the idea of a family conference in a few weeks. Until then, I shall...shall strive to contain my fiery impulses."

Yet contain them for how much longer? A Burn could mean many things. For him, now, his curious urge to nest, and also renew in the flames stemmed from vague future events that confused him. A hand fell to his midsection. What worried him was that he should not even be able to possess the divine insight of this happy event, since his space-time powers were so closed off. Currently residing inside this physical, humanesque form further blocked him from examining this un-chronological hiccup.

And...and how could he even Burn if he could not use his phoenix flame? This was all a quandary his brothers would not understand. He did not understand it himself.

The bell above the shop door jingled.

Frazil gave his shoulder a pat. "Thanks, Cal, for working on this with us. I've had my cig. We'll serve the last customer of the day. Come on, Maars."

It was only a few seconds later when both his brothers returned, looking as if they'd seen a ghostly specter.

"Well?" Calico retrieved a linen-covered bowl from the shelf. He dragged a spatula through the frosting dregs to get every bit of the sugary goodness, then slathered it over a tiny cake. He could not wait to eat them, for he decided this would be his final homesick indulgence.

"A rich bloke. He wants to talk to the owner."

"You know the ruse." Calico picked up a half-used piping bag. He added more frosting atop the spongy cupcake, creating a small mountain of swirls. "One of you place that cap on your head and masquerade as myself. We cannot lose the business over my offensive voice."

Conversation was the primary problem. The emergence of his magic when he was a child had forever altered his vocal notes. And the additional price of using a lot of magic was the loss of his voice. How long depended upon the might of the spell, and how well-rested he was.

Thankfully, the one thing the curse had not squashed was his magic.

His brothers shook their heads. "He's not human. Wants you."

Calico wiped his hands and straightened the scarf concealing his half-shaved head. He could do this. Taking a fortifying breath, Calico grabbed both his siblings by the arms. Pushing them ahead, and cowering behind, he marched them into the storefront.

Then froze, mid-step, at the breath-stealing sight before him.

Chapter 8

The Fiery Gentleman

IT WAS HIM. THE fiery elemental gentleman from the theater.

Calico's slumbering phoenix-self jolted awake, yet remained frustratingly imprisoned by the curse. He fiddled with his bib apron. Hot shivers spiraled up his spine. Why were his palms sweaty? Had he made a noise? He must have made a noise. Frazil marked him with a quick, strange glance. Thankfully, Maars had not noticed his clandestine alarm.

Despite that momentary agony, this was a delightful surprise, even if their customer not be phoenix. Truthfully, Calico did not think he would ever see this nobleman again. There was not much of a fiery community brave enough to live, or work upon the Peninsula's soggy landscape.

Perhaps that was why the man had sought him out. He had chalked it up to this gentleman merely passing through on business, and Calico had resigned himself to savoring that fleeting, bittersweet encounter. Could he hope, that maybe, this master of elemental fire was lonely too?

What if he was just passing through? If so, why even bother? Better to save himself the future heartache of that disappointment. For it would make the loneliness he already felt even sharper. Calico fidgeted. Why was he giving up before he even started?

Coward.

But now that he was on home grounds, safe in his little protected nest, Calico took a keener moment to observe. Why did this man feel so familiar?

Had they met? He was certain that was an affirmative. It must have had been during one of his space-time blinks. When had that happened? Further thought deduced it had been earlier today, but the details were fuzzy.

This gentleman overshadowed the sun's magnificence. His heart vibrated at the nearness of that inferno's might. The benign warmth radiating off this man was like a cozy security blanket. One Calico could pull over his head and hide away in. Alas, he had to remind himself the customer was not of a phoenix origin, and was most likely passing through.

The pit of his belly rolled with delight and stress, but it soon sunk back into the depths of disappointment. This was a fleeting joy. He had to remember that. One that deepened the well of his loneliness. He chased the depression out of his head. There was no time to socialize and eagerly discuss the essence of fire. He had a business to run and two brothers to look after.

Motioning his siblings to walk ahead, Calico lagged behind, putting the display counter between him and the patron. The much-needed barrier brought no solace. His place was in the kitchen. Not out dealing with the public.

The customer lifted his attention from the cakes left within the case, and Calico again felt as if he was lost in the waves of the bay.

Those eyes.

Sapphire-blue. Warm honey-gold.

Yes, indeed. A gaze analogous to his goddess aunt, Ysannee.

Homesickness swelled again. The sight of the lovely heterochromia, packaged with their shared elemental craft, branched out into a strange camaraderie, however imagined, between him and this gentleman customer. Somehow, it tempered the grief of being driven away from those he held dear.

Odd. This sense of comfort also gave him a small bout of courage—but not enough to come out from behind his protective glass barrier containing sponge cake and lemon ganache.

The paranormal gentleman who requested his presence was taller than Frazil and Maars. Their visitor removed his top hat. Calico's rapt gaze followed the downward path of that lovely accessory. Frazil and Maars had insisted such millinery was on a sharp decline, and here was a shining example to contradict them.

Calico adored that gray silk top hat with the shiny gray band, and the firm hand that held it. It proved that he should ignore the brotherly pressures to abandon the comfort of his older garb, in favor of the more modern styles. Which lead him to notice the attractive cut of the man's three-piece light gray suit.

The obviously expensive fabric showed off the gentleman's lean form, and highlighted the healthy radiance of dark brown skin. The suit was ironed by an expert hand, with a touch of magic sprinkled in to keep wrinkles to a minimum. Yet, there was more to this gentleman than physical appearances.

This customer wanted to talk to him. He could do this. Calico looked straight into that mismatched gaze and said in his guttural voice, "Greetings again, sir. I am Mr. Scrivens, the owner."

There it was. A flash. The customer's comprehension. Perhaps acknowledging the uniqueness inherent in them both, in addition to their shared element. Never mind the fact that his voice was jarring and hideously offensive.

"Good evening, Mr. Scrivens," the gentleman answered in a smooth baritone. "I see there aren't many staples left at the end of the day. Excellent for business, but not for those browsing at closing. Of the many cakes presented, there's no chocolate. The sponge beneath, perhaps?"

Calico shook his head. Responding to the customer's disappointed grimace, he straightened his bib apron and kerchief. He saw dollars fading from his cash register.

Frazil saved the moment, opening a case against the wall. "Might we interest you in our famous cinnamon bread?"

Black brows slanted downward now. "Hmm, perhaps another time." His gaze roved around the store, studying the remainders of the stock.

Calico attempted to observe from a buyer's perspective: tagged slots that read "dinner rolls," "bagels," "hamburger buns" and "sandwich bread" were empty, the basket of French breads not far behind.

He then noted the glass cases beneath his elbows. Sugary items such as doughnuts and cookies sat mostly full. All headed for the day-old slots. The cakes would be shifted over into the adjacent discount case. His brothers were correct, and he wished he had noticed this much earlier.

If the goods did not sell on the discounted shelves, he would make his weekly delivery to the soup kitchens. Grandfather Acanthus taught them waste, and especially hunger, was unacceptable.

The customer found something satisfactory. "Do wrap up the last of the French breads, and that lonely loaf of rye. The lot of pretzels, too."

Maars jumped into action to pack the accruing order while he and Frazil stood by.

"Would you care to sample anything?" Calico offered.

Those eyes lifted, and bore right through him. Calico felt a quick jolt fly through his brain. He likened it to the abrupt and forceful chop of a cleaver to a cutting board. Or when one's hat is suddenly pushed over one's eyes.

Another space-time blip snuck up on him, careening his current mind-self into future-time. He knew these hiccups happened. Ever since his injuries by the curse. But more often, he was not aware of them. But it was happening now.

Smoldering heterochromatic eyes in their true form, sporting one white sclera, and one black, caught, and held his gaze. Lazy smoke drifting from this demon gentleman's nose, coiling upwards.

A winning hand of the card game Hearts now spread across the table of Calico's cozy apartment kitchen. The radio belted out a song he could not hear. Because...because...

The demon's tongue flicked out in a humorous, teasing raspberry of triumph. Extra long and forked at the ends. The tines able to curl independently of the other.

How...how could he know about that tongue?

Calico gulped and adjusted his cravat. Why was his heart racing? He wrangled his mind back to this current timeline.

It was well and good his brothers were doing the majority of the customer service. He was holding onto an exploding mental escapade with all his might. Causing a scene would be very bad for business, indeed.

The customer's gaze fell back to the pastry case. "How about a croissant? Other than the doughnuts and cookies, do you have anything small and sweet? Or anything butterscotch?"

While Frazil fetched the last croissant, Calico again glanced into the display in front of him. Only whole cakes. Then he remembered.

"I have a half-dozen—" He recalled Maars had nibbled on one. "No, five cinnamon vanilla cupcakes cooling out of the oven, frosted with vanilla cream cheese." He was disheartened that he wouldn't be able to eat away his melancholy this night.

"Add those to the order," the man said.

"I shall fetch them." Calico hurried into the kitchen, where he rushed to top the rest of the cupcakes. Snapping out a box, he placed the goods inside.

When he emerged, the gentleman had finished the croissant and now rose from the small table next to the window. Frazil collected the place setting, butter dish, and serviette. His brother pushed in the man's chair and disappeared briefly into the kitchen.

The man approached. "I enjoyed that, and the chocolate cake I had this afternoon."

This gentleman was Triptych's guest. Calico swiveled to stare at his brothers. They too were wild-eyed and standing straighter.

"I would like to place an order."

Calico perked up at the indirect praise. He smiled at his gentleman customer while handing the box of cupcakes to Maars.

Pulling a pad of paper and a pencil from his apron pocket, he asked, "Shall I deliver to you, or will someone be out to collect?"

"Delivery, please." The man put a hand to his chin and grew quiet for a few seconds. "One dozen apple pies, one dozen mince pies, six dozen morning biscuits, a dozen French breads, and seven loaves of wheat bread. Oh. Six dozen of those croissants. And three remakes of that chocolate cake—minus the elaborate trees and dragons."

Calico shared another anxious glance with his brothers. This was such a massive order for a single person. Perhaps it was for a business or a social gathering.

The customer cleared his throat and continued, "An acquaintance of mine shared your work at tea this afternoon. I'm hosting an employee meeting and recruitment campaign, and I thought mass quantities of baked goods would settle interview nerves. It will also help take the pressure off my kitchen staff."

Calico took notes. "When will you need this?"

"By Saturday morning. Breakfast is served at seven a.m. and lasts until nine. Lunch will be from one to three."

His customer paused. As if striving to form his next words with care. "Would you agree to oversee and manage the servings? It'll be an all-day endeavor. My staff will be busy looking after those arriving. I will, of course, compensate you for your time, and your meals. If all goes well, perhaps you can assist my chef with a birthday-graduation celebration. I'll be hosting it in a few months. It'll last the entire week, and there will be several guests staying in residence."

The pencil tightened in Calico's hand. He had two days to deliver this special order. His brothers would be joining him in the back room, and they would have to run the bakery while he was away. They could not pass up this opportunity and the profits it would bring. He would be able to start saving up for a gas-powered delivery vehicle. One with his bakery's name painted on the sides.

Thank you, Mr. Triptych. Calico smiled. "I happily accept, sir."

"Splendid. My card."

Calico shoved his notepad back into his apron pocket and accepted the business card with both hands. The fancy script was too small for him to decipher at a glance, and he did not want to embarrass himself by squinting and scrunching up his nose to focus on the print.

His brothers clamored near to read it over his shoulder. Maars stifled a snicker, and Frazil gasped in shock. Calico wiggled his shoulders to fend them off and glared at them in reproach.

"How much do I owe you for the cupcakes and breads?" The man produced his billfold, ignoring their poor behavior because he was a gentleman.

Calico stared at the purchases bulging within the brown paper bags and calculated. "A dollar and a quarter."

The man handed two dollars to Maars, who was the closest. "Keep the change."

A shocking and most generous gratuity! Calico joined in with his sputtering brothers. All three of them stood straight and proper. Their customer donned that wonderful top hat. Touched the brim in a silent goodbye. Then collected his bundled purchases and strolled out.

Calico hurried over to the big, shopfront windows, sorry to witness this departure. It had been such a pleasant few moments, even if this fire elemental's flame had been banked. Even if he himself had been uncomfortable waiting on someone. He would miss—Calico gaped in surprise.

Their gentleman customer secured his purchases within a motorcar parked in front of the bakery! He even had a driver. Calico was mesmerized by the sleek lines and dark, shiny paint of that metal beast.

It almost distracted him from the fading fiery warmth that visited his shop. All that remained was the familiarity of the cooling ovens, and the small comfort of Maars's also banked and quiet presence.

Clenching his fists, and seeking gulps due to his shortened breath, Calico tried to calm himself. Of course he would see this man again. He had a generous order to deliver.

Yet, he did not wish to let go. Calico wanted him to stay, just a bit longer. To see him smile, maybe. To hover within the space of the first fire elemental he'd met since making their new home here in America.

Before he could stop himself, before he could think, Calico darted out the shop door. Without collecting his hat and coat, as proper.

Chapter 9

Show Me Yours

"Please," Calico called out, hands waving at chest-level. "Please, wait."

The raucous noise of the motorcar's engine ceased. The gentleman stepped down from the vehicle. "You wished to speak to me? Is it about the order? I can reduce the amount of—"

"Oh, no, no," Calico hurried to reassure. "My brothers and I are most capable, and we will have no difficulty filling and delivering your baked goods. On time. I..." He could do this. He had to do this. His loneliness would drive him mad before the curse could ever eat him into a permanent demise.

Perhaps it would be easier if they did not have the driver as an audience. Calico extended a hand to show his customer the way to the small strip of greenery next to the bakery. He could not be sure exactly what his intentions would entail, by waylaying a most important customer in this manner. It was indecent. Immoral. But Calico felt if he did not, he would lose something, or a moment, that was so dire, he would die.

He would die anyway... Calico bit his lip.

It was well and good his gentleman customer seemed to be interested in his most unusual inquiry. So that provided additional courage. Which came as a surprise.

In the heart of this little park next door to the bakery, his customer artfully arranged himself on the bench beneath the gaslight pole. Sitting straight and tall. Sophistication and elegance radiating as strongly as the furnace of his elemental aura.

The haziness cast from the street lamp created a most wonderful island against the coming twilight. It strangely made this rendezvous cozier. That alone bolstered Calico's courage another notch.

When the gentleman looked up at him expectedly with those mismatched eyes, Calico felt mesmerized. *Say something,* he demanded of himself. *Something witty and clever, so he will think me as gentlemanly and important.*

His customer appeared to be fighting the smile on his lips before clearing his throat. He turned his head away—just for a second, before facing him again, expression polite.

Say something, Calico pushed himself. *He is waiting. He will think me daft and even more unsound than I already am. Alright then. Here I go.*

"We are both fire elementals." The clumsy inquiry had Calico's cheeks heating in embarrassment. He bent his head at his failure.

"One moment," the gentleman said. He collected a small item anchored into his top hat and held it up. A blue gem embedded into a silver clip glowed, and the light circled around them like a curtain. Returning the jewel to its place on that magnificent hat, this man languidly leaned against the picnic table, and angled himself more in his direction.

Calico felt encouraged to pursue a friendly connection, but this intriguing magic had to be investigated. "What was that?"

"A spell my company uses. We call it the Curtain. It keeps our dealings private and unseen from the mundanes—ah, the general non-magical populations, I mean. Usually the humans."

"That is most ingenious magic," Calico exclaimed, leaning in. "I wonder how it compares to my Mirror Bubble?"

There was that smile again, most gentle, and prompting. "You wished to speak of magic? Or something more?"

"Ah, my apologies. Not magic. Will you show it to me?" Calico asked, knowing himself too eager. He tried not to wring his hands and appear desperate.

His customer's brows rose high, and Calico knew it was in utter surprise, and perhaps curiosity. "Show you...what?" The question was somewhat wary with a touch of amusement.

"Your elemental flame. You see, I too, am—er was once gifted with the flame. I am a phoenix, you see."

The man blinked. "A phoenix without a flame?"

Calico felt himself turn pink, and put a sheepish hand against the back of his head. "It is a most embarrassing admission," he rushed. "I did not plan on being so forward. I apol—"

There was a quiet whoosh. Another small circle of light rose, and Calico sensed the heat instantly. There, dancing calmly inches above the gentleman's gloved palm, was a tear-shaped flame. Flickering in shades of orange, reds, and yellows and blues. And...and yes. *White.*

He sucked in a breath. It had been so long since he'd seen such a flame. Curling, writhing in all its glory. Since he was cut off from his ability, Maars did not use his out of sympathy. At least in a sensory view.

Calico swallowed the hitch in his breath. How could this gentleman carry so many colors within? Was he that powerful?

"You're shaking, Mr. Scrivens." The flame disappeared, and there was a steadying hand at his shoulder. "Are you well? Perhaps you should sit down."

Calico touched that hand, as if to anchor it in place. "Yes, yes, I should." The wooden bench was chilly against his rump. "It-it is quite cold this evening. May I see it again?"

The request was granted. Calico stared at the dancing shapes. Wishing. Forever longing.

A few seconds passed before the gentleman spoke. "How long has it been since you were unable to create?"

Create. It was an elemental term Calico had heard bandied about the local wizard shops. The question sent warm tingles and shivers down his spine.

Staring at the flame so snug and content, curling about the gentleman's gloved fingertips, Calico suddenly found himself saying, "Sixteen months, two days, seventeen hours and 26 and a half seconds."

The gentleman lowered his hand, and the summoned fire faded. "That's quite precise."

Indeed! He should not be able to access any of his psychic powers. "I am the God of Space and Time," Calico said offhandedly.

There was an awkward pause. "Well, yes. About that. Mr. Scrivens, while we are here, alone, I'd like to take the opportunity to discuss your delivery further."

"Oh, yes," Calico replied with renewed energy. "What is it? Would you like to add my famous cupcakes to the order? It is no trouble."

"N-no. That's not it. Well, the baked goods are for a recruitment campaign."

"Recruitment?"

"Yes. My company has need of your skills."

Calico paused before he made a silly fish out of himself. As much as his mind was centered upon his magic, what if this man merely wanted an extra baker on his payroll, and not a wizard? He had to allow the man to formally extend the offer.

"I wish for you to sit in on the lectures—"

The ruby red ring on the gentleman's finger glowed, and he went silent. As he stared at it, his features schooled into a mask. When he slapped a hand over it, it stopped glowing. Calico could not be certain due to the loss of his empathic psychic abilities, but the gentleman seemed...agitated.

The man sighed. "I'm sorry. Something important's come up. But I will see you again? And then we will talk?"

"Yes, of course. I look forward to it. Sitting in on a lecture sounds most interesting."

"Excellent." The man nodded and turned, only to turn back. "One last thing before I go. May I have my glove back? It was a birthday present, you see."

"Glove?" Calico asked.

The man held up his hands, wiggling the fingers on his bare hand. "Maybe check your pockets?" The suggestion was simple, hopeful.

"I do not understand why you would claim I have your property." Calico patted down his pockets, as well as the ones lining his bib apron. Then pulled out the glove in question. "Oh," he replied. "Oh dear. How did that get in there?" Calico asked, truly mortified, holding it out.

The gentleman claimed it, thanking him with a grin. In a low, smoky tone, the parting words delved into the pit of Calico's belly and took up permanent residence. "Perhaps you can borrow it again sometime."

The gentleman was slow to take his leave, watching him with those eyes. He climbed back into the motorcar, it started, and they lurched out into the street.

Calico trailed after that gaze, wrapped in a lovely stupor of his own. But he stopped at the sidewalk when the vehicle turned a corner and was gone. It felt as if it would be forever before Calico saw this gentleman customer again. Sighing, he headed back inside his bakery. There was work to be done.

Chapter 10

Agustin's Giddy Euphoria

CLIMBING INTO THE PASSENGER seat, Agustin was only vaguely aware of Ramirez putting the motorcar into gear and heading home. The raucous motor sounded as soothing as a kitten's purr to his ears.

Agustin played with the surrendered glove, flipping it this way and that. His hands quivered with nervous excitement, well aware that his friend and fellow Infinity 8 member was giving him the side-eye. With a raised eyebrow to boot. Agustin had kept a tight grip on his euphoria until now. He chuckled, then started laughing.

Mr. Scrivens—Calico Winghorse, was indeed the triplet brother he'd met at the theater. Agustin wasn't sure exactly why that made him so happy. Maybe because it'd be nice to have another fire elemental to talk to besides Etney. They'd been the only ones residing on the Peninsula until now.

The brothers. A strange trio, to be certain. It'd been difficult to tell them apart. Perhaps he'd been too eager. No matter. This had been an initial reconnaissance. The favorable contact made it a bonus.

The feeling of freedom had returned when his assignment had stepped out of the back room. That feeling was still with him, the further away from the bakery they drove.

Perhaps it was Winghorse's perpetual zest for...something. It reminded him to look inside himself to achieve happiness. Glancing at Ramirez's puzzled face, he chuckled again and patted his friend on the shoulder. Ramirez returned the smile and elbowed him with a friendly bump.

Agustin knew his household and his Infinity 8 team would gossip about his behavior. Maybe they'd even think the forced outing had been a good thing. In a way, it had.

But he didn't care. They were free to debate. He was prepared for Etney to drill him for details. Oh, she'd have a thrill to hear that her summons through the ruby ring communications had disrupted a possible something.

He was happy, and his future looked promising. Still, he wondered why she'd been calling. He'd find out soon enough.

His mood immediately turned pensive. What happened to his staunch decision of quitting IC this very day? Agustin took a second to process that. He carefully measured the cost of such a delay to his psyche.

Agustin was aware of Harper's manipulative tactics. Of the hurt Harper had caused him throughout the centuries.

The announcement of his resignation would have to be postponed and kept a secret.

He'd grudgingly stay. Long enough to make sure Winghorse got a fair deal.

It'd be fine. He'd be okay.

He would.

Chapter 11

Brotherly Banter

WHEN HIS GENTLEMAN CUSTOMER was out of sight, there came a snicker. Calico snapped himself out of not just his motorcar euphoria, but the savored heat of his customer's elemental flame. He rounded on his brothers, who crowded him in the doorway. Ear-to-ear grins plastered on faces that were exact copies of the one he beheld each morning in the mirror when he shaved and washed.

"Well, now," Calico started, clearing his throat. "It is time to explain your earlier behavior. You dare insult and laugh at our customers? Like little children?"

"His name," Maars burst out, laughing.

"What about it?" Calico pulled the card from his pocket.

Mischief lit up his elder brother's eyes. "Agustin Chavez de la Cruz. Doesn't Cruz mean cross in Spanish? Hot cross buns? He had a nice a—"

Calico hissed, turning bright red. "Do not say it."

"Backside," Maars compromised.

"And what is your excuse, Frazil?" Calico demanded again.

"That was the Demon Lord of California." Frazil's low whisper revealed astonishment.

Calico held the card up to his nose and peered at the print. "Demon lord?" That meant notoriety and influence. So what was this recruitment gala all about?

Both his brothers rolled their eyes. "He's the authority around here for our kind," Frazil said. "How could you not have heard of him? Especially since you've been trying to peddle your magic skills."

Maars grinned widely. "He was Trippy's tea time meeting? I wonder if it's just all business between those two?" He wiggled his pale eyebrows. "Trippy went all out and ordered a *chocolate* cake."

Calico squawked and covered his ears. Embarrassed heat remained in his cheeks, and he felt a light sheen of sweat gather at his collar. "We shall not deliberate over the private lives of our customers, or our benefactor!"

Frazil pursed his lips in thought. "This demon lord could be the reason you can't make contact with any other wizards, Cal."

Uncovering his ears, Calico whirled on his brother. "Why would he be responsible? He seems like an upstanding and nice fellow." He had been so accommodating by showing off his fire element.

"I've seen the wizard advertisements in the Paranormal Gazette—so have you," Frazil reminded. "If I recall, each advert bears a guild mark, with a small California state logo. You might have to talk to the California guild. Or even the demon lord himself, if you want to set up an official shop. Rumor has it Chavez de la Cruz has his own band of henchmen. They're also members of some corporation, I think."

"And henchwomen," Maars cut in.

"He is Lord California, after all," Frazil went on. "Everyone seems to answer to him."

Calico gulped and leaned against the display case. "I did not realize. And I am to bake for them?"

Frazil's face twisted. "He's hosting a recruitment bash? He wants you to stay and serve it? I'm getting a weird feeling about that."

Calico pocketed the business card for safekeeping. "Well, he has asked me to sit in on the meeting."

"Oooh, bloody hell." Maars's saucy demeanor vanished. "I hope this isn't about paying 'protection fees' or some sort of rent for living in his jurisdiction."

"Language," Calico reprimanded, deep in thought. "I have agreed to attend. I find whatever he wishes to talk about interesting."

"Do you even know what he wants to discuss? You didn't ask?"

Calico pursed his lips and splayed his fingers out in a quizzical response.

Both his brothers groaned.

"Cal, if Frazil's having another of his hunches, maybe you should send regrets. Maybe this demon lord's seen your wizard ads in the Paranormal Gazette. Maybe he sees you as competition and he's sizing you up."

Calico had forgotten about his placed advertisement, as no one had answered it. Perhaps Frazil was correct about guild membership. Leashed excitement simmered.

Perhaps this recruitment invitation was his way into the wizarding community. If he pleased this client, there would be more bakery orders. And more orders meant a wider reputation. That created prestige and approval. Especially if he could figure out how to synchronize his magic skills into his current occupation. He was a creative. He could work something out. Like tasty edibles to bolster one's courage for a job interview. The anticipation grew. Perhaps this was his job interview.

"Cal, are you even listening?"

If he could build a client list for selling his magic services, it would bring in twice the salary the bakery did. Perhaps then he could purchase the home they lived in.

And...if he was regarded as a wizard and not a baker, then perhaps their kind would not take such offense to his voice. Quirks and oddities were expected when one practiced magic.

Yet, there was also the fact of his debilitating curse robbing him of most psychic senses. And eventually his life. His fingers fluttered against his lips. Hmmm...what to do, what to do...

"Cal." Frazil was waving a hand before his eyes, demanding his attention. "We know that look."

Calico flipped the shop sign to closed, and locked the door. "Of course I have been listening. I will heed the hunches, but we shall not decline the income offered in the meantime. And if I can finally make contact with other magic makers, perhaps I will find a way to unlock the other powers denied me." *And in doing so, rescue my life.*

His brothers were frowning at him. "Cal," Frazil tried to reason. "We've discussed this. Magic is *not* a substitute for fixing psychic powers. What you need is another veteran telepath."

The rehash of that discussion brought on a flash of self-doubt. Was his course of action a correct one? "We have attempted to locate said telepathic individual since arriving in this world," Calico shot back. He caught himself in mid-whine and in the growing anxiety of a mid-pace. "Charlatans or novices, all of them. Even as blocked off from my powers as I am, I can see through them."

"We'll keep looking for someone equal to, or above your talent—"

"If at all," Calico sniffed. He knew he was getting testy. Allowing self-importance to get the better of him. But he had bottled it for so long. "This could be the chance I have been searching for."

He had been denied the bulk of his powers, thanks to the curse. However, his space-time abilities were a cosmic gift beyond the curse's reach. For his soul, his very existence was a manifestation of Time itself.

But he was still trapped within a physical form because of said curse. Accessing the powers of his godhood were questionable at best, especially with his psychic ones so damaged.

And sometimes not so damaged.

Like that magic or telekinesis business with his cupcakes earlier.

Calico worried. Was he deteriorating faster than expected?

His future-self *had* jumped into his current-self at least once since coming to Earth. That happened after escaping Great-Grandfather's attack. His brothers had alerted him to that particular incident. And he had experienced and remembered another such transaction at least once, after that.

So it was of the conclusion this affliction was an ongoing affair. And with it, questionable access to the psychic powers of his empathy, telekinesis, and maybe even his telepathy.

Curious. And how many times had he come to this opinion before his mind time-skipped elsewhere, and the cycle started all over again? Further alerting his brothers to these additional episodes would make them worry more, so he would keep silent.

Just like he hid the fact of his approaching permanent demise.

Regardless, the time hiccups remained alarming, especially without his wizard's familiar to monitor and guide him. It was all so excruciating, and Calico was surprised he had not had a full-blown meltdown and panic yet. Perhaps it was his future-self holding the pieces together.

"We'll keep trying to fix you." Frazil drew him into a hug. Maars joined them.

That drained all the fight out of him. The loss of his powers had also taken a toll upon his siblings. As united as they were, because they were identical triplets, his pain was often theirs.

Their powers were their own, but mainly, their abilities fed his. Grounded his. To keep him from becoming lost in the endless sea of space and time. It was a quirk of their being. They were all connected, physically and mentally—or at least they used to. Before this most unfortunate curse...

Concealing his frustrated melancholy, Calico clapped them on the shoulders, lingering a moment to convey his agreement. "I have been working hard on my patience. We will find the key to repair my powers, sooner or later. Now then, get a wiggle on, and help me clean up for the night," he urged. "There is so much to do tomorrow."

Yet they stood there, looking at each other, their apprehension seeding. Until Maars sighed, grabbing the broom.

Frazil opened the cash register and collected the receipts. "I suppose we can discuss this again later."

Calico ignored their continued silent criticism. For in a few hours' time, he would need to do inventory and order extra supplies for the demon lord's employee gathering. A good night's sleep was next on the list.

Tomorrow, as he worked, he would mull over a new course of action in regaining the full power of his psychic abilities. Rehearsing his wizard guild inquiry speech was also of importance. And most of all, he would work to curtail the irrational guilt he carried over Great-Grandfather Rupart's curse.

Chapter 12

Harper's Phone Call

FINISHED WITH HIS SUPPER, Agustin returned his empty plate and serviette to the wheeled serving cart parked beside him. Shoving the signed and completed trade agreement with Lord Canada into its official mailing envelope, he placed it into his out box. His butler would post it with the morning mail. He plucked the next folder off the to-do stack. It was Calico Winghorse's dossier.

The low buzz of his desk lamp was exceptionally loud in his otherwise quiet study. The light bulb's glow through the verdant glass shade cast a small bubble against the darkness. It cultivated a better focus upon work.

Chilly night air circulated through the open window, and the moon hid behind the thick clouds and rolling fog. His mansion, Demonym, was at the base of the northern Santa Cruz Mountain range. Beyond those rocky peaks to the west, was the little agricultural town of Half Moon Bay and the vastness of the Pacific Ocean. To the north was San Francisco. And about an hour south of San Francisco, was Winghorse's little town of Redwood City.

The mountains and low temperatures surrounding Demonym kept Agustin from being too comfortable. He preferred it this way. If he was too content, his mind would turn toward tears and regrets better left to the past.

The small, clear glass paperweights he'd picked up in France kept files from scattering from the occasional gust of wind. Rising above the towering layers of paperwork was the mouthpiece and receiver of his black candlestick telephone. It rarely rang after 9 p.m. Which was yet another reason he worked late.

Agustin sucked the salt from a pretzel purchased from Scrivens Bakery, letting the flavor gather on his tastebuds. When the minerals dissolved, he crunched the airy shell of bread. The maids would be annoyed when they found scattered crumbs and grit. In an odd mood, Agustin finished the after-meal snack anyway, and studied the portrait-sketch of his assignment clipped to the cover.

Opening the folder, it was a surprise to learn this was a handwritten report. Official documents and reports were always typed. Which meant everything before him was the only copy.

Agustin flipped back to the image. Calico Winghorse was indeed something else. He was quite handsome, in a quirky sort of way. Eyes that he once thought were troubled, now seemed very sad. His heart jolted, and he ran a finger down the image's cheek.

The gold ring on his pinky flashed in the lamplight. No. Agustin couldn't let himself get involved like that. Not ever again. Especially with someone who may choose to join IC when he was on his way out.

He scrabbled to mull over his resignation letter now, but he dare not pen it yet. Harper's spies were everywhere, and his household staff wasn't exempt from suspicion.

Once his decision was announced, he'd kindly ask the unknown(s) to leave. Of course, bonus packages and glowing references would be provided. He'd permit them to save face in the departure, by stating that now that he was no longer affiliated with IC, he needed to downsize.

He was upsetting himself. So he pulled himself away to read. Frowning, the second sheet of Winghorse's file was completely inked out. Curious, he held it up to the light, trying to see the words concealed behind the blocks. Nothing.

The telephone rang, spearing the night with its sharp shrill. Surprised, Agustin checked his wristwatch. 10:58 p.m. It had to be an emergency. Pressing the bell receiver to his ear, and raising the mounted mouthpiece level to his lips, he said, "This is Lord California."

"Have you finished reading over the files Triptych provided?"

Harper.

Etney had been waiting, pacing in the garage to warn him Harper was more agitated than usual. Agustin caught himself before his sigh broadcasted over the line. "I'm going through it now."

"This was priority, Agustin, or didn't you know that?"

He mentally counted to three before replying. "I'm aware this is important, but I do have other duties." Before Harper could waylay him with objections that there was nothing more important than the Corporation, Agustin asked, "Why is there an entire page blacked out?"

There was a pause, then an angry grumble. "Triptych was not to give that to you—never mind. It's not important. How're you planning on accomplishing our goal?"

Agustin grimaced and rubbed his eyes with the back of his hand, still holding the candlestick telephone. If the page wasn't important, why was it blacked out, and why would Triptych place it in the file when Harper told him not to? Agustin didn't push for an answer. It was too late, and he was too tired to get into yet another fight. So he informed Harper of the first initial surveillance at the bakery, and of their target's arrival in time for the recruitment drive.

"As expected of you," Harper said. "Because the Amaranth have increased their efforts in trying to breech our protection wards. They've broken through a weak spot over England. Our regional Infinity teams are dealing with that as we speak."

That was disconcerting. "Do you think they're tracking the triplets?"

"I know so, because they're already poking at the wards over the Bay Area. The barriers are holding strong for now and our Infinity teams are watching. But we need to procure this rogue gateway before the Amaranth do. That is your sole assignment. We cannot allow the empire to steal anyone else to bolster their armies. I'm trusting you to take care of this, Agustin. I have my hands full dealing with New York business."

"What's going on in New York?"

"Oh, tireless drama with the Phoenix Forges—those damned false gods. They refuse to acknowledge our superiority, but I have it under control. I'm reviewing employment records to see who to transfer—"

"Etney's needed here," Agustin interjected, fists clenched around the telephone earpiece and neck. This was why she was upset. She should've come to him. Said something. "She's not ready to resume active duty. None of my team are."

There was a long pause. Through it, Agustin agonized over the whys of the silence. And for a moment, he thought, maybe, Harper would allow him some leeway. Just this once.

Then, "Her name's the first on my list. If I have to reassign employees, that's my right." The disconnect tone buzzed in his ear.

He'd thought wrong. Agustin mulled over that dark, empty feeling that boxed in his gut, his heart, and his mind, all at the same time.

Absently, he remembered to hang up and returned the candlestick telephone to his desk. Triptych's hand-written report bothered him. Harper wouldn't approve anything hand-written. But there was Harper's signature, scrawled at the bottom of each page, and authenticated by his personal seal. And most alarming, that included the blacked out page.

Agustin read through several more pages before tossing them back to his desk. He couldn't get Harper's intrusion out of his head.

With a grumble, he opened a drawer and pulled out the bundle of palo santo his son, Ganymede, had sent him. When burned, it was supposed to be a remedy for stress, and dissipate negative energy. He doubted it was strong enough to clear Harper's vibrations from the room, but it was worth a try.

Placing a small metal tray on his desk, he used a lighter instead of his elemental flame. Smoke began to rise. Leaning back in his chair, he closed his eyes and breathed deep.

Someone knocked at his door. Agustin hadn't realized he'd been staring at, and contemplating, the thick layer of ash in the tray. He rubbed his face and checked his wristwatch. Nearing midnight. The knock echoed louder this time, more urgent. His valet, who was accustomed to seeing him naked, or in various states of undress, wouldn't knock twice.

Agustin buttoned his shirt and vest and wrestled his long hair into some measure of decency. "Enter."

Chapter 13

Etney

THE DOOR FLEW OPEN. A familiar silhouette strode the distance into his office. Etney. Her men's shoes clacked purposefully across the tile. Golden irises against darker gold pupils reflected in the weak light. Those eyes set within a glossy black sclera made her appearance much more striking.

Sweeping over her forehead and down the bridge of her nose was a birthmark of orange-yellow and red. Charged with solar energy even at this late hour, she, and the facial splash faintly glowed. The illumination increased when she crossed into his bubble of lamplight.

The awe-filled visuals of her phoenix heritage meant she'd put away her communication ring for the night. The jewelry did double duty as a concealment spell, making her appear human. Her fiery red updo and outgoing personality marked her Irish among the humans, and that was fine with Etney, even though she didn't have the accent.

The Winghorse file mentioned the triplet brothers obscured their avian and mixed-blooded nature by a stud earring in their left ears. The jewelry was invisible to the eyes of the mundanes.

Etney rolled her sleeves. "We were on our way up and smelled smoke. The guys are waiting out in the hall in case of a flare up." Oil and grease splattered her baggy blue jeans and buttoned up shirt. She'd been tuning up the automobiles again.

He pointed toward the tray that held the smoldering palo santo. "A gift from Ganymede."

"You gave us a panic," she said. "Doctor E—"

"I'm well aware of Esteban's orders about using my flame." Agustin cut off that avenue of conversation before it became another lecture.

She eyed him before running her finger along the ashy residue, and popped it into her mouth. Her brows flexed. "Tastes of anxiety and indecision. Let me guess. Harper's sent down more of his bullying orders."

Reading ashes, and an ash's former vibrations so precisely was a unique talent only phoenix possessed. It unnerved him when she did that.

He froze. He wondered about that inked out page. If he burned it, would she be able to tell him what was on it—no. He couldn't. Harper said it was none of his business.

Hmmm...

Then why had Triptych...?

Annoyed, he pulled that blacked-out page from the file and slammed it in the drawer along with Winghorse's portrait. Out of sight, out of mind.

"Agustin? Are you all right?"

Agustin ignored the inquiry, and leaned back in his chair, preparing for yet another round of attack, dodge, and chase. "Harper doesn't bully me."

"Okay," she replied with a long sigh. "We'll keep filing this problem away in your desk drawer, Lord Ostrich, like you do all of your problems, and I'll keep trying to get you to see reason. Maybe someday." She slouched atop the edge of his desk instead of sitting in the guest chair. "So. What assignment has you so stressed?"

He allowed for a weighty pause to gauge her reaction. "Have you ever heard of a Breese phoenix?"

The sparkling and vibrant young woman evaporated right in front of his eyes. She transformed into his second in command. A second in command he often referred to as the grizzled old general. Her gaze flittered back to the fine traces of soot on the metal tray. The smoke curled lazily into the air.

As expected, she dodged and attacked. "You ditched supper. Neglected a meeting *you* scheduled. Ramirez said we had an assignment. The team's waiting in the hall for me to make sure you haven't fried yourself."

The danger of frying themselves was something they had in common. There was a reason their suites were side by side. To keep watch upon each other against a rogue inferno. Even if they both occasionally griped about their quarters being too close together.

He had to tread carefully here. "Our assignment is of the Breese lineage—well, a mixed blood, I'm told."

The Breese were a branch of phoenix he'd never heard of before Triptych's report. Which meant the Breese line was as scarce and unique as the research stated. But that was all it revealed. The why remained a mystery. He hoped Etney could enlighten him.

But as soon as he'd said the forge's name, she turned cautious. He'd knocked her off guard. She'd always been tight-lipped about her race. He realized he was holding his breath.

Etney tilted her head with a distant aloofness. "You know I won't get into my kind with you."

"Yeah, speaking of that. Harper's poking at the forges again. Why didn't you tell me he was harassing you?"

"I already told him no. That's the end of that, Agustin. I mean it."

So much for that. He'd give a little push. Hard gaze affixed to hers, he slid the file towards her.

"Okay then. A local resident. Calico Winghorse," Agustin said. "Baker. Wizard. God of Space and Time. We're to acquire his inter-dimensional portal, and keep it away from the Amaranth Empire."

Her mouth twisted, and he watched that raptor-like attention strike across the pages as she read. "And apparently, he's a Breese phoenix," she said after a long moment. "Go on."

Agustin wasn't about to crow over a victory yet. At least she was talking. "I thought that—"

"Because I'm phoenix too, that he'd cooperate with giving us his portal?" Her tone was marginally combative. Now on the receiving end of that idea, Agustin realized how silly it sounded.

"Oh. Is that Diana?"

Agustin startled at the jarring question, his chair slightly rolling in his shock. Etney pointed toward the open door of his bedroom suite. There, on his nightstand, was Diana's framed portrait.

He'd purposefully arranged the furniture within the two rooms so he could see it from his desk as he worked. That way, he wouldn't forget to tuck it out of sight. He didn't receive visitors at his private bedroom suite office, which was why he kept the connecting entrance, open. Etney had won this round. Agustin got up and closed the doors.

"Diana and I parted ways a long time ago. You know that." Etney was gifted at turning the tide against him.

"Not on good terms, thanks to Harper," she pressed on. "Why do you still wear her communication ring if you've let her go? While hers sits on the display rack with the spares."

Irritated, Agustin pulled the simple gold circlet off his pinky and shoved it into his desk drawer. It rebounded off of Winghorse's portrait, leaving a noticeable tear in the image. He grumbled at the damage. As if it were a foretelling he'd forever be alone. "I wear it because it's a reminder not to get so romantically attached."

"Because Harper refuses permission?"

The drawer handle cracked in his grip. "I didn't invite you in to speak of Diana. *Or Lord Gardenwood*," he hurried, before she brought up that heartbreak as well.

Palms up, and out, Etney surrendered. "I know both relationships still sting," she said softly. "Every once in a while, I can tell you're reminiscing. Agustin, sometimes, I hear you crying in the middle of the night. I—"

"That's quite enough," he snapped.

For the most part, he'd gotten over Diana. He knew she was gone for good. She'd dubbed the Corporation "the other woman". Something no one could ever compete with, she'd accused.

His gut twisted.

He knew now Diana had been right about that. Infinity Corporation had ruined his life. A life with her. Or a life with Gardenwood. Even though he knew for certain he'd never see Diana again, how it all unraveled would forever scar him. But he was thankful that he'd come to his senses now, after so long. The sooner this assignment was over, the better.

Etney let his temper cool for a few seconds before she said, "I wish I'd known her."

She wasn't going to give up. Agustin countered with the only defense he knew. Work. "I need your input. Calico Winghorse. A phoenix—a Breese phoenix, please."

It was her turn to keep silent, so Agustin tapped the pages she'd abandoned for her quest to torment him. When she picked them up, the papers crinkled in her fists. "H-how? W-where—who gave you this information?"

"That's classified." He crossed his arms before she protested. That shut her down. He didn't often assert authority over her. He didn't like doing it.

Another few moments passed as she chewed on her lip, eyes downcast. She took a soft breath. "I've always assumed the Breese were a myth—something the Dasheel forge made up so people wouldn't be afraid of us."

"Because the Dasheel are like roving mini suns?" It was one of the few things she'd shared with him, because of the dangers the Dasheel power presented.

She nodded. "The Dasheel and Breese originated off-world—there aren't any Breese here on Earth."

"There are now. The Winghorse triplets."

She didn't respond. And her expression was unreadable. He knew he had to nudge her again.

"So you'll help?" There were a few times Agustin cursed that he'd trained her against telepathic scanning. This was one of them. Her mind was locked tight.

Maybe he should let her read the complete file. There were still several more folders to examine. But being handwritten, it had obviously been classified. For his and Harper's eyes only.

"Etney?"

She looked up from her inner contemplations. "Yeah," she said faintly. "Fine. Yeah, I'll see what I can do."

Agustin acknowledged her surrender. He knew that compromise had been hard for her. He caught her gaze, then glanced at the closed bedroom door.

"You would've adored her."

He cleared his throat and checked the time. One a.m. This was going to be an all-nighter. "Bring in Ramirez and Joe Mist for our meeting, and I'll ring for a pot of coffee. We have a lot to go over before the recruitment drive."

Chapter 14

Nightmares

THE ANGUISHED SCREAM ASSAULTING his ears was his own. Agustin bolted upright from bed as the flames licked around him. *My heart. Oh gods. Is it going to burst from my chest before or after I burn to death?*

Thirsty. He lunged for his water. His element often left him parched, dehydrated.

Clumsy, numb fingers failed to make purchase and knocked the delicate tumbler off the bedside table. It careened into the pitcher on its way, causing them both to fall. The sound of glass shattering against his tile floors made him wince.

That was when he noticed the ash across his blankets.

Blast it.

Farming reports, profile applications for the upcoming recruitment drive, trade agreements with Lords Nevada and Oregon, *and* Calico Winghorse's entire file GONE. All gone. His secretaries were going to murder him and bury him on the estate's back acreage. But he couldn't deal with that right now.

Between the sobs and squeezing pain, his sleep-deprived brain realized he was awake, and it had been yet another nightmare. Agustin struggled for calm, even as the real flames around him swirled in the air.

His tongue stuck to the roof of his mouth. Pawing at the sweat-saturated strands of hair crisscrossing his face, he tried not to gag as he pulled them from his lips. He really needed to start sleeping with it braided.

With concentrated effort, he only had to think of snuffing his fiery elemental ability, and the room fell into muted shadows. Most of his private bedroom was spelled against burning—so was Etney's.

Weariness and gravity felled him back to his pillow. He grimaced and moaned. His sweaty nightshirt plastered against his faux human shell made him feel worse. But it was either that, or dealing with his true form.

The single ram-like horn on the left side of his head, and the curved twin spikes on each side of his head, usually cricked his neck and ripped his sheets as he slept. Not to mention fussing with his wings and claws. His dark mood escalated. Those twin spikes were more antler than horn, and he was due to shed them soon.

Agustin pulled himself up and reached for his wristwatch on the nightstand. Five o'clock in the morning. He'd gotten two hours of sleep.

Yanking away blankets fireproofed by magic, he peeled himself out of his nightwear. Avoiding the broken glass, he shuffled into his robe. Absently, he wondered if there would be a dustpan and broom in his walk-in closet. It was more his valet's domain than his.

The nightmares made him cranky. Every night for the past three nights, the visions had haunted him. Chased and attacked by a large white wolf that morphed into a large white bird was bad enough. What was worse was his suspicion that the wolf was no ordinary beast, but lycanthropic in nature. Whipping silvery flames surrounded both creatures. Annoyed, he eyed the ashes among the shards and watery mess.

Fire. Agustin knew fire could never hurt him. He couldn't be burned. Maybe it was the smoke-related respiratory afflictions of his childhood illnesses that caused the anxiety and dark dreams. As well as Esteban's age-old cautions about the use of his elemental fire powers. The Menehune doctor monitored and watched him like a hawk.

A deep breath further shook away the illusions, even as Agustin attempted to examine them. All through his childhood, his mother had urged him to heed his dreams, for they always had meaning.

In this vision, he'd been horribly disfigured by flame. The pain had been so real. Intense. The magical wrap of his human skin had melted right off, showing the scales and flesh of his true form. Until that, too, dissolved. Tissue and muscle oozed out of him, leaving him a sentient demonic skeleton. Spiky wings of polished white bones flexed and creaked.

Agustin plowed through the memory. Forcing himself to face it. To fight it, even though a sob threatened. Somewhere in the darkness of that dream, a sophisticated lazy laugh had reverberated, and it replayed in his mind.

He remembered a wolf howling. It snarled at that grim nightmare of foreboding joy. The canine beast then shifted its shape; a white firebird arose, filled with vengeance. A piercing avian cry echoed, filling the space around them. The phoenix took flight, vanishing into the darkness to seek the mirth. And then, he, in turn, whole and re-fleshed, had shed his human guise to chase the phoenix.

Agustin shivered. It didn't make any sense. He glanced to the ashes of the files. At this point, his decision to leave IC for good was the only thing grounding him from a breakdown. He wanted nothing more than to go back to sleep.

But the nightmare memory flared again.

Birds. Fire. Phoenix.

He was surprised he'd made the connection on half a brain, and without a cup of strong coffee. Perhaps Etney might help interpret the vision.

Or...maybe this was a mission he could assign her to lead. Wean her into the leadership role, and give her full control of the project. From the few pages on Winghorse he'd read so far, they'd make a good match.

The thought of that immediately annoyed and surprised him.

A quiet knock at his bedroom entrance had him quickly cinching his robe. "Enter," he called.

It was Etney. Dressed for the day in women's wear. She ignored the stink face he made. In turn, he discounted her cross expression of *I-know-you-were-using-your-fire, do-I-have-to-call-Doctor-E?*

Thankfully, she opened with, "I think we're going to have to move your bed away from the wall. Neither of us is getting any sleep. Especially since you're having multiple nightmares a night. It's taking a toll."

He folded his arms and absently waved two fingers. Using his meager talent of magic, he levitated his massive, four-poster ten feet further.

"Are you happy now?" Goodness, he was worse than cranky.

"No. I should have asked you to do that three nights ago. Here, a peace offering." She held out a mug.

"Peace," he agreed, taking a rejuvenating sip of black coffee. "Thank you."

"Agustin..."

He knew that tone, and his shoulders sank. "What?"

"Maybe...maybe you should see someone. About more than the nightmares, I mean. We're worried about you. Doctor E might be able to recommend—"

He stared down at her. "Why are you wearing a dress?"

She let her hesitant suggestion go and forced a smile before she flared the floor-length dark blue skirt. "Don't you like it?"

The corset she wore beneath her high-collared blouse hugged her too-thin frame and did odd things to her back. The elaborate laced cuffs of her long sleeves seemed to siphon the life out of her.

She was wearing women's shoes. The delicate, high-heeled, and narrowed style looked like it was squeezing her toes into oblivion. She'd wrestled her hair into an updo of curls that reminded him of the pale flames raging through his nightmares. He shivered for the second time since waking up. Or was it the third? He'd lost count.

If she went without her parasol, which wasn't often, Etney would have to wade into the estate's lake, sometimes twice a day. To keep those around her, and his mansion, safe as she shook off the vast amounts of energy she accumulated daily.

So she wouldn't burn out and die.

It was the precarious, sad fate of the Dasheel phoenix forge.

"Your chosen attire is unnatural and scary." He lifted an eyebrow at her while taking another sip. "Go put your trousers back on."

"I changed because we have a guest."

He glanced at the grandfather clock. "At five in the morning?" His inquiry echoed into the cup as it hovered at his lips.

She shrugged. "You're well aware IC never sleeps." She glared at him. "And apparently, I don't anymore either. I happened to be up when Mr. Triptych arrived. He's quite an interesting gentleman—wants to talk to you about our assignment. So I left him in the parlor with the morning paper and hightailed it to change and wake you."

Agustin choked and spilled his coffee. Getting feedback on his nightmare would have to come later. He pulled a handkerchief from his pocket and dabbed at the front of his robe. He opened his mouth to offer her the assignment lead, but closed it. Because the drawing of Winghorse tucked away in his desk now filled his thoughts.

Dammit.

So instead he said, "Show Mr. Triptych to my private dining—"

"He presented his corporation ID; he's a higher up. So I already told the maid to bring him in after she brews more coffee."

"—while I get dressed." He turned to her. "I'm curious. Is he still wearing his hat and veils? Did his identification have a photograph attached?"

She shook her head. "No photograph, and yes to the hat and veils. The team's bursting with excitement about the possibility of hot-off-the-grill-barbeque."

"Etney," Agustin tried, rubbing his forehead. "Those stepping back from their Infinity teams shouldn't be referred to as—"

"What can I say? Ramirez and Joe were up all night gossiping like schoolboys. When Triptych knocked on the front door, I had to beat them off the poor man by singeing their eyebrows. They've asked if he's one of the candidates. What do you want me to tell them?"

Agustin grumbled, his mind still reeling from his nightmare and lack of sleep. "Mr. Triptych's not a candidate, but the new regional manager."

When she jerked, her skirt hem swirled about her women's shoes—Agustin did a double take at her feet. He supposed the change of footwear made sense, since she was wearing a dress.

"WHAT?" she cried. "Harper fired you? When? Why am I hearing about this now?"

Because he had to calm down enough to swallow the bile and accept it first. "I wasn't fired," Agustin protested. "There's been a shift in staff. I'll explain everything this evening, after the candidates have left."

"You better," she demanded. "Then I'll buy you a beer at Raynard's. I can play counselor since you're too busy and stubborn to see one."

"What I need is for my damn secretaries to get back from their honeymoon," he mumbled, glancing at the mess on the floor again. They certainly wouldn't have allowed him to sleep with their precious paperwork. Dammit. He didn't want to be buried in the backyard. He had too much work to do.

Esteban had to go and rave at how beautiful Hawai'i was in front of two of the hardest working demons on his payroll. Then, bam, the question was popped and eagerly accepted. That meant two to three weeks on a boat to get to the islands, a week of fun and sun, and additional weeks to return.

Agustin grunted. To hell with it. The stress was going to kill him sooner or later. He'd been keeping his team on a tight leash lately. Working them as hard as he himself toiled. Trying to prepare them for their re-training, and for them to assist with the recruitment. It was why they kicked him out of his mansion.

Etney wanted to socialize at Raynard's with the rest of the crew? "Why not?" he relented. "Go ahead."

"You mean it?"

He nodded. "Tell Ramirez to arrange it."

"Hot damn!" she yelled and bounced out the door. "It's my turn to drive the Wolseley!"

Chapter 15

Good Morning, Mr. Triptych

As soon as Etney shut the bedroom doors behind her, Agustin yanked off his robe. There was no time to ring for his valet or clean up the mess.

Agustin knew keeping Triptych waiting would make his servants uncomfortable. They'd had a hard enough time adjusting to their lord's half-angelic nature. It would be cruel to ask them to wait on someone who might be the real thing while he was fooling around getting dressed. He still wasn't sure of the man's background, and coming right out and asking would be rude and disrespectful.

He finished tying his tie when he burst into the dining suite. As he surmised, his servants had gone into hiding after the side bar had been re-stocked.

Triptych and Etney stood on his arrival and paid their respects. Etney curtseying to him was disturbing. It was uncomfortable to see her act with such subservience.

Triptych was in another crisp white suit and still wore his signature hat, hood, and scarves. While the headwear was rude indoors, Agustin felt it would be equally impolite to bring attention to it. It was clear now, though, that Triptych was deliberately concealing his face. A disfigurement, perhaps?

"Good morning, Mr. Triptych. What brings you to my Demonym?"

"Your recruitment drive, of course," Triptych said. "Ms. Dasheel was kind enough to invite me to sit in on breakfast. We had a lovely chat before you arrived."

"Well..." Agustin hedged. "I usually have a working breakf—"

Etney motioned their guest toward the buffet station. Then glared at him from behind Triptych's back with a warning to be civil. Agustin produced a silent grumble and fell in line, more obedient to the scent of spiced sausages and strong coffee than to Etney's harassment. His stomach growled at the sight of Portuguese sweet bread and scrambled eggs.

A stack of dirty dishes on the corner table signaled that his Infinity 8 crew was quite awake and had already eaten. Perhaps it was better that way. To leave their ill-tempered, work-driven Lord Beast to snarl and gnash at his meal while he loomed over paperwork like a raptor guarding a fresh kill.

Agustin collected a plate and waited his turn at the sidebar. He spied Triptych avoiding all the offered meats. Interesting. The man looked up at him, then. Agustin had the sense there was another grin behind those ivory scarves. He found it suspicious.

"Our roster's been empty for years," Etney said to Triptych.

She was piling her plate high with scrambled eggs, bacon, and well-done fried linguiça. Dammit, she was taking all the good crispy pieces.

Etney had the nerve to deliberately look at him as she fished out another piece. "Especially since Agustin assigned half our team to guard

Syd Badweather off-world—ah, she's Agustin's former ward. We could always use more teammates."

What Etney didn't say outright was that not many in the Corporation wanted to work with him, specifically. There was a host of issues over that. They were too intimidated by him being his father's son. Partially because he was half demon. They didn't know him. They only knew of Harper's unyielding reputation.

Agustin poked around in the serving tray. Success. There were several pieces Etney had missed.

"That is news indeed," Triptych said. "And another reason for my visit. Ms. Badweather will be coming home soon. If we can arrange it through Calico's portal."

Agustin paused over the tray of mixed fruit. It had taken forever to find someone better suited to hone Syd's powers. He counted back the years. She was an adult by now.

"That's great!" Etney cried. "I'll ask the maids to start airing out her suite. I doubt she's into dolls and stuffed animals anymore. Oh! We can redecorate before she arrives."

Agustin flinched as the excited, discarded threads of Etney's thoughts shot out of her head like fireworks. Companionable appointments to the most prestigious clothiers. Trips to the milliner. Hair salons. Society socializing and lunch at Raynard's. Then onward to Sally's Place for darts, bocce ball, beer, and barbecue. Teaching her to drive.

Gods save them all.

"I don't want to clip your wings, Etts, but shouldn't we let Syd choose her suite's new color scheme?"

"Oh, sorry, Ms. Dasheel," Triptych hurriedly interrupted. "But Ms. Badweather isn't going to be staying after her debriefing. She's needed in New York."

Etney's shoulders fell. "Ah, that's too bad."

Agustin lifted a brow. It sounded like Harper had recruited his former ward for that mysterious mission in dealing with the phoenix forges.

Triptych selected four slices of Swiss cheese. "Mr. Harper says you've hosted a recruiting drive every year with little results. I thought I would see if I could help with that."

"That's true, we have," Etney replied. "Ramirez and I asked around about the poor attendance. Either the majority are afraid of Agustin, or they don't want to work with a group of has-beens."

"That's disheartening." Triptych stared at her a moment before turning back to him, perhaps wanting him to explain.

"It's the eyes. Always the eyes," Agustin mumbled, adding a second sweet bread roll to his already crowded plate. He didn't want to get into the gritty details.

Etney nodded. "They come for the free food and listen to what Agustin has to say easily enough. They just can't get past the fear of those intense and moody eyes, watching. Or admit to themselves they burned out bad enough to get kicked off their teams. And no one wants to admit they're an I-8er. We've basically been tagged as the shame of IC."

"Well..." Triptych claimed an apple and a bunch of grapes. "That being said, I think a change in tactics is what's required here. Ms. Dasheel, I'll need you front and center, taking over the hosting duties from Lord California. Joe Mist will assist you."

The three of them made their way to the long table and settled into their breakfast.

"A leader should lead," Agustin protested, reaching for the coffee pitcher. "With his people supporting him from behind."

"There's some truth to that," Triptych agreed. "But we're not here to get into the specifics of leadership. We're here to strengthen Infinity 8 as a whole.

"Swapping you out for Ms. Dasheel and Mr. Mist—a phoenix, and a full-blooded human—will silently show the recruits that everyone is welcome. Your actions will speak louder than any honeyed words, Lord California. Doing so removes your intimidating glares from the stage, gives prospective recruits time to get used to you, and see if they can take commands from a woman."

"Oooh!" Etney perked up, turning to him. "I rather like that idea."

"This is a rather...unusual tactic," Agustin began reluctantly. However, it was the perfect opportunity to start shifting his duties over to her, and to get Etney used to leading I-8 full time. Establishing her as the authority figure to any incoming recruits was the goal. "On second thought, that is the best idea. Etney, the floor is all yours."

"Really?" She put down her silverware.

Agustin nodded.

"Fantastic." Etney jumped up. "I'll go brief the team on the changes before the recruits start banging on the gate." She pushed in her chair, collected her breakfast plate, and ate as she dashed off.

Chapter 16

Preparing For Demonym

THE NEXT TWO DAYS flew by much quicker than Calico hoped. The normal banter that usually circulated among them had been put on hold. The mood in the bakery turned somewhat tense, but focused as they went about their work. By mapping out a plan and assigning the baked goods, they completed the demon lord's order the night before.

Pleased, Calico knew the compensation he made on this exchange could be stashed away to save for a motor vehicle delivery transport. His pony, Dot, would no longer be subjected to the ill tempers of his brothers.

Calico observed the neat stack of boxes along the workbenches, doing a quick mental tally to make certain all were accounted for. When the silence beckoned, he looked up. His brothers were nowhere to be seen, and the morning darkness still blotted out the sky. Which meant they were on schedule.

"Frazil, Maars," he called. "If you are finished hitching Dot to the cart, we must begin loading the pastries."

More silence. Tilting his head, he made for the back door, only to have it open before he reached it. The reek of wet straw and fresh manure wafted in on the predawn breeze, causing him to gag. It was a proper smell for the outside, but not when combined with his precious confections.

Calico used the hem of his apron to cover his nose and mouth while raising his other hand to bar his brother entry, even backing away a little to avoid contact.

"We have to get a wiggle on," Maars said. "It's three o'clock. It's going to take you a couple of hours at least to reach the reservoir area before daybreak. Longer if you insist on leading Dot instead of riding."

"And you were supposed to sweep Dot's stall after helping me load the cart," Calico said from behind his linen shield.

"I haven't shoveled yet. I was helping Fraze with the tack. You might want to get out there before she murders him and buries the body."

Calico shook his head. "You will not come into my pristine bakery, or touch my faultless creations, while covered in unmentionables. Go to the outside hose. There is a cake of soap next to the nail brush on the little shelf. I use them after attending to Dot. Wash up and change your clothes."

"Aw, Cal, it's not my fault you bought the orneriest, most foul-tempered monster in the city. No wonder you got her for practically free." Maars glanced over his shoulder, grimacing. "Fraze's probably dead by now. How are we going to function without him?"

"You exaggerate."

"Do I?" Maars's voice was oddly pitched higher, but it felt like a mild reprimand.

"There is nothing wrong with Dot's temperament. She is the sweetest pony."

"Sweetest pony my arse!"

Calico gasped. "Watch your tongue. Dot is very sensitive."

Nose scrunching, Maars shot back, "She's only sweet to you because you know a few Winghorse guild secrets. The rest of us have to throw food and run."

Frazil appeared behind Maars, his chest heaving. "The old nag bit me!" He raised his arm to show the bleeding flesh.

Calico put his hands on his hips. "You did something to offend her. *I* will hitch up Dot. Off with you, too. Both of you wash up at the hose. You are not entering my bakery in such a condition."

"Really, Cal," Frazil complained. "You're as fussy about a few measly traces of dirt as Great-Grandfather Rupart—"

Frazil stopped talking as soon as the name left his lips. Maars went three shades whiter than his fair complexion, and Calico felt as if he could not breathe. Frazil, on the other hand, turned bright red, and he looked as if he was going to start babbling apologies.

"Great-Grandfather would agree with Cal," Maars managed. "Come on." He grabbed Frazil by the shoulder and ushered him away. "Off to wash."

Calico slumped against the wall. As he slid down to the seat of his trousers, he pulled up the apron hem and hid his face in the linen. He would not cry. He would not. Perhaps his refusal to whimper had caused his palms to perspire.

Great-Grandfather.

Calico recalled when things had gone...ugly. He had been brimming with magical abilities even then. When that awkward event known as puberty occurred, it awoke the full magnitude of exactly where his magic stemmed from. And thus, activated Great-Grandfather's curse. Then, they were either on the run, or taking magic lessons from Grandfather Charade.

But, before that, it had been Great-Grandfather Rupart himself who helped coax his wizard's familiar into being. Calico's lip quivered when that bittersweet memory surfaced.

Calico had been hiding. All day. Even from Frazil and Maars. Bawling his eyes out because Grandfather Acanthus's lessons had been too difficult. Too advanced for him.

His brothers had understood the instruction and excelled. They had tried to show him how, even though they did not care to take the last step required to create a familiar.

But he wanted one. So badly. He desperately needed a friend who would completely understand him. Not tease him because he had 'quirks' and often fumbled the simplest of tasks.

His siblings and Grandfather Acanthus had all been so understanding. Comforting him at his failure. That had made everything so much worse. So he had run away. He could hear Grandfather Acanthus calling to him. He sensed his brothers' empathic quest for him. Still, he had fled. In shame and embarrassment. Why was he so dense and brainless? So dumb?

"Cally? Dearest?"

Calico gasped and looked up. The gruff endearments sounded so comical coming from Great-Grandfather Rupart.

Sniffling, Calico hid his head back in the cradle of his arms, utterly horrified. "Another witness to my misery?"

Rupart called to him telepathically. :Come here, my dear chick peep.:

So Calico did. He launched himself into that embrace, ignoring the elemental cold of Great-Grandfather's self, and cried some more. Then comforting flashes of light and emotion filled his mind. The projection of understanding of that hurt itself, and best of all, the recognition that Rupart did not know what hurt Calico was going through. The telepathic exchange helped soothe and settle, and Calico realized he was hiccupping less and less.

:I'm here for you.:

:Help me Great-Grandfather. Help me fix it. I am broken.:

A big, calloused hand smoothed his hair. :I know what broken is,: the gruff mental reply came haltingly. :You are not broken.:

:Then what am I?: he wailed.

:Beautifully unique, my child. Doing things in your own way, in your own time.:

:But I have failed! It is over. Finished. What will become of me?:

:Oh Cally. Failure is such an ugly word, bringing ugly feelings and despair. You fail only if you stop trying. Come. Show me your hands.:

Calico did as he was told, presenting them, palms up. Then, Great-Grandfather did something that confused him. He took an item from his pocket and held it out.

"Take it," Great-Grandfather said aloud.

Calico did.

He was even more confused when Great-Grandfather repeated the task four more times. A bit of candy. A hair tie. Half of a charcoal writing stick. A clean handkerchief.

Calico tried to quell the sadness still leaking from his eyes. Following suit with the verbal communication, he said, "I do not understand."

"The handkerchief is to dry your tears," Great-Grandfather said kindly. "You've used your left hand each time. You've shown me you're not naturally ambidextrous like Acanthus and your brothers. I'm surprised Acanthus didn't pick up on it. Show me, try your lessons again. Primarily using your left hand."

Calico dried his face, then sat cross-legged. Centering himself and quieting his mind, he let his magic breathe. Outstretching his left arm, he coaxed

*the energies from without and from within. Letting them gather and grow.
Then, leading with his left, he slowly made the motions around his skull,
then at his heart.*

*When the casting was done, he once again outstretched his left arm, his
right beneath it and supporting. Instantly, there was a coil and pop of the
most beautiful blue light.*

*There, in his palm, was his familiar. The most adorable and perfect
pink bean of a newborn kangaroo rat ever. Like the one big sister had
created for herself.*

*The familiar's pink little toes twitched and its closed eyes fluttered.
Slowly, fur was beginning to cover its tiny, fleshy body before it doubled
in size. Then, the big, beautiful black eyes slowly opened. She squeaked a
greeting. And blinked, acknowledging him, gazing at him with such love
and understanding. For she was a part of him.*

*Calico laughed. And cried. Then hiccupped and laughed again in such
relief. Such amazement.*

*"Gigglemug," Calico muttered in awe. "I am so pleased to meet you,
Gigglemug."*

*The kiss dropped atop his half-shaved head drew Calico out of his jubi-
lation.*

*"Well done, my little one," Great-Grandfather said. "I'll leave you and
Ms. Mug alone now to get acquainted."*

And then Rupart tread away.

Dot's whinny landed Calico back into the present. With an aching
heart, he fidgeted, further crushing his apron against his face. Something
in the pocket nearly poked his eye.

Absently thinking it was his notepad and pencil, he instead pulled
his new customer's business card into view. He stared a moment at the
smashed corner. This was the future. He had to keep looking forward.

Pulling himself off the floor, Calico composed himself and wiped his eyes. He pocketed the card in his vest, this time for safekeeping.

Stepping outside, he felt the rise of gooseflesh all over his body from the brisk early morning breeze. He changed into his barn boots and set out across their small yard. Shivering at the cold, he gave poor, miserable Dot a pat and combed her forelock with his fingers.

The pony was glad to see him and greeted him with an anxious nicker. After fixing the tangled tack hanging off her at odd angles, he returned to the porch. There, he removed his boots for his more sensible shoes, discarded his apron into the laundry bin, washed up, and headed inside.

Once back in the kitchen, he encountered his brothers, who scrambled to attention with their hands held out, ready for his inspection. He examined beneath their fingernails and nodded approval. Then together, they carried out dozens of twine-bound boxes to the cart.

Calico stored fresh aprons in a box under the bench of the pony cart. One was for working, and the other was an embroidered masterpiece by Frazil's own hand that read *Scrivens Bakery*.

Calico straightened his cravat and put on his best everyday jacket. The high-quality coal-colored garment had been a smart find back in England. The gentleman merchant in the shadowed alleyway had given him a good deal, even if Frazil had had to stitch up the small rip in the pocket and launder out the smell of formaldehyde.

His wound washed and bandaged, Frazil covered the load with a clean blanket. "Are you sure you don't want me or Maars to go with you?"

"The bakery requires you both while I am away. If need be, I will use my magic."

"You're confident for once. That's something." Despite loving the cooler temperatures, Frazil's teeth were clenched. That meant he was upset.

Calico tried to reassure him. "This is a demon lord's estate. I doubt the manifestation of paranormal or magical talents will send anyone into apoplexy."

Frazil tied down the load as he talked. "That's not what I'm concerned about. Best do such an important delivery manually, Cal. Please?"

"I will be fine. Go on. We will open soon." Calico countered with an affectionate peck to his brother's cheek. "Do not leave Maars unsupervised. You know how he panics if he must run the till and make change."

Chapter 17

Escape From Demonym

THE MISMATCHED WROUGHT-IRON WINGS affixed to the demon lord's gate was an impressive sight. Even if somewhat menacing. The larger than life-sized appendages stretched across the black bars, two spread on the left, and one on the right. Calico detected faint traces of a protection spell woven into the metalwork. A rather weak one, in his humble opinion.

As he drew closer, finer details emerged. On the right panel, the sleek, smooth bat's wing arched into acute points with a small hook at the crest. It shimmered with dark, oily blues and purples in the early morning sun. On the left, two avian wings sported a matte-ivory finish. The fine craftsmanship of the individual feathers appeared to be ruffling in the wind.

Calico wondered if the white wings upon this majestic showpiece symbolized a phoenix, but he knew it was unlikely. Frazil and Maars had informed him the beings with such appendages in this land were not phoenix.

What had his brothers called them? Angels? Whatever the title, the grand sight before him revived a bout of homesickness.

Calico shook out the memories rattling around in his skull case. Frazil and Maars would be unhappy with the direction of his gloomy thoughts right now. No matter how much he hoped, or prayed to their mother goddess, they could never go home. Not as long as Great-Grandfather Rupart suffered under the death god's possessive curse.

Drawing a semi-depressed inhale, Calico stepped up to the demon lord's own impressive entrance. In his homeland, demon lords were also powerful, influential. But even they could not break a vengeful god's curse.

Calico pinched his cheeks to distract himself, determined to keep moving forward instead of dwelling upon a traumatic past. The polished brass plate affixed to the stone wall guided him away from his misery. Crisp, embossed letters read *DEMONYM*. Below this, the mismatched trinity wing motif carried through, showcasing the buzzer bell. Calico pressed it.

An old man shuffled out of a small building several yards up the driveway. This gatekeeper looked at him and his confection-filled cart and disappeared inside. Seconds later, the motorized gates clunked open.

"The kitchens are around back," the gatekeeper said in a thick Spanish accent. "You're expected, Mr. Scrivens. Follow the smaller driveway for deliveries."

Calico hesitated before answering. But politeness mattered more than embarrassment over his voice. "Thank you, kind sir."

As he drove the pony cart up the bricked driveway, he enjoyed the view of big oak trees and manicured greenery. A gravel path forked from the main drive, around to the back of the mansion.

Pulling Dot to a stop, he disembarked at the servant's entry. Someone had left the door open, so he hurried inside. As he suspected, flies buzzed the center of the room. With a disgusted snort, it took two attempts to concentrate. Using his magic, he herded them together and shooed them out. His control did seem to be deteriorating further, but he was content he did not cause harm to the creatures. He would have known had he did. His mother was the life goddess, after all.

That done, Calico marveled at the impressive kitchen. Colorful ceramic tiles dominated the large space. A diamond-pained window highlighted a wide copper sink. Ovens spanned an entire wall; some were even warming up. Pots and pans hung from wrought-iron ceiling racks in the middle of the room. Meat and vegetables were strewn over chopping boards. Cooks were not present. Someone had to be here, as evidenced by the open door.

"Hello?" he called.

No answer. Perhaps they were out collecting more fare. The estate was massive enough to host several acres of food plots and flower gardens.

Well, he'd best get the order set up before guests wandered in searching for refreshment. Donning his work apron, Calico stacked four boxes in hand before he remembered his brothers cautioning him. Finding his inner balance and calm, the remaining packages floated out of the cart and trailed behind via his magic.

Each box lined up on the open counter space along a back wall, and all the lids opened at once. He was most pleased with the results. He would sound like a monster bullfrog at the end of the day, but it was what it was.

After washing up, he manually plated confections on the silver trays and platters that had been awaiting him in the butler's pantry nook. Calico stepped back and admired his work. He reveled in the sweet scents that uncurled and lingered in the air. Content and ready to start his day, he slapped his hands together and rubbed them. He could not wait to change into his serving apron that boasted the name of his bakery.

Now that his important duties were out of the way, he let out a little chuckle of excitement. He eagerly switched gears to mentally rehearse his wizard application speech. He adjusted his baker's cap to appear extra sharp.

The far door leading into the mansion swung open. Two rough-looking men walked in—humans. Their auras conducted an undercurrent of danger. Calico wondered if they were his customer's bodyguards. Their flawless matching uniforms consisted of dark blue trousers and buttoned-up coats. A brighter blue patch on their collars drew his attention. It was an infinity symbol.

Calico did not sense any magic within them, but it concerned him. It had been decades since he had trained for combat. Those rusty skills saved the lives of his siblings. But he was no longer as acute and swift as he once was.

"Buenos días—uh," the Mexican gentleman's greeting trailed off before switching to English. "Hello, good morning. I'm Ramirez. Are you one of the new recruits?"

"He's awfully skinny to be a recruit," the blue-eyed, brown-haired man added. "Definitely doesn't have the cracked open and wrung out IC look about him."

Attempting bravado, Calico threw back his shoulders. "What was that?"

Both men flinched at his gravelly voice. Calico cringed, too. The bullfrog was creeping closer. Would his interview speech be ruined?

"Ah! He's the boss's assignment." Ramirez motioned to his companion. "This is Joe Mist. We heard you have a portal. How easy is it to control? Is it a lot of work?"

Ramirez stuck out a hand in greeting. Calico recoiled instead, his gaze darting between the men. The blood drained from his cheeks, leaving him clammy. Only he, his brothers, and Mr. Triptych knew of his otherworldly gateway.

"What are you saying?" Calico asked.

"Welcome to Infinity 8." Joe Mist bobbed his head. "The boss said a new recruit would be here today—one who stood out from all the others, and you're certainly that. They work us hard, but it's all good. We gotta keep on our toes to protect Earth from the Amaranth. And there's always perks." He was staring at the goods on the trays.

"The A-Amaranth?" Calico's heart skipped an additional beat and his palms went clammier than they currently were. How were they aware of the cruel otherworld empire from his homeland? "I do not understand," he said. "I am here to serve pastries."

The men looked at each other. "Aren't you Calico Winghorse?"

They knew his real name. He took a step back. "I-I am Mr. Scrivens, the baker."

"Oh, right. Etney said you had an alias," Joe Mist replied.

Calico frowned. "Etney is your employer?"

"No, Lord California is," Ramirez said.

A ruse. The man who had been his customer. But not a customer. A man who had walked into his bakery and lied to him. Fingers curled into his palms and turned white from the pressure.

Then terror flooded through him, and his stomach soured. This Lord California knew of him and his portal. These men spoke of the Amaranth Empire. Were they spies for Great-Grandfather Rupart? Rupart would never work with the empire though, would he?

Calico wished he could warn his brothers via telepathy. Would they have to run again? His lip caught in his teeth and bled. If Rupart caught him this time, his great-grandfather would succeed in shutting down his mind. This time for good. If that happened, his siblings would be next.

His hands would not stop shaking. The desperation to protect his siblings allowed the dread to escalate. He had to make an exit. He needed a distraction. Calico lifted his arm in one fluid motion, grasping for more than his magic. Mild pain lanced through him and he grimaced as he felt his telekinesis attempt to flip on. Behind him, the confections tumbled into the air—pies, cakes, breads, and biscuits.

The duo froze; Joe Mist chuckled. "Hey, mister, you have a wicked sense of humor, but no need to get steamed."

Steamed indeed! Huffing, Calico let his arm drop. All his hard work rocketed through the kitchen and slammed into the men, knocking them off their feet. Sugary-sweet smells rose further in the air.

Wiping fillings out of their eyes, the men sat there, stunned. Their mouths opened and closed, but no words arrived. They looked at each other, then turned to stare at him.

"You shall be billed for my goods and services. Good day, gentlemen. Inform your boss I do not appreciate being lied to."

For added measure, Calico mentally grasped the bakery boxes and hurled them at the duo. He scurried out, not waiting around to see if his defective telekinesis obeyed. He jumped into the pony cart and snapped the reins. He was halfway down the driveway when the rush of running boots sounded behind him. His telepathy may now be useless, but he knew it was his ex-customer.

"Wait!" Lord California cried after him. "Please, wait! I can explain. Mr. Scr—Mr. Winghorse, please wait!"

A quick glance over his shoulder revealed the man waving his arms and hopping about like a complete lunatic. Calico's jaw clenched; his vision was starting to go fuzzy from the stress. He snapped the reins again. Dot picked up speed.

Then he heard Lord California's desperate order. "Marco! Hold the gates."

No...won't be trapped!

Calico gulped, his heart pounding. Panicked, he gathered the surrounding energy. From within himself, and from without. Praying that somewhere inside of him his telekinesis would function, providing a boost to his magic.

Pain from the curse shot through his limbs and his concentration scattered into the wind. He waved a single hand with far more panic than he'd intended. Metal creaked and groaned, then screeched for the both of them.

Calico bent his head and covered his face with his arms, knowing what was coming, but unable to stop it. Dot screamed, pranced, and half reared. The gates burst open with the force of a magic-induced typhoon, slamming into the stone walls. Bricks cracked; a section collapsed. Dust billowed. One gate hung sadly as a hinge shattered.

Another glance. Through the rising dust, the California lord slid to a halt, his mouth agape and his eyes wide at the destruction. Calico gulped, and flicked the reins. Dot hopped through the wreckage, still shrieking from the aftermath. The little cart jostled roughly over the jagged debris. Once clear, his badly shaking hands snapped the reins several times in a row, and Dot took off at a full gallop.

Once far from the estate and feeling safe enough, Calico wiped his eyes and started shivering. He'd not just used his telekinesis in the destruction, but had inadvertently added a small fireball into the mix. His hands were still tingling from the force of magically created fire—something his innards and elemental self had always revolted against.

Fear slid into his heart. At his loss of control. Of what this demon lord wanted so much that he had to lie to obtain it. Then try to imprison him inside the high walls.

Dot snorted and slowed her pace when he ceased holding the reins so tightly. Calico wished Gigglemug was awake. He missed his familiar with her wisdom and guidance. Frazil and Maars often referred to her as his security blanket, or another big sister.

Perhaps...

No. He could not risk waking her up, especially with his powers in such a sorry state. Doing so would cripple her, just as he was currently incapacitated. He would have to deal with this scare all on his own.

Calico pulled Dot to a stop. He couldn't see the road through his tears. He didn't want to drive into the ditch. Dot would do so, if he asked her to, she trusted him that much. How would he explain that accident to his brothers?

His fingers trembled, and he shoved them beneath his armpits. His legs shook, even as he tried to brace them against the footboards. He struggled to force away the traumatic flashes of his past: *Chased. Hunted. Trapped. Hearing, seeing, up close, the creature that was once his great-grandfather. The creature's grotesque, wheezing laugh. The creature forcibly peeling back the layers of his mind like an overripe fruit and the only thing he could do was scream helplessly into the void...*

Terror smothered him, sinking into the pit of his belly. His vision wobbled and darkened. He couldn't take the stress any longer. Calico leaned over the edge of the pony cart and dry heaved. He clutched at the emptiness and grief inside. All the while, he prayed to his mother goddess that his legs would hold him up by the time he made it back to the bakery. If he made it back...

Calico glanced over his shoulder. Rupart was the most powerful telepath in their homeland. If his great-grandfather wanted to find them, he would.

Emotions, horrors that were too fresh and too raw, arose. He wasn't sure he could be strong enough to save himself, or his brothers, again. Rupart had stolen more than his psychic powers. His great-grandfather had robbed him of his courage.

Laying his head against his knees, Calico quietly sat there, shaking. And tried to breathe.

Chapter 18

Brotherly Support

CALICO LIFTED HIS HEAD off his arms and gazed skyward, sensing an emotional pull so strong, it was not to be ignored. Even in his poor psychic condition. Wiping away the tears obscuring his vision, he saw them. His brothers.

Maars and Frazil approached, from high in the sky. Maars in his phoenix-self, wings spread wide. Frazil stretched prone across the human-sized feathery back, holding on for dear life, arms around Maars's neck. It was strange to see Maars's natural form, and without flame. But Frazil was the reason for it. Their ice-affinitied sibling would not have survived if Maars had been alight.

It never ceased to amaze Calico of the lithe grace of the Breese. With their massive wings, impressive train of tail feathers, and the long, slender, stilt-like legs.

The sight assuaged some of Calico's nerves into the mild humor of memories. In the third week of their arrival on Earth, Mr. Triptych suggested a trip to the zoo. It would aid their familiarization with their new home.

He and his brothers had soon been forcefully removed from the premises after they arrived to view the aviary exhibit. For within, had been the native beauty dubbed the Secretary bird.

The wonderful creature was so similar to their kin, Calico remembered being distraught, thinking the poor dear was a Breese chick. So he had leapt over the fence and attempted to liberate it. His brothers whisper-yelled at him from the viewing patio as he chased the little thing around the enclosure, trying to calm it in their native tongue. Once again, Mr. Triptych had to produce the bail to spring them from the human jail.

Calico was jarred out of his reflection; Maars banked swiftly and landed. Those wings beat furiously as his talons touched the ground. Those whipping wings showcased two or three dazzling blue feathers among their snowy brethren. The blue indicated they weren't technically a true Breese, but passed enough to be accepted as one. At least with the forges back home. Calico wondered of the forges here, and another bout of homesickness flared like a phoenix from its ashes.

Calico was aware of Frazil running toward him. And of Maars bouncing and trotting along after him on his long phoenix legs. Sharp talons clicked against the scattered rocks and pebbles of the dirt road. The feathered crest on Maars's head and the long tail train bobbed as he went.

Calico could not say a word as Frazil launched himself into the pony cart and locked him in a hug. He reciprocated, squeezing harder as he hiccuped and started bawling. His brother was sweaty and damp from being in close proximity to the shape-shifted Maars. Even though Maars was not ablaze, his body temperature was enough to cause Frazil some discomfort.

Calico should have known his brothers would rush to his rescue, for his terror sent a tidal wave punching through their disrupted bond.

Maars leaned over, his avian head butting against them. Calico put an arm around that feathery neck.

"Cal," Frazil pulled back, looking him over. His brother was inadvertently knocking him to and fro, rubbing at his numb arms, trying to get some heat back into his shocked system. "What happened?"

Unsure if he wanted to delve into the hurtful subject, Calico replied, "Who is running my bakery?"

"No one," Frazil said. "We barely got the doors locked before Maars was tearing off his clothes and taking flight. I was lucky enough to hold on."

Maars let out a low avian screech, and Calico knew he'd been instructed to stop stalling.

"I..." Calico had to rub his eyes and straighten his coat.

It was painful, but he revealed the entire story of the demon lord's ruse. All the while Frazil patted circles over his back, and Maars paced, making chirping noises.

A low rumbling from deep within both his brothers followed, and the feathers around Maars's neck ruffled. Calico found a small measure of courage in the quiet support. He slowed down to tell the tale. Until finally he could raise the most important question.

"Dearlings," he asked haltingly. "Do you think Great-Grandfather Rupart is coming for us?"

His brothers looked at each other thoughtfully, and Calico worried as the seconds ticked past. It turned into a moment before Maars chirped, and the feathers unruffled.

Frazil nodded in agreement. "There's no way he could get through the portal. Not after you locked it behind us."

Calico shivered, remembering the Rupart-creature swiping and beating at the closed gateway as they huddled inside it, recovering from the shock and trying to make sense of the brutal attack.

"Frazil?" Calico asked. "I am sorry I did not properly heed your premonition."

"No, I'm sorry, I should've reflected further before I opened my mouth. The hunch was over your fright and flight from the mansion. It wasn't about this demon lord."

"But—"

"No second guessing my powers, chick peep," Frazil said warmly. "Why would this noble go through all that trouble for you to bring an entire cart's worth of pastries if he didn't mean to eat them? If he wanted to take you, he could've had his henchmen grab you coming in. Or sent them to chase you when you left. Do you see anyone following?"

Calico turned around to check. The only presence on the estate's miles-long road was a group of bunnies sitting in the middle of it. Calico slowly nodded. "That is true—oh! My bakery! The wasted pastries. The lost wages and time."

"Don't worry about the bakery. Maars and I'll get back there soon."

Stark embarrassment overcame Calico's fear. His head sunk into his hands. "This is all my fault. I allowed my imagination and terror to rule me."

"Oh, Cal." Frazil hugged him again. "Don't regret taking chances. We want you to live, and learn about this world firsthand. Let me drive back. Maars will take you home."

"Home?" Calico squared his shoulders in surprise. "Oh, no, no, I must return to work!"

"Are you sure?"

Calico whipped out his handkerchief and dried his eyes. "A cup of calming tea and a biscuit, and I will be fine."

"Well, if you're sure." Frazil reached for the reins, but Dot snorted and shook her head, shuffling back and forth and rocking the wagon.

Frazil backed off. "Cal, would you do something??"

"Now, Dot, I know we've had a scare." Calico jumped down from the cart and gave her a pat, combing her forelock with his fingers. "I am sorry I put you through that distressing hubbub. Would you please take Frazil back to the mansion estate, then bring him home without fussing? I would be most grateful."

"Back to the estate?" Frazil asked in surprise. "What do you mean?"

Maars made a low grumbling noise.

Calico looked at his brothers. "Have patience. She's thinking about it."

"Wha—no, I mean me going back to the estate?"

"You must apologize for me until I can gather my wits," Calico sniffed. "I am too embarrassed and upset to face him. Not to mention I must calculate how to repay him for destroying his property!"

"Leave the monetary worry to us, Cal. Maars and I will figure it out. But you're right. I'll go talk to the demon lord. We don't want him filing any charges."

Calico waved his hands in near panic. "Are we going back to jail?"

He could not contain his nerves as his brothers looked at each other.

"I'll do my best to calm the situation," Frazil said. "Will Dot let me drive the cart?"

Calico looked at his pony, then to his brother. "She is ready."

Chapter 19

Dual Apologies

His gatekeeper had been clear of the blast. That's all that mattered. Marco had used the teleport tunnel to jump to the north entrance gatehouse the second the brick wall vibrated. Thank goodness for elemental-sensitive employees.

Ramirez and Joe Mist, however, were helping with the clean up and repair. It was their punishment for loose lips. His people should've known better, but he was also to blame. Ramirez and Joe were still used up from their time on active combat teams.

He and Etney were about to assign them light duties. Helping with the recruitment drive would've been their first assignment.

Agustin glanced up from the rubble when his on-sight maintenance foreman called out. The same horse and buggy that fled the estate was now returning. His heart sped up.

But soon, he realized the driver wasn't Calico Winghorse. White hair stuck out from a dark blue bandana. One of the brothers, then. Agustin walked out to meet him.

"Mr. Chavez de la Cruz?" The voice was different, too. Not the grating, throaty tones he'd expected.

"Mr. Chavez will be fine." Considering, he wasn't a stickler for using de la Cruz outside of his IC status.

"Is everyone all right?" the brother asked, setting the little wagon's brake to keep it from rocking back and forth as the pony fidgeted.

"We're all fine here. No injuries. A bit shaken up, though."

The brother glanced at the mess, fists tight around the reins. "I'm so sorry this happened. Cal apologizes too. He was just—"

"Scared," Agustin finished. "I take responsibility. I am truly sorry I wasn't clear with him, and I paid a price."

The brother clenched his teeth now. "About that. If you can work with us on installments—"

"No. This was my doing. I don't expect you to pay for my mistakes."

"But sir—"

"I won't hear it. And I can only apologize as well."

The brother nodded, the relief evident in his manner. "He's beside himself, and wants to apologize personally when he's had a moment to catch his breath."

That the baker wished to talk to him was more than a surprise. Strangely, Agustin didn't feel so tense anymore. There was still a chance to salvage this assignment. "Then I shall come by later this afternoon, with your permission?"

"That can be arranged. Mr. Chavez, thank you for being so reasonable and understanding." The brother released the brake, turned the pony cart, and bumped back down the road.

Agustin watched him go until he was so far down the driveway, he was merely a speck on the landscape. Then he beheld the destruction again. His heart sunk lower. The stink of fear and violence held this area in thrall.

Which meant he had to cancel the recruitment bash.

He had to keep the buses from arriving to witness the carnage. He had to keep those with sensitive psychic powers from detecting this mess. Because it would trigger negative flashbacks. Ruin any chance for them, and him, to aid their effort to strive for healing.

Agustin telepathically alerted two of his employees to see to the task. Less than a moment later, two motorcars exited the garage, and hurriedly rambled down the same road the brother had taken. At the public intersection, one vehicle would go north to intercept the group arriving from ICHQ. The other would head south to waylay the bus from Cooley Landing.

Agustin headed back into the house. He ignored Etney standing there in the main foyer, at the threshold of his public office. Triptych had apparently left during the drama, as he was nowhere to be found.

Walking past Etney, Agustin took a seat behind his desk. All he could think about was Winghorse's terror. And of how he'd personally let down the dozens of people who had looked to Infinity 8 as an avenue to regain something they'd lost.

Stomping all over that was the sudden vision of Harper. As if on cue, the telephone rang. And rang. Etney moved to answer it, but Agustin raised a palm.

"We know who it is," he said quietly. "I'll take it. My responsibility." He cleared his throat, then lifted the receiver to his ear. "This is Agustin."

"I will see you in my office. One hour." There was a click, then a dial tone.

Slowly, Agustin leaned over and hung up.

And felt very small.

Chapter 20

Reporting To Harper

AGUSTIN DROVE HIMSELF INTO San Francisco for the most difficult trial of them all. Facing Harper. He parked and entered the building. The colonial-style house had additional floors and wings added since its original construction. Which made the place a bit of a maze at times.

The narrow, sterile halls of Infinity Corporation headquarters always gave Agustin a stomachache. He felt eyes on him. Heard the dozens upon dozens of thought-threads from employee to resident that had broken free of their sources, and attempted to wriggle into his brain. None of which he'd been even remotely tempted to read.

He already knew what these angels were thinking, and rumors spread fast. Seeking escape, no matter how brief, Agustin hurried his pace.

Perhaps his sick stomach had something to do with this being angelic territory. Perhaps it was because of the many summons he'd received as a small child.

Even back then, he'd had to wait. Judged, and glared at, by the angels who loomed over him as they went about their business. Even back then, there had been nothing to do but pace to burn off the nervous energy to keep from going mad.

Of course, he could have sat on the floor as a child, but that brought on more trepidation. He'd always imagined that if he had, he'd have melted into the surface and lose himself. The floorboards would consume him, become a part of him, as punishment for his demonic blood. Then the angels would have been able to wipe their boots on him before they cast him to the fiery landscape of true Hell.

Agustin's polished leather oxfords strode across the cold, ugly tile as he paced. The tile's new, he thought. Fresh-painted white walls were so bright they were blinding. The stink made him dizzy. In his childhood, magic had lit this corridor of doom. Now the flicker of electric bulbs caused it to be colder and more unfeeling.

He had to pull it together. Focus on why he was here: his screwup with his assignment. Of not having Calico Winghorse, and the portal that Harper wanted, already secured. The baker may accept his apology, but it made the yet-inquired-about-portal-purchase all the more complicated. Winghorse would be wary of his intentions now, which would slow negotiations even further.

Agustin noticed he was wringing his hands and forced himself to stop. He removed his sweat-soaked gloves and shoved them into his coat pocket. Meeting with Harper shouldn't have him sweating like a schoolboy sent to the headmaster's office. Not anymore, at least.

He looked at his wristwatch. Eleven a.m. He'd made the hour deadline. That was one tiny detail that had always irked him: always having to wrangle an appointment with Harper's secretary, even during emergencies—unless he'd been summoned by Harper himself.

Taking a deep breath, he knocked on Harper's office door and strode in. He was surprised that Triptych was here. Harper laughed with the liaison as if they were old friends. Triptych's hat bobbed in greeting. But Agustin waited awkwardly for Harper to acknowledge him.

Harper sat straight and tall behind his desk. His black dress shirt contrasted with his gray vest and silver tie. The angel's appearance was what one usually saw depicted in Renaissance paintings. A fair complexion. Slim, yet muscular. Classical features set with blue eyes and sandy-brown curls sweeping his shoulders.

Another dollop of sweat gathered behind Agustin's tie. He forced himself not to pull the handkerchief from his pocket to dab his face.

Harper's mirth vanished. He motioned toward the extra chair against the wall. "Sit down, Agustin. Mr. Triptych has informed me of the disastrous state of your assignment. Frankly, I'm shocked at your incompetence. The situation with the Amaranth Empire is dire. We need control of that portal."

"The fault is mine, sir." Agustin fetched his seat and settled next to Triptych. "I was on the telephone conducting urgent California business. I was unable to greet Winghorse when he arrived."

Triptych's shoulders hunched, and his body language went rigid. "Maybe I should just tell—"

"No," Harper interrupted. Triptych jerked at the booming response and cringed in on himself. "If Agustin can't handle this on his own, I wonder about his competency to run this organization."

An embarrassed flush crept all the way down Agustin's neck. He knew better than to debate the harsh criticism. It always stung, but he was no longer a child seeking comfort in his mother's hugs as he sobbed and asked why. His fists curled tight.

Agustin held back the words itching to spring forth. A declaration that would free him from Harper's toxicity and the crushing weight of what was Infinity Corporation. *Not yet*, he told himself. *Have patience. Make sure Winghorse gets a fair deal, in writing, before Harper throws everything into chaos with his affronted outrage over the announcement.*

Harper spoke through Agustin's dark thoughts. "You're more committed to your demonic thugs than doing something worthy of the people."

Agustin's frustration and hurt almost had him blurting out a barb in response. He wasn't the one who hobnobbed with nobles to produce heirs solely to make rigid alliances.

Instead, he forced his shoulders to relax, and tempered his reply, striving to be the adult he was. "I respect and believe in what IC is attempting to do. I'm here to protect the people, sir. Both as Lord California, and as Infinity 8's team leader." *For now.*

"Well, I think you need a little help," Harper snapped. "Infinity 3—"

Agustin leaped out of his chair and leaned over the desk. "I-3? No! You can't. Winghorse seems a simple, gentle man. He's just a baker. We're in the middle of negotiations. I've been told on good authority that Mr. Winghorse does wish to meet again. There's still a chance."

Agustin hoped his emotions wouldn't disrupt the magic that sheathed his claws. Harper would make him pay for a new desk.

Winghorse was simple, gentle, yes, even if the man had blown a new hole into Demonym's front gate with a wave of his hand. He'd been frightened. Agustin knew what could happen to downtown Redwood City if Winghorse felt threatened again. It damn well wasn't making any shred of sense why Harper wanted I-3 involved, when he was to handle this on his own.

Harper hadn't even twitched at his plea. "He's a wizard. And a phoenix-demon-lycanthrope hybrid-thing. There's nothing innocent about him."

Agustin tried one last time. "I-3 are front line warriors. They'll accost him, strong-arm him. I just finished telling you he wants to see me. We should coax a potential ally, not—"

"The orders stand. Do I have to remind you IC's primary and single function is thwarting the Amaranth Empire and safeguarding Earth? Their attacks and abductions are why I've built this corporation with my own hands. Our goal is to close off all avenues of their arrival, and that means obtaining that portal.

"So no, we don't have time for niceties. People are at risk. Time will tell who'll succeed—I-3 or I-8. And we'll see if you truly have what it takes to run this organization. So do the job you were born to do, Agustin. Dismissed. Both of you."

Agustin couldn't bring himself to face Triptych. Surprisingly, the liaison spared him further humiliation by racing out on his own. But as the man exited, Agustin startled and jerked.

A fleeting tendril of strong emotion escaped Triptych's otherwise vise-like grasp. Agustin's parched telepathy whipped out and latched onto it before he could stop it.

While Agustin was definitely not empathic, he translated the broader signals with ease. *Anger. Embarrassment. Failure.* Directed at Triptych himself, and at Harper. It appeared Triptych was just as rattled with Harper as he often was.

Agustin sighed, and nodded to Harper, who was already buried in paperwork and paying him no mind. Clutching his top hat, Agustin made his way out into the parking area and got in his automobile.

There was a baker awaiting his apology. He only hoped the brother was correct, and that in these few short hours that had passed, Calico Winghorse was ready to see him again.

Chapter 21

The Back and Forth

LOITERING ON THE SIDEWALK leading up to Scrivens Bakery, Agustin took a deep breath. He tuned out the rattle of motorcars and horse-drawn carriages. Ignored shoppers with packages making their way up and down the creaking, wooden sidewalks.

Coming here sooner than permitted might not be in his favor, but with Harper's threats swimming around in his head, it was only right to warn the baker of potential trouble storming onto his doorstep.

Pressing a hand to the brim of his hat, Agustin tried to ignore the brisk, cool bay wind and the dust that it kicked up. Dark clouds rolled in from over the coastal range; rain was certain.

Calico dabbed the perspiration from his brow before shoving the linen handkerchief back into his pocket. His brothers had said Mr. Chavez de la Cruz would arrive after closing to apologize. He too, so dearly wished to apologize. Glancing at the clock, he then consulted his pocket watch. It felt as if the hours had dragged.

Waterlogged with calming tea and stuffed with sandwiches and biscuits hadn't settled the minor tremors in his hands yet. Perhaps he was still too overwhelmed with panic and embarrassment over the drama.

He slowly circled the multi-tiered basket display on the sales floor. Frazil and Maars had instructed him to fill it. *Before* they returned from escorting the morning's draw of cash and checks to the bank before it closed for lunch.

A simple task for him, they said, as he waited for the pies to finish baking. It was proving not so doable.

Agustin truly wished to apologize. Leaves and other debris tumbled along the street, as if urging him to get on with it. Or maybe it was a signal to run, but he squashed that thought quickly.

He still hadn't put his gloves on because his palms were damp. What must he look like, standing here, working up the nerve to go in? More importantly, why was he having to build himself up to do this? He needed courage for what, exactly?

Calico permitted a small grin. Finally. Success. The loaf stood tall in the middle basket. Now for the next one. He glanced at the trolley full of French bread, then back to the baskets. But all Calico could see was the little granules of crust crumbling off the cooled loaves.

It reminded him of the rubble and ruin of Demonym's gate. With a huff and a shake, he picked up the second loaf and debated which box he should place it in. Why was this decision so difficult?

It wasn't his fault the demon lord had lied to him. Calico shoved the bread into the basket. The demon lord tried to keep him from departing the estate. Yes. This was his false customer's doing, creating this catastrophe. Not just for the gate, but for all his destroyed hard work. For all the wasted confections! And for upsetting poor Dot!

Perhaps it wasn't the lack of courage that kept Agustin out on the sidewalk. Perhaps it was the guilt of failing his assignment and having another team come in to fix the results of his incompetence. Or his shame to prove himself as the future leader of Infinity Corporation.

And he briefly wondered if that was a small part of why he was going to quit. Because he'd been unable to bring I-8 the true success that its members so needed.

He pushed the negativity away a second time. The frustration over his appointment with Harper should have abated by now. Damn it all. He was acting like the wounded, moody child he'd once been.

What to say to the baker? A heartfelt apology to start. Be honest, respectful, and willing to accept compromises. Accept another dressing down.

Tinkering with the bread placement was no longer daunting. Because Calico knew he was in the right. Another loaf made it into the basket. Then another. He was curious as to why the tremors in his hands hadn't abated by now. The bells above the shop door jingled. He took a breath, and turned to meet his customer.

Chapter 22

The Conflict

AGUSTIN OPENED THE BAKERY'S door and stepped through—only to be a few feet from his intended target. Who stood at a half-constructed bread display. He instantly knew the man before him was not one of the brothers.

The siblings were tangible, whereas Calico Winghorse was ethereal, empyrean, and smelled such. Looked such. *Felt such* down to the depths of Agustin's being. Beyond the mundane soap and shampoo were breezy, celestial spices. It wasn't any common mix, but one infused with the writhing, wild element of life.

And...something else that was difficult to even describe. It surrounded Agustin's senses, ensconcing him in a euphoric calm that had no ending or beginning. The bliss of pure existence. Perhaps that was because of Winghorse's godhood.

Agustin had grown up around all sorts of spices and herbs—due to his mother's herbalist hobby. He'd never encountered any so coiling and vibrant—as if they were alive. Not from Etney or any of the other phoenix he'd met.

Dwelling on the sensations left him breathless. He was even more winded as he delighted in a face that was so engaging and animated.

Agustin unpacked these feelings for what they were. This man's celestial essence had drawn him, awakened his angelic half—a piece of himself he had long ago denied and rejected—and showed him he shouldn't be ashamed of his demonic self, either.

A length of French bread forcefully thrust a foot away from his nose knocked Agustin from his dreamy contemplations. It smelled delicious, and fading warmth radiated off the crust.

"Well?" Winghorse demanded, waving the bread in his face, as if it would keep him at bay. "Speak up! What are you doing here?"

Agustin asked himself if he had lost his mind. He'd let his wits wander away so much that he'd forgotten the baker was standing there, addressing him. He didn't know why his heart thumped faster. Sweat beaded his brow, and his stomach was doing delightful somersaults.

Agustin met this man's infuriated glare, especially since the baker was using a loaf of fresh-baked bread as a weapon. It took all his control to ignore the double entendres bombarding his thoughts.

"Are you here to pay me?" The bread was jabbed forward a few more inches.

Agustin clenched his fists. The man was taunting him. With French bread. And didn't even know it.

He had to banish additional innuendos out of his head. *Great gods, Gustin. What's wrong with you?* He had to do something—something that was practical.

He casually lifted his hand, as if to brush loose hair behind his ear, aiming a quick glance at his pinky. Dammit. The gold ring was sitting in his desk drawer. He could do this.

One deep, calming breath. Agustin removed his top hat, shut the door, and flipped the business sign to 'Closed'. High-pitched sputtering blistered his ears as Winghorse worked to form words.

"Additional compensation is required for private consultations!" The baker stepped closer, invading his personal space.

More heat crept up Agustin's collar, and his palms were still damp. The scent of cumin sat beneath a fainter scent of...he wasn't quite sure. Seared steak? Gunpowder? Welding fumes? Burnt charcoal? Perhaps all the things a phoenix should be, but it was so much more than that.

Whatever these smells were, they were hot, metallic, and celestial, as if they were the very universe itself. *The God of Space and Time.* The fine hairs on the back of Agustin's neck rose. He turned away, politely clearing his throat to compose himself.

"Can I surmise you are here with my payment?" Winghorse demanded again.

"Yes, and to pay you for your time. However, the truth is, I'm here to apologize. Mr. Winghorse, I apologize for not being up front with you."

There was a snort. "Sorry for lying, or sorry you were discovered?" the baker pushed back.

"For lying, and for misleading you. The blame is mine. I didn't think things through when I was handed this assignment. I didn't devote the proper time to investigate. I admit I haven't been my usual, methodical self." *Since I was demoted. Since I encountered you.*

Winghorse lowered the bread. He stepped back and folded his arms. "You speak of time? What do you know of time? Do you show her the respect owed?"

Winghorse considered time a feminine entity? How odd. "I'll have you know," Agustin countered, "my time is precious."

"How so?" came the challenge.

Was he really having this debate? Of being called on the carpet yet again over how he managed his daily affairs?

Jaw clenched, Agustin silently counted to ten. "I wanted to try to make things right by coming here, and to warn you that my corporation is going to try again."

The man shrunk in on himself and became more wary. That hurt Agustin's heart. For Winghorse had seemed to have confidence in himself until Agustin had wrecked it.

"Try again?" Winghorse asked. "For what?"

"To recruit you into our cause. I had intended for you to do more than serve my guests, but also to sit in on the orientation. To join us—them."

"For use of my portal." Winghorse surrendered the bread, placing it back into its display basket. Then the baker retreated behind the glass cases, using them as a shield. Fear and vulnerability were evident on his face and in his body language, and Agustin was sorry for that.

"You know what we're after?" Agustin asked.

"Yes. Your Demonym bodyguards answered that for me."

Winghorse meant Ramirez and Joe. Agustin motioned with his palm out. "Again, I apologize. But lives are at risk."

Winghorse lifted his head and stared. "How many are you referring to?"

"Hundreds, if not thousands."

Winghorse's mouth flattened with disapproval. "What is this IC your people spoke of?"

"The acronym for Infinity Corporation. It's an organization created to keep Earth's residents from being harvested."

Alarm splashed across Winghorse's face. "From whom?"

The words stuck in Agustin's throat. "An otherworld empire. They've been raiding Earth for eons, stealing people for their genetic armies."

Fear bloomed in Winghorse's blue eyes. His body language changed. He looked ready to run. "This empire wouldn't happen to be the Amaranth, would it?"

Agustin startled. "You know of them?"

Winghorse paced, fidgeted with his apron hem, and mumbled worriedly. "Of course I do. They were a burgeoning presence in my native world before I was forced to leave."

"So you can understand the urgency of our requests."

Those blue eyes flashed. "That was not a request," Winghorse argued. "You and your corporation attempted to manipulate me."

Agustin winced. Was he becoming more like Harper than he realized? It made him feel dirty. Was that another reason why he wanted out so badly? He tried again. "I admit I should've been straightforward with you. I will strive for honesty going forward. Please, accept my deepest apology."

Winghorse nodded, crossing his arms. "Yes, you should have been straightforward."

Agustin welcomed the dressing down, as long as this man kept talking to him.

An instant wave of anxiety crossed Winghorse's features, and the baker began to crowd him, herding him toward the exit. "Now shoo! You are costing me customers!"

Agustin turned around to look in the direction the baker faced. Two gentlewomen were at the door. With one look at him, they ran. Dammit. "Um, Mr. Winghorse, perhaps we can still meet after closing and I could tell you more."

"Would this have anything more to do with my gateway?"

"It could, or it couldn't," Agustin hedged, then wanted to slap a hand over his eyes. Why did he say it like that? "The portal is what my boss wants."

Winghorse stopped crowding him and sighed before scratching his chin in thought.

Agustin tensed as the man turned to survey a row of pies on the counter. "You're—not going to throw a pie at me, are you?"

"You can afford it. Now, where are my American dollars?"

Agustin pulled the money from his wallet. Along with another two dollars to compensate for the customers he'd chased off. He slid the stack delicately across the top of a glass case. Winghorse seized the bills and shoved them into his apron pocket.

"Well, how about we meet for dinner tonight?" Agustin invited. "Say, eight o'clock at Raynard's?"

"Raynard's? Ah…"

Agustin realized it had been stupid to assume. Even if Raynard's was a gathering place for their kind, it still cost money and catered to a higher class. Even if this man owned his own business, he was probably not quite breaking even, having been open only a few months. He wasn't even sure if Winghorse lived in the back of the store or not.

"You'll be my guest." It was then Agustin remembered the brothers. While they seemed like nice fellows, they hadn't begun to needle at him like this baker had.

The truth struck him like a lightning bolt, and explained why his palms were sweaty and his stomach flopped. His interest in Winghorse went beyond business.

"Just—you," Agustin clarified. "I would talk to you privately."

"I do not think that could be arranged." Winghorse herded him towards the door. "I am most busy running Scrivens Bakery."

"I understand, but Mr. Winghorse, please, I remind you, my company wants this portal. They're sending a team—Infinity 3 to come and ask again—perhaps demand use of your gateway."

The baker shook his head, waving a hand with dramatic effect. "Joining an organization is not what I want to do, nor is my portal for sale like some bit of inanimate object. It is alive, it is primal, fragile, and tamed only by myself. Now, if you please, good day. I have bread to place." He opened the door and flipped the sign.

Defeated, Agustin frowned a little before he remembered himself. The delightful somersaults transformed into cement bricks. He needed to retrieve his gold ring, as a reminder. He nodded, placed his top hat on his head, and returned to his motorcar.

Chapter 23

The Second Chance

CALICO RUSHED TO THE oven and opened it. The apple pies wore a smoking, crispy black crust. He pulled them out, pivoted, and dumped them straight into the big metal trash bin, cooking tin and all.

The man was insufferable! Demon lord indeed! Smoothly waltzing into his bakery with the proper grace and looking so smart in that top hat. Demanding the purchase of his portal! A portal no one but he and his brothers knew about!

And...and...the man wouldn't stop oozing sexual pheromones while trying to conceal the fact that he'd become...er...quite aroused! While the nobleman might have gotten away with his sudden indiscretion among humans, Calico had his lycanthrope heritage and the sensitive nose that came with it. Thankfully, his brothers were not currently in the store! All three of them had a lycanthrope's sense of smell. It would have made the situation even more awkward.

Calico wiped sweaty palms against his apron. His hands and knees were shaking, and he wasn't sure what to make of the visit. Perhaps because he was still trying to deal with the odd flutters dashing around in his belly. They were fluttering their way northward, mailing a proper invitation to his heart to join in on the confusion.

He pulled a clean cotton rag from his multi-pocketed bib apron, retreated to the storefront, and began the mad quest of wiping down display cases. Yet, the demon lord had genuinely apologized. He'd kindly asked him for another chance. Invited him to sit down to a fancy meal and discuss the use of said portal.

Because lives were in danger. People could get hurt.

The demon lord also warned him this Infinity Corporation would send bullies to threaten. Calico chewed on his lip. He was not prepared to handle such a boisterous confrontation. He froze for a moment before truly throwing himself back into cleaning.

Which confrontation was he referring to? The surprise of the demon lord popping up in his shop unannounced, or the men he said were coming to strong-arm him?

Calico was too used to defense, not offense. Doing his best to not harm Great-Grandfather Rupart while trying to break the curse had tempered that behavior. He would have to plan a strategy. Should it be magical or physical? Subtle or straightforward? He missed being able to talk it out with his familiar, Gigglemug.

It puzzled him that this Infinity Corporation wanted use of his portal. Shouldn't they have resources of their own? His was not like other portals. It was a dangerous and chaotic thing, controllable only by something as equally chaotic in nature. He could not hand over access like they were a neighbor requesting a cup of sugar. No. His answer to their pushy inquiries was most certainly a no.

Yet...

The shop bells rang. His brothers entered, having completed their banking. "Cal, did you burn the pies?"

Agustin had said people were in danger. On both sides of the portal. It would be horrific and selfish of him not to act. Even if it brought the

Rupart-creature back down upon him and his brothers. Even through his terror, he could not risk all to stay hidden away. It was not right. It was not how he was raised. *Oh, mother goddess, was it too late...? Please do not let it be too late!*

"Cal?" Frazil tucked the bank receipt under the cash register for safekeeping. "We're talking to you."

"Ooph!" Maars suddenly held his nose, but there was a big grin on his face. "Burning pies isn't the only stench in here. I thought he'd visit nearer to closing. You're too tidy for a quick tryst, brother dear. Cal? Are you even listening?"

His second chance was slipping away. Calico leaned against the picture window, hoping to catch a glimpse of the demon lord. There had to still be time. There had to be. Before he could permit himself to think of the social scandal, Calico dashed out of the store without his top hat and coat.

Stressed, he glanced up, then down Main Street, praying he would not be run over. Automobiles rumbled past, their engines roaring enough that he had to cover his ears. He leaped out into the street, straining his eyesight, wondering if he should call out.

Scanning the rows of parked vehicles for Agustin's motorcar would not do any good, since there were handfuls of others parked along the street. He had to calm down, or else he would miss him.

Calico looked toward the grocery mart. A tall, lean, dark figure towered over the crowd. It had to be! Calico squinted further, concentrating on the fuzzy shapes. Yes, a possible top hat among the sea of the rounder, more streamlined modern styles!

Yet he was too nervous to solely trust his poor eyes. He had to be certain. Calico sought the safety of the sidewalk. Inhaling through his nose, he engaged his lycanthrope senses. The demon lord was hot ash, wood smoke, cedarwood, and butterscotch.

Yes. There!

Abandoning his beloved bakery without a backward glance, Calico sprinted, dodging the gentlefolk still strolling the walkways. Why was he doing this? He wasn't sure, but he knew it wasn't just the use of his portal to protect people. The deep need inside him to reach this demon noble was paramount.

The figure he had seen was the demon lord. Calico was too self-conscious to call out. His voice was hideous. Unworthy. The populace would fear him.

It was fate that Agustin was still here. It had to be. Calico made a note to deliver fresh cinnamon rolls to the grocer. For Agustin was securing a crate of dry goods into the back boot of his motorcar.

"Mr. Chavez," Calico cried, breathless.

Startled, the demon lord looked up, and waited in silence.

"Please return to the bakery and have a cup of tea."

With that, Calico raced back to his shop, only to find his grinning brothers had been watching him from the window.

Chapter 24

Pre-Negotiations

THAT WAS...PERPLEXING. AGUSTIN WONDERED why the immediate change of heart. Did the brothers have another talk with him in the short space of their parting?

Securing the extra groceries his chef requested inside the motorcar, Agustin curiously strode back to the bakery. He bent, looking through the window before he dared to enter.

He certainly didn't want another encounter with artfully jabbed French bread. Or suffer the indignity of a pie to the face. His cheek ached from a stressed grin. He was eager to take that chance, but he had to remember to control himself.

Centering himself with an easy draw of breath, Agustin opened the door, the bell signaling his presence. The sales floor was empty, but oh, the noise!

From the curtained kitchen, came chaos. Tables and pans rattled as if someone had bumped into them. Voices. Rushed. Excited. Cautious. Among them, the sweet, guttural tones of his assignment. Agustin felt his cheeks heat. *Stop that,* he told himself. *This is business.*

"Hello? Mr. Scrivens?" He figured it was better to use Calico's human alias, especially during bakery hours.

One of the brothers suddenly poked his face out from behind the curtain that separated kitchen from storefront. There was a werewolfy grin beneath that short crop of white hair and bright blue eyes.

A husky chuckle shot across the room and vibrated through Agustin's chest. The brother abruptly retreated to the kitchen in a choppy, bird-like motion. That unique, harmonic laugh mesmerized before Agustin shook himself.

Lycanthropes, like tigers, had the exceptional talent of infra-sound—sound waves that emitted frequencies beyond the hearing range of most bipedal races. While it could be used for a number of instances, a growl could cause disorientation or fear enough to stop you in your tracks. A perfect tactic to stun prey, or give warnings.

But only positive sensations circulated through the air and sang along his veins. He should be annoyed that they'd reversed the talent to draw him in.

Agustin scanned his surrounding for discarded thought. As he guessed, the brothers were nervous and upset at the damage caused to his estate, and were working hard to make amends. Agustin harrumphed and squashed a laugh. They didn't want to go to jail again, and they'd been incarcerated a few times for the most bizarre reasons.

Calico appeared. Minus his apron, and looking like a gentleman in his worn, outdated jacket. "Tea and sandwiches are presented on the backyard veranda. Would you care to join me?"

Agustin found his shoulders straightening, and he smiled. "I'd love to."

Seated at the cozy luncheon table with the wobbly leg, the faint whiff of manure from Dot's barn caused Calico a mild panic. Because their business was on the main shopping thoroughfare, and because he ran a food establishment, he and his brothers did their best to keep things pleasant.

The smell wasn't overpowering, but he hoped his guest would not be put off by it. Once a week, usually on a Sunday because they were closed, they would hitch Dot up to the designated manure cart, and dump the waste in the neighboring farm lands. With permission, of course.

Dear mother goddess, I am thought-babbling.

The demon lord's most wonderful eyes twinkled as he hid a smile behind his hand. Those eyes went downcast for a moment, and his guest cleared his throat.

Despite his baker's cap covering his half-shaved head, Calico went through the motion of tucking strands behind his ear. Shyness consumed him from the inside out, and his hands felt clammy. So he fiddled with his hastily arranged place setting instead. Then took a sip of water.

"Thank you for changing your mind and inviting me in," the demon lord said. "It means a lot to the—I mean me. I also wanted to apologize again, for scaring you. That was never my intent."

Calico nodded, still trying to bolster himself to use his voice. The demon lord knew what he sounded like, so why was it so difficult? Perhaps it was because of their current close quarters. The patio was cozy, barely enough room for three chairs and three meal plates.

Be brave, Calico told himself. "It is my turn to humbly make amends for the destruction of your property."

"Then we're even."

Calico looked up. Was it all that simple? "Ah, will you tell me about this recruitment drive you are hosting?"

The demon lord's jaw clenched. Only briefly. "Well, unfortunately, I had to cancel it."

The heat rose so much in Calico's cheeks he thought he would combust. "Oh my, I have caused more disruption—"

"You're fine." The demon lord spread hands upon the freshly laid tablecloth. "We've both made mistakes. Grave ones. Luckily, no one was hurt. Let's put it past us. Moving forward and learning from them is what matters most."

Calico nodded with relief. "That is true. I am most thankful for it."

An awkward silence followed. Calico felt the blush burn hotter as the demon lord's lips met the rim of the teacup.

"Quite a lovely cup of green," his guest prompted lightly. "Wonderfully hot."

It was he who invited the demon lord to refreshment to talk business. That meant Calico needed to direct the conversation. He was no good at such things. "Ah. Um. So what is the purpose of the recruitment?"

The teacup returned to its saucer. "I do hope we can come to an agreement. Infinity 8 helps those who need gentle guidance. Especially after high levels of stress and conflict."

"So you are lacking team members?" Calico asked.

"Currently, yes. Most of my team is off world, protecting our oracle. At a place called Temple Prime."

"Temple Prime?" Calico exclaimed, leaning over his yet untouched sandwich. "Why, that is the temple home of the Staritti goddess, my very dear mother. It is also the sacred avenue where Grandfather Acanthus grew up."

"Then this realm is your home," the man said, shoulders relaxing a bit. "And you know of the area well."

"I do."

"It's the realm where we'd like you to open your portal so we may ferry people across—that is, if you'll permit us its use."

Calico sat back in his chair. "Oh, I could not do that."

The demon lord paused before answering. "We'd hoped for you to see reason—"

"Oh, my pardon. I see you misunderstand." Calico drummed fingertips upon the table, his nerves rising. "I would like to discuss the use of my portal, but I cannot operate it at this time. I...am not certain I wish to reveal the reasons quite yet. It is a sensitive and private matter, you see."

"That is troublesome." The noble tapped his chin. "For now, why don't I get you familiarized with the Corporation, and we'll come back to that at a later time."

"Yes," Calico felt the burden lifting, only a little. "That suggestion sounds doable. What exactly does your Infinity 8 do?"

"I-8 is a gathering of recovering wounded and cast offs," his guest began. "From our regular corporation divisions, and from the Infinity teams themselves."

"Then it is a rest and recovery group?"

"Not quite. We do have certain assignments, such as investigations, research, or ferrying VIPs to events. Nothing too intense."

Calico pondered that. "Do they get a choice to return to such a high-tension duty? Or are they told?"

Another sip of tea. "I don't push my people. They leave or stay at their own will—but it's my call to decide when they're fit to return to service."

Calico quirked his brows. "Is there an Infinity 9?"

A head shake. "There's been no need for additional team numbers. At least not yet."

"So what assignments do the other seven teams specialize in?"

The noble leaned back and crossed his long legs. "Combat, mostly. I-6 are diplomats. Infinity teams are scattered around the world."

"Oh! So there is more than one Infinity 8?"

The demon lord chuckled. "There's two other I-8 teams on the other side of the world. They also work with those traumatized."

"A most needed haven, for certain. How many have left your nest?"

"Dozens." The bittersweet joy alighting the demon lord's face jumped into Calico's heart. He didn't need his crippled empathy to sense the affection the noble had for those under his care.

"Our most recent graduate—Cadence—returned to his old Infinity team. I couldn't be more proud. Cadence started out with the Corporation, young. Too young. He was transferred to I-8 not long after his first assignment, so I'm a bit nervous for him going back, as his team is a front line patrol."

"Poor lad." Calico poured his guest more tea. It was the only comfort he could offer. "I hope he is doing better."

There was a grunt of acknowledgment. "I as well. I haven't heard from him since. I took him in as a personal fosterling. Got too attached. Perhaps because my own son had set off on his own."

"A son?"

The demon lord's bittersweetness unfurled into pure joy. "Ganymede. He should be home soon from university for seasonal break."

"It can be emotional when chicks leave the nest." Calico chuckled softly. "Doubly so when they return to visit. My own parents had difficulty letting go. What was the nature of your fosterling's affliction?"

The demon lord's lip skewed now. "Telepath breakdown. I've become kind of the magnet to try and heal those with psychic powers."

The words struck Calico's ears, causing him to jerk to a sharper attention. Had he heard correctly, or was he dreaming his most wanted desire? He could not appear overeager. He had to remain reserved. "Oh? That is most interesting. Are you a telepath?"

"I've been since my time in the womb."

"That is...fascinating." Calico put his fingers to his lips in thought. Could this demon lord be the one he needed to help him? Teeth grit, he worked himself up to ask. "Ah, about my portal..."

Calico almost cowed when the man looked at him funny.

"What's on your mind?" the demon lord asked.

The blunt directness nearly had Calico fleeing back into his shell. But he had so many people counting on him for care and protection. His brothers. His wizard's familiar still in a healing, stasis sleep. Those the demon lord mentioned that needed his portal.

Calico took one ragged breath. Then a second. "Ah. Might I ask something in return? My psychic powers are broken. Can you fix them? Or know of someone?"

The man looked at him again, then away. "Fix them how?"

Calico opened then closed his mouth. Now or never. "My great-grandfather tried to tear them out of me—tried to kill me. In doing so, I was infected with the curse he carried. A curse from my homeworld's death god. And...well, I have not shared this with my brothers, but I sense it is slowly killing me. Eating me from the inside out."

The incremental silence had Calico on edge.

Then, "This curse. It sounds contagious."

Calico shook his head. "It is bloodline related. A very specific bloodline."

"That's reassuring. It keeps me open to the possibility of helping you."

Nodding eagerly, Calico rushed on to explain. "Your response is promising. But you see, there are several obstacles...well, I am a god. And...I cannot assist you with your portal crossings. Or even access the gateway until I am healed. Also, upon our side, my gate is currently anchored upon English shores. Beyond, it rests upon the acreage of my childhood home, and I am estranged from there. To use it will take strategic planning—with help from those from my homeworld."

"Hmm." The noble studied him. "Detailed planning we can accomplish, yes. I have to be honest with you. The Corporation has a file on you. I was able to read some of it."

Calico worried at his jacket hem. "Oh dear. They've been spying upon me?"

"We had to be sure you weren't a threat, or in some way connected to the Amaranth."

Calico tucked his thumbs behind his jacket lapels. "I assure you, I am a proper and upstanding gentleman. I do what is right."

"That wasn't detailed in your file," the demon lord grinned. "But noted."

The encouragement and gentle humor rallied Calico. "It would be a pleasure to call Infinity 8 my fellow team mates. However, what would be expected of me were I to join—in a reserve capacity, mind you. I do not wish to see people hurt, but I must care for my family. To me, they are foremost. The bakery takes up the majority of my time, and I must begin brushing up on my wizardry."

"Your magic practice...right." The noble pursed his lips. "I hope we can sit down to discuss that, and your interest in the Corporation. Shall we return to my office to start planning? You are free to depart?"

Calico looked up at the afternoon sun. "Perhaps we could schedule an appointment? Not only do I sense these negotiations may monopolize a full day, I feel guilty leaving my brothers alone to sweep and lock up for the night. We must also prep for tomorrow morning."

"That we can do. Why don't I call on you tomorrow night? I need to inform HQ of your interest—"

"Ah, yes, you did mention other visitors would inquire about my portal."

The man tapped the table, thinking. "Not visitors, but another team. I'll take care of it. Tomorrow, I do have several conferences to attend, and a meeting with the Queen of Mexico's emissary, but I will be here."

"Goodness. We are both very busy."

"We have an appointment then," the noble said. "To further explore an agreement. Thank you, for changing your mind."

"I too, found it more enjoyable than I thought."

"So meeting adjourned?" the demon lord asked.

Calico blinked. "Yes."

"Wonderful. I've been waiting to dig into this marvelous-looking lunch." the demon lord picked up the toasted bread fully loaded with meat slices and fresh vegetables, and took a robust bite.

Calico blushed when the crisp crunch from lettuce, onions, and pickles reached his ears. There was a lovely riot brewing in the pit of his stomach, because he watched this demon lord enjoy the roast beef sandwich he had assembled with his own two hands. To help dispel the visible shine at his hot cheeks, Calico picked up his own sandwich and crunched right back.

Chapter 25

Infinity 3

IT HAD BEEN A productive morning, baking and watching the sunrise sweep with glorious beauty through the bakery's kitchen windows. Calico took a sip of his breakfast tea. The chat with the demon lord yesterday showed promise, and he looked forward to their next meeting. He paused a moment, blushing, before shaking his head. It was time to work, not daydream.

With a spring in his step, he finished packing up the luncheon for his brothers. Frazil would be accompanying Maars on the neighborhood rounds today. Then they'd be off to the dock warehouse to pick up the weekly supplies. That meant he'd have a working meal, himself.

It was likely his brothers would be out of the bakery for the rest of the day. Besides waiting in line, it would take time for their order to be unloaded from the boat and the paperwork processed. Even longer since they would have to walk alongside the pony cart on the return trip.

Calico had provided Dot with her weekly bribe of an apple along with her regular alfalfa. Frazil and Maars had also promised to be on their best behavior. It made Calico smile when all three of them were in good spirits.

Hearing the hose turn on outside, Calico knew his brothers were washing up. So he hurried to finish their food basket, double checking the water jugs and the two books to stave off boredom while they waited. On second thought, he rushed over to the small desk by the telephone box. There, he ripped several pages from the Sears catalog and tucked them under the basket handles. He doubted there would be fresh corn cobs available in the outhouses.

Frazil met him at the door. "Cal, you sure you'll be all right on your own? I have a feeling I should stay today. In fact, maybe the pick up could wait until tomorrow."

Those beckoning words brought Calico up to a pause. Faint and foggy images swam through his vision, and he sensed a hint of Future Time in play. But with his powers so broken, it was difficult to interpret them. He forced himself to remain cheery. If something were to happen, he would prefer his family at a safe distance. So he shoved the picnic basket at his brother. "Nonsense."

But Frazil wrinkled his brow at that. "Really, Cal—"

"Shoo!" Calico ushered him out. "We need those supplies. Maars will hurt himself if he hefts those monstrous flour sacks all alone. It is worry enough that Dot has to pull such an overloaded cart, which is why we must keep saving for a motorized lorry. You take care with my pony." He gave his brother a peck on the cheek. "Don't forget your hat. It will be a wonderful, sunny day."

Too nervous to have a proper luncheon after the noon rush, Calico opted for a spot of calming tea. So far, everything had been dandy. But he remained on edge. Frazil was not often wrong; be it from a stubbed toe or a misunderstanding—such as the incident at Demonyn—to warning them of Great-Grandfather's transformation and attack. Although they had not known the danger was the rise of the Rupart-creature's coming assault at the time.

Calico glanced over to the empty day old and discount shelves. His boisterous regulars, Mrs. Wright and Mrs. Brown, along with their marriageable daughters, had cleaned out the section. But even their usual, overly fussy visit had not been able to distract him.

The entrance bells above his shop door rang. Four men entered. Calico immediately sensed they were angels.

Dressed as dockworkers in simple sweat-soaked trousers and shirts, they were hard-eyed and hard-faced. Scars layered on their hands and faces enhanced their brisk, jaded auras, informing him they were not here to purchase bread and trade small talk.

Was this Frazil's concern, then? He clenched his fists and hid them behind his back. Maybe his voice alone would scare them away. "Good afternoon, gentlemen. Welcome to Scrivens Bakery. How may I serve you?"

They didn't even flinch. The men took up strategic points throughout the store; one blocked the entrance, flipping the sign to 'Closed' like the demon lord had done. Another headed straight for the kitchen and disappeared behind the curtain. The remaining two crowded him, causing him to bump into a display case.

One palmed a knife hanging on his belt, and the other drew back his coat to show him a holstered gun. Guns were such strange, frightening things. They did not exist on his homeworld. He imagined they were originally miniature cannons shrunken by some sort of dark magic so one could conceal them in one's pockets.

Inside himself, Calico panicked. All around them, his telekinetic power seeped out on its own, rattling the dishes and display cases, vibrating the very bones of the building. Terrified that this was even possible, he tried to pull it back in. But as expected, he could not grasp control. The more nervous he got, the more dust and debris sprinkled down from the ceiling.

No. No. He could not do this. He had to stop. What he had done to the gates of Demonym had been shameful. And flesh and bone was not iron and steel that could be replaced. *Pull it back, pull it back. I am a god. This is wrong.*

"Now s-see here," Calico protested.

"Silence," the leader demanded in raised, sharp tones. Other than raised eyebrows, the group did not seem to care that the building shuddered around them.

The second man reappeared from the kitchen as fast as he had gone in. "He's alone."

"Where are the other two?" asked the youth, who was watching the door. "The ones who look like you?"

Calico was prompted for an answer by the thug's fingers tapping on the knife. "Where they are every Thursday afternoon." Calico swallowed, staring at the sharp blade. "D-driving the pony cart to the docks to restock the bakery supplies."

"He's telling the truth," the youth by the door said.

Calico locked eyes with that young man, and somehow, he knew. Was allowed to know. A telepath. One much stronger than he, since the Rupart-creature had crippled most of his powers in their bloody campaigns against each other.

I am a god. I am a god. Do not hurt them. Calico inhaled, then let it out, hands at his sides and pressed calmly into his apron. Thank his mother goddess his brothers were safe. Away from here.

"Gentlemen," Calico inquired tentatively, "I assume you are of Infinity Corporation? I have been informed you would be visiting."

The men looked at each other in surprise. Calico experienced a greater wave of ill ease as they worked out how and who. Would this cause the demon lord trouble?

"We're Infinity 3," their leader confirmed. "If Lord California told you of our arrival, then you know what we want."

"Ah yes. I have had a chat with Mr. Chavez de la Cruz. We are in pre-negotiations."

"We know. He told us. But that's not good enough."

Calico tried to catch his breath. "I offer my apologies, then, as my answer to you will be the same as it was to the demon lord. My portal is not for sale. He still wishes to talk, however, and I am open to the subject."

"Mr. Harper wants that portal," the telepath said. "It'll keep us all safe."

Calico shook his head. "The portal is not for the hands of the rational and sound. It permits a single virtuoso."

"Mr. Harper extends the offer to join. Sell it to us," the leader demanded, grabbing his arm.

Calico said nothing more, because there was nothing more to say. He had already informed them he was working with the demon lord. They would not accept his answers.

"Villani," the telepathic youth called, "he needs more convincing."

Calico's attention rocketed back to the men threatening him with weapons when dry, cracked hands seized his neck. Fingers curling around his throat, cutting off his air. The rest of his protest was shaken out of him. He was slammed into a display case, and the glass shattered under the force.

Calico tried to throw off the heavy arm imprisoning him, but the two men now held him immobile. His fingers twisted into his flour-encrusted apron. Heat rose in his face, and he found it harder to breathe.

Dishes and display cases rattled again via his unresponsive telekinetic ability, and he candidly sobbed. *Pull it back, pull it back. Do not lose control. A god cannot be allowed to lose control.*

Villani called out to the man who'd searched the kitchen. "Waltzer, get his attention."

Waltzer left the kitchen entrance and headed for the shelves along the wall. Baseball bat in hand, he started whacking at inventory. Shelves splintered and came crashing down.

Calico screeched and fought to extract himself from the crushing force of the men who restrained him. His struggles were for naught. More shelving units were destroyed, more breads trampled underfoot. Display cases cracked and shattered as the warnings continued.

"Stop, please!" Calico sobbed harder. "This is all I own, my livelihood. It is how I provide for my family. Please, they need me to take care of them."

"Then maybe this will help convince them to convince you. Mr. Harper *will* have that portal."

One of them grabbed him by the neck again; Calico felt the sharp sting in his face. It took a full minute to realize his assailant had slammed his head through a glass case.

Frosting made its way up his nose and blurred his vision. Perhaps he shouldn't have brushed it away from his eyes. It would have spared him the sight of the iron-like fist speeding toward his cheek.

Chapter 26

Picking Up The Pieces

SEATED AT THE DESK in his bedroom suite, Agustin examined a series of land grant requests sent to Lord California. That was when the telephone rang. The shrill screech shattered the silence. Groaning, he leaned back in his chair, closed his eyes, and pinched the bridge of his nose. He needed a minute to regroup. But the blasted contraption kept ringing.

And ringing.

And ringing.

Etney pounded her fist on the connecting suite wall. "Answer your damn telephone!"

The shouted reprimand reached his ears in a muffled outrage. His head dropped forward and clunked the desk surface in the admission of defeat. He was a self-made billionaire on the brink of inheriting an angelic army that protected the entire world, a responsibility he never wanted—still didn't want—and his mansion walls were built thin enough to hear a delicate cough. Where had he gone wrong?

Being born was the answer.

Taking a soothing breath, and glancing at his wristwatch. He had an hour before he had to leave to meet Mr. Winghorse.

He picked up the receiver. "Good evening. You've reached Lord California himself."

What funneled into his ear was a jumbled rage in a most curious and strange language—the language he'd encountered at the vaudeville theater. Where he'd met Winghorse. Again, snippets did seem semi-familiar, his mind grasping at mutilated root words that may have had a previous life in Latin. And Greek. Oh. Some Mandarin flew by. His brows fell when Japanese and Hawaiian also seemed to worm their way into the verbiage. He immediately singled out short phrases that were distinctively German, but the screamed meaning was beyond him.

"Please state your grievance in English, French, Spanish, Portuguese, Mandarin, Elven, or any of the demonic tongues."

There was a high-pitched whine where the person apparently tried to calm down enough to switch languages. Then in English, *"WE'LL RIP OUT YOUR HEART WITH FIRE AND ICE."*

Agustin pulled the receiver away from his ear. His daily routine hadn't changed any. "Please describe the nature of your complaint," he recited. "I'm sure we'll be able to come to an agreement."

"WHAT DID YOU DO TO HIM?"

Do what to whom? Wait. This voice had a familiar accent. "May I ask who is ringing?"

"IT'S FRAZIL, YOU..."

Colorful insults and additional threats filtered out of Agustin's brain, as usual. But it was that heavy British inflection that further ensnared his attention.

Oh, right. This was the baker's triplet brother. "Frazil? Winghorse?"

"YES!"

"Please," Agustin said. "Stop shouting. What's going on?"

"What're you, dead from the neck up? What did you do to Cal, and how do we undo it?"

"I've done nothing to your brother."

"We've been gone all day today. I knew we should've never left."

Agustin recalled Infinity 3's planned visit, and alarm rose. But he'd taken care of that. Personally. *Infierno.*

"So you're denying you trashed our bakery, pummeled my brother, then stuffed his body in the pantry?"

Agustin's fingers whitened around the receiver. He pushed out of his chair and stood up. "Body?"

"We thought he was dead he was so still." Frazil's voice broke into restrained tears. "He's not under any sort of spell, we know, we checked. But he won't respond to us. It's like he's stuck inside his head."

Agustin clenched his teeth and paced two steps before he had to reverse and start over. Cadence was I-3's telepath. Cadence, the youth he'd taken under his wing in I-8, and the one he'd told Calico about.

Damn it all to hell. It was probable Cadence mentally knocked out the baker as a warning, and as punishment for refusing their demands. And a psychic attack took longer to recover from than a physical blow.

"I'll be over shortly."

"We expect it."

He winced when Frazil slammed down the receiver. Taking a deep breath, Agustin clutched at his head before smoothing back his long hair.

"Ramirez!" he shouted as he picked up his hat and coat and strode into the hall. "My motorcar!"

〜—♡—〜

Ramirez hadn't even decelerated the vehicle before Agustin leapt from it. "Wait here," he told his man. "Whatever you see, do not interfere."

"Sí señor." Ramirez turned off the engine.

Through the shattered shop windows, Agustin witnessed overturned cases and trampled bread. He rushed inside. Cake and pies coated the walls and floor. Eggshells crunched under his shoes. As the broken door swung shut behind him, he saw the cash register on the floor. Upturned, smashed, and empty. The I-3 bastards had even robbed him.

"Mr. Winghorse?" Agustin called out. "Are you here?"

The space in front of him shimmered slightly. One of the brothers appeared out of nowhere, advancing on him with grim purpose.

Magic. He should have known.

The brother shoved him. Agustin shuffled backward into the arms of the second sibling. In that instant, Agustin cried out. Bolts of ice blasted him. In multiple layers. The sheer speed of its manifestation was incredible.

Ice enshrouded him from feet to neck, and he could not move. "I'm here to help," he rasped.

"Does this look like helping?" The first brother he encountered motioned around the wrecked bakery; his voice did not match the one who had telephoned him.

Agustin glanced at the destruction, and his heart sank. "No. This isn't helping at all."

"So if you didn't do this, who did?" The brother behind him demanded.

The frigid element emanating from this ice-affiliated sibling was shutting down his mental faculties. It was getting harder to think. Which one was which? Frazil. Frazil ice. Maars. Mars. Planet. Fire. Right.

"I had warned your brother that I-3 could be...brusque."

"Brusque!" his captor exclaimed with shocked disbelief. "Look, you elitist turd goblin—"

Agustin's jaw locked in a grinding slide, scoring deep rents into his cheek. Apparently, the trio had been here long enough to identify the deeper cultural and racial slurs. The heat of the insult cascaded across Agustin's cheeks and around his collar, despite the enclosure of his ice prison.

Where compassion lay, anger and impatience took over at the vivid disrespect. "¡Basta! Stop this!"

Agustin called forth his inborn ability: flame. As his flesh heated, his clothing smoldered. Through it, the ice binding him immediately sluiced away. The heat magnified the scent of his cologne, and the burning stench of fabric filled his nose. What a damn waste of a perfectly good suit and hat, but he was through coddling the outrage.

The ice wielder—Frazil—shrieked and released him, then scurried to hide behind his sibling. Maars had fists raised that manifested crackling blue-white fire.

Mundane scents that once arose from Calico Winghorse now emerged here: charcoal, ash, and perhaps a faint whiff of peppermint. Maars also favored his phoenix bloodline, but at nowhere near the same level of ethereal and celestial power as his absent brother.

Agustin pulled at his saturated sleeve. The warm, damp, clinging linens sticking to his pseudo-human form made him irritable. "Mr. Winghorse? Are you set to burn down the building and put yourself out of business? Now. Where is he?"

The two identical faces before him snarled at his demand. The phoenix brother snuffed his fiery element and pointed sharply to the back room.

Removing his favorite hat and slapping the bit of smoke coiling off it, Agustin flung the curtain aside and scanned the repeated chaos. Tables overturned and splintered. Oven doors torn from their hinges and slammed through windows. Pots and pans and hanging frame ripped from ceiling hooks and strewn across the entire room. Sacks of flour slashed open and tossed about. He pushed away the simmering rage because he had to be the calm one. The voice of reason and guidance.

Tempering his tone, he called out, "Mr. Winghorse, are you here? It is Agustin Chavez de la Cruz."

Something off to his right shifted inside the partially closed pantry door. Agustin approached, swinging the barrier wider. Looking down, he saw the baker curled into a fetal position. Dried blood caked his half-shaved head; a trail of it crusted over his cheek and under his jaw. Sweet blue eyes were glazed over and drooping.

When Winghorse spoke, the words were broken, dazed, and foreign to Agustin's ear. It was the language he'd heard when the brothers telephoned him, and from the theater. Squatting down, Agustin touched the head wound to gauge its severity. The baker winced and curled away.

Agustin sighed. "I'm sorry. I'm so sorry this happened, but I will make it right."

"He won't come out."

Glancing over his shoulder, he noted one of the brothers crowding him. With them powered down, it would be easier to ask. "Which one are you again?"

"Maars," was the brisk response.

"Maars. What did he say?"

The man sneered at him. "It was nonsense in our native tongue."

The answer came too quickly. He let it pass. Calling the man a liar would not help the injured brother. Agustin lowered his eyelids a little, and permitted his telepathy to loiter outside the baker's cowering form. He sought the discarded and unguarded thoughts and emotions, the ones no longer anchored to the source.

He didn't want to spook Winghorse any further than he already was. He wanted the invitation to mindspeak. Faint pictures manifested in his mind's eye. Agustin cleared his throat and gave a little shake as he attempted to interpret them.

"He wants something," he told the brothers. "A rat of some sort, but not a rat. It represents safety." Agustin thought about that, and Triptych's claim the baker was also a wizard. "A familiar maybe?"

"Stinking telepath!" Maars cried.

"Stay out of his head," shouted Frazil. "We should ring for the bobbies."

Maars whipped out an answer before Agustin could. "No. No law controllers. Dammit, we don't need the mundanes nosing around in our business. I doubt even Trippy could shield us again."

"Maars is correct," Agustin said. "Humans nowadays have guns."

A small whine from the pantry speared through Agustin's heart. With it followed Calico's extreme terror and frustration—at not being able to summon the fortitude to protect himself. This wish for courage and the familiar seemed to go hand in hand before the mental residue faded from existence.

Agustin fished about for any more abandoned threads, and witnessed the scene clearly in his mind's eye. The Infinity 3 bastards had joined forces to secure him. Threatened to shoot off his fingers, with the barrel pressed against his flesh. All the while Winghorse mentally chanting to himself about godhood.

And...and Cadence had indeed been the team telepath. Disappointment and sorrow choked him.

Additional jarring rage swept over Agustin and he bit his tongue. A single pot still hanging from the ceiling rack caught his eye. Agustin steeled himself. There were four bullet holes in it.

He had to keep a level head.

Agustin glanced at Maars. "He wants—needs his courage. What are you planning to do about it?"

Maars turned to Frazil. "Gigglemug."

"You'll have to get her," Frazil replied softly. "I can't get past Cal's safeguards."

Agustin narrowed his eyes at that confession. These two were fire and ice. Calico was fire. Frazil was the oddball.

"Where is this Gigglemug?" Agustin asked.

They both stared at him. "At home."

"Then I'll have Ramirez drive you."

Agustin stood up and strode back into the storefront. The brothers were on his heels. Agustin motioned to his man and pointed to the siblings.

"Well," Agustin said. "Get going."

"Watch him," Maars instructed Frazil before moving out the door.

Agustin heard the motorcar fade into the distance, and he returned to the kitchen. Frazil was his shadow. He turned to the man, preparing for a hostile debate.

"I want your permission," Agustin stated.

Frazil's eyes drew into slits. "What for?"

"To talk to him."

Frazil inhaled through his nose and puffed out his chest. "Telepathically?"

"Yes. Once I'm in, I don't want to be disturbed, even if Maars returns. I want to assure him," he motioned to the baker, "that you're here, and that I don't mean him any harm."

"Why should I allow it?" Frazil demanded.

Agustin curtailed his impatience. "Because it's proper form to ask the closest relative, and the polite thing to do. Because I could just as easily make you forget and do what I will. But I will not because I am a gentleman. Because right now, I am the only one who can reach him. Because this is about your brother's well being."

Agustin took a sick kind of satisfaction watching that realization skitter across the man's face. Yet he regretted being so harsh. For the face he was looking at also belonged to the baker.

The blasted baker who was beginning to interfere with his better judgment—or *had* interfered since the moment they met in the vaudeville playhouse.

Agustin gave himself another little shake. He had to deal with the situation right in front of him, and with its aftermath—and of Harper's acute criticisms of this mess later.

"Well?" Agustin prompted. "May I try to reach him? Soothe the psychic bruising caused by Caden—I-3's telepath and draw him from his trauma?"

The brother had the grace to look embarrassed, then exclaimed, "Go ahead. But remember, this is your doing. You're the reason this happened."

Agustin inwardly winced at the reprimand, and the absolute truth of it. This was his fault. This was his assignment, and he kept botching it.

Badly. Because he was too concerned about his departure from IC. And Calico had paid the price for his choices.

Sitting on his knees, he put his hat and coat beside him. Agustin took one last look at Winghorse's pale, slack expression and felt sick at the sight. He had to fix this. To make amends.

Resting his fists atop his lap, he bent his head and closed his eyes. Reaching out with his mind, he tentatively circled the form huddled on the floor of the ransacked pantry.

{Hello, Calico? May I call you Calico?}

For a long moment, he was denied a response. Then the other mind stirred and swung toward him. Agustin wheezed at the incredible onslaught of it.

This...this was Calico's self, his core consciousness. Ancient, yet not. Encompassing and frightening in its expanse. Agustin sensed his physical body jerk from the impact. Twitch as if he were being electrocuted. He wasn't being attacked or beset with retribution and revenge; it was merely the overwhelming sensation of the leashed power washing through him. It was terrifying. Exhilarating. Of meeting a mind so foreign, so celestial, he nearly forgot how to breathe.

Agustin was picked up from his mental stumble by a simple, static-filled greeting. It was difficult to interpret; he compared it to talking through a wall while first-year orchestra students practiced different musical selections. All at once. On both sides of the barrier.

:It was the other telepath: Calico's weak reply referenced Cadence. It was full of disgust and disdain. *:I could not sense him until he permitted it, and I still cannot sense you. Even when you came to the bakery.:*

{I've had centuries of training.}

There was a soft growl. Agustin was taken aback. There it was. A sharp thread of envy and frustration.

{You too, are telepathic,} Agustin sent to the baker, trying to soothe him in this deeply traumatic moment. *{I sense its vibrant notes, however fractured. But, I'm astonished. I've never encountered such an incredible difference in mindspeak! Even when the languages differ.}*

Another gruff dismissal from Calico.

Agustin listened, sensed the muted pulses directed at him through their not-yet-established link. They were communicating on the outside, through discarded mental thought. He wasn't permitted near, but in examining these threads he noted locked links, thick barricades, extensive psychic damage, and the battle scars were not recent. He would not ask for details. Not yet.

Gathering his wits, Agustin verbally asked, "Are you hurt badly?"

Again, a delay before the man answered in kind with that deep, grating, raspy voice that plucked the strings of his gut in a curious, pleasant way. "I prefer to be addressed as Mr. Scrivens."

There was a relieved sigh from the brother loitering above them.

"I deeply apologize, yet again," Agustin said. "The blame is mine. Infinity 3 will be hearing from me. *Again.*"

"I will not give up my portal. No matter how much harm you or they cause."

"I have not harmed you, nor will I do so. However, as of now, I claim you as an honorary member of Infinity 8. Any further aggression against you, your family, or your property, will be met with extreme discipline."

"Your useless declaration is hours too late." Calico panted a little as he pulled himself out of the small nook he'd been stuffed in.

Those words cut Agustin with the sharpest of slices. Yes, this was his fault. His over-inflated ego and arrogance because of his birth status had harmed this man before him. Because Agustin considered himself so important that his orders to underlings, who weren't even under his command, would be obeyed without question.

Subdued and quiet, Agustin offered his hand.

"Leave me be," Calico demanded.

Frazil pushed in and took his brother in his arms, muttering something in that foreign language of theirs. Calico sluggishly replied in the same tongue.

Agustin stood and flipped a chair upright; Frazil eased his sibling into it.

Calico squinted and blinked as he carefully looked around, holding his bleeding head. Then he groaned again. "My kitchen..."

Agustin suddenly sat back and reexamined the damage. His heart sank, and he clenched his fists. *He'd allowed this. This was his doing. His fault.* Maybe Harper was right all along that he was a screw up. Because that's all he'd been doing lately.

"Hey, demon lord—I can't—my powers won't fix this," Frazil demanded, fussing and fawning, pressing a clean linen to his brother's bleeding scalp. "Not strong enough. He needs a doctor. One for our kind."

Watching, Agustin agreed, and made note of Frazil possibly being some sort of Healer. Calico was not batting away his brother's attentions. He was leaning into him for support.

Striding over to the telephone box on the wall, Agustin stopped. It was smashed. He wondered how the brothers had rung him. Magic, probably.

Releasing a pent-up breath, and deciding what demonic torment he could inflict on the Infinity group responsible, Agustin removed one of the rings on his right hand. Staring into the red gem, he waited until it glowed.

"Etney," he called, "I have a task."

"What is it, boss?" Her voice rose from the ruby as clearly as if she were standing in front of him.

Agustin sensed Frazil watching, perhaps out of curiosity, or making sure he wasn't up to no good.

"Please bring Doctor E to the Scrivens Bakery in Redwood City, immediately. We're on Main Street."

"Agustin!" she cried.

"Don't worry, I'm fine. It's Mr. Scrivens who needs medical attention. Have Joe Mist rouse and supervise the construction crew. Divert them from my gate and to the bakery. They'll need wood for shelves, new glass for shop windows, and new display cases. Ovens need repair."

Agustin walked a little farther and looked down as his oxfords collided with broken tools. "Also, we'll need to be fully restocked on flour, sugar, rolling pins, measuring cups, muffin pans, things like that. Baking racks. A wall telephone installed. I want it complete before morning, Etney. Do what needs to be done, and do it all behind the Curtain."

"Will do, boss."

He secured the ring back on his finger and turn to find the brothers staring at him.

"You're gonna...our shop?" Frazil scratched at his cheek, watching him askance. "What's this Curtain?"

"The Curtain," Agustin replied. "Haven't you wondered why the human police have not arrived? Especially after all the noise this ruckus would've produced?"

"Now that you mention it," Frazil said.

Calico sat up as straight as possible despite his injuries, listening to their exchange.

"The Curtain," Agustin continued, "is a spell used by the Corporation to keep our activities secret from humans. It's available to all the operatives within an Infinity team."

"Yes, that magic." Calico was looking at him differently now. "I meant to inquire in the park. What root origin does that magic curtain stem from? It sounds similar to my Mirror Bubble."

"Cal!" Frazil touched his brother's shoulders again. Words in their native speech came forth in warning.

The baker put the bloody rag back to his head and turned eyes on him. Agustin met that gaze and shivered from the crushing scrutiny. It was like a hand had plunged into his heart and sorted through his emotions. But the invasion felt sloppy and rough. There were holes and sharp edges, as if something had corrupted the talent—that curse Calico had mentioned. Details had been in the dossier before he'd accidentally set it afire.

Freed from the damaged inquest, Agustin wheezed and steadied himself against the leg of an overturned workbench.

"He is sincere, Fraze," Calico said. "I think we can forgive his peccadilloes. He is, after all, taking it upon himself to repair my bakery and restock it. And to keep this from happening again."

Frazil shook his head and tossed up his hands. "You know he's doing all that because he's the one who led them to us."

"Guilt," Agustin replied simply. "And regret that I neglected my duties and your safety. I am to blame, and I will make it right."

His words were met by silence. He dismissed Frazil's damning sneer, lured instead by the slight upward curve of Calico's mouth. It felt like forgiveness, and he clung embarrassingly to that notion. Agustin turned away the instant appreciation and admiration swirled, making his cheeks burn.

Agustin cleared his throat. "The Curtain originates from Earth and nature-based magic."

"Earth-based, you say?" The baker's eyes lingered on him, blazing with interest.

Agustin studied the man's head wound. The bleeding had slowed, thank goodness. The panic of the evening was subsiding.

Calico's wild black hair tangled and flowed past his strong shoulders without that baker's cap. Agustin resisted the urge to touch those locks and sweep them back from those blue eyes. In some sort of...what, he wasn't sure. Comfort?

In the distance, the sound of a motorcar approached. It was the brief escape he needed. "My man returns. Perhaps we can discuss it another time."

Agustin's words, spoken much too gruffly, broke the building interlude. Needing a moment to regroup, he strode out to meet the automobile. And he sensed the baker's forlorn gaze eagerly trail after him.

Chapter 27

A Wizard's Familiar Sleeps

THIS DEMON LORD HAD ridden to his rescue. Well, drove. The noble had been full of worry and guilt. For him.

Calico stood at the curtain partition between the kitchen and the storefront, his heart twisting. He was vaguely aware of the events happening beyond his damaged shop windows. And of Frazil hovering beside him, keeping a hand on his elbow to steady him.

Perhaps the demon lord's temporary departure was to escape the tension between them. It made the few moments' reprieve the perfect opportunity to ask himself important questions.

Tonight had been emotional. The demon lord's more intimate feelings were running as high as his own. Calico shivered a little as his empathy drew back from the nobleman, to linger on the additional discord bouncing around in his own heart.

His empathy had been blazing strongly. His telekinetic ability nearly shook down the building. His doing, but not his doing. Perhaps with his powers so closed off, he was reaching out to his other selves across the dimensions for help?

But wouldn't they, too, be cursed? Past. Future. The now and in-between. He was the God of Space and Time, after all. There was hope to undo what had been done to him. But it was a consideration to ponder on another occasion.

Calico pursed his lips, pressing his arms against his stomach. It was important to focus upon the present. He looked back out the window.

The demon lord was attracted to him before this unfortunate circumstance. He himself had noticed the strong hand that held a wonderful top hat when the demon lord first entered the bakery. Even then, those comforting, mismatched eyes permitted him to not feel so lonely.

The impromptu situation with the loaf of French bread had shaken both of them. Now that Calico had had time to process this sparking attraction, he wondered. Was the demon lord's yet unconfessed affection something that he wanted? Heat swarmed across Calico's cheeks, and the smile already curved his lips.

Perhaps.

Maybe.

Yes.

But where to find a proper chaperone?

No, no, permitting himself to think in such a direction was most improper. Due to the demon lord's higher social standing in this society, it was the nobleman's duty to procure one. Calico's delight put up a fight and remained visible.

Maars jumped out of the noisy machine, then barged through the door. His brother rushed to his side. "Cal, you're all right?"

"I am fine, now..."

He had been squirreled away in a dark place until the demon lord nudged his mind and freed him. It was marvelous to have conversed with another telepath while trapped in that gauzy gray despair. It had been sooo long since he had experienced telepathy. Calico decided he was pleased that this demon lord was telepathic.

His joy faded. I-3's telepath had cushioned his psyche from the brunt of the physical violence doled out by their leader. Calico didn't want to delve further into the exact whys. Casting heroism on someone who was part of a mob that had harmed him wasn't a deed he wished to examine right now.

His boots crunched on shattered glass as he surveyed splintered wood and the wasted labor of ruined pastries. It was too bad his bakery had not weathered the conflict as fairly. But wood and glass could be recycled and replaced. Most of his customers would return. Still, the inconvenience and disruption of his routine was an unfortunate setback.

What was important was dealing with this Infinity Corporation. If he had learned anything from this encounter, it was making sure future incidents did not escalate toward an aggressive and destructive scale.

It was in his best interest to investigate this intrusive gathering of para-normals. Calico glanced out the broken front windows at the two men talking beside the motorcar. ...And learn more about the Corporation's handsome demon lord as well. Not just for the safety and welfare of his family.

Where was this sudden bravery and self-assurance coming from? Maybe from the need to be more than a simple baker, hiding himself away, quietly nursing his wounds. Patiently waiting to grow older and stronger to one day save Great-Grandfather Rupart.

It was not solely the presence and kindness of the Demon Lord of California. It was something much, much more that fueled this action blooming inside him.

Ms. Mug?

She was near.

"Cal?" Maars's sweaty fingers stroked his cheeks and cupped his head. "Cal! Look at me. Talk to me."

Ah, yes, his brother had returned from his motorcar ride. Had it been as enjoyable as Calico imagined it would be? Maars had brought something with him—a tiny box. Blue and white flame coiled from that one hand. It encircled the box that did not burn.

Calico closed his eyes, leaning toward his wizard's familiar, and the element itself. Ever so much hotter than the ovens he often huddled around. Comfort. Safety. Family.

"Cal? Cal? I'm getting tired. The whole town'll combust if you don't take her. Cal, snap out of it!" Then came the desperate call. "Frazil!"

There was an icy, jarring slap to his buttocks. Calico yelped at the impropriety, and the fog in his mind cleared.

"Here!" Maars thrust the little jewelry box at him. *Much. Too. Closely.* All the while the cobalt-and-ivory-colored flames in his sibling's hand writhed and crackled.

Calico recoiled. Hands raised to shield his face. The heat, the dancing light—he choked and mumbled. When…when had he become afraid of fire?

Maars did not realize how much of an agony this was. Within reach, yet unable to interact with the spiraling light. Calico wanted to feel its burn firsthand, but the consequences were fatal.

"Cal," his brother said kindly. His chest heaved at the exertion of summoning his flame for an extended period. Especially while in a human form. "It's Gigglemug."

Ms. Mug. His familiar. His courage. His protector now that the Rupart-creature had paralyzed most of his powers.

Calico knew he would have to use Maars's spark in lieu of his own. Cupping his brother's elbow, Calico closed his eyes and focused inward, seeking the element that was his very being. Within his mind, he stood before a glowing door. Seared into the wood, the image of an alabaster phoenix signaled what lay inside. White and blue fire licked around the gaps. If he touched or even tried to bypass this seal created by the curse, he would suffer more than third-degree burns.

But he had to get close to it. It was the only way to take the box from Maars. He neared the door; the flames lunged at him, singeing his human flesh and he whimpered.

Maars crowded closer. "I'm here," his brother whispered. "Don't be afraid. You can do this."

Calico channeled his magic. Fueled by gathering energy from an outside source—his brother. But with fire as the foundation, the magic lashed out and attacked him. Calico ignored the gaping holes and fresh tears cleaving, coursing through his system.

He took sole possession of the little box his sibling offered with his free hand. Sweat beaded on Calico's cheeks. He brought the box to his lips, still clutching Maars's elbow. Calico mumbled a spell in his birth language that removed the safeguards and traps. Once that was complete, he stepped back, avoiding the flame's deadly temptation.

Maars's fire flashed out. Freed from the responsibility, his brother exhaled and staggered over to the righted chair.

Calico spared the jewelry box a glance before hiding it away in his pocket.

"What is that?"

Calico shivered at that rich, deep baritone inquiry. Through sweat-laden lashes and stinging eyes, he saw the demon lord standing at the bakery's entrance. Metaphorical red-hot coals delightfully stirred in the pit of Calico's belly, further soothing his brief agony.

The lord's tall, straight form stood at attention, yet a curious expression lit his features. "Why the phoenix fire?" the man asked.

That heart-stopping, diverse gaze representing blue sky and warm honey. Calico wished he could sense the man's thoughts without outside telepathic assistance. Feel that part of himself that was not a lifeless one-dimensional picture.

It had been some time since the Rupart-creature had cut him off from his psychic senses. It had been just as long trying to adjust to his new one-dimensional world. Forever watching the empty husks of his brothers try to assist in his recovery, to a point where he could at least pretend to function normally.

Calico wanted to reach out, to share, to sense, to feel. *To...love.* To not just view the elements and emotions on the surface. But he could not.

"Perhaps you should sit down." The demon lord presented another chair.

"Yes, you are correct." Calico put a protective hand over his pocket. "Why the combustion safeguard, you ask? To protect my familiar from being spirited away should a prowler break in. Only a phoenix manifesting their flame at full power may touch the box—I had to use Maars as an intermediary. Only I may open it."

"You imprison your familiar?" came the surprised inquiry.

"Imprison?" Calico snorted. "Certainly not! Why would one not safeguard their soul?"

"Your soul?" the demon lord exclaimed, tilting his head.

"Of course. Ms. Mug is part of me. Born from my essence, from what I am, as I grew into my magic when I was a young lad."

Those magnificent black brows highlighted eyes wide in shock. The demon lord looked over his shoulder and around the room, his gaze flittering to Frazil and Maars, then back to him.

"So you and your familiar are connected? If something happens to her, it happens to you?"

"That is how it works," Calico confirmed. "Is it not how wizards of this realm acquire their familiars?"

The demon lord shook his head. "Familiars in this realm are partners. They're more like spirit travelers or lesser beings. Usually in some sort of animal form—like your pony. They are their own entity, entering into contracts with a caster."

Calico curled his lip in distaste. "How peculiar. So familiars here are slaves?"

Those mismatched eyes squeezed shut briefly. "N-no. They have free will. Does your Ms. Mug have free will if she's merely an extension of you?"

"Ms. Mug certainly has her own mind and lives separate from me," he replied, somewhat offended. "A familiar's creation is quite common and known in my homeland."

"Well, it's not here. This...anomaly..." The man stopped and started again, his tone urgent. "Mr. Scrivens, this magical practice must remain a secret. Tell no one, understand?"

Frazil wrung his hands and paced. "Maybe we should stop talking about this."

The demon lord's worry, along with his siblings', seeped into Calico. "W-why?"

"Your life may depend upon guarding this knowledge," the demon lord explained. "Here, if an adversary were to know of Ms. Mug's origin, a spell that weakens or incapacitates her could be easily modified to do the same to you. Even if you function independently, she's still mentally and physically part of you."

Calico recoiled. "That is terrible!"

"So you understand the seriousness of this request?"

"Yes, I should say I do."

"Good." The noble's brow seemed a little less pinched but remained crinkled.

Calico clutched the jewelry box against his heart. His brothers had reunited them, but if Ms. Mug would not be safe in this world, perhaps it would be better if she continued in stasis.

Her skirmish with the Rupart-creature had taken so much out of her. She deserved her rest. Besides, he could not wake her in his current condition. His brothers had merely brought her to him for comfort.

"I see you're having second thoughts." The demon lord's voice lowered. "Something more to think over. And, well, if you revive her now, won't she be angry about all this?"

"Oh, no, no, no." Calico paused. "Ah, yes, she will become aware of the circumstances through our psychic link. But it will take several hours for the knowledge to catch up in her memory, since she has been in stasis for so long."

"Cal," Frazil waved his hands to garner his attention. "Again, it'd be wise to stop talking about this."

"Thank our mother goddess he hasn't had a chance to meet other magic makers yet," Maars slouched against the broken bakery case.

"Indeed." The demon lord agreed.

The bell above the shop door jingled, and the noble turned to block the way. The Mexican gentleman Calico had seen before at the mansion leaned through the broken entry.

"My lord." Ramirez looked back over his shoulder. "Brace yourself. Etney's coming."

Chapter 28

Phoenix Foreplay

"I THOUGHT I'D WARN you," Ramirez announced. "I'm sure it's Etney. I see the Daimler Phoenix coming up the street."

The demon lord groaned, his fingers pinching the bridge of his nose. "She's going to want to be buried with that thing."

Ramirez muttered. "I think that clause was in her renewed IC contract, señor. How could you have missed it?"

Calico perked up. Had his ears deceived him? A Daimler Phoenix! He headed for the door to get a firsthand look. The demon lord's protective, outstretched arm halted him.

Frazil, too, yanked at his apron, barring him from leaving the shop. "You need a doctor, Cal," his brother admonished gently. "Stay close, and try not to impale yourself."

Calico's excitement dulled the warnings as he craned his neck, eager to see.

"What's a Daimler Phoenix?" Maars asked, also trying to get a look out of the jagged glass still slotted in the window frame.

Frazil joined Maars at the window. "Are they one of the Earth forges?"

"Oh, no, no," Calico cut in eagerly. "It is a motorcar. They named a motorcar after our kind. It is so delightful!" He glanced at the demon lord, seeing him in yet another light. Calico smiled as the noble's eyebrow lifted. "Sir," he asked, "Do you also have a fondness of motorcars?"

Their eyes met.

"I do." The demon lord gathered his hat and coat, looking at his driver, before his gaze lingered a little on Calico. "Thank you, Ramirez. Please wait in the automobile."

Ramirez complied.

Placing that magnificent top hat back on his head, the demon lord explained further. "Etney's arriving. She's my second-in-command of Infinity 8. Since two of you manifest phoenix heritage..."

Calico could not focus on the nobleman's words, as smoke still coiled off the man's sleeve. It added an extra layer of attraction, and Calico nervously fiddled with the bib of his baker's apron.

"Another phoenix, driving a Daimler Phoenix?" Calico cut in, trying to dismiss the allure of the demon lord's top hat, and struggling for a smidgen of cheer. It seemed good news for a rather harrowing night. "How wonderful! We have not seen another of our kind since departing England."

"Well," the demon lord cautioned. "If you aren't aware, the Dasheel line can be...too energetic."

"Demanding." Frazil offered.

"Pushy," Maars clarified, tilting his head and crossing his arms. His grin signaling he was familiar with the subject matter. "Proud. Arrogant."

"Well-meaning," the noble finished. "Then I see you're already acquainted with this specific forge."

"Oh, we certainly are. Intimately." Maars half-laughed before Frazil elbowed him into silence.

Calico felt the demon lord's heavy stare.

From this man, there was an instant flash of disappointment. A psychic wall of the demon lord's creation rose to part them.

Calico was all too aware of when his empathic flashes came and went. He often pondered if the power had tangled up with his magic and space-time abilities over the years. Which might have shielded it from the curse.

However, with weighty guilt, Calico had an inkling of why this man was disappointed. But he could not be certain. Was it really so wrong of him to *avoid* thinking of this demon lord by his personal, given name? Mentally referring to him as just his title? Especially when he could not control the firestorm of flutters the proper monikers caused?

"The Dasheel and Breese phoenix lines are of an extreme symbiosis, you see," Calico said, trying to renew the communication.

"Cal," Frazil and Maars interrupted simultaneously. They diverted their attention from the approaching motorcar, vigorously shaking their heads at him. "No."

Calico pursed his lips and steepled his slender fingers at the reprimand. Revealing to outsiders that the two branches needed the other for long-term survival could be dangerous. They were also in hiding, and should not be advertising their heritage. Especially since Grandfather Acanthus counted on them to help revive the Breese bloodline.

The demon lord was about to speak again when this Etney pulled her Daimler Phoenix motorcar up to the storefront, right behind Ramirez's vehicle. The machine sputtered and fell silent; she and a little man jumped out.

Yes, clearly the woman was of the Dasheel line, even if there was some sort of concealing magic around her. Calico knew his brothers saw through the ruse as well. Phoenix were in tune with each other. Especially the Breese and Dasheel lines.

The woman's blunt, commanding aura was every bit as assertive as the demon lord warned them of. Fascinated, Calico peered a little harder to see through the concealing magic. He was surprised at the pale red, yellow, and orange facial markings that decorated her forehead and the bridge of her nose.

His brothers were staring at the bold colors as well. The brighter the hue, the more energy one could wield—at least that was the common thought. It was most unusual for matrilineal lineages to have any markings at all, or the vibrant hair color. Or be able to manifest the fiery element. But it was not unheard of.

"Boss," she greeted, walking into the ruined shop, the doctor at her side. "You took ten years off my life when you called."

The demon lord nodded. "Etney, Doctor E."

She drew herself up. "Hey, thanks, Etts, for bringing the doc here as fast as you could."

Frazil and Maars smirked and snorted. Calico's eyebrows rose at the sass, despite having grown up around this forge. The demon lord bowed his head at that moment, and his shoulders sagged further.

Waving her hands, she droned on. "I mean, if you'd sprouted wings, Etts, you could've gotten here much faster. But then poor Dr. E would need a doctor of his own."

Maars's smile went wider as he watched the woman rant, and his blue eyes were intense, amused.

"I'm fine with you giving your passenger third-degree burns," she continued. "As long as the doc gets here like I asked."

"Gentlemen," the demon lord interrupted her, "this is Ms. Etney Dasheel, and Dr. Esteban Makani. Mr. Scrivenses," The demon noble addressed the brothers, but did not meet Calico's gaze. "Dr. E is formerly of Oahu, Hawai'i, and my personal physician—Demonym's resident physician. Dr. E, please see to Mr. Winghorse. He's been—he's met Infinity 3."

Calico shivered at the mention of I-3. And when the doctor's expression turned to dread, Calico hugged himself.

The little man drew him back down into a chair, and studied him with critical eyes. There were a few questing pokes around his limbs and torso. Calico sluggishly shied away, but he was no match for the swift examination.

A palm with stubby fingers pressed over his heart. Then hands urged him to bend forward before clutching onto his scalp. The palms grew warm and energy gathered at the fingertips. There was a sharp sting.

Screeching, Calico jerked at the zap, but the pain and fog had abated. Ah, so this man was an actual Healer, someone who had the gift of fixing most injuries in mere moments depending upon severity and skill. The tension cascading along his nerves lessened, just a little.

"His noggin'll ring with a headache for a while." Dr. E wiped the sheet of sweat off his brow with a handkerchief and slumped against the side of the chair. "The major wounds are closed up. Physically, he'll be fine."

"Esteban," the demon lord said, "Excellent work. Thank you."

The small man nodded before turning to check his own pulse, for Healers used their own vitality and inner strength. Frazil brought him a glass of water and a few unscathed, and still-wrapped oatmeal cookies for quick energy. The Healer accepted the refreshment, and sat quietly in another chair to recuperate.

"So, now that the bleeding's stopped," the noble said—he spared Calico a quick look. "Please allow me to drive the three of you home. Etney—"

Maars jumped forward at that. "Miss Dasheel, now that I know my brother is well, I must convey it is a great pleasure to meet you."

His brother held out his hand. In place of a farewell handshake, a small sprig of blue and white flame swirled around Maars's palm. In the shape of a rose.

Calico did not understand why the demon lord immediately face-palmed himself and took a deep breath. The doctor smothered a chuckle and suddenly found interest in his water glass.

Calico then beheld his elder sibling. Maars's ridiculously embarrassing grin revealed he was already falling head over feet. The woman, too, was wreathed in distant mirth.

Frazil made a sound like an overloaded garden hose, hand over his mouth. Then laughed under his breath in their birth-tongue about Maars being a lascivious and oversexed monster-dog marking his territory.

The woman lifted a brow, but there was a smirk on her lips.

"L-Language!" Calico cried out in English, horribly embarrassed. Especially now since the demon lord suddenly looked at him, eyes going strangely dark with something as equally intense.

Calico did not understand all this behavior. Had he missed something in his stupor? He pulled a handkerchief from his pocket to head off additional nerves sprouting on his brow.

The awkward silence yawned on. Calico feared Ms. Dasheel had been grievously offended by the fiery elemental offering. Ever since he was a child, Calico had been told to keep his fire to himself. Exactly why, he never understood. He began to reach out to smother his brother's questionable and too intimate gift. He was also terrified Ms. Dasheel knew their Nuran tongue and the foul words.

But her salty laugh had Calico drawing back.

"Really, Mr. Scrivens?" she asked of Maars. "In front of everyone? You're a firecracker, aren't you." Ms. Dasheel blatantly stated that as a fact, not a question. "Well, let's hope you don't have a short fuse."

Her dialog left Calico puzzled. What did Chinese explosives have to do with the situation?

Maars's eyes sparkled and clouded over. Frazil's attempt to squash his raucous mirth with the back of his hand failed. The demon lord's face went bright red, and he turned away and loudly cleared his throat. The doctor studied his water glass as if it were a new never-before seen invention.

The woman ignored all of them. "Hmm. How pretty." She reached over, beckoning the flame to her fingertip. Her gaze pinned solely on Maars.

Frazil and Maars choked on restrained laughter, with Maars grasping at Frazil in order to remain standing.

Ms. Dasheel twirled the element around as she studied it. "But I prefer red."

Instantly, the blue-white fire changed color to reds with highlights of orange and yellow.

"But more are even lovelier." The rose multiplied, and the woman cradled a dozen or so duplicates in her arms.

Maars clutched his chest and wheezed, gripping Frazil tighter to keep from falling down. Concerned, Calico patted his back, for Maars's face was turning as red as Ms. Dasheel's hair.

"Etney," the demon lord said with exasperation and flushed cheeks. "We're not hidden behind a Curtain. Please extinguish your gift. There's been enough of a show tonight."

She rolled her eyes with good humor. With a short exhale, and like candles on a birthday cake, she blew out the fiery roses Maars flattered her with.

The demon lord cleared his throat, again. "As I was saying, Mr. Scrivens, please allow me to drive you and your brothers home. Etney, please escort Dr. E to your vehicle and collect Ramirez."

The woman took one last lingering look at Maars. "You got it, boss."

She and Dr. Esteban moved out the door. Maars's euphoric state hadn't faded, and he wandered outside next.

"Shall we?" the noble asked, motioning to the exit.

Frazil shrugged and followed Maars.

Calico remained rooted to the spot. After a moment, he listened to the group outside making small talk; Frazil speaking to the doctor about Healing techniques, and Maars engaging Ramirez and Ms. Dasheel about the daily grind of the bakery.

Calico prepared to follow. Yet blocking his path was the most incredible pair of honey gold and sapphire blue eyes that drank him in.

A gaze that purposefully drew his attention away from the smart, still-smoldering top hat. Drawing him into that hot and inviting stare that sent Calico's heart into beating triple time.

Chapter 29

Calico Out Of Sync

HE HAD BEEN LEFT alone. With the demon lord.

Calico witnessed the nobleman flinch, again, but he could not help it. It was important to remain formal and polite when thinking of such a distinguished and helpful gentleman. It was respectful, after all. Because their close proximity caused a double dose of emotional upheaval. It was too much to deal with all in a single night. Calico prepared to depart by fumbling with his keys.

"That won't be necessary." The nobleman flinched, yet again. "Your front door is beyond damaged."

"Quite right." Calico shoved the keys back into his apron. This was it. Their parting. Calico was sorry to see him go. The demon lord had been the light in the darkness this day. "Ah, thank you for taking my brothers home. But I must attend to Dot and unload the wagon—"

"Mr. Scriv—Winghorse. Calico. May I call you Calico?"

Startled, Calico spun, hands on his hips. The sound of his given name spoken by this man brought happy, scandalous goosebumps. "Well, that is quite forward, I think. We have known each other for hardly a week."

The demon lord's husky reply—the man winced again—was low, sending exciting shivers through him. "Would you call me Agustin?"

Call him by his given name? He felt light-headed. "That is even more forward."

Calico looked about and found a torn apron on the floor. He picked it up, shook it out, and started dusting around the debris. How could personal names be bandied about when they had not even gotten to the chaperone stage yet? The demon lord remained in place as Calico put a little distance between them.

There was another sigh. "I don't want a title between us. I would be pleased if you called me Agustin."

"Why?" Calico asked absently, barely listening.

"Because I would rather have you thinking of me as Agustin than 'the demon lord,' 'Lord California,' or 'the nobleman.'"

Wide-eyed, Calico dusted faster. He'd been found out! But of course, the man—was a telepath. But this request was much too intimate so soon.

"I would prefer my given name to 'the man' as well. If you must, a compromise of you only thinking of me as Agustin will do nicely."

Thinking of him as his given name when they barely knew each other? Now that was excitingly naughty. "How are you reading—?" Calico asked faintly.

It was a moment before he answered. Arms folded loosely, he shifted his tall frame. "You're a telepath, but you've been denied your talent. Reading discarded thought is my first language, and difficult to suppress. Demonspeak and Spanish are my second and third."

Calico straightened his shoulders, hooking his thumbs through the shoulder loop straps of his apron. "I see. Well, under the circumstances, a first-name basis would not be proper."

"Why?"

Calico had to pause at the disappointment radiating from the man's—Chavez's—Agustin's—brow. "Because while you have proven you are willing to do what is right, I still do not know if we can fully trust you."

A distressed dent appeared on Agustin's cheek. Calico found it attractive, but knew he could not be distracted by a handsome dent.

"Because I'm with the organization that harmed you, and we still want something from you."

"Precisely." Calico nodded smartly.

"Well," Agustin said. The man—Agustin—then abruptly stopped to reward him with a wide, secretive smile.

Calico blushed at thinking of the man by his first name. It had been so forward and improper that his heart pounded at the daring move.

Agustin's expression softened further. "Thank you, for accommodating me."

Calico inclined his head and continued to dust among the broken glass. Finding someone attractive, someone who considered him pleasing in return, was quite...exhausting. He did not know how much longer his chore could hide quivering hands.

"Calico?"

Oh, that low, husky accent! Calico huffed with nerves and busied himself further. "Mr. Scrivens," Calico corrected, his guttural voice surprising him by going a tad squeaky.

"You are extremely forgiving, Mr. Scrivens." The voice was soft. Too soft!

Agustin was watching him with a leisurely smile, his form relaxed and arms bent at his sides. Calico fumbled for something to say before his scrambled brain lured him into further trouble. "Grandfather Acanthus says forgiveness can unburden the soul."

"Your grandfather is wise. I admit that I will try to get you to join our cause. But I must be honest. I'm attracted to you. On a personal level."

The apron-turned-dust rag fell from Calico's hands. His heart kept pounding triple time. This was it. Agustin was going to inform him they would need a chaperone!

"I have been wrestling with myself about this conflict of interest," Agustin went on.

Calico threaded his fingers together and stared at the wall. He couldn't look at those eyes now. The flutters had returned and had decided to play football in his stomach.

"And-and what do you wish to do about it?" Calico inquired.

The man—Mr. Chavez de la Cruz...A-Agustin—walked around to face him. Those blue and honey-colored eyes saw right through his naming hiccup, and kept smiling knowingly, warmly. Calico lost himself in the sizzling, comforting gaze. Agustin's wide chest drew a breath to answer.

The crunch of glass sounded from within the kitchen. Frazil and Maars pushed aside the shop curtain. Maars cleared his throat. On purpose. "Cal, we need to get you home."

No, not now! Shoulders sinking, Calico mourned the loss of this tender moment. Agustin had been seconds away from announcing his quest for their chaperone. His brothers had wrecked the mood. Could his heart take the additional wait for the next rendezvous?

After a thought, Calico decided he was grateful for the interruption. Tonight had taken a toll. He could not handle much more. He touched his head and winced. Still tender.

"Cal?" Frazil's voice sounded far away...

...Calico's entire body felt like lead weights, and his mind like runny scrambled eggs. He would consume two aspirin tablets with a spot of tea while he watched the cooking channel on the telly.

Tonight was the microwave baking challenge special edition finals. It pitted the top five chefs from last season against chefs from the current season.

If he inquired nicely, Ms. Mug would bring him the remote control so he could turn up the sound. Then a nap before luncheon at the new Asian-Mexican fusion restaurant with Gus sounded dandy.

Frazil patted Calico on the back. "We finished unhitching and feeding Dot and closed the side gate."

Calico's fingers clenched at his apron. A small noise escaped his throat. Oh! His sweet pony! How could he have forgotten her?

"Don't worry." Frazil offered a comforting squeeze. "She's okay."

Calico frowned, scratching his cheek. Dot had passed over a century ago. What a sweet little pony...

"It's been a long day," Maars said. "You need to rest."

Yes, it had been a stressful day. Misters Hagen and Smith had been most generous, towing his '57 Chevrolet work truck to their repair shop—on their day off, no less.

Gus was here to take him home, and cold beer, takeout barbecue, and streaming a romantic movie from the telly sounded lovely.

Home. With Gus.

The three of them exited the shop and his brothers hopped into the automobile. The second vehicle transporting Dr. E, Ramirez, and Ms. Dasheel was gone.

Why was Agustin—Gus looking at him funny?

It was difficult for Calico not to lock up, but he closed the shop door as best he could. Why wouldn't it engage? Curious. He'd have to alert Ms. Penny and she would summon the repairman.

He worried about the computer, but if it was stolen, it was safely password and magically protected, and his office door with the paper files had a sturdy lock. He fiddled with the door some more until Gus's hand gently laid atop his own.

By the time Calico reached Agustin's motorcar, he noticed his brothers squeezed into the secondary seating behind the driver. That meant he would sit in front. Agustin settled himself in the driver's station.

Frazil had the nerve to grin and wiggle his eyebrows at him. Calico clutched his chest. The nerves making him unable to enter the vehicle. His middle brother suspected what would be taking place tonight between him and Gus.

Calico blushed. Gus watched him, too. A gentle, but highly amused smile was still on his face, his elbow braced against the steering column. Calico took a deep breath, then smiled back. He could not wait to get home and snuggle.

Agustin suddenly tilted his head, a concerned, curious expression crossing his brow...

Calico inserted himself into the front seat, still holding himself stiffly. The fit was cozy. And it was difficult to decide what was more exciting: sitting in a motorcar machine for the first time or being this close to someone whom he wasn't sure he could candidly inform he was attracted to.

The trip home was too long and too short. Rubbing shoulders with this man—Mr. Chavez—Agustin—as the automobile encountered every rock and pothole in the road thrilled and exhausted him. And when the motorcar rolled to a halt at their tiny house, Calico didn't want it to end. But it had ended.

At the close of this most unpleasant day, Calico exited the vehicle and waited, looking at the demon lord—Agustin. Trying to figure out the best words for their parting. But Agustin's tender smile was gone. Concern now reflected in those marvelous eyes.

Calico hadn't realized his brothers had disembarked. Frazil and Maars were already at the stoop and fumbled with their keys.

A small tick flexed in Agustin's cheek. "I know you think I'm only doing this to—"

Calico held up a hand. "I do not wish to end a rather exhausting evening with a harried debate. Your actions tonight speak well to me, Mr. Chavez de la Cruz."

Agustin's eyes narrowed slightly, and the concern appeared to lift. "I like hearing you say my name...and thinking of it, too."

His cheeks pinkening, and not knowing what else to do, Calico stuck out his hand in proper greeting. They shook. "I imagine we have gotten off to a chaotic beginning," Calico said. "But chaos is my nature. Restarting can be easy, if we wish it. So, yes, please." He breathed in a deep breath. "I would consent to you addressing me by my given name."

The front door opened and his brothers went inside. Leaving him alone. Again.

With—Gus.

Chapter 30

The Gentle Rebuff

WORRYING ABOUT THIS MADDENINGLY fussy baker was playing havoc on Agustin's emotions. There had never been a mind he couldn't read. Since leaving the bakery, Calico's mind felt out of reach, more than once. Normally, abandoned thoughts drifted with aimless direction before fading away.

Tonight, the baker's discarded thought-threads would cut off sharply, like scissors severing paper. Then snap back into existence. It was as if Calico had been some place else, then returned. But he had faith in Esteban's diagnosis. Still, Calico had been through a past trauma. Now a current one.

The brothers were correct. It had been a long day. The guilt Agustin felt over Calico's assault, and the stress of trying, however lamely, to make it right, took its toll. It was so much harder on Calico.

Agustin wrestled with a sense of anger and betrayal at IC. At Harper, and at Infinity 3. Most of all, the fury was directed at himself, and at Cadence. No, not at Cadence. He was more disappointed in the orphaned youth he'd taken under his wing, even if he knew Cadey had been following orders.

"Thank you," Calico said. "For motoring us home."

Calico interrupted his reply by walking around to the driver's side. Agustin tensed; Calico leaned into his personal space, wrapping his arms loosely about his waist.

Heat gathered at Agustin's collar, making it difficult to respond. This was certainly out of the baker's character. Or was it? Yes, it was, despite how their first encounter at the theater went. Agustin still needed to mull over that. Calculate when in this budding friendship he should bring it up.

While Calico's embrace was welcome, Agustin knew he shouldn't allow this to proceed any further, given tonight's assault. "Calico, I don't expect you to—"

His guess was correct. Calico lifted himself up on tip-toe and offered his face, poising himself for a kiss with eyes at half-mast.

With slow kindness, Agustin halted the advance. "You don't need to do that," he said with soft quiet. Then, gently, he removed Calico's arms from around his waist. He didn't let go of the baker's hands, but stroked them with his thumb.

Calico blinked at him, affronted at the statement. And the rejection. "And why not?"

"Because I don't want any type of repayment, thanks, or reward. What I did was because it was the right thing to do. And you need to recover from the shock."

Pulling away and arms crossed, Calico shifted his weight to one foot. "Gus," he reprimanded matter-of-factly.

"Gus?" Agustin asked, somewhat surprised. It was the name Calico used at the vaudeville theater. Agustin wished he hadn't agreed to close off his telepathy at that time, for then he'd have a basis of comparison to go by. Right now, he was in the dark as to what was happening.

"Yes, Gus. How else am I to address you?"

Agustin opened his mouth to reply, then shut it. He didn't know what to say. What was there to say, anyway? As much as he wanted, this wasn't the time to get into this confusion. Calico needed to rest.

His heart jumped when the smug smile lit up Calico's thin face. The baker's low chuckle melted his insides. Why was Agustin wishing this interaction could be real?

"I thought you would not have an answer," Calico said. "Now, if I may continue?"

Calico's quest for something more intimate, quickly cleared the fog. His adorably blushy baker wasn't in his right mind.

I-3 had given Calico a hard hit to the skull. Between that and those acute, out of sync thought-threads, it was time to say good night. Summoning all his willpower, Agustin once again sought those questing hands, and gently took hold of them. He didn't want to upset or offend this man he was starting to like. No, care about.

With a slow grace, he lifted Calico's palms to his lips. This close, the scents were welcomely magnified. That vibrant aroma of fresh ground cumin. The exciting rush of burnt charcoal, smoke, and heated metals.

Calico's skin was warm. Sadly, though, he somehow knew it was not warm enough. It should be hot for a phoenix-blood. And now, more than anything, Agustin wanted to help this baker heal, and be whole.

Thankfully, He was saved from further action when the porch light suddenly lit up.

"He's practically attacking him. Has him pinned in the driver's bench seat."

"WHAT?" Frazil rushed to the window.

"Shh, keep your voice down," Maars ordered. "And do not turn on that light."

"The bastard's assaulting Cal and you're just standing there—?" Frazil had a hand on the doorknob.

"No. Cal's the one," Maars said.

Frazil turned back. "Come again?"

"Have a look for yourself." Maars puffed out his chest with pride.

"Dear mother goddess." Frazil frantically peered through the window slats. "Why are we watching our little brother have his first plow?"

Maars put a knuckle to his chin and considered it for a moment. "I'm not sure it'll go that far."

"You think? Cal made a grab for him. That's looking pretty serious."

Maars shrugged. "I don't know, but it looks like the demon lord's slowing things down, so I think it's time for us to go to bed."

Frazil grunted. "Is this wise to leave him unsupervised? His powers have been so out of whack since we left home."

Maars shrugged again.

Frazil bit his lip and abandoned his grip on the front door. Frowning, he peeked between the wooden slats a second time. "His mind's wandered off into the future again."

Maars joined him. "That could be a sign of why he's going at it like he is. Do you think there was any tongue?"

"Maars!" came the fierce, whispered reprimand.

"What? If he did, I'd be proud."

Frazil folded his arms. "Did you stop and think that maybe your exhibitionist tendencies, and your near-phoenix copulation with the Dasheel woman—in front of non-phoenix strangers!—broke something in Cal, and now he's horny?"

Maars braced himself against the wall, held his belly and laughed so hard he bent over. "Cal? Horny? Two words I'd thought I never hear strung together in my entire lives. Besides, you know my little tryst went waaay over his head."

Frazil grumbled. "If he's interested in this demon lord, maybe we should start talking to him about playing with fire. Literally."

Maars snorted and went back to looking out the window. "Do you know how difficult it'll be to even get him to understand a real condom? Let alone having the concentration, and understanding enough to create the ethereal one needed so flames don't mix?"

Frazil threw his brother a disgusted look. "The condoms are for the demon lord. He'll find Cal's womb sooner or later, and we don't want any accidents."

Maars closed the slats. "Maybe this demon lord is family, after all. If Cal's mind did wander into the future..."

"Caused by IC's assault, you mean? That was a pretty bad blow to the head."

"That doesn't help matters." The delight of his brother finding his first love interest faded from Maars's demeanor. The terror of the day flared back into memory. "We know Great-Grandfather's curse only exacerbates Cal's mind time-skipping."

"Yeah," Frazil agreed. "It was pretty harried there a few times in England. Don't want any repeats of that."

"But since he's going at it like this," Maars declared. "it only means our baby bird did find someone he can be happy with. Hmm. On second thought, we might need to have a little chat with this demon lord. And soon. Yeah, maybe we should call Cal in before anything escalates further. Flick on the porch light."

Chapter 31

Reporting To Triptych

AGUSTIN'S GUT TURNED WHEN Calico closed the door and the flickering porch light went off. Would this gentle man be able to strengthen his own resolve and courage and take a place within their nym society? He hoped Calico had that strength.

Leaning back in the driver's seat, Agustin took a deep breath, letting all the stress and shock exit his system. This had gone too far, and he wasn't just talking about Calico's questionable behavior. Fingers curling around the steering wheel, he knew what he had to do.

The drive into San Francisco allowed him to collect his thoughts and decide how he was going to confront Harper. Such a confrontation further twisted and rolled his stomach. But it wasn't as much of a twist as what Harper's assignment was doing to him.

He pulled into the car port of his reserved parking space. The office windows on this side of the building were dark, and the doors locked. That didn't mean Harper wasn't here. If the head of IC wasn't toiling in his office, Agustin would invade the onsite private residences.

Using his key, he took the stairs to the fourth floor. With his hand to the gold latch of Harper's office, a light in his former office—now Triptych's office—distracted him.

He knocked.

A file cabinet drawer slammed shut much harder than it should have. There was a thump, a crash, a gasping, and a shouted, "A moment, please!" A few seconds later, the new occupant directed him to enter.

Triptych stood up from behind the desk. The gauzy black hood, and wide-brimmed hat and veils were back in place. Remembering his manners, Agustin removed his own hat. What were those veils hiding?

"Lord California," Triptych greeted. "Surprising to find you here so late. Please have a seat."

Triptych meant it was surprising because Agustin was no longer the regional manager, and that there usually wasn't anyone in the offices at this hour besides Harper.

"I'm here to talk to Harper."

"Oh? He left early today. Molly's school play."

Hell and damnation. He'd forgotten with everything going on. His five-year-old sister was going to have his scaly hide for a Halloween costume. Or maybe a throw rug. He'd buy her some new boxing gloves, and she'd forgive him.

Sighing, Agustin wanted to get the argument with Harper *done*.

"Anything I could help you with?"

Gritting his teeth, Agustin settled into the chair. He felt he was taking the coward's way out. Maybe he was. But he also wanted to go home and unwind in his private conservatory and hide among the greenery. "It's about Calico Winghorse—the phoenix-werewolf-demon with the portal."

"Yes, I remember—having given you that assignment."

Agustin detected testiness seeping into that tone. "Have you finished the daily team reports?"

"I've been out of the office most of the day finishing my introductions to the Infinity groups. I still have to read and file I-3's and I-7's. I was about to get to I-7's."

"Why don't you pick I-3's first? I'll wait." Agustin leaned back in his chair and dared to prop his oxfords up on the corner of the desk he once sat behind. He had a hunch that Calico was Triptych's pet project.

Triptych shuffled through some papers, then went silent. A few minutes passed while he read. Putting the file down, he folded his hands. "And your thoughts?"

Agustin shared the encounter: from the brother's harried telephone call, to the time it took him to drive into the city and file his own report. He watched in fascination as those clasped hands got tighter. Whiter. Those manicured nails dug into lily-white flesh and drew blood. When Agustin finished, it was eerie how silent the new regional manager was.

"I understand," Triptych said after a few moments.

Agustin felt the fine scales on the back of his neck rise at that slow, dangerous tone, even down through the magic that stuffed him into a human shell like an uncooked ravioli.

"I was not aware of this happening," Triptych went on, more to himself. "It wasn't in the archives."

What a strange thing to say. Agustin studied the hatted man from under lowered lids. Triptych was much too calm, but with a rage loitering beneath the surface. And that behavior offered a clue that made no sense whatsoever.

Triptych asked, "You're certain Calico is recuperating?"

"My personal physician looked him over."

"Good. Thank you for bringing this to my attention, Lord California. Don't concern yourself any longer. Rest assured, *I will* handle the issue from here."

When Triptych stood, so did he. Adjusting his veils, Triptych strolled over to the office door and held it open. Agustin debated those dark, cryptic undertones as he headed back down the stairs to his motorcar.

Triptych was quite the conundrum, and he mentally filed this meeting away. This new liaison was not one to be crossed.

Chapter 32

Unexpected Help

CALICO CREPT OUT OF bed hours earlier than when they normally rose. Leaving a note for his brothers, he donned his heavy coat and walked to Main Street in the brisk chill of predawn. He shivered with each step, and hurried his pace a little, trying to keep warm.

Thankfully, his headache had subsided. His precious top hat covered the shaved side of his head and helped buffer him from the early morning dew. Having his phoenix bloodlines at the forefront of his heritage often made for uncomfortable mornings and even more distressing winters.

There were times he toyed with wreathing himself in fire via his magic. It only produced lancing pain, anxiety, and frustration. What he needed, required, was a flame created from within, a flare birthed of his inner psychic abilities. Not one formed with energies taken from the natural vibrations of the world around him.

His anxious desire to reach his bakery surpassed the fear of his assault. Even if the gloomy dark and fog filtering through the treed landscape made his knees knock, he soldiered on. He had to provide for his brothers. They had two building rents to pay, Dot to feed, and bills to mail.

He wished for his gentleman's bicycle, for it would've shortened the journey by a substantial margin. But the vehicle had been left behind at the bakery, just like the two owned by his brothers.

He was glad he had not been able to eat anything before his departure. His stomach had remained in knotted butterflies since last night. It wasn't merely his concern that his entire shop needed replenishing.

It was the demon lord hovering within his thoughts. Agustin. A name he could cherish, but one that played havoc with his tongue. He found it most difficult to pronounce. There had to be an easier way. Though he had to tuck that quest away for another time.

Calico was uncertain. He trusted the man, yet not. The thought of sharing his portal—with the hostile strangers of Infinity Corporation—made his stomach ill.

He equated his circumstances with his gateway to a parent protectively cradling their newborn, a vibrant, fragile presence that filled one with awe and wonder. A spark of creation waiting, trusting, to be properly shaped and tempered by a firm, loving hand.

Sharing his portal with Agustin? Maybe not so bad. Even if Agustin was a stranger, too.

Calico chewed on a thumbnail. Perhaps not a stranger for much longer, though. This new acquaintance was weighted and examined. Agustin admitted the Corporation still wanted access to the uniqueness of his portal entity, but Agustin also conveyed a personal interest. In him. What did a nobleman see in a humble baker?

Or, perhaps Agustin wasn't seeing a baker at all. But rather someone with a shared demonic heritage—albeit a much diluted heritage on his end—and telepathic powers. Although, his mind was currently a broken one.

There was also the fact they shared the ancient element of flame. Calico quivered at the thought of maybe not being so lonely now. Because there was someone like him, who understood the intimate soul of the conflagration itself.

He believed Agustin's intentions were genuine, and the thoughts of a chaperone in their future were bringing back the flutters.

No. He should not be thinking of such social luxuries. He had a bakery to run and two brothers and Dot to take care of. That was his priority. Work was never-ending. There was precious little time to acknowledge the loneliness long buried in his heart.

Because the majority of Time itself was a fleeting, chaotic beat currently denied him. He pushed away the frustration and loss. To dwell upon it would do no good, other than further upset him.

Forcing his thoughts to measurements, flour, and water, and what he needed to produce this morning, he sorted through his keys as he rounded the corner. His feet stopped. A silhouette lingered at the door of his business. Calico's hind mind urged him to flee.

The shadow wore a large floppy hat that was familiar. It was Mr. Triptych.

Muscles he did not know had tensed, relaxed. He found he had a death grip on the small pendant box in his pocket. Giving Ms. Mug's accommodations an apologetic pat, he moved forward.

"Good morning, Mr. Triptych. What are you doing here so early? I do not open for another six hours."

Their benefactor's voice shook. "Are you hurt? How are you feeling? I had a personal visit from Lord California. He told me what happened when he submitted his daily report. I am so sorry."

"I am well. Thank you for inquiring. The demon lord—Agus—Mr. Chavez de la Cruz—had a Healer see to my injuries and sent someone to repair the bakery."

"Oh, I'm so glad to hear it!"

Triptych briefly patted him on the shoulders, and for a moment, Calico thought the man would hug him. Ducking his head and turning away, he unlocked his new door.

He was not able to see within, as shades had been added, and they now shielded the newly installed shopfront windows. The interior smelled of fresh paint, making him eager to view the finished product.

Mr. Triptych followed him inside.

Glass did not crunch beneath Calico's shoes as he sought the light switch. Once he'd flicked it on, he was speechless. New shelving units lined freshly painted walls. The color was a wonderful warm cream that suited the bakery atmosphere well. New display racks and glass cases wrapped around the entire storefront, providing him with more retail capacity than before.

His heart swelled with a mixture of gratitude and expectation. With the added equipment, he would no longer have to house merchandise awaiting shelf space in the storerooms.

Triptych's voice was much calmer now. "Lord California's construction crew worked wonders in a few short hours."

Calico tested the paint with a pinky finger. Still tacky. This would not do at all.

Ignoring Triptych, Calico took a slow, steady inhale and closed his eyes. Reaching deep within himself meant focusing upon that core of his being that was space and time.

Time.

His even slower exhale cast forth his request. Coiled within that ex-hale, Time inched and stretched throughout the bakery. The age-old fingers of the universe ignored Triptych, cured the paint, and drove away the smell. Calico opened his eyes to see Triptych standing in front of him, arms crossed, and foot tapping.

"Mr. Winghorse. Calico."

"What?" he inquired innocently. Calico dismissed the wobble in his limbs as he briskly moved into the kitchen to begin his day. "I will not have my confections spoiled by smelly chemicals."

Triptych trailed close behind, the veils flowing with the motion. "Should you be doing that without Gigglemug to spot you? Especially since your great-grandfather Rupart blocked you from accessing your other gifts? You shouldn't be using such cosmic energies without your magic and psychic abilities being a buffer! Especially while in a mortal, physical form. I can see the tremors in your hands."

"Bah," Calico drew his arms behind his back and out of sight. "It is nothing to be concerned about. I only used a minuscule portion."

But maybe his ex-benefactor was correct. His psychic powers did buffer the celestial from the corporeal, and did well to keep the two halves of himself in harmony. Right now, he felt...squeezed and torn all at the same time. He grabbed onto his mind as it attempted to drift away from his physical body and revel in the realm of space-time. He discreetly swallowed some bile.

Triptych swayed back and forth on his feet in indecision. "Well...as long as you don't do it again, I won't mention it to your brothers."

"We have an accordance, then." It was the last thing he needed, some-one reporting his slip ups. He certainly wouldn't be courting Time again anytime soon. Not without his psychic powers. He did not enjoy the residual sensations while trapped in a physical body.

"Speaking of your siblings, they're not here?"

"I could not sleep. I would not disrupt theirs."

Mr. Triptych motioned around them. "I'm here. I'd love to help get you started."

Calico was already handing the man an apron. "Oh, do you bake?"

"Actually, my papa taught me. All sorts of breads, cakes, cookies, biscuits, tarts, and even the cooking basics." There was amusement in Triptych's answer as he folded the full bib apron and tied it around his waist, for it would not go over his large veiled hat.

"Oh, how delightful. Was he a baker?"

Triptych washed and dried his hands. "Umm...uh. Baking is only one of his many talents."

"Let's start then, shall we?"

The kitchen was just as renovated as the storefront. Calico hurried to his precious ovens and tested the doors. Good as new. He found the fireboxes were already filled. He wanted to get started. There was so much to do. So, using his magic, he ignited the wood with a touch of his hand. Then ignored the small riot turning over in his gut at a flame unpalatable.

"Caaaall...I see what you're doing."

Caught. Calico hunched his shoulders and peered over. His ex-benefactor was busy hefting a sack of flour to the counter. Apparently paying him no mind.

Triptych sliced open the burlap and poured the contents into a large tub for easier access. "Stop hurting yourself before you do serious damage. Do your brothers condone this behavior?"

"Alright, alright, I promise." Advice he had best follow after the jolts of a moment ago.

Calico sought to discover if his bank of yeast starters had been com-promised. He had to kneel and lean over to reach into the back of the cabinet. With a sigh of relief, he noted they were untouched.

"What's first on the list?" Triptych collected several measuring cups.

"We'll start with bread loaves," Calico said as he washed up.

"Wheat? French?"

"Affirmative."

"With luck, we'll get a decent quantity on the counters by lunch." Triptych filled a canister with water.

"We will be fortunate to meet the demand of opening rush," Calico added. "I am not certain if Maars will be able to take the cart out on rounds today."

So they toiled. As the hours went by, spilled flour and water arched across the work benches. Stacked pans teetered as they were put aside to cool. By the time his brothers arrived, batches of goods were already out of the ovens and ready for the sales floor. Calico took their reprimands of coming in alone in stride, and for a while, light banter between Triptych and his brothers filled the kitchen.

As the hour to open approached, Frazil and Maars adjourned to or-ganize the shopfront. Calico and Triptych kept baking.

Calico paused, then suddenly said aloud. "Perhaps I should learn more of the culinary arts. It would be nice to have something different for dinner for a change. Between the three of us, there is not much variety in our home kitchen."

"No need to overextend yourself," Triptych advised. "But I'll bring you a cookbook on my next visit. How are your reading skills in English coming along?"

"I shall get the hang of it, just like I finally mastered the English tongue."

Triptych snorted a short laugh, as if he found humor in the statement. "Uh, erm, I wanted to ask. Word in the nym realm says you've been contacted by Infinity Corporation."

Calico raised an eyebrow. Pursing his lips, he said, "Yes. Infinity Corporation is interested in my portal. I have been giving it some thought."

"It's an unusual creation, one you should keep close to your heart."

Calico knew, sensed, that Mr. Triptych was watching him intently.

"Do consider sharing it—though only with those in need," Mr. Triptych clarified. "Um..."

Calico stopped kneading the dough, and waited.

Triptych placed his trays in the oven. "Calico, I take responsibility for your assault."

Calico shook off a shiver at the memory. "Pssht," he answered. "You did no such thing."

The man was fidgeting with his veils now, and genuinely appeared nervous. "Please, please don't be mad at me. I was the one who alerted the Corporation to your portal—after I took employment with them. I'm deeply sorry. I never knew you'd been coerced like that. Nor was I aware of their vile recruitment methods."

Calico gasped. "It was you! Of course, why did I not realize?" His fingers squished right through the dough in his shock, leaving it a lumpy mess he paid no mind to. "No one else knew of my otherworld quintessence!" His vision blurred slightly in his stress and he drew a double breath, but still choked out, "W-why would you do such a thing? I trusted you. As did my brothers."

This did not make sense. There had to be a good reason. Mr. Triptych had been so protective of them in the past.

Their ex-benefactor held out his hands. "Please, p—you have to un-derstand, millions of lives are at risk—our kind and humans—in two separate worlds."

Calico's blood ran cool at the reminder. "Mr. Chavez de la Cruz had said, but...that many? All because of my little portal? Something that brought me years of joy and exploration as I honed my craft?"

Mr. Triptych removed his apron. Placing a hand to Calico's shoulder, he said, "Cal, this portal may be the crux of you experimenting and honing your powers, but it's someone else's weapon. In the wrong hands, it will lead to many suffering."

Leaning against the table, Calico pulled off the excess dough stuck to his fingers. "The Amaranth Empire." he said quietly.

Mr. Triptych's hat nodded. "I sent Lord California to you because I knew he'd respect you. Provide you the time you required to make the right decision. What I failed to consider was Mr. Harper's impatience. He sent in a team who patrols the veils between worlds. A team that monitors the gateways to the lesser portals IC already operates."

Calico grunted with dissatisfaction. As his quick fingers shaped dough and set it aside to rise, he considered the respect shown to him by both Mr. Triptych and the demon lord. Of the countless lives that would be on his soul should he continue to ignore the need for help.

Mr. Triptych and Agustin were in high standing within this corpora-tion. They had influence. They believed in him. Then he, too, should place his trust in them, even if they both went about the request for it in the clumsiest of ways. Calico pulled off his own apron and faced his benefactor.

"You are wise to bring this to my attention further, and I thank you for it. I do not want to see anyone harmed by something I created. However, you must ask yourself, Mr. Triptych—have you implemented this course of action in the correct manner? You manipulated Mr. Chavez de la Cruz, and most especially myself. I agree it was for the greater good, but you have done so at my expense."

"My reasons for my actions are my own, Cal. Please don't ask me to explain. *I can't.*"

Calico looked at him. "Is it that important?"

Mr. Triptych crossed his arms.

Calico would not stand down and kept staring.

It was Mr. Triptych who folded first. His shoulders rose at this scolding, and his head dipped. "P—Cal, I would never do anything that's not in your best interests. You must believe that."

"Oddly enough, I do," Calico said without a qualm. "I am merely upset with your methods. We shall strive for better communication in the future."

"Indeed." Mr. Triptych wiped his hands on a towel. "Well, I should be going. It's getting late and I should be on my way. Oh, before I forget." He pulled a piece of paper out of his pocket and slid it across the workbench. "A check. Mr. Harper rejected compensation for the destruction and business losses, but Lord California covered it."

Calico picked up the bank note and glanced at the amount. "More than generous. I cannot accept it."

"Think of it as also payment for your time. You know all about *time*, yes?"

It was a small joke. Calico chuckled. "Of course I do."

"Then why not humor me and agree to meet with him? Lord California, I mean. Perhaps in doing so you'll get to know the nym community more. Find other wizards. And you and your brothers won't be so lonely."

So Mr. Triptych had seen the loneliness within him as well. Was his behavior so obvious? Reluctantly, Calico nodded. "You may inform Lord California I still plan to meet with him."

Excitement seemed to radiate from Triptych. "How about dinner? To be fair, I'll spring for Maars's and Frazil's meals elsewhere, since all three of you work too hard—to make up for my serious blunder."

"You mean I'll be meeting him alone? To dine?" Calico was aghast. He and Agustin had not yet employed their chaperone. "Oh dear, no. That would be much too intimate! I have become a wholesome figure in this community, and Mr. Chavez de la Cruz's noble reputation—"

"Er, a business dinner then," Mr. Triptych rushed. "Yeah. To talk about business."

Calico thought about that. He was doing nothing tonight. Well, other than wrapping himself in a warm blanket while he practiced his reading in the small parlor of the rented house he shared with his brothers. It tended to be a little quieter in the evenings, being on the outskirts of town.

It was Frazil's turn to cook, and his brother would be pleased to abandon that duty. But...Calico could not afford to break their strict budget and indulge.

"Lord California would pick up your tab," Mr. Triptych hurried again. "Also as an apology for not being straightforward."

Calico found this acceptable. Perhaps he should remove himself for a few hours, then. A short intermission from the catch-up baking would be nice. "A business dinner will be satisfactory."

"Good. I'll have him pick you up, here, after work."

Chapter 33

Agustin vs Harper Round 1

AGUSTIN'S MIND WAS MUCH too busy to be driving himself into the congested city this early morning. Because of his tense mood over Calico's injuries and mental state, he had Ramirez drop him off at ICHQ. He wasn't sure how long this confrontation—ah, unscheduled and unplanned meeting—was going to run. Harper might even turn him away.

Still, Agustin sent his man off to enjoy the sights. At least one of them should have a pleasant day. He hoped Calico was coping with his trauma, and not because the sweet baker was quickly waltzing his way into his heart.

Agustin pressed a hand against his chest to keep his heart from pounding right out of it. Oh, he was falling fast. Did Calico even have an intimate regard for him? What if Calico's feelings had changed after the incident with I-3? When would be the appropriate time to introduce Ganymede? But shouldn't they discuss the incident of their first meeting before bringing Ganymede into the fold?

What was he even doing? He was getting way ahead of himself. It was past time to get his mind out of the clouds and pay attention to his duties. And especially to Calico's well-being. He continued to mull over those missing gaps in the baker's discarded thoughts.

Angels striding through the hall on business jarred him further from the clouds. Had Triptych placed yesterday's field reports on Harper's desk yet? Most likely not. He'd not received one of Harper's brutish telephone calls all night or before he left home. Which meant he might have to relay the disaster all over again.

Shoulders straightened and head lifted high, Agustin struggled for neutrality. Maybe his mother was right. He always went to Harper looking to pick a fight. Always on the defensive. Unfortunately, it would be one of those types of visits.

He traversed the corridor leading to Harper's office. The door swung open before he could reach for it.

What. In. The. Name. Of. Heaven?

The drama within had him frozen in surprise. Seven members of Infinity 3 hobbled past him and down the hall. Two of them were on crutches; one had a leg cast. Three others had an arm in a sling, and their leader had a broken nose. All of them had a black eye. All of them burned. And according to his affinity with the fire element, some of the wounds held the whiff of third degree damage.

Cadence was among them. With a black eye. Agustin could discern no other injuries.

"Cadey?" Agustin reached out, but the youth pulled away and refused to make eye contact. Agustin stared, dumbfounded. They were angels, beings created of light—well, all except Cadence. Had they been human, they'd be dead. Only something as equally celestial could do such damage. Yet they were currently in a physical mortal form. Had they just returned from a mission he hadn't been informed of?

I-3 mumbled subdued greetings and respect to him as they went, keeping their eyes downcast.

Triptych careened into him, also on his way out. The liaison still wore his black hood, white hat, and veils. The man's shoulders were thrown back, and his arms were stiff at his sides.

"Greetings, Lord California," Triptych snarled through clenched teeth. Did Agustin imagine that demonic, wolf-like growl?

"Mr. Triptych," Agustin greeted. "What—"

"If you'll excuse me, sir, I have papers to push," the hatted man snapped before he shoved past. There was a fraction of a second's pause. "Oh, you're taking Calico to dinner tonight."

Agustin leaned against the open door. *All of those curt responses had been entirely in Spanish.* He was more surprised that Triptych was fluent in the language. Native speaker fluent.

By the time Agustin glanced over his shoulder, Triptych had retreated to his office. Slammed the door shut hard enough to shake the walls.

Wide-eyed, Agustin gaped. The liaison's thoughts continued to rail, and a cabinet banged open and shut. There it was. A loose thought-thread. Detaching from its source. Just waiting to be read.

Like a carrot dangled in front of a horse, Agustin hesitated before reaching out for the straying temptation.

"Agustin!" Harper yelled from his place behind his desk.

The shout disrupted his concentration. This disturbance also jarred Triptych. The thoughts were instantly yanked back and sealed away. The liaison's mind went silent. Agustin regretted his hesitation, but it was due to his strict telepathic training.

"What are you doing here?" Harper demanded.

Collecting himself, Agustin entered the room. "I told you, I'm here to go over what IC will offer Mr. Winghorse for his portal. I also was going to discuss I-3, but..." He gestured toward Triptych's office. "The bakery incident, I assume?" With all that occurred yesterday, Agustin fig-ured the drama was related.

Harper tapped a stack of papers straight and shoved them into an outbox. "Our dearest Mr. Triptych had an issue with I-3's recruit-ment methods. I've docked his salary and placed him on probation. More than fair, since it's going to take months to get I-3 back into the field."

"Shouldn't I-3 be the party disciplined?"

"It seems like they already have been, by Triptych. This behavior was unacceptable, especially coming from a regional manager! Our target is to blame for this squabble among us."

Harper was testing his decision to strive for neutrality. "Mr. Winghorse wasn't giving us trouble," Agustin protested. "If you'd been patient—"

"Trouble?" Harper exclaimed. "Our target blew up your home! What if Ganymede had been present? It was bad enough Triptych was there. He could have been harmed in the melee!"

"Ganymede's away at school," Agustin replied calmly. "And obvi-ously, Triptych can take care of himself. It was my gate blown up, not the house. Winghorse only did so because I'd foolishly trapped him inside the compound. Frightened him. The error was mine."

Harper continued shifting things around on his desk in his upset. "Ganymede's due home for winter break, and his birthday is coming up. I will not have him put in danger."

"Are you saying I ignore my son's safety and well-being?" Agustin asked hotly. Of course he was. Ever since Ganymede was born, Harper had instructed him on the proper way to raise a child. That had forced Isabella to move back to Mexico and seek the queen's protection. Izzy took his son with her when she left.

Five terrible, long and lonely years without his son. Missing his first steps. His first word. His sweet face. Only the magic of the communication rings had kept him sane. Agustin clenched his jaw shut.

"I'm saying you invited a stranger into your home!" Harper stressed. "An otherworld demonic phoenix god wolf-thing who commands incredible power should he choose to release it, and owns a dangerous inter-dimensional portal. I won't have my grandsons influenced by such chaotic forces."

Agustin shook the flashbacks out of his head. He turned back to the door and looked out into the hallway. Assured they were alone, he shut and locked it. Looming over the desk with arms crossed, he asked, "When did this become an attack on how I raise my son?"

Harper gave him an exasperated, familiar, and long-suffering look. "When you decided to be irresponsible. When you forced me to take matters into my own hands and send in I-3."

"Now this is about my assignment?" Agustin shouted. "Make up your mind, old man."

Harper's reply was sharp and slightly elevated. "I sent in the team I considered the most capable of handling our target's temper."

Agustin slammed his palms onto the desk. "You gave this job to me, remember? Why did you usurp my authority? I had it under control."

"Moving much too slowly for my liking. I expect better of you."

Agustin flinched.

Harper gestured with acute resolution. "I cannot have my right hands go around bashing in the heads of my combat teams," he said. "I expect more of my managers, and I expect much more out of you."

Harper was too at ease with this, which meant he was manipulating his operatives again. Manipulating him.

THE DEMON LORD OF CALIFORNIA

Agustin bit the inside of his cheek as a reminder to keep calm. "You did this all on purpose."

"Yes," Harper said easily.

"*Why?*"

"Simple. The target needed the proper motivation. Provide him a friend, and an enemy. The friend instantly becomes the ally."

Agustin shook his head, feeling sick to his stomach. "Winghorse would've come around. He's a compassionate soul. There's no need for games."

"This isn't a game, Agustin, this is a war. Earth is at risk—"

"You speak of games when you play many yourself," he snapped.

Harper ignored him. "The Creator's children, the humans, and even the nym, are at risk. I want that portal. It's the only one left unsecure on the planet. The Amaranth will discover its existence sooner or later. And when they do, I will have control over it, and block them from returning to this world."

Harper was in the right, and in the wrong at the same time. Agustin put a hand to his temple in disbelief. Was this what it took to run the Corporation? Always pushing? Well then, he would push and not look back.

He collected his hat and fiddled with the inside liner. Looking at the angel who was his sire in the eye, he said, "I'll return with Mr. Winghorse tomorrow, promptly at ten o'clock. I request you be cordial, and respectful, and that his contract of employment with IC be ready for his signature. I've already assigned him to Infinity 8, and that's where he will stay. I also bid he receive a generous and regular salary for the indefinite rental—*and I do mean rental, Harper*—of his portal."

Agustin paused at the door. "I'm meeting with him this evening, so I'll send along any addendum paperwork for you to incorporate. Your secretary will be working late tonight." He didn't wait for protest or argument; he spun in dismissal and departed without another word.

It was his turn to ignore Harper's rails of anger. The noise growing ever fainter the further he walked. This action should have been a small victory. But it only left the foul sensations of a long, familiar anxiety and resentment festering inside him.

Chapter 34

Starting Anew

CALICO STOOD AT THE window of his bakery, waiting. Shadows had begun to descend, and he bid good night to the life-warmth of the sun. Shop lights across the little street had gone out hours ago. Neighboring proprietors had locked up and gone home. Everything was quiet, still.

The lone street lamp flickered on the far corner, strongly reminding him of the emptiness that had once been in his heart. Pacing kept the butterflies from launching another chaotic flight around in his stomach. He settled into an uneasy routine, procuring a dust cloth and absently swishing it across the sales counter.

He had pedaled home after the noon rush to fetch his good suit. Changed as soon as his brothers had locked up and left. They had wanted to stay and keep him company, but he would not have it. It was embarrassing enough to face the demon lord after the frightening drama, but hold court with an audience? Unacceptable.

Twice he had fussed with his appearance in the wraparound mirrors Agustin's crew had curiously added to the storefront's decor. It was much better than trying to check himself in the small mirror hanging on the back patio.

The crickets buzzed as the evening grew. Calico turned to the clock ticking away on the wall: 6:58. He consulted his pocket watch to be sure. Worry gave way. Had he been duped by his own benefactor? Or had something happened? Was the demon lord lying dead in a ditch from a motorcar accident? No, no. He could not think such things.

He moved to ring Mr. Triptych to see if there had been a misunderstanding. Yes, just a misunderstanding, even though he could not shake the idea of a mass of twisted metal burning on the side of the road.

A raucous rumble perched on the edge of his hearing grew louder. Motorcars weren't common on Main Street after businesses closed for the day. Perhaps it was a lost tourist. Much to his surprise, the gasoline-filled beast stopped in front of his bakery.

It was the demon lord.

The engine went off and the man disembarked. Calico flung open the shop door. Mr. Chavez de la Cruz was not expired in a ditch after all.

The not-corpse wore a black suit behind a long, heavy motorist's coat. The white shirt collar and shiny silver-and-white necktie against Agustin's darker skin made Calico's heart flutter faster. He was anxious for that driver's coat to come off in order to view the suit's style. Was it of a modern cut, or was it older? His attention shifted upward.

Another top hat. Calico was excited to see it was decorated with a matching white-and-silver band. The brim concealed a braided bun at the base of Agustin's neck. Those golden upside-down double triangle earrings made that one honey-colored eye sparkle brighter and highlighted that one blue eye.

The car, however, seemed vaguely familiar. No, another automobile. A vehicle much bigger, more comfortable. Completely enclosed, with a wonderful heater contraption built into the

dashboard. Calico blushed furiously, wondering why he knew the intimate feel of the slick leather upholstery against his naked back.

Calico hurriedly shook the most distressing, Time-snapped thoughts out of his mind. He had become a trollop! Such an act was most improper!

He re-centered himself, recalling he was supposed to be worried, and angry. He put his hands on his hips. But his voice went squeaky-gritty, and he wheezed, "Good evening. Are you all right?"

Agustin gave him another one of those peculiar glances. "I'm well. Although it's a question I want to ask of you."

"I...I am managing. Thank you for inquiring."

That honey and blue-eyed gaze lingered. "No more...ah, for the lack of a better description, flashes or blackouts? Last night, I sensed your mind drifting off and returning."

"Oh dear!" Calico exclaimed. "I did not do anything untoward, did I?"

There was a muted smile and a brief downcast glance. "Nothing that I couldn't handle. You do seem more yourself today." His chest rose high, then fell. "I'm glad."

"It—it pleases me you are concerned." Calico knew his face was redder than a tomato. He cleared his throat and tried to remember his upset. "With the pleasant greetings behind us, why are you two hours and seven and a half minutes late?"

Calico motioned with restless hands. He'd had nothing to do but listen to Ms. Dasheel's cuckoo clock tick and tock and cuckoo every hour. It had come in the post and Maars had been giddy and distracted the remainder of the day. "Mr. Triptych said our meeting would begin after the shop closed."

Those marvelous bi-colored eyes widened, and Agustin's mouth dropped open. "I-I'm sorry. There was a last-minute summons from the Demon Queen of Mexico," he rushed to explain. "I had to use all my charm to move it up to next week. Didn't Etney telephone and tell you? I told her to call you."

Calico gestured toward his little bakery. "The telephone has not rung."

Agustin's broad shoulders drooped, the weariness overtaking his trim form. "She's had her head in the clouds since she drove Dr. E over to assess your injuries. Again, I apologize."

Calico's heart jolted with disappointment. The demon lord would be too exhausted then for their meeting. Before he could still the thought, Calico was already replying. "Then there is no charm left for me? Perhaps we, too, should reschedule."

The regret and dejection radiating off the demon lord like a phoenix flame was too much to bear. To Calico's surprise, his ears popped and there was the presence of magic coming down all around them. A blue jewel tucked into Agustin's hat glowed. He had not noticed before that the tiny gem was a mainstay of Agustin's style.

The demon lord slowly glided into his personal space. "My magic has us behind a wraparound Curtain spell. To the mundanes, we've already entered the bakery. Calico," Agustin's large, dark-skinned hands rose to touch him, but paused. Instead, they began to drop back to his sides.

Calico surprised himself when a soft whine of protest left his throat. The hands halted again, then slowly, ever so slowly, graced his cheek. Calico leaned into the caress, enjoying the calloused thumbs that stroked his face with feather light touches.

"Calico." Agustin's voice had gone deeper, gruffer. "There is a special charm, in abundance. All reserved for you."

So this was what it was like not to breathe, Calico thought. To be riding on the clouds of the universe itself, the multi-verses itselves, suspended in Time like no else. Here, he was no god, just a man who desired another.

Agustin gently bumped his forehead against his own. "We're not getting off to an easy start, are we?"

"Well." Calico thought about that, answering just as dreamily. He took his time, enjoying the heat, the little touches, the nearness of another. "One could agree our exchanges have been most rocky. However, I would like to think we are participating in a marathon, and not the one hundred-yard dash."

Starting over was a task he and his brothers were well acquainted with. New beginnings were nothing surprising to a phoenix. From fleeing their home and living in England, then traveling to America with Mr. Triptych, they had done their share of resettling.

Drawing a deep breath and standing straight, Calico outstretched his hand. "We shall start anew. Good evening, sir. My name is Calico Winghorse. You could say I am new to town."

He was rewarded with a gaze of smoldering silence, before cozy amusement followed. They clasped hands. It was a handshake, yet not. Agustin's touch was as warm and gentle as Calico had felt seconds ago, and the sensation set his stomach back to chasing butterflies. They were slow to part, and Calico mourned the loss.

Calico cleared his throat and motioned to the bakery behind him. "I own and run this shop with my brothers. Saturday mornings are our most busy days. The adorable little children line up, squawking and pushing like chicks in the nest, to purchase a day-old and deeply discounted frosted cupcake."

Calico's cheeks went rosy as a wide smile graced Agustin's lips. That smile transformed the handsome man before him. While some of the weariness remained, the frustration and regret melted away.

"It is a pleasure to meet you, Calico. My name is Agustin. My hobby is collecting motorcars, and I live for my work. However, lately, I've realized I would enjoy the opportunity to slow down and socialize. It's a delight to learn you run a bakery, because chocolate cake and butterscotch pudding are nearly my most favorite things in the world."

Joyful that Agustin had followed his lead, Calico was now stunned and terrified because he was unsure of what he should do next—other than make a mental note of stocking up on said supplies.

Agustin's manner morphed into cozy enjoyment. "You have patience with children."

"Oh, yes, of course. They are most chaotic and easy to get along with."

Agustin snorted with humor. "I can tell you don't have any of your own."

"Not currently. I do hope to marry someday. I require heirs to revive the Breese heritage."

Agustin's eyes went thoughtful and somewhat veiled. Sad. He seemed to close in on himself. Calico tried to understand why sharing the fact that he wanted marriage and children would be the cause of it.

"It's so different when they're your own," Agustin said. "I wish you the best of luck with it. I have a son myself."

Calico's empathy cleaved him with another jolt. Agustin had opened back up to him. Perhaps it was best to try to tamp down the ability until he had a few days of rest. Especially since the emotional impacts were so empty to him. "Thank you for the well wishes. Ah, your son! Do you have a photograph? May I meet your family?"

"Ganymede will be home in a few months. His mother, Isabella, lives in Mexico and visits on occasion. Mostly when Ganymede takes university breaks. His portraits hang on my walls," Agustin replied. "Or framed on my desk."

"His mother does not live with you?"

"We aren't married."

"Ah, I see."

"Do you? It was an arrangement for heir purposes only."

"Ah. Such agreements happen on my homeworld as well." Calico reached for his billfold. "I managed to have this photograph-image on my person when we first arrived. It is of myself and my brothers when we were small lads. Would you like to see?" He removed the frayed bit of paper and held it out.

Agustin did a double take. It took a moment for him to speak. "This is in color. Full, clear color. The lines. They're so crisp and defined. As if the art had already been perfected."

"Yes."

Agustin caressed the creases. "This size is endearing and personal. I should get one like this of my son. Then I can carry him with me."

There was a short pause as Agustin seemed to be thinking. Absently, he fiddled with his wristwatch. "But color photography is only in experimentation now and not for the general public—you said you arrived here a few years ago—you have photography on your world?"

Calico nodded. "Of course. It was invented by our tinkerer god, Wolthwatt and his priests."

There was a moment while Agustin looked at him, those marvelous eyes full of questions. Too many questions. A soft grin soon measured across his lips, and he tapped the picture. "White-blond like your brothers, but even then you had your head half-shaved as a child." Agustin took his time, looking him over again. "I prefer the black hair."

Calico felt a happy blush bloom on his cheeks at the compliment. "It is an old photograph. I colored my hair to honor my father and Grandfather Myles. The hairstyle is to honor my father."

Agustin's tone went softer, and he handed back the printed image. "You must miss them."

"Yes. I am so glad my brothers are at my side. Without them…I…don't think I would have…"

Ah, what an emotional mess this was stirring up. Thoughts of home twisted his innards. Calico nearly stopped breathing when a gentle hand came over his shoulder to comfort him. For a moment, he thought there was the brush of a thumb against his collar.

"Shall we go?" There was a quiet huskiness to Agustin's inquiry. It brought the butterflies back.

Calico locked the shop door behind him and secured the key ring in his pocket. As they stood beside the vehicle, Agustin held out a helping hand. Calico once again swallowed the flutters before accepting the assistance up into the passenger seat. While it was difficult to let go of those warm, calloused fingers, Calico latched onto something almost as exciting, for these particular butterflies were much easier to manage.

This would be his second motorcar ride. He'd been too nervous before to admire the metal wonder. His fingertips stroked the sleek leather seats and caressed the glossy green chassis, fascinated with the incredible machinery.

When he poised to ask a question, he found Agustin's hot, intense gaze had been following the movements of his hands. The butterflies took another chaotic flight; Calico sat rigid. Agustin's eyes darkened, and he cleared his throat.

Calico pulled at his cravat. Why was it suddenly so tight? "How many motorcars do you own?"

Agustin slid into the driver's bench. Then patted the tight space beside him. "It's rather exciting, isn't it?"

What was rather exciting? The volcanic gaze he'd encountered? The hot future-memory of their intimate rendezvous? Here in this very motorcar? Yes, yes indeed, that had been rather tingly. Wait...or had they already...? Oh dear. Oh dear...

"I have ten more back at my estate."

Oh, had Agustin been referring to the motorcars? How embarrassing. Even more embarrassing to realize, the Curse was messing with his space-time awareness. Again.

"Ten motorcars?" Calico exclaimed in a rather croakier voice than normal. "My goodness! Might I view them?"

"I can arrange that." Agustin's eyes were half-lowered, and a clandestine grin edged his lips.

Calico couldn't breathe. Was he breathing? Fuzzy space-time memories were being most naughty right now. "Er. Um. Will those little lights be enough? We shall be getting back after dark."

"The headlamps work well. We'll be fine. I can see in the dark," he said. "I am, after all, a demon."

Perhaps Calico could not see in the dark because his heritage was such a jumbled collection. He sat awkwardly with his hands in his lap as Agustin started the machine.

"Hang on to your hat," Agustin said. And then he smiled, offering a slow, sensual wink. Calico knew it had to do with him thinking of his name. So he gulped with nervous, giddy joy. And hurried to do as instructed the second the engine sputtered to life.

Chapter 35

Cooley Landing

CALICO HELD FIRMLY ONTO his top hat as they bounced down the thoroughfare. They passed the occasional horse-drawn taxi. The evening wind was brisk, and the cold was making its way through his clothing layers. So he buttoned his coat as best he could with one hand.

Agustin drove them south along the waterfront and marshlands and turned onto Bay Road. The jolting ride rattled the wax in his ears and the change in his pockets. Calico gripped his hat tighter. The close quarters in the motorcar kept his breath short, especially since he was unable to escape rubbing shoulders with an extremely attractive man.

Images of a rather er, most graphic coupling suddenly arose in his mind's eye. A passionate union between him and Agustin. In this very motorcar.

The disjointed Time-mind jumps were happening again. Calico fought to swim back into his present self. Praying to his mother goddess he was scrambling in the correct direction.

Once grounded, it was a difficult task to decipher where he was. And in what timeline and dimension. Especially anchored into a physical body as he was. Calico turned his head to the side, lest his companion notice his agitation. It had been harder to return this time, and he gripped his fear close. He pulled out his handkerchief and dabbed his brow.

Had this carnal event taken place here, or was it going to happen in Future-Time? He grit his teeth and thought hard. No. The incident was Future-Time. He was certain. Because that motor vehicle was different from this one. It was all so confusing. Was he going to turn into some sort of wild and brazen hussy? Oh, dear. It was vital he get a handle on these Time-blips.

"W-where are we off to?" Calico asked, trying to distract himself. Agustin was providing him a lengthy side-eye. Was he aware that his mind skipped? Had he done anything offensive towards Agustin during this intermission? He was too nervous to inquire.

"To Sally's over in Cooley Landing. It's a small bayside strip of land near Menlo Park."

"I thought this area was unpopulated."

"Yes and no," Agustin said. "There are several human places scattered about for shipping and industry."

Calico detected the spell half a second before it engulfed them; he jolted at the benign intrusion and found himself poised to leap from the moving vehicle. The gloppy, clinging sensation of this magic reminded him of the time Frazil had become cross with him and upturned a pot of warm molasses over his head. This magic had to be the Curtain. But it was much stronger than his previous experiences. Perhaps because it contained something big.

Agustin reached over and touched his knee in reassurance. "Easy, there."

The contact was another jarring spark. Racing through his entire body quicker than lightning.

"You'll get used to it," Agustin said.

Get used to it? Oh dear mother goddess! What did he mean? The pat to his knee or the Curtain spell? It took a moment to settle down from the drama.

Calico hoped the Curtain's gloppy weight would not cause him a headache. The magic of his Mirror Bubbles worked in the same manner as the Curtain, yet were light and unobtrusive.

Agustin pulled into a graveled parking lot. Ahead of them, two- and three-storied buildings topped a wide wharf. Thick wooden piles followed the shoreline, and flights of stairs reached out to the parking area at evenly spaced intervals.

Bright lanterns hung along each set of risers, and Calico sensed more magic at play. Water lapped quietly against the support pillars. Quiet voices drifted.

"What is to stop humans from building nearby or attempting to move into our Curtained landscape?" Calico asked.

"The Curtain encourages the mundanes to think the area is un-suitable, and to work around us. It can be used for many purposes." That was followed by a longer than usual look.

Calico pursed his lips, trying not to blush as Agustin lead the way to the first bank of stairs. Only this one business appeared populated, with lights blazing through the long line of windows. The name *Sally's Place* stretched across the side, in a glowing bright blue paint. A few women and men loitered around on the deck, smoking and talking low.

"You can be yourself here," Agustin told him. "It's not as classy as Raynard's, but I thought you wouldn't want to go too far from home. Since you get an early start, I mean. We can talk freely. Sally's Place and the surrounding businesses here are specifically geared toward serving IC employees."

Inside and away from the brisk chill, Calico surveyed the long hall. The building followed the shape of the pier, with walking decks on both sides. Wooden tables and benches matched the planked floors, and never-ending windows reached end to end. He tensed at the crowd of people in the corner, and at the presence of more scattered throughout. He was about to ask, but Agustin held up a hand.

"I specifically barred anyone in I-3 from being here tonight. Be at ease."

Once seated, Calico opened the menus left on the table, and once again, he inwardly cringed. The fuzzy writing was in script, and it took more effort to translate. He squinted.

Frazil and Maars had picked up the language much better than he had. He was still struggling with the native communications—their written word being the most troublesome. He had not bitten his lip and betrayed himself, had he?

"The fried chicken looks good," his dining companion suddenly announced.

Calico lifted his attention from the menu, shoulders back and spine straight. "I do not eat birds of any kind, thank you."

"Oh! My pardon." An endearing flush graced Agustin's cheeks. That mismatched gaze quickly re-scanned the pages. "Then perhaps you might enjoy the prime rib?"

Did Agustin suspect he could not read this language? Or was he reading discarded thoughts again? Calico wanted to dab at the light sheen of perspiration gathering under his collar. "A-are you always this chatty?"

"I've always adored the English accent," Agustin replied in a tone of smooth, heart-pounding silk.

Of course Agustin suspected he could not decipher this fancy writing because he was too quick to change the subject, Calico realized. Yet it was a pleasant subject.

Calico lowered his menu. "You do not speak like most of the locals here. It rolls nicely. Like music. It—it is lovely."

Agustin laughed quietly. "Because I was born, raised, and educated in Mexico. Although I have family from countries like Portugal and Spain. I visit them frequently, and also conduct business there."

"Is Mexico the country south of us?"

"Correct." Agustin closed his menu. "I think I'll have the roast beef and potatoes."

Calico decided to conclude the awkward situation. "Then I shall have the roast beef and potatoes as well."

With their order placed and their drinks presented, Calico took a moment to study his surroundings. Two demons with spiraled horns greeted people around a cluster of tables in the drinking area. A waiter with green scales hurried across the room with trays of food.

Calico squinted a little more. A tall, red-haired woman who could be a giant, worked the bar, giving out alcoholic drinks.

"That's Sally."

He swung back to find Agustin had been watching him. Intently. With those lovely heterochromatic eyes. Calico was embarrassed at getting caught squinting.

"So, Lord California," he tried to fill the awkwardness. But he lost himself studying the downward curve of the man's soft lips.

"Please, less formality if we're going to be working together. Especially among the nym. We're safe here."

Calico again rolled Agustin's given name around in his mind, still failing to come up with an alternative. "Mr. Ch—A-Agustin—why should I join Infinity Corporation?"

Their meals came and there was a moment of delay while serviettes were unfolded. Calico partook of his water, and Agustin sipped wine in a fancy glass. Then, Agustin slowly reached across the distance between them, and waited, palm up.

For permission, Calico suddenly realized. He offered his own, and welcomed the tentative stroke against his skin. The warmth between them seemed to provide them both courage.

"Why should you join?" came the soft question. Then there was a pause, as if Agustin had to ask himself. When he found the answer, their eyes met again. "So I can protect you, even when I am not at your side."

Fragmented pieces of future and past memories clashed, taking that second to swirl around in Calico's damaged brain. Were they moving too fast? Was he moving too fast? Or not fast enough? Deep down in his soul, he knew he could trust this man.

As much as Calico wanted this, he had to focus on why he was here. "About your leader's need for my inter-dimensional gateway..."

The hand withdrew, and Calico was instantly sorry. He wanted to take his words back, but it was too late.

"Yes, you're right. We're here for business. ICHQ is in psychic communication with our oracle. She's currently on the other side of your portal, in your dimension. She sensed the existence of a power bridge between worlds, but couldn't find it. When word of her discovery worked its way through the Corporation, Triptych stepped forward and said he knew you. He told us of your portal's stability."

Indeed. Calico still had to find time to invite Mr. Triptych to tea and talk about sharing private matters with strangers. He would bake the man's favorite scones with an additional batch to carry home.

"Your oracle," Calico inquired. "You want to bring her back to Earth?"

"Yes."

"And you need my portal to do it? How did she get there in the first place?"

"We once had our own networks, created by powerful psychics from both worlds. Stable networks anchored by ancient magic. But the Amaranth Empire destroyed them because they could not control them, and that connection was lost. Our psychics and wizards have resorted to manipulating natural vortexes. But we dare not permit more than two or three people to traverse them at a time, for they are dangerously unstable. We generally have...casualties...because transfers often fail."

"I am so sorry," Calico said to comfort him.

"Thank you. There are many Infinity Corporation operatives trapped on the other side, including members of my own team."

"So IC searches for a more stable avenue of transportation?" It was clear Infinity Corporation's need had become clearer. More desperate.

"Yes," Agustin said. "We need to rebuild a stable gateway that the Amaranth won't have control of. Bolster our ranks with Healers who wish to cross over. But more importantly, we must begin rescuing and returning the people they've stolen from this world."

Calico tapped his chin. He decided he would do this. People were suffering. But while helping innocents was the right thing to do, it did present a lucrative opportunity to make sure his brothers would be cared for when he expired. "What compensation would I receive?"

It was most curious when his dining companion hesitated. "What would you like? Infinity Corporation does wish to purchase your portal outright, and'll push for it. You and your brothers wouldn't have to work for the rest of your lives if you did sell."

Flatware clattered. "It is *not* for sale. If that is what you have brought me here for, then our business has concluded."

Chapter 36

Negotiations

CALICO STOOD TO DEPART, but Agustin touched his hand. The sensation was like another electric jolt all the way into his gut, and his face flushed. Calico retracted his arm and rubbed it. Agustin's elemental ability was too intense for him to handle as he was. It was too yummy. Too improper!

"My pardon," Agustin said. "Please, I won't demand a purchase. We'd like you to be part of our Infinity 8 team. I apologize for yet another clumsy attempt. Would you consider discussing terms for an indefinite rental?"

"Rental?" Calico sat back down. This could be acceptable. Could he use this to his advantage, and safely, while still helping innocents? "You inquired as to what I wanted for this transaction. My brothers and I would require protection. I would like to expand my bakery and purchase a delivery truck for them. I've saved half already. I desire to socialize with other wizards and make connections to practice my craft."

"Protection from whom?" Agustin asked, attention centered upon his wine glass.

Calico wadded up the serviette nervously, and his hands quivered. "My great-grandfather, Rupart Bright Terra. He is the high priest of the goddess Rattani, and once king of the elves."

That someone cared enough to ask him. That he could finally share this heavy burden with someone he cared about—with someone who seemed to care about him back.

The tale rushed out of him before he could center himself. "When Rupart was a lad, he served the death god, Nolth. When he and his lover, Charade, escaped that service, Nolth placed a terrible curse upon them."

His lip quivered and the grief pressed down.

"Take your time," Agustin offered softly.

Calico glanced up through teary eyes, grateful of the offered comfort. It was the strength he needed to continue. "If the death god could not have Rupart, neither could Charade. They were driven apart by that curse, for Rupart now wants to destroy the one he loved the most.

"Myself, and others have been trying to break that curse. But my abilities are not yet seasoned. Worse, the Rupart-creature deprived me of several of my talents—while he was under control of said curse."

"Your telepathy," Agustin stated.

It took a moment to get the words out after that confession. "My telepathy completely. I have a small tether to some of my empathic talent, although not much."

Agustin toyed with the wine glass stem, obviously thinking over that information. "Why would Rupart wish you dead?"

This was painful to speak of aloud. His guilt. His shame. The curse fully manifesting was his fault. Because he existed. "Charade may have been Rupart's lover, but he—ah, Charade—is my grandfather. It is where my lycanthrope and my demonic heritage stem from."

Silent seconds passed as Agustin took a slow sip of his wine. "So Charade married Rupart's daughter?"

"Yes. But that union happened many centuries later. And they had a son. My father."

"That's quite a unique and complicated bloodline you have."

"Oh, it is even more complicated than you realize."

"Let's keep focus upon the curse heritage," Agustin reminded.

"Yes, right. Half of my magic is inherited from Grandfather Charade," Calico continued. "When it manifested within me, its signature was easily recognized. And, well, the presence of Charade's bloodline activates the curse within Rupart."

Agustin touched his hands. "I'm sorry you're suffering through this." The quiet murmur strangely made everything right. "But safety is what Infinity Corporation can provide you."

Calico helplessly shook his head. "Rupart is the most powerful telepath in our land and a formidable warrior priest. If I utilize the portal, it will open up where I originally anchored it—upon the acreage of my childhood home, which is Rupart's estate. The Rupart-creature will sense our whereabouts and come to harm us. I went away to grow stronger, so that one day I will be able to return and save him."

Agustin leaned across the small table for two. "Then I'll be there to protect you should you decide to open it."

Calico trembled. "How could you possibly protect against—?"

"Infinity Corporation was founded by, and is run by angels. Angels are a divine army of their own. It is my blood as well."

Calico recalled the winged emblem on the gates of Demonym. "So you are also a warrior priest."

Agustin's eyes narrowed. "That's a curious way to describe us, but yes." A few seconds flit by. Then Agustin put his elbows on the table, hands clasped before him. "I've decided. If you want me to unbind the blocks this Rupart-creature placed on you, I will."

Wide-eyed now, Calico drummed nervous fingers. Could he hope? "Y-you would?"

"I would do so as a gift to you. Even if you decide not to contract yourself and your portal out to us. I cannot conceive of how you're functioning without your telepathy."

So Agustin had suspected. Of course he would. It was any telepath's worse nightmare. "I...I have retained a faint psychic connection to Frazil and Maars—because we are identical triplets. In his cursed state, the Rupart-creature was attempting to obliterate that to weaken me..." Calico pushed his plate away. "I must save him."

The memory flashed. *His childhood self hiccupped and tried not to cry.*

:You saved me, Great-Grandfather!: Calico sent his joy and gratitude telepathically, for he could not verbally speak while in phoenix form. Not yet anyway. It was difficult, and he was too young.

Calico flapped wings wildly, trying to sit up, but he remained pinned. He was just a little phoenix, and the enemy warrior priest was a full-grown adult. A dead adult who still had a hand wrapped around his thin, stilt-like leg.

Rupart had killed the priest who tried to harm him.

"And you saved the temple trainees by revealing yourself as a Breese and flying away." Rupart's voice cracked as he freed him, lifting him up, and hugging him tight. There were rivers of tears tracking down great-grandfather's face. "I was so scared when I saw you take flight. You took a hundred years off my life! By all the gods, please. Please. Never risk yourself again. I couldn't bear to lose you, Cally."

Agustin's touch on his hand tightened, clearing the flashback out of his mind. "You will save him, someday, that I believe. But you must take care of yourself first."

Calico glanced down. Strong fingers revealed calluses and minor scars among Agustin's manicured nails. Calico's heart skipped yet again, then fell over into somersaults.

"You do realize fixing me will be a monstrous task."

"Monstrous tasks are what I do."

The man winked at him! Calico gulped as Agustin lightly stroked the back of his hand. The sensation was too much. "About..." Calico tried. "About myself joining your Infinity Corporation..."

"If you join us, we'll provide you a regular paycheck so that you can expand your bakery."

Calico reminded himself he had a family to care for and support. With a motor delivery vehicle in their future, additional expenses for gas and maintenance would increase his bills. "That...that does sound agreeable. However, exact numbers should be involved."

Agustin leaned back in his chair. His glass of wine went with him, and he swirled it gently as he contemplated. "How does a salary of three thousand dollars a year sound to you?"

Three thousand dollars...! Shock erupted through every nerve in Calico's body. Dizziness briefly dimmed his sight, framing the demon lord in a fuzzy gray box. He waved Agustin away, who was half out of his seat in effort to assist him.

He could buy his little rental house. Add on bedrooms for his brothers, and a private work space for his wizardry practice. The addition of a new-fangled fancy, indoor toilet so he would not freeze in the middle of the night! Purchase his bakery building and a motor vehicle transport.

With that paycheck, he could split it evenly with his brothers and still have more than enough of his own to play with and set aside for a rainy day. He wondered if that dangled carrot was what Agustin had in mind when he offered.

No, he had to slow down and think about this.

He could begin considering the idea of offspring—although repairing the damage done to his mental powers was a priority. And his recovery would take a good wedge of time. Years, perhaps.

"Do we have a deal?" Agustin inquired.

Calico could not let quivering excitement and ugly greed rule him. Or the fact Agustin was becoming dear to him. He could not be distracted simply by having the damage of his mind repaired. Money was materialistic. It did not produce genuine happiness for the soul. However, currency was what was required to survive in this world. And he reminded himself innocent lives teetered on his decision to share his portal.

"If a contract is offered, I would consider this."

"One is being typed as we speak. Amendments are simple enough."

Calico took a gulp of water, this time to fortify himself. "May we begin the task of psychic repair now?"

The startled pause was longer than Calico would have liked.

"Now?" Agustin asked, confused.

Calico glanced around to see if they were alone, then lowered his voice and leaned in. "Truth be told, I will not be able to awaken my familiar in my current condition. Nor work properly with the portal. It was luck extreme that we managed to flee to Earth safely."

Agustin stared at him for a second longer. "Ah. Well, from what I've encountered after the bakery incident, removing those blocks will be strenuous on us both. We would need a quiet and comfortable place. Somewhere we wouldn't be disturbed."

Calico thought about that. "While Mr. Triptych was fortunate to se-cure our one-bedroom rental home, with a marvelous parlor to perform this ritual, we would have no privacy."

"That is a problem." Agustin sipped his wine.

Calico averted his eyes from the soft brush of those lips on the glass rim. It would be far better if he thought of the man's top hat.

"We wouldn't be disturbed at my estate if you care to have the proce-dures done there. And I'd have Etney and Ramirez nearby if we should need assistance. I trust them completely."

Procedures—plural. Agustin was correct. This would not take a few hours, but a few months. Perhaps even a year or longer. It was delicate work. There was not only the damage the Rupart-creature had done during their battles, but the safeguards he and Rupart had built prior to the curse activation. Agustin would need time to study each signatured thread and be sure he wasn't unraveling the wrong foundation.

"Demonym does sound like the most secure location. And another phoenix nearby—a Dasheel one, brings additional comfort."

Lips he had been trying to ignore widened into a most endearing smile. "We should alert your brothers to our agreement. It may keep you from working for several weeks—at least until we find our rhythm. There's a high possibility you'll be sluggish, and mentally fatigued for a few months."

Calico sighed. "I had not realized I would have to leave my bakery."

"Your brothers seem capable."

"Yes," Calico replied absently. "I still worry. This avenue of employ-ment was my decision, and is ultimately my responsibility."

"You and your brothers'll be quite comfortable with IC's salary. Transform the bakery into your playground. You may take risks without the concern of them not paying out."

Agustin dipped into his inner jacket pocket and produced a checkbook. He wrote out an amount and handed it to him.

Calico seized his water glass and took a double gulp. "Five hundred dollars?"

"An opening bonus." Agustin draped his serviette atop his empty plate and signaled the waiter. "I'll take you home so you may inform your brothers. Then I'll call on you in the morning, and we'll meet with Harper. Afterwards, we'll retire to Demonym." Then he stood up and held out his hand. "Once you're settled in, we may begin your healing."

Chapter 37

Maars and Etney

CALICO FELT AS IF he had cast off his human-self and was finally soaring. Fluttering. Tumbling into the ethos of...what he was not certain. But he wanted more of this incredible feeling that excited him from brain to toe.

He took a deep breath before curling his fingers around Agustin's roughened palm. Tenderness and warmth pulsed between them. Agustin's thumb brushed across his goose-bumped flesh. Calico was rooted to his chair. His quivering legs would not lever him up.

This seemed a perfect occasion for Agustin to announce his procurement of a chaperone—

Across the restaurant, there was a clatter, and a squeal.

Someone yelled, *"PHOENIX FIGHT!"*

Jarred from the commotion and losing his newfound courage, Calico regretfully withdrew from their private moment. Glancing toward the windows that overlooked the water, he saw brilliant red flashes of fire with small amounts of oranges and yellows arcing past.

Curious. The signature and color belonged to Agustin's Dasheel phoenix friend.

Chairs scraped back; diners raced to press their noses to the glass. Customers started placing bets. Others exited the restaurant for an unobstructed view on the outside deck.

There was laughing. Cursing. Commentary on technique, then a collective, *"Ohhhhhhhhhhhh!"* when a massive flash of red lit up the evening sky.

Agustin bowed his head sharply. "Please tell me that's not Etney."

Calico glanced back out the window, examining the energies to confirm for certain. "The signature is of a Dasheel origin. Surely, she is not the only family member in the area."

"She's been the only phoenix in the region—until you and your brothers."

The scarlet flare was followed by a more dramatic one, this time in swirls of deep, vibrant blue edged with white. The crowd let loose an impressed, *"Ahhhhhhhhhh."*

Calico jolted on witnessing the azure color. And its rather familiar energy identification.

"Blue fire?" Agustin asked. "Am I correct in guessing that's a Mazarine phoenix?"

The strength in his legs returned, Calico leapt up. He yanked the serviette from his collar, and threw it to the table. "That is Maars out there."

Agustin tilted his head. "Aren't you of the Breese forge? I thought the Breese were of an alabastrine-colored flame?" He was mindful enough to push in his own chair.

"It is highly complicated." Making his way to the windows, Calico searched the shoreline. He sensed Agustin hovering behind him.

It was there the shocking scene assaulted Calico's vision. His brother. Frolicking in the water. With Ms. Dasheel.

In their phoenix bodies.

Without a thought, Calico was out of the restaurant. He was aware of Agustin following as he pushed his way through another spectator throng along the wharf. They clamored down the stairs leading to the water's edge.

Ugly, revolting envy. Instant remorse and guilt.

His brother had not shifted to torment him. Maars had never once done so since the curse felled him. It was fact that his sibling was careful not to transform in his presence, unless under emergency.

The sharp sting of the cacophony boiled in Calico's gut, causing his knees to shake so much that his boots had to find firmer footing on the spongy marshland. He quickly extinguished the emotions and fought not to cry. If he fell back into a depressive state, he was no good to anyone, especially himself. He had to have patience.

When they approached, Maars squawked, stamping his long, stilt-like legs in shock at his arrival. Alabaster-colored wings flared, showcasing the handful of blue feathers that revealed their Mazarine phoenix genes. Flapping for balance, Maars made it to the shoreline. In a flash of whipping bluish-white fire, he became humanesque once more.

"Ohhhhh, hi, Cal," his brother greeted sheepishly and somewhat tense. He bent down to grab his underdrawers and covered himself. "Fancy meeting you here."

Thoughts of the transformation slipped right out of Calico's noggin. He gasped, one hand covering his eyes, the other pointing. "Maars, put your clothes on this instant! There are observers. Think of your reputation!"

"Okay, okay, Cal." Calico listened to the rustle of him getting dressed. "I'm covered."

Calico peeped with embarrassment and discontent. Maars stood there solely in his front-buttoned bodysuit undergarment, but at least he was no longer exposed.

Then it was Ms. Dasheel's turn. Calico gaped when that eagle-like form rose out of the water. Feathers of reds, mixed with accents of orange and yellow, glittered and glowed. Whipping red flame and the rush of magic engulfed her, momentarily obscuring her from view. When the energy faded, in its place was a woman fully clothed. Calico spied the ruby red ring on her finger and sensed the numerous spells within it.

Ms. Dasheel frowned. "Beat it, guys," she demanded. "We're busy having a pissing contest."

"L-language!" Calico briefly put hands over his ears. Agustin stood at his side, quiet and watching. Calico could not discern the expression on the demon lord's face.

"She's letting me win," Maars said flatly. "I know she can piss much farther than the building."

"By our mother goddess, brother, language!" Calico rushed over and collected the rumpled pile of Maars's clothing. He let out another peep of distress. "Why are you wearing your Sunday best when it is not Sunday? Shall I assist you in dressing?"

Maars only laughed. "And why are you wearing *your* Sunday best when it's not Sunday?"

Calico gaped and sputtered. "I am not!" He looked down at himself then. Oh, he was. Imagine that.

"Overdressed is more like it," Ms. Dasheel announced. "Let's remedy that and finish this the hard way—in people form. And of course I'm letting you win. I can't go full flame without hurting myself and you know it. Also, it's polite to let the man have the upper edge on the first date. It keeps them coming back for more."

Maars outstretched his arms wide and whooped. "I'd adore a second date with you, Etney."

A twinkle sparked in her eyes. "Let's resume the challenge."

Calico screeched and covered his face again when the woman began unbuttoning an article of clothing at chest level, and sloshed closer.

"Here you go," she said. "Hang onto that for me, please."

Agustin's exasperated groan rose. "Etney, I don't appreciate being used as a coat hanger."

Coat hanger. Sans a jacket outdoors was scandalous, but he could be a gentleman and overlook it. It was safe to open his eyes then. But he squawked in dismay. Ms. Dasheel had removed more layers from her torso and was standing there in her corset. There was cleavage! And actual flesh! Calico sputtered and turned away a second time.

"Boss, that blouse is expensive silk! I bought it this morning to wear tonight! I can't have it lying around on the rocks."

"Yet you wade into the mucky bay wearing it," Agustin replied.

"I'm not stupid," she said. "We're in the water because if I burn down Sally's boardwalk, IC will dock my salary—mind my shoes over there. Don't step on them. A cleaning bill is less expensive."

"Because, priorities," Agustin snorted. "If you two haven't noticed, you've drawn attention."

"And they are betting!" Calico put in. "Think of the additional scandal! Think of Scrivens Bakery! Please put your clothes on, both of you!"

His brother sighed dramatically. "Dammit, Cal, I hate it when you use logic," Maars said. "Etney, sweetie, I'm sorry. Thanks so much for the dinner invite. Can we rematch some other time?"

Her eyes beamed brightly with mischief. "Sure. Loser buys dinner and drinks at Raynard's."

"Whaaat?" Maars started laughing. "Damn, Etney, Raynard's? Cal, may I have an allowance raise?"

"She got you there," Agustin said. "I should've warned you."

"I should've known, given her family line," Maars replied.

"Language," Calico whined softly with his guttural voice, knowing he was being ignored. "And we shall discuss your allowance anon."

Collecting her garments from Agustin, Etney suddenly shouted, "Last one to the motorcar buys the gasoline!"

"Not going to happen," Maars hollered, then ran after her, leaving his clothes and shoes behind.

The crowd on the dock above meandered back into the restaurant. Calico knew the horrified flush was still spread across his cheeks.

"You can open your eyes now." There was muted amusement in Agustin's voice.

"They-they were naked!" Calico cried with indignation, clutching at Maars's abandoned garments. He had not realized he was pacing frantically until Agustin sighed, taking him by the shoulders. Halting him with a gentleness Calico easily responded to.

"It's been quite the evening, my friend."

Calico knew he was correct. "But—!"

Agustin draped an arm over his shoulder. Startled, Calico quieted at the sudden nearness. He found himself eagerly leaning against Agustin's tall, sturdy form. Savoring more than the woodsy cologne. He sought comfort from the natural, heady scent of smoke and char beneath. Unable to help himself, he slowly coiled an arm around Agustin's waist, quivering fingers gripping the back of his jacket.

"A good night's sleep will help soothe things over. Come," his demon lord coaxed softly. "I'll take you home."

And Calico willingly followed.

Chapter 38

One Spouse Is An Absurd Idea

TUCKED INTO THE MOTORCAR, Calico leaned his head against Agustin's strong shoulder. Maars's antics had exhausted him, and he was glad of the companionable silence. He fidgeted with his brother's clothing folded across his lap.

A touch to his hand had Calico lifting his head. There came another reassuring pat, then a slim, subdued smile. Agustin understood how upset this scenario had made him, and was trying to make amends.

When they glided to a halt outside the home Calico shared with his brothers, the front door was just closing. The vehicle Ms. Dasheel drove was just pulling back out onto the road. But it suddenly stopped. The woman flung her arm over the seat and twisted around to watch them, delight roaring across her face.

Calico flinched, eyebrows bent nervously at the scrutiny.

Agustin grumbled. His fingers tapped on the steering column. "Let's not give her something to gossip over. Remember, I'll pick you up in the morning. At the bakery. We meet with Harper to discuss the contract."

Calico got out, Maars's clothes clutched against his chest. Mourning the privacy of bidding Agustin farewell. "Very good then. Good night."

Agustin nodded and steered back onto the street. Ms. Dasheel followed behind.

The second Calico walked into the house, his brothers pounced.

"How was your date?" Maars asked as Calico shoved the clothing bundle at him.

"Cal was on a date?" From the couch, Frazil put down his newspaper. "You didn't tell me it was a date!"

"I got in less than a minute before he did," Maars declared. "I didn't exactly have the time to fill you in on all the details."

Calico removed his coat and brushed off some of the road dust. A ride in Agustin's motorcar was quite fun. Perhaps he should have negotiated driving lessons into the contract. Perhaps he still could.

"I had a lovely time." Calico secured his garment in the hall closet, as proper. "It was not a date, but a business meeting."

"You're flushed," Frazil said.

"That noble was sure dressed to impress," Maars added. "It was a date. Despite being an older style, his suit must have cost a bundle."

"Ah!" Calico exclaimed. "Did I not say the top hat was still an acceptable accessory?"

His brothers ignored the old debate over proper fashion. "Where did you go?" Frazil asked.

"Our business meeting was at Sally's Place."

"Etney took me there, too." Maars settled on the couch next to their brother.

"So you seriously think it's serious?" Frazil, face pensive, turned to Maars. They shared a look, and Maars wiggled his eyebrows.

Frazil grunted before turning the question on him. "Is it serious? Cal, if this is getting serious, you need to start telling him about our customs."

Calico tilted his head. "Customs?"

Maars groaned, and rolled his eyes. "Great gods, how many more talks are we going to have to give him?"

"Shh, shhh. Okay, okay, Maars, we'll get him through this."

"Are you sure, Fraze? Because even explaining Earth's cultural taboos to him in our native tongue didn't do any good. We need to have that talk with the demon lord. Bloody hell, we need to explain Cal's naivete and frustrating quirks before we all end up shackled in his dungeon."

"Language!" Calico protested. In his distress, he sought a glass of water from the kitchen.

His brothers followed his mad dash. Frazil took him by the shoulders, then gently gripped his chin. "Cal, look at me. Yes, customs. Like how it is back home compared to here? Remember in England when Maars got gutted by that woman's husband because he gave her flowers and asked her to dinner?"

"Certainly," Calico said. "The law controllers got involved, and we were jailed. It was a most unpleasant row and extremely confusing. Thank our mother goddess that Mr. Triptych arrived with the currency for bail."

Maars let out a little whimper. He sat and put his head down on the kitchen table.

"Cal," Frazil went on. "In this realm, people have one spouse at a time, not two. Got that?"

Calico paused before replying. "Yes, I understand, but that is most absurd!"

"Then is the demon lord married?" Frazil asked.

Maars's muffle came from under his folded arms. "Etney said he's never been married."

"He has a son attending university," Calico added. "Ganymede. Gus says we can be ourselves in this community. We do not have to hide what we are."

"Oh, he's Gus now?" Both his brothers stared at him, then gave each other a long look.

Calico blinked. "When has he not been Gus?"

His brothers glanced at each other again. They both suddenly looked tired.

"That's because your 'Gus' isn't aware of our culture." Maars slumped over the back of the chair now.

His brothers stared at each other. A slow half-grin stretched across Frazil's face. "This *is* getting serious."

"Of course not," Calico repeated. "Our meeting was strictly a business venture. They wish me to join their corporation. I will be paid well for it. Expanding my shop and purchasing a motor delivery vehicle are waiting upon my to-do list."

His brothers looked at each other, again, faces tight and eyebrows crinkled. "You're just telling us this now? Are you joining?" they asked.

"I may. The salary is most generous for all three of us."

"He's smiling," Maars said to Frazil. "I never thought I would see him happy again."

"I don't know." Frazil crossed his arms. "I think...this could be moving too fast. What are you supposed to do at this IC? Will it interfere with the bakery? Cal, we need to have a talk with your demon lord."

"Of course you should," Calico said. "It is all friendly."

"How friendly?" Frazil suddenly demanded. "Did he take advantage?"

Calico thought about how the demon lord touched his hand, and how he liked it. He hoped when next they met, Agustin would finally get on to announcing his intentions to employ their chaperone. It was an Earth expectation, after all. "Well...he was quite forward."

Still in his bodysuit undergarments, Maars headed for the door. "I'll kill him—"

Calico squealed, blocking his exit and gripping the doorjambs to bar Maars from his prey. "You will do no such thing! And you, you cannot run around naked! It is indecent!"

"Cal." Frazil intervened, separating his flailing siblings. "Maars didn't mean it that way. We only want to be sure you aren't being bullied into something that would make you uncomfortable. Maars, please remember this is Earth. Put some clothes on before you rush out the door."

"Right," Maars said, obviously ignoring his brother's advice. "He didn't take advantage of you, did he?"

Calico winced.

Maars's eyes darkened. Teeth bared, he growled low. He was frightening enough to make their lycanthrope grandfather Charade proud.

Frazil stepped in again. "Maars, this is Cal we're talking about. His powers have been out of whack. Remember the sideshow the other night...?"

Maars snorted through his nose, but his jaw remained clenched. "You're right. So what did he do to you?"

Trying to calm his flutters, Calico mumbled. "He touched my hand. He was quite forward. I was quite forward in instigating it."

Maars turned to the wall and started ever so gently bumping it with his forehead.

Frazil only laughed. "Told you so."

"So do I have your blessing if I wish to pursue this job with IC?" Calico asked, hands spread in a query. "I would dearly love to expand the shop."

"Well...again, what does this IC want you to do? Will it interfere with the bakery?"

"Gus says it will not."

"Well?" Frazil prompted.

"They have need of my talents."

There was silence.

"Which talents?"

"My inter-dimensional gateway. Gus assures me safeguards will be in place."

More silence.

"I think it can be worked out," Frazil said carefully, glancing at their eldest sibling for permission and clarification. "It is your portal after all, and you know it intimately, so you don't need our consent. But shouldn't Gigglemug be spotting you when you use such abilities?"

"Wonderful," Calico waved his hands in excitement. "And yes, about Ms. Mug. Tomorrow, you both must be at work extra early and get things moving along."

"What? Why?" his brothers demanded unhappily. "And you need to answer the question."

"Because I will be in negotiations with Gus all day."

His brothers looked at each other, smirks beaming, but cautious. "Another date."

"Do not be silly. Courting requires a chaperone, and he has not yet introduced me to the one he has arranged."

"Uh-huh," they said in unison, deadpan.

"Um. Cal, you really should—" Maars started.

Frazil wrapped an arm around Maars's shoulder and covered his mouth so he would not speak. "No. Let's see how this romance plays out."

"Romance?" Calico blustered and sputtered.

"Sorry. Business meeting."

It took a moment for Calico to compose himself. "Yes, well, tomorrow morning, I am going to meet the head of IC, Mr. Harper," he announced. "Then, at the end of the week, Gus is going to assist in repairing the damage done by the Rupart-creature."

He was instantly surrounded.

"Repair! Is this what it's all about? Cal!" Frazil clenched fists.

Maars was not as excitable; he was wrapped in high caution and concern. "Cal, isn't this something you should have told us before?"

Hands to his hips, Calico chastised them. "I thought I had. You asked me about Ms. Mug. Of course my powers need to be repaired before her awakening."

His brothers shared a glance, looked at him, then back to each other. Exasperation and additional worry washed over their faces. They appeared doubtful and wary.

"We'll go with you," Frazil insisted. "Cal—"

Facing both his siblings and patting their shoulders, he said, "I thank you for the concern, but I will be fine. I do not wish an audience for this, even from those dearest to me. I need you both to stay here and run my bakery. It is decided."

With a final pat, he nodded and ambled off to bed.

Chapter 39

Meeting Mr. Harper

THE NEXT MORNING, CALICO stood in front of his shop. Dressed in his Sunday best, he braved the frigid bay breezes. The collywobbles fluttering around his nerves were threatening to devour him so much that he barely made it through his bakes.

Agustin was coming to pick him up. He was going to take another jaunt in a motorcar, this time into San Francisco.

With Agustin.

Would Agustin devouring him be so terrible? Calico drew his handkerchief to dab his cheeks. *Devoured.* Oh my, why did he consider such a naughty thing?

Calico had never experienced such gut-wrenching nerves before. Had never been this moved by another. Dare he even think it consciously? Were his brothers correct? Romantic notions?

He blew into his cupped palm to smell his breath. Onions from his breakfast omelet. He slipped one of Maars's peppermint candies into his mouth. Nodding, Calico touched the brim of his top hat as two early rising humans entered his shop. Beneath his hat was a linen bandana to conceal his half-shaved head from the mundane population.

The roar of a motor broke the stillness of the morning. He crunched the mint, swallowed, and yanked at his coat sleeves. Would he be more nervous when Agustin collected him to begin their psychic sessions? His knees wobbled as soon as the thought entered his brain.

Agustin rounded the corner and pulled the motorcar over to the curb. The extended carriage top swathed the man in faint shadow. Sunlight bouncing off the shop windows found the golden shine of Agustin's dangling earrings. The upside-down double triangles swayed from the rattle of the vehicle.

"Buenos días, Calico."

That voice was full of husky velvet. As if he had just woken up a short time ago and hadn't had the chance for a cup of tea or coffee.

"G-good morning," Calico greeted back. He was barely aware Agustin drove a different motorcar this time. He was too busy watching the lazy bay breeze run gentle fingers through Agustin's long, unbound hair. Tousled from either sleep or the zephyr. Enthralled, Calico delighted in the strands hovering on the drafts.

"I almost asked Etney to come with us, but decided that wasn't the best of ideas. She poured fruit juice into her coffee instead of creamer."

Calico's heart went aflutter at the spoken affections. His brother wasn't the only one absorbed in the excitement of courtship. "Maars mistook salt for sugar this morning and ruined the entire batch of wedding cake. I banished him to the cash register as punishment."

"Dear heavens, I'm glad you caught that." A grin crept over those lovely lips. "Maybe we should put them both out of their misery."

"Oh my goodness, no! That would be most—" Calico paused. Agustin's grin morphed into a heart-stopping smile. "You were jesting."

"I was." Agustin balanced an arm over the motorcar's steering tiller. Then winked at him.

Was he breathing? Calico was certain he was, for he liked breathing. He was dismayed at the fact that his palms were sweaty.

Agustin took pity on him. "Come," he said, offering a gloved hand to pull him into the vehicle. "Harper's waiting."

"Yes, the employment contract." The brief clasping of hands made his stomach somersault.

Calico slid onto the bench seat, aware of Agustin's hot, fiery warmth. But without his empathy, he could not sense the emotion beneath it. He was looking at nothing more than a picture in a book.

The joy within him wilted. He could not perceive this man any other way. It was as if Agustin wasn't real. The acute emptiness inside kept him from truly feeling the man next to him.

It tore that pain open all over again. The butterflies also seemed conscious of this, and their wings slowed. He had to distract himself from being foolish.

"Er, ah, the vehicle's canopy top is quite cozy. But it blocks the incoming sun."

Agustin turned onto the main road and swerved around slower-moving horse carts. "That's the point of it, for shade."

"Toast and strawberry jam, how shocking," Calico babbled over the engine's roar as they bounced along. "I say, keeping off the sun! How is one supposed to bask in its wondrous rays?"

Agustin stopped in the middle of the road. Early risers in other motorcars honked and swerved around them. Horses snorted as coachmen yelled. Agustin disembarked and folded down the canopy.

The touch of the morning light filled Calico. He closed his eyes, humming as the energy caressed his skin and sang along his veins. Moaned before tilting his head up and rubbing the back of his neck.

This was the one thing that could soothe his phoenix-self, if temporarily. Even if he could no longer absorb the sun's gift, it kept him from succumbing to the grief of his fate.

Calico jolted when Agustin settled back into the driver's station. Then noted the stunned, hungry gaze. "What? Is something wrong?"

It was a full minute before Agustin spoke. "You're right. I was missing something special." His voice was rough and halting now. "You glow when the sun kisses you."

The flush of pleasure seeped into Calico's cheeks. Kissing? By the goddess, the man threw around that word so casually! Such an idea was indecent at this stage in their acquaintance. It was wrong, yet why did it bubble such forbidden excitement?

Calico tried to still his nerves. All he wished to do was study Agustin's handsome face, highlighted by the sun. Words failed him, so he only bowed his head and tipped his hat a little lower. They would need a chaperone soon! He hoped Agustin would hurry the task along.

The bay breeze intensified as they continued northward. It assuaged the burning heat in his cheeks and helped divert improper musings. Calico buttoned up his coat as additional armor. Agustin's companionable silence helped redirect his thoughts to more proper ones.

It only took an hour to get into San Francisco this early, yet there was a slight delay on the road once they arrived. Horse-drawn wagons and delivery vehicles clogged the way along the docks. When they finally turned onto Market Street, Agustin slowed the motorcar.

Infinity Corporation headquarters was an impressive four-story manor with blue shutters. Tall white columns supported wraparound decks. Farther up Market Street, taller buildings provided a backdrop to the rolling fog.

Adjacent to the IC building was a small parking lot. Agustin pulled into a space with his name on a signpost. Disembarking, they passed through a locked gate guarded by two men. These sentries bowed low to Agustin before permitting them to pass.

They strode into a massive foyer. Black-and-white floor tiles accented mustard-colored walls. The black-and-white theme repeated along the balusters and railing of an imperial staircase. Dark green carpet edged up the steps.

It was cold and too businesslike. Grand. He did not fit in here, and he deduced Agustin did not belong here either. The man was too warm and vibrant for such stuffy pretense.

Calico hurried to brush minor road dust from his jacket. "Am I presentable enough?"

Agustin's gaze rolled over him and lingered. "You are quite proper."

Calico still felt the need to fidget and adjusted his cravat.

The foyer's focal point consisted of a large oak secretary's desk and a crystal chandelier. A little farther back, in the alcove created by the flanking staircases, was a sitting area. Two red settees butted up against the staircase walls.

The clerk stood and bowed. "Mr. Harper awaits you and your guest in the sunroom, Lord California. May I take your coats and hats?"

"Hello Andre," Agustin greeted. "Excellent, thank you. Please be sure to send tea and refreshments."

They did not climb those impressive stairs, but made their way down the hall, their footfalls clicking, clacking, and echoing throughout.

Agustin pushed open a door, and Calico relaxed the moment he entered the massive room. The high glass ceiling had to have eclipsed the entire height of the building. Soft shades of greens and golds worked well with the jungle of trees and plants filling up the tiled floor.

A thin man dressed in a white suit turned away from the bright windows. "Welcome to Infinity Corporation headquarters," he said. "I am Mr. Harper. I thought having our meeting in the sunshine would benefit your primary nature."

How nice. Mr. Harper was aware of his phoenix heritage and was open to accommodating his comfort.

"Would you care to sit down?" Mr. Harper pulled a chair out for him.

The sun shone down on the head of IC, casting him in a soft, ethereal glow. The nimbus of light around the angel's head was even brighter, but Calico did not blink at the majesty of it. An adult phoenix was not blinded by any luminosity, even ones of a celestial nature.

Calico stepped farther into the room, shivering as he crossed through the magnified morning rays. Oh. A second lovely dose of the early sun. So welcoming yet so far away. Its touch instilled vitality and hope to fortify him for the healing ahead. Somewhere in this sunroom, Agustin gasped, and Calico wondered why. He was not able to inquire.

Gulping, Calico fussed with his Sunday best jacket as Mr. Harper's gaze pinned him down like an entomology specimen. The sensation was intense, drilling. Calico felt the inquiry dive deep toward his soul. It was primitive. Custodial. Judgmental and wary. Edged with a peculiar kind of cold welcome he could not place.

Calico's gut turned at this personal invasion. But something within him bloomed then. He, too, was able to see inside the heart of this warrior priest. Calico did not want to probe deeper, yet his squirrelly empathy had other plans.

Through the ages, the crushing duty on Mr. Harper's shoulders had picked away at his fortitude. It jarred Calico to encounter such stark and ugly fatigue when he was so de-powered. He feared what turmoil he would see if he had been at full strength. Could Agustin see this? Could anyone?

Agustin coughed. For what reason, Calico did not know. The demon lord had not seemed ill in the short time they had known each other.

Mr. Harper's quiet, looming presence jabbed at his weak, empathic wave and squashed it. As if offended Calico had seen what lay under the surface. That earlier perceived welcome faded. In favor of...he could only translate the brisk, yet reluctant feeling into a...fortification of duty.

Seconds ticked by. Calico sensed his energy ebb, as if he were sinking beneath the waves of the bay in a blissful daze. As if the sunlight's embrace was being sucked out of him. His legs wobbled.

Agustin cleared his throat, louder this time. "Harper, that's enough."

Calico resurfaced from the fuzziness.

"Mr. Winghorse?" Agustin gathered up the paperwork from the long table in the center of the room. "Why don't we sit over here, out of the distracting godrays—er sunrays—so we can all concentrate on our meeting. Harper, please join us."

Calico allowed Agustin to seat him at a smaller corner-side table. His chair faced a grandfather clock tucked between thick layers of leafy greenery. In the presence of time, it seemed to return a little of the energy that had drained out of him. His fingers touched his pocket watch for reassurance.

After two or three more beats of that inscrutable stare, Mr. Harper joined them. His tall, straight form stepped out of the light and into the shadow, and he glided into his seat. Now that the head of the company sat in front of him, Calico had a clearer visual.

Mr. Harper actually wore a pale blue shirt set off by a white vest and a bi-colored matching tie. His sandy-brown curls were pulled into a single braid.

"Tea and refreshments to break our fast will be served shortly," Mr. Harper announced.

"Thank you," Calico said.

"Has Agustin informed you of the reason we wish to meet?"

"You want access to my portal to ferry employees home," Calico replied.

"It's more than that. Your talents and unique heritage will assist Infinity Corporation to better protect the people of Earth. A band of field operatives need to return as soon as possible."

"How many individuals are you planning to bring over in a single passage?" Calico asked.

A man in a dark blue business suit entered, placing a silver tray on the table. He poured tea, served croissants, and departed.

Mr. Harper only resumed their meeting once the man closed the door. "Around twenty. They've been running and hiding from the Amaranth Empire for some time now."

The teacup rattled in Calico's hands at the mention of the empire. "So these people you have on the other side, where exactly do you need the portal to reach into?"

Harper seemed intrigued with the clattering cup and saucer. Calico tried to take a sip of his tea.

"What do you know of the Amaranth?" Harper leaned forward, his hard gaze spearing him.

"N-nothing." Calico said.

"Are you sure?" Mr. Harper prompted. "They are a presence of your world. So you should be aware of at least something. Think hard. Do they have any weaknesses?"

Calico shook his head. "I am sorry. I do not know. They were emerging into power as I was leaving."

"Hm." Mr. Harper looked over his papers. "Well, the area we need access to is called Nura. The northern region. Near the mountains."

Calico had known where this company needed to go, but he had to put down his clattering teacup. The thought of interacting with his homeworld so soon...with Great-Grandfather Rupart...even though he and Agustin had discussed it, was a gut-twisting hurdle to leap.

"Are you all right?" Agustin inquired, putting a hand on his arm.

The sensation of the touch shot straight to his belly. Calico nodded before addressing Mr. Harper. "Y-you are aware of my specific requests?"

Mr. Harper pushed a stack of papers toward him. "Agustin telephoned them in last night. They're merged into the contract. You have our complete protection from your high priests, and the warrior priests."

Calico slowly flipped through the contract pages. There were lots of long paragraphs in small, typed print. It caused the words to bleed together. Perhaps if he asked questions, he could learn what the deal detailed.

"What is the official offered compensation? Maintaining and controlling the energies is quite taxing."

"Oh?" Mr. Harper asked. "How is that done?"

Agustin's chair creaked as he moved around in it. "Sir, shouldn't that be—?"

"I am merely curious." Mr. Harper cut Agustin off. Then the angel pressed a long look at Calico.

Calico glanced between the two, withdrawing his hands from the contract and placing them in his lap. Agustin's face was pinched and displeased. Mr. Harper was eager for him to chat.

The portal was dear to him. But Mr. Harper's drilling eyes and sour expression pressured him. Calico forced himself to take his time. Reminiscing over the social lessons Grandfather Charade had taught him. And the ones Rupart had instilled before the curse.

"Mr. Harper," Calico began. "With all due respect. I am uncomfortable discussing the portal's workings. Not even my brothers know—"

"Perhaps another time." The head of Infinity Corporation offered a pen.

Calico started to sweat. There were so many words. Tiny words that ran together. Blurred together. Long words he wasn't sure of. He leaned forward and squinted. He was to sign each page beneath Mr. Harper's elegant and neat loops and lines. He reached for the writing instrument.

He startled when Agustin stayed his hand. Agustin took the contract and flipped through it. Minutes passed by, counted by Mr. Harper tapping a pen on the desk. Agustin ignored the irritating sound, so Calico tried to, as well.

Then Agustin spoke. "There's nothing here about payment for his time and services."

Calico squirmed in his chair. There wasn't? What should he do?

Distracted, Mr. Harper got up. Searching through the files on the other table produced two more sheets. "My mistake."

"Oh, that is quite the relief," Calico said aloud, then shrank into himself when Mr. Harper and Agustin glanced at him, as if surprised he was here.

Agustin stood and seized the pages out of Mr. Harper's hands. "I'll make sure these get back to you, sir."

Calico cringed at the heavy and grotesque undercurrent oozing out of both men. It was so powerful, even he could detect it in his sorry state.

"Why are you in a hurry?" Mr. Harper snapped. "I thought you were here to sign documents. I've cleared my morning schedule for this purpose. I'm a very busy man!"

Calico thought the same, but Mr. Harper's fury stole his tongue.

Agustin came to his rescue. "I promised Mr. Winghorse a trip around the city."

Calico tilted his head in question. He had? A small tour would be nice now that it was mentioned...

"He's still new to the area," Agustin went on. "It's in the Corporation's best interests to better acquaint him with our community."

"Mr. Winghorse, will you excuse us for a moment?" Mr. Harper asked. "I would like to confer with Agustin in private. My secretary will escort you to the parlor. You'll be more comfortable there."

"O-of course." A man Calico had not noticed before approached from a small desk blocked by tall foliage.

Unsure of what was happening, he glanced at Agustin for assurance. When Agustin offered an encouraging smile, Calico wavered a moment with confusion, then followed the secretary out the door.

Chapter 40

Agustin vs Harper Round 2

AGUSTIN DIDN'T LET HARPER get the first word in. "Why are you trying to cut him out of a salary owed? What other deceptions and loopholes riddle this contract?"

Harper fired back a question of his own. "Why are you turning this most important deal into your paramour?"

"He's not my lover."

"Don't lie to me. You were laughing with him at Sally's. Holding hands. How serious is it, Agustin?"

Damn Harper's personal spies. Staging a meeting on IC property was a stupid mistake. He'd only been thinking of Calico's need to get a good night's sleep.

"We had dinner and discussed the use of his portal."

"And?"

Agustin leaned an elbow on the small table. "All right. Out with it, old man. I can see it in your eyes. You're about to combust."

"Seeing your recent obsession with...this...this..."

"Watch your words," Agustin warned with a severe, weighty sharpness.

Harper sighed. "Gentleman foreigner." He motioned toward Calico's exit. "Aren't you moving too fast? Or maybe not fast enough. Have you pounded him?"

Agustin's control over his human form wavered. His claws broke through the magic and scored the chair's upholstery. "That's none of your business, and a vile way to phrase it."

Harper lifted his chin. "It is my business, and you'll do as I tell you. Like produce respectable and proper heirs."

Startled, Agustin leaned back, shaking his head. "Why is Ganymede never good enough for you? He loves you."

"I love him as dearly, but you disobeyed me. Saddled me with an unacceptable bastard. What you find yourself incapable of comprehending, is that Ganymede—and even your sister—understands. The divide between family and business is necessary. You've never grasped that concept. Ganymede holds no ill will, which makes me love and respect him more.

"My corporation requires a legitimate male heir, and I want him of age before I retire. That way you can concentrate on running the company." Harper tsked. "Pity about Diana. She had the focus and drive. Those traits would've produced a strong and stable heir."

Agustin floundered. The jarring remark knocked him further off balance. Scored him with ripping swells of loss and grief that tore open a wound that had nearly been healed. "Y-you chased her away. Threw a tantrum and raved the world would end if your grandchild had fae bloodlines. Against my better judgment, I kowtowed to your demands.

"Diana was devastated when I backed out of our commitment to each other. I irreparably damaged our relationship because of you—for you! She wanted a baby. And a family so badly. Ganymede should have been hers." He stopped, horrified. "It was her right," he whispered to himself. "And I took it away."

Harper scoffed. "A baby she would switch for a human one the first chance she got!"

"How dare you!" Agustin's voice deepened, echoed. "Diana and I were to marry. I loved her, and she loved me."

"I will not be denied my blood relations. I do not trust the faerie, especially when it comes to infants!" Harper sprang out of his chair, leaning over the desk. "I will not have an impostor, a changeling, inherit and rule my corporation. You pick women I do not approve of! You deliberately defied me, bred with the peasant class—"

"I won't stand here and listen to you condemn Isabella, either," Agustin cut in. He vacated his chair, standing, just as Harper was doing.

"Then sit down," Harper shouted back.

Agustin only loomed further. He planted fists on the table's polished surface. "Isabella deserves respect. So does Diana."

They stared each other down until Harper relented. It wasn't due to a weakness in his character. Agustin knew that. Something else was afoot.

Harper made an insincere coddling noise. "Isabella. Thank the heavens you didn't marry your childhood friend. A scullery maid's daughter is a terrible choice for a bride."

"*STOP.*"

"It's past time you settled down and took a proper consort for your regal station."

There it was. Agustin felt the pain in his jaw from clenching it. "I've already submitted to your demand for an heir. I will not do so again. I'm not a prized stallion you can breed on command, and by hell and damnation, I will not allow that fate upon Molly."

"Molly is not my firstborn. You are now my heir. You'll do as I tell you."

Agustin flinched. Was this why he'd put a blindfold over his eyes and stayed with IC for so long? To keep Molly from suffering his fate? He still wasn't sure.

As much as his father kept him under an iron fist, Agustin knew Harper would have no problem marrying again and producing more offspring. But why would Harper do that when he already possessed the perfect puppet who was already of age?

A puppet who had forgotten until now that he'd planned to quit. Where had he lost track of himself?

Agustin rubbed the sharp ache between his eyes. "Here we go again. Only the daughter of your proxy back East will suit you, am I correct? The full-blooded angel you've shoved at me since I came of age."

An obscure expression crossed Harper's face. "I've canceled that agreement. There's a grander fish to net."

Startled, Agustin's voice wouldn't work.

"But this person remains under observation and judgment."

Agustin couldn't shake off the shiver. Those were the same cold words Harper had said when he'd begun courting Molly's mother.

Could he ask? Did he finally have the courage to open this ancient wound? But why torture himself when he knew the answer, deep down? Closure, maybe? Diana had once pushed him to seek it. He'd rebuffed her. That had been the beginning of their personal discord.

"Harper, did you love my mother? You wed that sea dragon goddess before Lady California's casket was even in the ground! If you despise mongrel offspring so much, why have them?"

Harper waved him off as if he were a gnat. "Where is this nonsense coming from? You've never asked such questions before! Oh, I see. Diana's meddling rising from the grave? Or has she come crawling back?"

The thought of her return punched a gaping hole in Agustin's gut. "I want an answer."

Harper grumbled. "I do not despise you, or Molly. You still don't understand. I soil my angelic blood so our nym brethren will help strengthen the Corporation."

"Because they see themselves represented within it." Agustin rubbed at the dull pain now growing at his temples. It was an ideal motive for all the wrong reasons.

"Correct. It brings unity, and that unity will fortify us against the Amaranth Empire. However, you are only half angelic. That makes the situation and my ultimate decision more complicated."

"Harper. I continue to respectfully decline an arranged marriage."

"By God in Heaven, Agustin!" Harper shouted. "What's gotten into you? You've been so unruly and combative lately. Why can't you accept the way things are done? It would be a solid, smart match. For the good of the Corporation. You may even be surprised at the new candidate I have under consideration."

His palms were sweating. Why didn't he just quit? Right here, right now? Agustin opened his mouth to do so, but the words failed him. Something kept him from the declaration. Exactly what he couldn't figure. Instead, he found himself biting back with, "I do not care who it is. I will not do this again."

Harper railed with fury. "You put the safety of us all at risk. I won't have it. You will marry an acceptable choice, and then produce more offspring." Harper pushed the contract closer. "I want this on my desk first thing in the morning. Signed."

Chest tight, Agustin stormed out the door and into the parking lot. His hands shook; a full-blown headache exploded. His vision blurred he was so distraught. If his mother—a demon oracle of noble blood, with dreams of future sight that were never wrong, knew Harper never loved her, why did she marry him?

Why?

Agustin leaned against his vehicle and cursed his fate. His life would never be his own. He was simply a means to an end. A depressing cycle passed down to his beloved Ganymede, because Harper would use him too, at some point.

He couldn't keep his thoughts from tidal-waving. His jaw trembled as hope slipped from fists that could not hold on.

A companion. One of his own choosing. Fat, happy babies that became children who lived with him full time before they went off as adults to start families of their own. Then grandchildren to thoroughly spoil as he dodged the wrath of his own offspring.

He wanted to love. To *be* loved.

But it was not to be. Grief ate through Agustin's heart. It traveled with a sharp sting through his nose. The pain further lanced across his jaw, locking it tense.

He would die alone. Unloved.

Agustin startled as a strong, sure hand pressed against his back. It offered a defective and broken calm, ready to flow into his being at the first sign of permission. He rejected the comfort out of shock. Spinning around, he braced himself against the cold metal of the vehicle.

It was Calico. The baker's thin body shuddered visibly. Without a thought, Agustin took him by the elbows. It was just in time, for Calico collapsed.

With the baker wrapped in his arms, Agustin slid to the ground from the momentum. Leaning against the motorcar's tire kept them from falling over entirely.

Those sweet and gentle blue eyes were dazed and unseeing. The look on that dear face was slack, and his mouth agape. Calico was cooler to the touch than normal. He didn't seem to be moving, or...or...Agustin gave him a little shake when he realized.

"Calico? *Calico! Breathe!*"

He was rewarded by gasping, heaving. The tears in Agustin's eyes stung again, and he pet the man's hair. His shoulders, his face. Trying to brush away the invisible maladies. Trying to bring at least some warmth into that chilled body.

"Calico, I have you. Are you alright? What happened?"

"I-I apologize," Calico said, caressing the hand that stroked his cheek. "I did not mean to intrude."

Embarrassed, Agustin slipped on the stoic mask of his noble station. But there were cracks. "You're not intruding."

"I...could not block out the frustration building within you as I was escorted out. It clung to me as I paced in the parlor. When you raced by, it cleaved me in half. Such sadness, such spiraling despair. Please, allow me to comfort you."

Calico had access to his empathic abilities? He'd been led to believe his psychic gifts had been turned off or weakened by Rupart. Too bad there wasn't anything left of Calico's file to review.

"...How? If you're...?" Agustin asked, confused.

Calico's brows bent, and he appeared as perplexed. "My lycanthrope sense of smell picked up on the shift of your pheromones."

"But that fractured calm offered?"

How had Calico done that without the use of his abilities?

Calico's face contorted with puzzlement. "I am...unsure. Perhaps—it is because we have been working together in the last few days. Perhaps not all my powers are completely muted. I still possess my magic and a smidgen of my empathy. My space-time abilities often play peek-a-boo."

Agustin reminded himself Calico had blown a hole through Demonym's gates. What incredible power. He studied the man's lowered gaze, feeling his own heart quickening. That made it easier to read the discarded thought-threads dangled right in front of his face. The baker decided the strong attraction between them was what heightened his abilities.

It was imperative Agustin keep his attention focused on this mission. Earth's safety and the oracle's return had to have priority. So did Calico getting a fair deal for his portal.

But meeting Calico's concerned and sweetly naive gaze did him in. Agustin wanted to reassure him. The noise and hustle of Market Street faded from his ears. Tucked between the carport pillar and the vehicle's wheel allowed some cozy privacy. There was only himself, and Calico.

"Your eyes are still wet," Calico noted softly. "Alas, I do not have a fresh handkerchief. Agustin, would you share your sorrow with me?"

He didn't answer. If he opened his mouth now, everything would spill out, making him look like a crazy fool to someone who was still a new...what? Friend? Acquaintance? Employee of the Corporation? If it had been Etney or Diana or Isabella standing before him, would he confess? Maybe.

"Do not feel pressured. If it is quiet company you seek, I am here." Calico's gentle thumb smoothed away a tear. "Oh." Calico said, and Agustin watched him swallow. "I had forgotten you are so warm."

"Warm enough for the both of us," Agustin replied quietly. "Your hands aren't quite as chilled anymore. It comforts me to see the bloom on your cheeks. It reminds me of your true self. And the elemental fire that we share in common—"

Agustin froze. It was all so clear to him now. Of why he'd forgotten about leaving IC for good. This time, the banked tears were of cautious affection and elation.

"What is wrong?" Calico dabbed at his damp lashes before there could be a watery track.

"Nothing." Agustin let out a quiet little chuckle. His shoulders weren't so tight. "I've just realized that being with you makes everything else easier to bear."

"I am honored by your omission." Calico ducked his head. He petted Agustin's hand before leaning against his shoulder.

Calico's delicate weight was comforting, if still a bit cool. Agustin inhaled slowly, drinking in the faint peppermint of Calico's breath, and the faded echo of char about his skin.

He'd been waiting for this gentle phoenix to cuddle up in his arms, and it was happening. Here, like this, Agustin didn't feel so torn and empty. Calico brought him a calmness, a reflection of the will to live. And a dreamy peace of mind.

Yes. Calico was the reason why he'd remained with the Corporation. Why his resignation had never even made it into written form. Agustin wanted so much to guide him. Protect him from those who'd use him. Once again, he explored the planes and angles of Calico's sweet face.

Calico willingly reciprocated by playing with the smooth and silky texture of his dark hair. A slim, finger soon traced the patterns engraved into his gold earrings. Then a thumb rubbed gently against his mouth before a brighter flush spread across those pale cheeks. Agustin pursed his lips, causing the questing fingers to quiver.

Wanting to reassure, Agustin cupped that hand. Lazily caressing. Slowly, he leaned in, nuzzling Calico's temple.

The sound of rushed footfalls drew closer. "Lord California! Wait!" Calico jerked away and made it to his feet.

Agustin grit his teeth and pulled himself up as Harper's secretary came running through the parking lot. He carried their hats and coats along with an attaché case.

Agustin fought back a snarl. At the interruption, and at his own actions. He'd forgotten to take the contract because he'd rushed off in a snit. This was his fault—permitting both Harper and Calico to distract him. Pushing away from the vehicle, Agustin met the clerk halfway and collected the items. With a curt nod, he dismissed the secretary.

Stowing the briefcase in the motorcar, they donned their hats and coats. Calico was much slower to dress. Agustin noted this. It made him aware he'd again acted foolishly, and it was hurting the man beside him.

"Perhaps we should regroup," Agustin said. "Have a proper meal as we review the contract—it's nearing lunch. I'd like to take you to Raynard's. It's only a short drive. The repast is a corporation write off."

It disheartened him when Calico got into the motorcar without a glance or comment. And it made Agustin think, especially after what had transpired today.

It was good he had the contract in hand. Calico needed to fully understand what he was getting into before signing himself, and his property away. But whatever Calico's decision, Agustin would stand at his side in full support.

Chapter 41

Re-Negotiations

AGUSTIN BYPASSED THE RESERVATION rule by handing the club's host a wad of bills. The harmless bribe secured them a private dining room. Being Lord California, and the future head of IC assuredly helped as well.

Calico remained reserved and silent, even as they finished their coffee, salads, and roast beef sandwiches. Agustin shielded a grimace behind his cup and checked off the baker's preferences via the discarded thought-threads. Calico would have preferred tea. He also didn't consume birds, but did eat meat. He'd have to remember that.

In his head, Agustin reviewed how the assembly soured. Harper had turned it into a pissing contest. Pushing and poking at Calico's weak spots. Looking him over. Holding their meeting in the sunroom to gauge just how much of a phoenix the phoenix was. All the while showing off a small piece of his own incredible angelic being.

...Or had the odd exchange been something more than that? No. He shook the absurd idea out of his head.

With the dishes cleared, Agustin dumped the contract on the table. "Before we begin, I must be completely honest. Harper runs the Corporation with an iron fist. Everything that happens within it benefits only himself, or the humans. Combat teams are run past their breaking points, which is why I founded Infinity 8."

Actually, he'd co-created it with Diana, but that memory was moot.

"I-8 is a buffer from that torment." Agustin sorted through the contract to make certain all the pages were there. "Do you understand?"

"I do," Calico nodded. "This is a most important venture. People's lives are at risk. It is the correct thing to do."

Agustin studied him a while before nodding. "I wanted you to be sure."

"I am."

"Then let's begin." Agustin turned to page one of a forty-seven page contract. As he read aloud, Calico sat, sipping his unwanted coffee and not interrupting. Once done, Agustin bumped the pages into a neat stack.

"What are your thoughts on these terms and conditions?"

Calico didn't answer, and he was starting to worry. "Please," Agustin coaxed. "I don't want you pressured into anything you're not comfortable with."

And that was the problem. The way Harper had worded the contract, it teetered on the verge of transferring rights. The prose was subtle, but the baker had picked up on it. It made Agustin more angry at Harper's deception. Just because Calico had trouble with this language, and was unable to see it clearly enough to read it, didn't mean he was stupid.

A moment more before Calico spoke. "I cannot offer my portal under those terms. I am sorry."

Agustin took up a pen. "Then we'll change it."

Calico's brows rose. He leaned forward and his fingers fluttered atop the table. "That is permitted?"

"Of course it is. I won't have you cheated. What would you prefer struck out?"

"I do not care for the addition of this portal janitor." Calico sat up straighter. Agustin could tell he was more engaged now. "I am quite capable of operating and maintaining my own creation. I do not require or want a partner, or assistance of any kind."

Agustin flipped to the telltale section and ran neat lines through the paragraphs. The text faded, and disappeared. Calico leaned closer, the force of his excited laugh caressing Agustin's writing hand.

"That is most curious magic!"

"It's handy," Agustin said, trying to keep himself under control. That gritty, husky chortle had shot through his spine like a lightning strike. "Harper has a duplicate copy. What I cross out here is also removed off the page on his. It saves time."

Calico sat back, thinking. "What is to stop the contract from being changed or tampered with after my autograph—ah, if I sign it?"

Fanning out the pages, Agustin pointed to the infinity symbol at the top of each sheet. "See how it's in that brilliant glowing blue? This marks it as the master copy. Only the master copy is valid in editing. When you sign a page, it cements that page against tampering elsewhere."

"I see." Calico stroked his chin.

"And, well," Agustin went on. "I shouldn't be saying this, but Infinity Corporation needs your portal more than you need them."

There was Calico's mischievous joy, but then it sobered. "Mr. Triptych tells me I should help for the good of the world. And I shall—on my terms."

Agustin's heart swelled at Calico's renewed enthusiasm. Perhaps, in time, Harper would warm to this sweet baker.

Calico poked at the pages. "About that notification of usage clause. Emergencies are acceptable. Regular operations must take place after the bakery's business hours."

They set back to work, moving through negotiations and edits with ease. When there was a knock at the door, Agustin bid them to enter. It wasn't the wait staff, but one of the owners who appeared.

"Pardon the intrusion, Lord California," the woman asked. "Would you and your guest like to see the evening menu?"

Agustin checked his wristwatch. Six o'clock. Heavens, they'd been tearing apart Harper's one-sided deal for hours. Glancing over to ask if Calico was ready for another meal, the sight stole his voice. Weary, yet willing blue eyes did something pleasant to the pit of his belly.

"Ah. Um. Yes, Ms. Raynard," Agustin replied. "I think we do. Please send in a pot of green tea. We're going to take a short break and stretch our legs, but we'll return shortly."

"Very good, sir," she said, closing the door.

"We are nearly done." Calico motioned to the final sheet of paper.

All it needed now was Calico's signature. "So, are you feeling better about joining?"

"I am." Calico laughed.

Agustin froze at that rich, guttural sound. Dear heavens! Calico had to be aware of the romantic longing lighting up his face.

Their introductions in the theater never strayed far from his heart. Neither had the encounter this evening in the ICHQ carport.

He wanted to discuss it, but his courtship skills were too rusty, overshadowed by the desperate need to forget his past failed relationships.

Calico lifted a brow at him before reaching for the pen. Agustin knew he'd sensed the mood turn. Or even scented his rising desire. Damn the lycanthrope nose. He didn't want to scare the man away.

Turning back to the contract, Calico signed his name at the bottom of each page. The papers glowed a final time, and the heading morphed into a mundane blue ink.

Calico put down the pen and announced, "I am not eager for the wealth, although it does cushion my worries. My foremost concern is making sure my brothers are financially stable. That has always worried me. Especially should I expire due to bloodthirsty footpads bashing me on the head and leaving me for dead. When that happens, please inform my brothers. They'll know what to do, so do not worry."

This man was too adorable. "You have quite the imagination, Calico."

"What?" He was confused. "What did I say?"

Yes, so adorable his heart thumped. "Nothing. Never mind."

Calico tapped the stack even and carefully aligned it next to the pen. "I would enjoy remaining for dinner. Frazil and Maars know I may be out late tonight."

Agustin rolled sore shoulders. They'd been sitting too long. His entire body was stiff—not the correct word to be thinking of. Calico was now a corporation employee. Besides, pouncing on the man like a sex-obsessed deviant was wrong.

"You told them not to wait up?" Agustin asked.

"Someone must prepare tomorrow morning's bakes."

They strolled out to the private gazebo. Fresh-cut grass drifted on the evening's cool bay breeze. Calico lifted his attention skyward. Agustin followed suit, admiring the stars shimmering in the darkening sky. His companion cupped his hands and blew on them.

"Are you cold?" Agustin asked.

"I have grown used to it. We will be back inside soon enough. I can endure."

"If you're sure."

Calico awarded him a dazzling smile. "Some things are worth braving the frigid frosties for. May I ask a question?"

Whatever it is, yes. "That is?"

"A stipulation the contract did not indicate was a team assignment, and I did not think of it earlier. I do not want to associate with those who destroyed my bakery."

Agustin nodded. "You're still under my protection, and you'll remain a part of Infinity 8. That way, I can be sure you're not being taken advantage of—if that is acceptable to you. You've already met Etney, Ramirez, and Joe Mist."

A light sheen of red crept into Calico's cheeks. "Ah, yes, the chaps I had wearing the desserts I carted to Demonym. I will have to apologize for my short temper."

"They understand, but would be grateful if you talked to them. You couldn't meet two more forgiving souls."

"I shall do so. Um. Might I also, perhaps, learn to drive?"

The anxious desire. The fidgeting. It was the most adorable thing. "Something I can offer. Whenever you're ready."

Agustin settled on the gazebo bench. Barely a heartbeat had passed when Calico followed suit. Sitting together was a lazy pleasure, even if a little more intimate than in the dining room. Hoping to initiate further conversation, Agustin poised to shift the topic. The scents of cumin and lavender drifted—they came from Calico.

It reminded Agustin of home, where it had been safe, comforting. That was before Harper's won't-take-no-for-an-answer apprenticeship.

His mother, despite her Lady California title, cooked with spices and herbs hand-picked from all over the world. Her ability to teleport permitted her obsessive hobby.

With her permission, he'd turned that into a thriving business. It made them richer and nobler beyond words, raising them into the elite of the elite.

Her nobility, and her teleportation talent drew Harper's courtship. They married months after. Not long after that, he was born. But unfortunately, like most teleporters, she passed away at a young age. Before he even started university.

Agustin had traveled home for the funeral. The Queen of Mexico urged him to witness the body's physical condition firsthand. A lifetime of constant teleportation had torn his mother's body to pieces. And he'd never known. She'd hid it well. Traumatized, he swore then and there he'd never use his teleportation talent ever again.

Calico took his hand, bumping him out of his thoughts. "I did not mean to cascade you into melancholy."

Escaping the memories was a relief. Calico's touch soothed the old wounds. Agustin was grateful for this fleeting companionship. A life under Harper afforded him few friends, and even fewer lovers. Etney and Diana had been his supporting rocks of stability.

Diana.

Harper had ruined any chance of her forgiveness.

"My mind wandered," Agustin replied.

"May I inquire?"

"Family," Agustin said. "My mother was forever cooking. The scents you wear are nostalgic."

"Yes, cumin and lavender."

The baker's words came with reluctance, so Agustin ignored the discarded thoughts. Avoiding mental discards was so much more difficult with the people he liked and cared for.

"It's comforting," Agustin repeated. "Safe. It reminds me of when I was free of expectations and responsibilities. I could laze about in the meadows and watch the clouds. Sneak into the cornfields for a quick snack, then run away from irate farmers.

"Mother allowed me to leave home for days at a time, immersing myself in life. I eagerly explored ancient ruins throughout all of South America via my teleportation ability."

Of course, that freedom had all been before puberty and Harper.

"Ah, how wonderful! It is something we have in common."

"I don't teleport anymore. It's much too dangerous."

"That is too bad." Calico patted his hand, then kept it there. Agustin relished the offered coziness.

"My brothers and I often journeyed about our own countryside," Calico continued. "More often, I tiptoed away upon solo adventures. I traveled by portal to visit other times and other realms as a child."

Responding in kind, Agustin caressed the back of Calico's fingers. Calico's body language showed him willing, attentive. They turned toward each other.

One small kiss couldn't hurt, could it?

Agustin dipped his head. All he saw were Calico's inquisitive eyes, watching. Strong peppermint wafted nicely. Agustin felt his lips quirk. He hadn't noticed Calico slip a bit of the candy. But he liked it. Wanted to taste it.

He inched closer, ever closer.

A loud squeal scored his ears.

Then Calico shoved him right off the bench.

"No!" The baker was up and pacing. "No!" he cried again. More frantic steps to and fro, arms bent and locked against his sides. "I will not marry you. We do not even know each other! We have not properly courted!"

Wincing, Agustin struggled to pick himself up. Dusting off the seat of his trousers, he tried four times before he could reply to the crazy accusation.

"Marry you? Calico, what—?"

"Dear goddess, we have no chaperone!" The man's arms waved in distress at waist level. "My reputation, your reputation! You will take me home this instant! And not a word to anyone!"

Speechless, Agustin watched as Calico fled back into the dining room. It was tearful, devastated chaos. Panicked, incoherent thought-threads rocketed through the suite, spearing Agustin in the chest. Ones in Calico's native tongue that he could not translate. But they cleaved and bruised his heart all the same.

His gentle, quirky, yet bafflingly sweet baker scrabbled at the pages of his contract. Fumbled with his hat and coat. Then rushed out the door without looking back.

Chapter 42

Permission To Be Naughty

CALICO SLAMMED THE DOUGH onto the counter with extra force. Once. Twice. Then plunged both fists into the spongy mass and tore it in half before kneading it back together.

"I think you've killed it," Maars said from the doorway.

Calico glanced up, knowing there was a nervous scowl on his face. He could not help it as he eyed Frazil's approach to the cooling bench. His middle brother tapped on the baked goods there, checking the crispness and color of the crust. His sibling sighed in disgust at the splits on the sides of the sandwich loaves.

Casting a critical eye over the finished products, Calico took a deep breath. He knew he was in for a talking-to. Everything was over-baked, under-baked, under-proved, over-proved, oddly shaped, or pathetic. Perhaps he had misplaced his senses.

Frazil surrendered the subpar bakes to their elder brother for inspection. The two looked at each other, then turned to stare at him.

"We didn't hear you come in last night," Maars went on. "We also didn't hear you leave this morning. You need to stop sneaking off without us."

Drat. He did not want to explain himself and expose the scandal. "I returned home at 8:30. I saw no reason to wake you, you were both hibernating soundly. I awoke before three. I saw no reason to wake you."

"Touchy, isn't he?" Frazil said to Maars.

Frazil came over. Shooing him away, his middle brother poked at the dough he was currently crafting. "You really have killed it. It's over-worked," Frazil reported. "See what you can salvage for donation. The rest of the failures are straight into the bin."

Calico growled low and moved to obey.

"Delay that," Maars rushed. "Cal, you keep attending to whatever's bothering you. Fraze and I'll get on to re-baking." The elder brother quickly sorted the breads, and pitched the rest into the designated com-post. "We'll chat about this disaster after we have the proper stock to sell today."

Calico frowned. He slammed the dough against the table with addi-tional force.

Maars spun and shook a finger. "Don't talk back to me, Calico Acan-thus. Look at the money and supplies you've wasted. Not to mention the time."

Calico continued to put the spongy matter out of its misery. Yet he was keen on the short reprieve. Perhaps the day would be too busy to delve into the tale. But when Maars warned there was a dressing down in his future, it was likely to happen.

So as the hours passed, he watched his brothers perform duties he had neglected in his upset. All the while, he beat anything remotely viable out of the dough. Or washed the pots and pans. Or swept. Or feasted on cake scraps or week-old sweets. He did anything but bake—to mentally run from the demon lord who twisted his feelings into a mass of jumbled tummy aches.

How was he going to explain Agustin's behavior to his brothers? And what did that mean for him? He did not want to be forbidden to ever see the man again. But initiating a kiss when they'd barely known each other a handful of days? Perhaps...perhaps Mr. Chavez de la Cruz was not the gentleman he had envisioned. His jaw trembled, and he bit his lip.

Soon, there was enough new merchandise to carry out to the storefront. Both his siblings turned toward him as one, their arms akimbo. Calico took that as his cue to man his post at his baking station. Quivering hands resumed folding and kneading the substance no longer deemed bread dough.

"Well?" Maars asked, glancing at the wall clock. "You have seventeen minutes to bare your soul and get it out of your system before we open."

"You know it has something to do with the demon lord," Frazil said.

"Of course I know that. Which was why we waited until now to talk about it."

Sixteen minutes and four and a quarter seconds, Calico thought. His gaze shifted back and forth between his talking brothers and the ticking wall clock.

For once, he didn't dare draw attention by checking his pocket watch. He continued to squash the upset that he required such crude devices to keep time. Keeping up the steady pace of working the dough he had previously killed was a fine cover to hide.

Thinking about the incident had Calico all in a stir. But when his brothers finally pulled the truth out of him, what then? Agustin had been so close that he'd felt his body heat, scented his woodsy, hot-ash, and cologne. And, and the...the...arousals! That smoky, heady campfire aroma of the demon lord's exhaled breath. The man was the embodiment of fire. Of burnt wood and scorched earth.

Oh dear. Oh dear. Would his brothers notice the slight upheaval in his breathing? It was all too much—especially since he was unable to mentally sense the demon lord's mind. He'd never be able to hold on to this disgraceful secret.

"Agustin tried to kiss me," he blurted out.

Silence.

Aghast, Calico bent his head and kneaded the dough faster. This was it. He'd never be allowed to tootle off and see the man alone again. He should have kept his laughing gear shut. He was a disgrace.

When the silence dragged on, Calico's stomach rolled. He had to peek. His brothers were staring at each other, as if figuring out what to do.

Until Frazil tittered and patted Maars on the back. "You're the one to handle this, being love-struck yourself. I'll open the shop for the day."

Maars put a finger to his lips and grimaced.

Oh dear. A sure sign the lecture had arrived. Calico picked dough residue from his fingers. Awkwardly trying to appear casual, he rested his chin on the palm of his hand. Then decided to place his elbow in his other palm.

"Cal," Maars began.

"Yes?" he squeaked.

His brother started and stopped several times. With the frustration building in them both, Calico's shame tugged on his conscience.

Finally, Maars asked, "Do you like this demon lord?"

"Yes."

"Hmmm. An immediate answer."

"A definite answer," he inserted.

Maars put both hands on his shoulders, and Calico raised his eyebrows.

"Cal, I'm going to go over this again. Here, kissing does not mean marriage."

His brother's words sent blinding white shock waves behind his eyes. Calico sputtered and blustered.

Maars held on to him, and his voice rose slightly. "Neither does sleeping in someone's private bed."

Calico didn't think he was breathing. "Oh, my. Oh my."

Maars ushered him to a chair. "Cal, do you trust me? Completely?"

"Y-y-yes!" His baking cap was in his hands now, and he wrung the fabric. "Of course! What a silly inquiry, my dear, silly pumpkin!"

"Frazil and I love you." Maars squeezed his shoulders. "We want you to be happy. If you and Lord California like each other, go ahead and kiss him on the mouth."

Calico let out a small whine of distress.

"Hell, Cal, get naked. Plow him if you both want it. In his personal bed."

Maars's voice sounded as if it was coming out of a tunnel. The sight of his little kitchen was going dim.

"L-language!" Calico's guttural voice squeaked in protest.

Glasses clinked. The faucet ran. Then a hand thrust a glass of water beneath his nose. Calico claimed it and took a long drink.

"Are you all right now?"

He nodded. "Thank you."

"Calico, please. Listen carefully. While we're here, in this realm, how you conduct yourself with Lord California is entirely up to the two of you. Ah, um." Maars ran a hand through his shaggy white-blond hair while his teeth scraped his lip. "Uh, I know this is going to confuse you further, but remember. Please, please, keep your activities confined to the bedroom. Or to the privacy of his mansion. No public displays of affection, especially around the humans."

"Why?"

His brother appeared troubled. "Let's just equate it to back home. Where larger human populations fear mixed breeds because of the Amaranth."

"Oh." Calico stared at the droplets upon the glass. "But what about chaperones? It is an Earth activity, is it not? Are they not required here?"

"Another complicated question, Cal, and it has complicated answers. For a woman, yes, chaperones preserve their reputation. For a man?" He shrugged. "Frazil and I still don't understand everything about this world. A lot confuses us, too.

"Right now, let's concentrate on you and the demon lord. Frazil and I won't object to your lack of a chaperone. Just like we won't object to you kissing Chavez de la Cruz on the mouth, or having sex in his private bed. We're just concerned about you having trouble readjusting to our birth customs. Especially if we ever go home."

Maars dropped a rough kiss atop his hair. "Sit here a while. Think about it." He patted his shoulders, then strode out to the storefront.

Calico only sputtered some more, feeling the heat creeping into his cheeks. He reached into his pocket for his handkerchief and dabbed at his nervous sweat. The room continued to spin. It was a tremendous amount of knowledge to consider. Was it something he thought he could handle?

He wanted to pursue these feelings, and the chat with Maars had settled the more frantic part of his doubts. To be a little freer than before, to not always have someone looking over his shoulder. These were ideas that compelled him.

Calico fanned himself with his handkerchief, finally embracing Maars's lecture. By their mother-goddess, by the very universes. His eldest brother had granted him permission to be naughty.

Chapter 43

Agustin and Maars

AGUSTIN SAT IN HIS office, fountain pen flipping between his fingers. He hadn't been able to concentrate on any of his duties after the disastrous meeting with Harper. The outing with Calico was equally unfavorable. Agustin glared at his candlestick desk telephone. Willing it to ring, and telling himself to pick it up. He could call the bakery if he wanted to. He'd memorized the short sequence of letters and numbers days ago.

The baker was maddening. Going on about a simple kiss as if the universe would collapse. He'd taken Calico home. During that entire car ride, the man sat rigid, clutching his signed contract. Arms crossed over his chest as if to protect himself from being ravaged. Calico had held his head high. His blue eyes sparkled with unshed tears.

Agustin realized he was pacing a groove into his favorite antique rug. When had he even stood up? This was maddening!

The more Agustin tried to make sense of it, the more frustrated he became. Was the baker unsure if he wanted to be with a man? Agustin never had a lover—er, potential lover—who was so uncertain of themselves.

Etney's laughter rang out in the hallway.

Well, at least one of them was happy. And Ramirez and Joe Mist were enjoying a respite from training drills by helping with the gate repair.

How could two brothers be so different? He'd caught Etney and her beau in risqué situations around the manor in the last few days. Maars just laughed at his shock. Etney threw fireballs in his direction. The fiery projectiles couldn't harm him, but his expensive clothing would take damage.

His mind shifted back to the fussy man who twisted his insides. Someone knocked. Irritated, he didn't bother to stop pacing.

"Enter," he bellowed.

"Ooo-oooh, Agustin," Etney sing-songed. "You have a guest."

She swung in at an angle, holding onto the door frame, looking like a lovesick puppy. He was not in the mood for company; he didn't even have to utter a word.

"A handsome one." She giggled.

Calico was here? He pivoted toward her. "Don't stand there, Etts. Show him in."

Agustin stood straight and tried to finger-comb his hair back into its proper place. He rushed for something to say. To apologize for the offense. His palms went damp.

The stupid smile he felt on his face faded. The man crossing into his office had a shaggy white-blond mane. Not Calico. Damnation. He should have known who it was if Etney was tittering like a schoolgirl.

"Agustin will see you," Etney-who-thought-herself-funny said. "I'll be out on the grounds perfecting some new exercise drills. Ring for chef if you need anything."

"Oh, I'll be quick, Etts." Calico's brother actually made kissy faces at his second-in-command. "I should get back to the bakery."

Agustin wondered how long it took for Etney to even drag her new beau this far into the mansion. They'd been canoodling in the garage. Both were flushed and disheveled, and Maars was still semi-erect.

{Dammit, Etney,} he sent through their telepathic link. *{I don't care what you do, but I do care where you do it. Your phoenix fire and my precious automobiles do not mix. Do you want to set my entire estate aflame? Why can't you be historically accurate and seek a rendezvous in the stables—uh, scratch that. My prized Arabians and Andalusians wouldn't be happy, either. Try the pool house next time.}*

Her horrified inner gasp bombarded his mind. *{The stables?? A Dasheel would never stoop to something so tawdry as a peasant roll in the hay. My forge has a reputation to maintain. Besides, love among horse dung isn't romantic, boss. Or stimulating. I prefer the smell of oil, gas, and machinery. Now that's excitement.}*

{The gasoline is what I'm worried about, Etts. I know you have precise control of your flame, even under duress. But we know nothing about his restraint, his abilities as a phoenix. Please show some restraint and extra decorum.}

{You're right. Will do. Sorry, Agustin.}

"Um," Maars interjected. "If you two want to continue your chat, I can step outside. While I do have some time to spare, it's not much. Cal's going to question my absence."

Both he and Etney stared until Maars lifted his shoulders.

"I know you're in a telepathic chat. Probably about me, or Cal, or both. I can sense the patterns and undercurrents as it happens. But I can't hear or understand."

Of course he'd be able to detect the conversation, Agustin thought. His identical triplet brother is—was telepathic.

Maybe it was time for one of those newfangled headache pills Ganymede sent him to try. Agustin sat behind his desk and opened the drawer. Its original purpose had been to help him deal with Harper, but this was an emergency.

Etney winked at her beau. "Boss man's been distracted lately."

"Ah, right," Maars said. "That's why I'm here."

"When you're done, firebug, I'll drive you back to the bakery."

"You're a sweetheart, Etney. I spent the last of my allowance on a cab."

Agustin cleared his throat and motioned his Second to leave. The door closed behind her as he wrestled open the medicine bottle.

"So, you've come about Calico?" Agustin prompted. He downed two headache pills, washing them down with the dregs of room temperature coffee.

"Yesss. Ah. He told us you tried to kiss him. So I ask you, what are your intentions with my brother?"

This he was not expecting. Agustin tossed the headache pill bottle back into the drawer and slammed it shut. His table lamp wobbled at the force. "That is none of your concern."

Maars raised his hands, helplessly. "With apologies, Mr. Chavez de la Cruz, unfortunately, you must realize it is. I will protect him. But, Calico is Calico. He's—old fashioned and unique."

"You mean a god." Agustin cut to the chase. "One that is of space and time. Born from a line mixed with gods and other ethereal creatures." He rather enjoyed the color running out of Maars's pale cheeks. "Infinity Corporation is not without its own resources. Need I remind you, we're interested in his portal."

"Ah, right." Maars composed himself and was back on the offense. The man's next inquiry he wasn't ready for. "I repeat, what are your designs on him, Mr. Chavez?"

Springing up from his chair, Agustin reeled. The only people who had ever challenged his authority so were Harper, Etney, and...Diana. He did not appreciate it coming from a stranger.

Maars wasn't alarmed at his aggressive reaction, though. The brother had other priorities. "If you're looking for casual and quick releases between business dealings, I implore you, look elsewhere. Cal isn't the type. The heartbreak would destroy him. I need to convey to you that my brother is unquestioningly naïve and trusting."

Agustin was still perturbed at this man's challenge, but the words were starting to sink in. He debated over asking about Calico's hot and cold behavior. The sudden scowl on Maars's face bumped him into a continued reflection.

"Your silence worries me, Mr. Chavez de la Cruz. If the promise of fixing his powers was a ruse to get him into bed—"

"It was not," Agustin cut in.

"If you're seeking a thrill, I'll wear a wig and help you get him out of your system. You wouldn't even notice the difference, well, except for the wig, and if you wanted a plow by fire. My flame is bluish-white while Cal's is white-blue."

Then, Maars spoke in that familiar, guttural rasp that so enamored Agustin. "Or would you prefer magic to arrange the hairstyle and color? But you are a magic sensitive, are you not? I can do a color-and-limited shape shift instead via my Gerin heritage. I can do both with ease."

As Maars talked, Agustin felt the blood drain from his face. For as Maars chatted, one side of his head went bald. The white-blond hair darkened to a silky charcoal black, then grew, water-falling past his shoulders. "Either choice would present a more natural and satisfying feel to the deed than a wig."

"Don't." Agustin trembled in a banked rage at the shock to his ears. And at the affront to his eyes. He couldn't control his legs they were shaking so badly. *How. Dare. He.* "Don't ever do that, or talk like that again. Change back this instant."

Maars shrugged, obeyed, and switched to his own voice. "Vocal mimicry is a natural talent to my trio—to the Breese line. I've physically disguised myself as Cal before."

"Why?" Agustin didn't want to ask, but he had to know. Had to keep him talking long enough so he could calm down and think rationally.

Maars swayed on restless feet. "We don't like to talk about it. But if you must know, back in England, a rakehell elf noble with high connections wouldn't take no for an answer."

Maars's lycanthrope growl vibrated through Agustin's body. The brother's voice melted into a gravelly snarl before he collected himself. "He'd cornered Cal in a kitchen pantry at a soiree we were catering. I won't get into the ugly details. Trippy wanted to kill the bastard. I told him that would cause too many problems.

"Because of our class difference, we had to handle this with tact. So I shapeshifted. Went to the noble pig, and offered the perverted plows he wanted until he got bored, and threw me away.

"I will do anything to protect my brother, Mr. Chavez de la Cruz. Sex isn't special—although I do enjoy the physical rush of it. To me, it's the emotional connection I find most intimate. But for Cal, it will take time."

"A family man then?"

"Exactly. I've come here to try to help you understand him, and us, as a whole."

Agustin sat down, motioning to the empty chair in front of his desk. Maars sank into it stiffly, sitting on the edge. Agustin wanted to ask about the ramifications of a kiss, but he'd listen to what Maars had to say and go from there. No sense giving away his upper hand of neutral disinterest. Or mirroring Etney's lovesick demeanor.

"You see," Maars said. "In our culture, kissing on the mouth is an official cementing of marriage. Oh, and we often have two spouses."

Agustin thought back to when Calico mentioned marrying for heirs. How it'd sent a jolt of despair through him. Now, perhaps he needn't be so worried. But could he bring himself to share the affection Calico offered?

The idea was hard to stomach. If he cared about this maddening baker, he'd have to accept the man's lifelong ideals. Agustin wondered if he indeed was spending too much time among a rigid human culture himself.

"It rattles you," Maars said. "Let yourself get used to it."

"I see that I must," he murmured.

"There's more."

"Of course." Agustin picked up his pen again, and it was flipping between his fingers.

"Sleeping in someone else's private bed also means automatic marriage."

The pen slipped from his grip. He tried to temper his comment. "Does your culture even engage in casual sex?"

An ear-to-ear smile split the man's face. "You've caught me and Etney a few times. Many of us do it like bunnies. Some don't."

"But not in a bed," Agustin remarked, wondering if this brother had exhibitionist tendencies. On second thought, Etney's fireballs had been pretty pathetic and way off target.

Oh, dear lord...

"Sure, beds," Maars said. "Just not your personal private bed."

"Of course." Agustin opened the drawer to consume a third headache pill.

"There's been others vying for Cal's affections, both male and female. He hasn't shown any interest, or even any recognition to the heavy flirting. Until now. I think it was your eyes that drew him. They were a reminder of home—our aunt's eyes are like yours. That, and even I can detect the fire and ash of your banked powers roaring off you."

Agustin was thankful Maars wasn't eyeballing him like a hungry predator. "Calico has no sweetheart on your homeworld?"

The grin dissolved. "Cal was in training. To become a mental anchor to the white phoenix god. The choice was his from a young age, so there wasn't time for socializing. Only discipline and study."

There was a flash of sadness in Maars's eyes. "When he came into his magic, we found out he was a god in his own right. That crushed his dream. It also brought to light our blood ties to Rupart's ex-lover. Then we were on the run, but I digress.

"What I'm trying to get you to understand, Mr. Chavez de la Cruz, is that our culture permits two spouses, of any gender. We grew up in an extended family unit, with several adults looking after us. There were even more people around to tattle if we got into trouble.

"If we stay here, on Earth, for the rest of our lives, that's the path I can guarantee that Calico will end up pursuing. He found great comfort and support in it."

Agustin stirred. "He did mention wanting heirs someday."

"It's imperative my brothers and I have children. Hopefully, some will display traits of the Breese lineage and help keep it alive. Frazil and I, we've chosen to work within this realm's narrow-minded way of thinking. Because we're trying to fit in. We've tried to get Cal to conform to your odd customs—"

Maars rolled his eyes and looked worn out for a moment. "—dear mother goddess—it took weeks to wrangle him into a pair of trousers. Trippy even had to help chase him down a few times. Then another week to make sure he'd stick with a man's garb. He still hates it."

"He wouldn't wear trousers?" Agustin blinked, distracted.

"Traditional Gerin clothing for his sex are long and flowing skirts or robes."

Agustin leaned forward. "His sex?"

"Ahh...that's Cal's business. I'm getting off topic. Anyway, Cal either refuses to understand earth customs, or can't. But," he went on, "we're still young, so there's no hurry for marriage. He also wants his powers back at full strength before starting a family. That may increase the odds of reviving the Breese forge."

Agustin tapped at his lip. "That's unfortunate he has trouble understanding."

Maars got up. "Well, I have to get back for the lunch rush. We've been doing a test run with ham and cheese sandwiches wrapped in paper. 'To go' as Calico calls it. So you can take it to the park or wherever. Doing a brisk business with it."

The brother paused at the door. "Please, think on this. I've tried to convince him that human courtship rituals are okay here, when done in private. I suggest giving him a little space to get used to the idea."

"Wait," Agustin called. "I'll drive you back. I was going anyway. I'll just be early for my appointment."

Maars nodded. "His powers. Right. Thank you, Mr. Chavez de la Cruz."

The brother held out a hand. Agustin shook it solemnly.

It was past time to set this budding relationship right. Agustin finally knew what he wanted. Golden pinky ring be damned. He wanted to take the chance. To see if there was the possibility of a life with his maddeningly fussy baker.

Chapter 44

Navigating The Bakery

AGUSTIN FELT CROWDED AND closed in. The stares from the customers bored into him from all angles, and he pressed a hand against his wallet while they milled about on nervous feet.

There were at least a dozen humans crammed into the bakery this late morning, all from different walks of society. All clamoring around the counter or the bread displays in the middle of the shop.

Scruffy and unkempt dock workers sought the sandwiches Maars had spoke of earlier. Housewives and maids filling their shopping baskets for the week. And gentlefolk browsing until moving onto the other shops along the street.

Agustin stared at the empty slot between the sugar cookies and raspberry tartlets. Pushed up against the display case glass, in that lonely space was a small handwritten card that read chocolate cupcakes.

Dismayed, he wondered if the selection hadn't been stocked yet, or if someone had beaten him to the delights.

Frazil emerged from the curtained kitchen. "Acanthus'll be out in a moment, sir. He's in the back wrapping up sandwich orders." His manner was more formal in a shop full of humans, Agustin figured. As well as referring to his brother by his human title.

"Thank you," Agustin said. "I'd also like to inquire about these." He pointed to the empty slot of chocolate cupcakes.

The brother shrugged while on his way to the next customer. "I'm sorry. They were purchased right after we opened."

"Ah. Too bad. Perhaps next time." Although he was already talking to himself. His gaze soaked into the other sugary edibles, and he wondered if he should bring a selection back to the mansion with them. Something that would comfort Calico between their intense and rather exhausting sessions. The goods would also shield his nerves and stand as an apology at how poorly their last meeting ended.

The sensation of being watched had him dismissing the baked goods. The humans weren't only gawking at him. Some cowed and backed up to go around him. Frazil occasionally spied on him through the continuous strip of wall-spanning mirrors.

Mirrors he'd instructed his crew to install.

As a precaution.

Agustin knew the undead wouldn't make an appearance today. Or even tomorrow. But sometime soon. He didn't know why, but he felt it in his gut.

His attention dropped back to the confections to help ease the tension. It was finally his turn again. "Please wrap up a dozen oatmeal cookies." Then he decided on something Calico would find more familiar, and perhaps enjoy more with their tea. "And a dozen of the English biscuits."

He'd exchanged the currency for the bakery boxes when the curtain stirred and Calico arrived, a tray stacked with his "to go" sandwiches. Customers mobbed him as they collected their orders and departed.

Agustin took a second to enjoy Calico in his apron and cap, noting that a bit of flour dusted his cheek. How he wanted to stroll over and brush it away with his thumb, but the shop bell above the door rang continuously as humans came and went.

"Mr. Chavez de la Cruz," Calico greeted him.

Agustin's frown deepened. He wasn't the only one who was a little nervous this afternoon. Taking a subtle, deep breath, Agustin asked. "Are you ready?"

Maars exited the kitchen, stood behind Calico, and nodded. As if standing in as the authoritative father-figure. Agustin returned the greeting.

His baker was worrying at his apron now. "Ah. So it is time already?"

Agustin glanced at the brothers. Then at the milling customers.

He wished he didn't have an audience. He'd have to be careful in his wording. "Yes. Our business trip. Have you packed, or do we need to stop by your home to pick up your things?"

Calico continued to stare at him. "Business trip?"

Agustin was too afraid to reach out for any abandoned thought-threads to see how Calico was feeling. There were too many people in the room, and his own feelings might disrupt the signals. He didn't want to cause anyone a fright or panic if he latched onto the wrong thread. Or if there was a feedback loop because he could not center himself properly.

He hoped he hadn't confused Calico. Thoughts were discarded from the gentle baker as quickly as they were created. Whatever the man was feeling, Agustin knew the struggle should be a personal one until it was willingly shared.

But the dumped threads beckoned and taunted. Got tangled among the other thoughts from the patrons in the shop. The more Calico fidgeted, the more difficult it was for Agustin to ignore the delicious temptations.

"This will not be easy," Agustin said softly, and for his ears only. "For either of us. But we'll get through it. Ca—Mr. Scrivens, I apologize for the grave misunderstanding at Raynard's. Will you forgive me?"

Agustin controlled the urge to offer his hand. His height and fine clothes already had the attention of all the humans in the shop. It was worse now that the conversations halted completely. Their private business was on candid display.

Calico looked at his brother, as if for permission.

"Go on." Maars muttered with a gentle nudge of encouragement. He helped Calico shed his apron for his hat and coat. "We'll take care of things here. Be well, chick peep. We'll come visit you in a few days."

Calico nodded to his brothers, and donned his top hat. Agustin opened the door and motioned him through. But Calico surprised him by taking his arm. Agustin stiffened, subtly glancing toward the human customers. As one, the patrons all turned back to their business, and the noisy chatter resumed.

It was as if it were a signal of some sort. A blessing from some higher authority. Agustin's chest puffed out with joy. He felt more secure in the notion that this was meant to be. That this could be something that was beautiful and real. His concern now was solely for Calico.

Calico, too, seemed to recognize this, and embraced this gift of growing passion that was happening between them. His gentle baker gave his arm another little squeeze. Then they strolled out the door. Together.

Chapter 45

Sensory Overload

THE DRIVE TO THE house Calico shared with his brothers took only five minutes. During the short trip, Agustin further mulled over the delicate, telepathic surgery that would cement a deeper friendship between them—and how it might nurture the intimacy they were both experiencing.

Those musings vanished when Calico opened the front door. The thick smells flowing out of the home were enough to make a human gag. Burnt cheese and pumpkins. Seaweed. Black pepper. Wax. Fresh cut lemons. The clinging, leafy smell of broken tomato vines. And more he couldn't quickly identify.

Lavender and cumin scents also hung so heavy, he forced himself not to draw his handkerchief and press it against his nose and mouth.

It was the preparations of a phoenix burn.

Agustin choked, then faked a frivolous cough. Breathing shallowly, he glanced at Calico, who acted as if nothing were amiss.

Cause for alarm spiked.

After a few years of working with Etney, they'd become good friends. She'd warned him of the danger signs of an impending phoenix burn—just in case—such as if she started developing particular hoarding habits. She even set him with the task of impromptu and unannounced suite searches. They'd also trained some of the manor dogs to sniff out strong odors.

Agustin's fingers tightened, and he made another effort not to reach for his handkerchief. Etney had never been clear with why she needed him to monitor her for any flare-ups.

While Etney wasn't up front about the hows and whys of a phoenix burn, she said there were multiple reasons for it. She refused to go into detail. He knew that silence was to protect the secrets of their race.

Entering the parlor, the lazy creaks and squeaks of the floorboards were strangely comforting after the initial concern. A small, patterned rug did double duty to cushion his footsteps, and added some color to the wood floors.

"I will only be a few moments. Please, have a seat." Calico disappeared down a hallway.

Agustin glanced around the main room that Calico had dubbed a parlor. Sprigs of lavender were pinned to the walls, while some were spread pell-mell across worn rugs. Even more were shoved into crevasses along a bookcase jammed with a myriad of mismatched texts.

Open jars of ground cumin and cumin seeds held a special place on the shelves. Rotting miniature pumpkins decorated a nook, and as he looked around, he spied the sources of the other smells.

He could only hope the brothers had whatever Calico was planning, or unconsciously planning, under control.

Agustin worried about his servants. Not all demons wielded powers, and not all were immune to fire. And those that did possess the ability of flame tolerated it at different levels of intensity. His IC team did not wield the element—Ramirez and Joe Mist were human.

Once he returned to the estate, he'd leave Etney a note to ring the brothers for information. They would be more candid with her about Calico's condition, and he'd rather be aware of any impending infernos before they happened. It would also be prudent to have Joe Mist on standby. He would have to scribble a second note.

In this sitting room, Agustin had vaguely expected fancy wallpaper, not pale green walls. This didn't match Calico's fussy personality.

His gaze traveled over to the standing candelabras tucked into the corners—well-used from the faint scent of smoke and the short, melted candles. Ah. So there was the presence of his baker. Light bulbs protruded from the ceiling fixture to further brighten the room, if needed.

The two fat sofas looked drowsily inviting, but he dared not. He was sure the fabric had absorbed much more of the smell than what lingered.

Between the sofas, a low table hosted a stack of newspapers and well-worn child readers. A magnifying glass rested atop the children's books. It provided another clue to Calico's poor eyesight and highlighted the reason he lacked literacy skills. The long hours put in at the bakery obviously didn't allow an appointment with the optometrist.

A thump in the next room drew attention to Calico's fading, discarded thoughts that floated around the house. Agustin tried not to listen in, but Calico was projecting, blasting. *Too embarrassed to inquire if he should pack more than two days worth of clothing. And finally deciding to stuff the carpetbags full.*

Soon, Calico appeared, bags in hand, and glided toward the exit. "I am ready."

"Before we depart, I want to ask you something."

Calico paused at the foyer. "Yes, what is it?"

Agustin tried to build the words into something less frightful, despite their unity of a like heritage. "The more we psychically connect, the longer we stay connected, the greater chance that we're going to see each other as we really are," Agustin said softly. "Stripped bare. Are you truly ready for that? To reveal your all? The true form you hide beneath your human persona?"

His mouth bent, Calico lowered his eyes, and he clutched at the carpetbags. He also fiddled with the silver cuff earring in his left ear. "You ask that of me, but I pose that question to you. I am not what you perceive."

"I know. I've sensed it."

Calico shook his head, worried. "Are you certain you truly understand?"

Agustin nodded. "You are here, and there. The essence of the chaotic universe, of the in-between. Of past. Present. Future. I acknowledge that which is you. All coiled and contained within this physical presence standing before me. A combination I greatly admire."

Agustin took a step closer. Finally garnering the courage to touch Calico's cheek a little longer, and more intimately than the last time. Calico was freshly clean-shaven and silky smooth beneath his roughened fingertips. The contrast of their skin tones was exotic, exciting. Dark warmth against creamy pale.

He was delighted when Calico rested his head within his palm. And even more surprised when the baker raised himself up on tiptoe, ever so slightly, and offered his lips.

Agustin stared at that mouth, craving a taste. Wanting the texture, and the fire, however wounded and extinguished. But they both needed to keep their wits about them for the approaching task, and Agustin wasn't sure what reaction he'd get this time. With shaking hands, Agustin squeezed Calico's shoulders, sweeping his fingers up along the man's ears.

"I'm eager to accept your offer," Agustin managed to say, "but let's savor this." His thumb caressed Calico's bottom lip. "For a more appropriate time."

When he could be sure it was what Calico wanted. And that it was Calico who stood before him, asking. Not whatever had happened during those moments of disappearing thought-threads.

Calico gently bumping his forehead against his chest signaled total agreement. The romantic heat building between them didn't make Agustin's decision any easier.

Chapter 46

Settling In

IT WAS ALWAYS GOOD to be home.

Agustin greeted his head butler, and arranged for Calico and his luggage to be shown to the Yucca suite. With Maars's talk about beds, it was best that Calico differentiate his assigned private guest apartment, from the two connecting suites they'll be working in.

Entering his own bedroom, Agustin pulled a small trunk from his armoire and put it on his bed. His mind was so busy with planning and details, he jerked in shock when Calico's sweet, guttural tones reached his ears.

"Ah, what room is this?"

Agustin spun. Calico's arms were folded around himself in a protective hug. Obviously, he'd been too preoccupied to realize the baker had followed him. "Oh, Calico...didn't Alejandro show you to the guest quarters? I thought you'd like to relax and settle in."

"I would prefer that you take me. Where are we?"

"My private suite." Agustin glanced up from the nightshirt he'd packed.

Calico paced slowly, his body tense. Apprehension etched the baker's features.

Muffling a curse word, Agustin knew Calico was right. He should've been keeping communication open. It'd been far too long since he'd had someone to care about. His last romantic relationship had fallen apart just before he attended Ganymede's birth. He was out of practice when it came to letting another this close.

"I'd like to show you around our work space before you retire to your private suite. I apologize for the delay. I didn't want to delegate packing to my staff—I thought doing it myself would help cement my sincerity to your recovery. But I got side-tracked."

Calico's discarded, panicked threads eased their mad exodus when he confirmed they wouldn't be working here. It was one thing for Calico to offer a kiss. But it was a completely different level of trust and intimacy when it came down to a personal bed. Especially when their budding relationship was barely acknowledged. Or officially agreed upon.

Some cultural customs took more work to let go of. If that was what Calico wanted. The companion suite connected to his private suite had been cleaned and aired out, for when that time was right. The wait was more than fine with him.

"Ah, may I query?" Calico's attention was locked to the extra-large four-poster in the middle of the chamber. "Why is there so much...mattress?"

There it was again. The obsession with beds. "To accommodate my wings."

"Wings?"

"You've seen them depicted on the gates of Demonym. I often sleep in my natural form...although not lately." He thrashed too often during the nightmares. He didn't want his wings or horns to catch on or hit anything and cause sprangs.

The puzzled look was replaced by a small, delicate shiver.

"Do...wings bother you?" Agustin asked, somewhat anxiously.

"Why would wings bother me? I am a phoenix."

Agustin was disappointed when Calico turned to the picture window. Perhaps now wasn't the time to delve away from the preparation of healing. For the next few weeks or so, it was about Calico's comfort, not his.

"I want to assure you of your privacy," Agustin said. "In our connecting work-suite, there's a shared parlor. Both bedrooms have their own private bath. The lake view is breathtaking from the second floor, should you need time to yourself. And your personal private bedroom suite is down the hall from the one we'll share."

"You mean this lake?"

Agustin didn't have to look up to see the sliver of sparkling dark blue concealed by trees and brush. "Mm-hm."

Calico continued to peer out the window. "Why would you not take the best views in your own home?"

"If I did, I wouldn't get any work done. I'd just daydream of my beloved Mexico."

"You miss it," Calico said, voice soft. "Home?"

Agustin couldn't answer right away. "Yes." He almost felt himself drawn back into the mire of its loss. Of Harper's demand that he reside in this region instead of the Baja Peninsula where he belonged.

"When I retire from the post of Lord California, and when Ganymede takes my place, I might be able to...visit home, if I'm lucky. I may be too busy running the Corporation."

"And when is that? Your retirement as Lord California?" Calico turned around.

"Not for another hundred years or so, at least." Agustin shook off the melancholy.

He'd mourn quitting California. Hard. Too hard. He'd mourn becoming the head of IC. But he'd make himself come to terms with the decision to remain. For however long Calico wanted a place within the Corporation, he would be there to be sure this gentle man wasn't being abused.

He might as well dive into the misery of his fate and lesson any suffering. Dragging his feet over the matter would be too painful.

Agustin absently scribbled out two messages. He closed the small steamer trunk and pinned the notes to the lid—one for Etney, the other for Joe Mist.

"My valet will bring this and your carpetbags up later—securing them in separate rooms, of course. Now, let's get you settled."

Nine o'clock. It was the dead of night, and still he could not sleep. Calico ruffled the pillows and tossed and turned to no avail. He missed the company of his brothers slumbering within earshot. Frazil's quiet and even snoring. The warmth that Maars radiated, even at rest.

Calico beheld the empty space on this big bed. He ran his hand over the coolness of the sheets. The fine threads catching the callouses at his fingertips.

What would it be like to have someone curled up close beside him? It was so easy to picture Agustin there, with his dark hair fanned out around his face. The thick lashes brushing against those bronze cheeks in cozy repose. The slow, gentle, rise and fall of the blankets gathered about Agustin's chest.

Calico tossed and turned some more as the hours passed. His previous thoughts of loneliness greeted him with not so fierce a bite. Courage was something Calico knew he lacked after their harried dash through the portal to Earth.

Now, it seemed possible that maybe he could once again stand tall. He would think about it further. And to do so, a snack may help promote the decision-making process.

So Calico lit the small candelabra on his nightstand from the lighter he discovered in the drawer. Donning his robe and slippers, and with the candlelight leading the way, he padded down the grand staircase.

Once at the foyer, he noticed light seeping through the open crack of Agustin's public office door. Peeking, he witnessed the man who made his heart flutter. Agustin worked vigorously at his desk stacked with papers and files. There was strain around the corners of his mouth, and he often reached up to rub his eyes. Still, he toiled.

Agustin working late into the night was a common occurrence, the household staff had said. Ms. Dasheel also vehemently agreed to that fact. Perhaps Agustin would be favorable to a break with refreshment.

Calico headed to the kitchen and flicked on the light switch. There, he found an array of leftovers in the largest ice box he had ever witnessed. Chicken soup and a spot of heated bread should do it. He measured out two bowls and added the meal to the cook pot. In Agustin's kitchen was a fancy gas stove that took a moment to operate, but he managed.

He found a tall stool, and sat next to the warm stove, waiting for the vigorous boil. He squinted, frowning at the overly bright wall sconces. He preferred an oil lamp to the harsh glare of an electric bulb.

His brothers were not here to praise modern technology, and the silence was nice for a change. Calico closed his eyes, listening to the sporadic sputter of the gas-fed flames. The quiet curtain of night highlighted that he was alone in Agustin's kitchen.

Alone...

Breakfast with Great-Grandfather Rupart always had him leaping from his bed and rushing through his ablutions. But this morning had brought sorrowful news. "Great-Grandfather, why are you going away? I do not want you to go!"

"It'll only be for a few weeks, Cally."

"I want to go with you!"

"Well, we'll see what your mother says."

"Do not leave without me."

Calico's eyes snapped open.

The chicken soup boiled frothfully, so he removed the pot and turned off the gas. He was preparing a tray when someone knocked at the kitchen door. Visitors? Calico consulted his pocket watch. Nearing midnight. At this hour? Perhaps it was a delivery. Calico answered it.

His guest's white veils fluttered in the breeze. Glowed in the fog of the woodsy foothills. There was a book in his arms. "Ah, Calico, there you are."

"Mr. Triptych, it is a good night. How did you know I was here?"

"Your brothers filled me in."

Calico nodded, stepping aside. "They are more anxious than I over this outcome, it seems. Come in. Have you dined? I have made plenty of chicken soup and bread."

"Chicken soup, huh?" There was restrained humor in his benefactor's voice, why he did not know. But it was of no consequence. "I've eaten. I'm not interrupting your meal, am I?"

"No, of course not. Please join me."

"Thank you, but I can't stay long. I've brought you a cookbook."

"Splendid!" Calico flipped through the pages, seeing several mouth-watering drawings. "Something new to read tomorrow."

"I understand you signed up with Infinity Corporation."

Calico closed the door behind them, shutting out the chill. "Yes. Agust—Mr. Chavez de la Cruz went over the contract with me. Ah, please sit down."

The man pulled out a chair and flipped it around so he could rest his arms on the back. "What's your impression of Harper?"

"Mr. Harper? Why, he is a polished gentleman." Truthfully, he did not know what to make of the warrior priest—angel. He was still trying to figure that out.

Triptych adjusted his veils in the shadowed light. "Is that all you see?"

Calico placed the book upon the meal tray. "You think there is more?"

"You're a good friend to me, Calico. I wanted to tell you not to get too comfortable with Infinity Corporation."

Brows creased, he asked, "Why do you say that?"

"They are decent...people...but they'll not hesitate to put the needs of the Corporation ahead of yours."

"Mr. Chavez de la Cruz spoke of that. I will keep it in mind. It is good then I have secured a contract."

"Good, good." Triptych paused. "Are you falling for Agustin yet?"

The question embarrassed Calico so much that he started fussing with the stack of dishes in the drying rack. "Mr. Chavez de la Cruz is my boss and supervisor now."

"Agustin's different," Triptych said. "He's Corporation, but so much more. Trust in him. Don't shield your heart so much from him."

"I am unsure of such a conflicting relationship," Calico said absently. "Although I have been mulling it over. My brothers have also encouraged me." Encouraged him to be naughty, but it was not a subject he would repeat to his ex-benefactor.

"You need to live, Calico Winghorse. Not just exist and mourn the fact that you're unsuitable to keep a phoenix god grounded and sane, because you're a god yourself. You need to consider your own needs and wants for a change."

Calico leaned against the sink, hands tucked beneath his elbows. "I do miss Gigglemug's companionship and wisdom. She understands me more than my brothers do at times."

"Your familiar saved your lives and paid a small price," Triptych said. "But Agustin can help you to free her. Agustin could be more than a friend, and someone who helps you regain your true self. If that's something you think you'd want with him." Triptych stood up and pushed in his chair. "Will you see me out?"

Calico nodded, and held the door open, watching his breath puff in the cold of the evening. He pulled the night robe's lapels closer to his neck for warmth.

Triptych faced him but drifted backward into the fog, as if he were floating. "Perhaps you can find the perfect recipe. Fix dinner for Agustin sometime."

Without another word, Triptych literally disappeared. The faint impression of white feathered wings glowed and outlined his fading silhouette before that image, too, vanished.

Returning inside, Calico shut the door, contemplating Triptych's warning. And...most especially his advice. Calico tapped his cheek. He then squared his shoulders and headed for Gus's office, meal tray in hand.

Chapter 47

The Kiss

"Good evening, Agustin. I hope this is not an intrusion."

Agustin startled, putting down his pen. The use of his name sent a thrill all the way down to his toes. Although he preferred Gus, he'd take his given name in a heartbeat.

Calico was in his night robe and slippers. The hem of his long nightshirt offered a sexy view of the baker's bare ankles. Agustin didn't want to divert his gaze, but he did so, lest his desire wander any further.

"It's a good evening, now," he answered, voice low. "This is a nice surprise. Is there something I can do for you?"

"Yes, there is. It seems both of us cannot sleep."

Stacking the papers he'd been working on to one side, Agustin inhaled the aroma coming from the tray. "Chicken soup?" he asked with doubting amusement. "It smells lovely, but I thought you didn't eat poultry."

Calico strode forward, his shoulders squared and his chin aloft. "I said nothing of the sort."

Agustin schooled his response. "I see." He didn't think Calico outright lied. For the current discarded thought-threads held no deceptions or malice. He was coming to understand this man, and harmless little inconsistencies like this seemed to be his nature. Calico did believe he never voiced such a thing. Although, once they got to know each other better, Agustin did want to ask about such frivolous misstatements.

"I just bid farewell to Mr. Triptych."

"Oh? He was here? Quite a unique individual, our Triptych."

Calico arranged the bowls and spoons on the desk. "Well, I trust him implicitly, but he left me with a rather alarming warning. About Infinity Corporation."

"Oh, dear. Please sit with me. Let's eat and discuss it."

Agustin beckoned, and his magic pulled around the guest chair stationed in front of his desk. Excitement caused him to shake a little. This. Here. Now. Sharing a lazy, and so cozy meal with someone he cared about. Surrounded within the quiet embrace of night. Listening to the last few fading cricket songs. His heart had yearned for such tender moments.

Calico sat. He tucked the linen serviette into the collar of his nightshirt. "I wanted to clear up any misunderstanding, you see."

Agustin dunked half a roll into the soup, enjoying the sight of the liquid soaking into the crumb. "It pleases me you're asking questions. What more can I do to alleviate your concerns?"

"Well, why should I not trust Mr. Harper?" Calico took a spoonful of his meal. "Mr. Triptych reminded me of the chat you and I had, before I signed the contract. He was adamant that the Corporation would put their needs ahead of my welfare."

The legitimate question should have been a red flag, a splash of cold water to his face. Instead, Agustin found himself automatically falling back into the role of Harper's puppet. "Triptych's correct about Harper doing his best to protect the people—"

"It is good Mr. Harper wishes to keep us all safe," Calico interrupted, "but is that at the expense of those who he conducts business with? The first rendition of the contract—"

Agustin nodded emphatically. "That's exactly why I took the time to go over it with you. To make sure you were properly compensated."

Calico lowered his next spoonful. "So Mr. Triptych was correct to be wary of him? Even with a contract, I begin to feel uncomfortable about this partnership. What if Mr. Harper decides not to honor a signed agreement?"

Agustin wanted to ask if Calico was having second thoughts about him as well, but that was not the critical issue of the moment. "Harper's always held firm to contract rules. I've never once seen otherwise. I'm also here to make sure you're not taken advantage of. Remember the clause in Article Four. You're permitted to withdraw with a six month's written and verbal notice. During that time, you're only contracted to help with emergencies—if someone's life is at stake."

After a few seconds, Calico nodded back. "Yes, that is true."

Agustin clenched his fists, still hidden below the desk. He didn't want to show his concern over this questioning, even though he was glad it was happening. He wasn't sure how this made him feel. If Calico decided to withdraw from Infinity Corporation, would that mean a withdrawal from his company as well? Mild grief stirred in his gut.

"Would you like to submit a dismissal?" Agustin was surprised at how strong and even his question came. Because inside, he was a sorrowful mess. "I can begin the paperwork first thing in the morning, with it prorated to yesterday."

Calico didn't answer. Agustin felt the perspiration gather on his brow. He'd be truly sad if Calico exited IC. He would miss that smile. That laugh. The companionship between them that hadn't yet even begun.

"No."

The response jarred Agustin out of his gloom. Remembering himself, he hoped that the relief hadn't been visible on his face.

"I shall remain with Infinity Corporation," Calico declared. His shoulders back, and his head held high. "To help protect the people. With the contract in hand, and you to lead, I do feel much more secure. Thank you, Agustin."

Agustin hadn't realized he'd been holding his breath.

"Now," Calico said. "Since I am feeling settled with that matter, I wanted to inform you that I am ready to move forward with fixing my powers. That is, if you can set aside the time from your work schedule."

"For you, I'll make the time." The words were elevated and slightly rushed. He hadn't come across as a lovesick fool, had he? "We can start tomorrow afternoon, if you like."

The possibilities of Calico's telepathy repaired made him anxious and eager. Even with Calico's powers locked off, Agustin knew this man was of a high caliber. Agustin hadn't realized how isolated and alone he'd felt until now.

"Yes, tomorrow afternoon is agreeable." Calico abandoned his meal. "Thank you. Now that that is decided, I...I wish to speak of something that is not business."

"And what's that?"

"Our chaperone. Why have you not yet employed ours?"

"Chaperone?" Agustin blinked.

"Yes. We have been courting, have we not?"

Agustin took a second to process this sudden and self-confident request from this sweet, little, cinnamon roll of a man. His heart sped up, and he prayed this was heading where he hoped it was.

"I've been aware of the attraction we've had for each other," Agustin agreed carefully. "But because of our business agreement, I thought it wise to let you direct the course of anything...not business related."

Calico stood up. "Then I am doing so now."

Somewhat alarmed that Calico appeared to be on his way out, Agustin made it to his feet. It was only proper and respectful. But instead, Calico glided into his personal space. And hugged him.

Calico was touching him. Curling into him. And Calico's mind had remained steadfast. There were no mysterious mental-gaps present. No disruption in the flow of discarded thought-threads. This was real.

The offered affection was over before Agustin could process the joy.

"Oh, dear. Quite naughty," Calico mumbled, tucking hair behind his ear.

The scarlet stain across Calico's cheeks was the most endearing thing Agustin had ever seen. So had the hug he would replay and treasure. But he had to be sure his sweet baker was clear-headed for what he was about to ask.

"Calico, would you play along with a silly and bizarre request?"

"And what is that?"

"Say my name."

"Your name?"

"Yes."

Calico laughed lightly. "That *is* a silly and bizarre request. But one easily granted, *Agustin*."

A heartwarming thrill. His given name spoken. Not Gus, even though it was an endearment he hoped to hear in the future. "Thank you. Now I have another request. One with a deeper significance.

"Calico?" he asked softly, offering his hands. "If you'll have me, I'd dearly love to be your companion, your most adamant admirer. A suitor who's so enamored with your pure smiles and gentle nature that my head spins."

Calico surprised him by meeting his gaze. Agustin had expected shyness. Instead, he witnessed stunned and giddy blue eyes. Calico's chest noticeably rose and fell. It was rounded out by a quivering grin. His sweet baker accepted his offered palm and pressed it to his cheek.

"Oh, Agustin," Calico whispered. "Unquestionably yes! It would fill me with such happiness to be your sweetheart."

Small, jittery laughs from them both, as if they were fumbling schoolboys. Agustin wanted to touch this man. To kiss him. Feel the lines and weight of his body beneath his fingers, encouraging a dual exploration between them both.

But after this declaration, and Calico's quick withdrawal from a physical embrace, he didn't think he could stomach a rejection.

Calico was the type that required a proper bed for their first time together. Slow preparation and lit candles for mood. A little chilled red wine to calm them both. And certainly not a frenzied release propped up on the desk or against the wall.

Agustin froze when Calico slid back into his personal space. Touched his arm. Then raised his head, offering his mouth.

Agustin moistened his own lips. Could it really happen this time? He wanted to chance it. A small, simple brush would do. Tentatively, Agustin bent near before making a slow move to wrap an arm loosely about Calico's waist. When he achieved that and it was met with eager favor, he permitted his other hand to wander through the dark sheet of Calico's soft hair.

The closer they came, the more Agustin was inundated with Calico's scent. No. It was more than that. A life energy leashed. Imprisoned.

It reminded him of Calico's essence when viewed through his psychic senses.

Then it happily happened.

A press of lips. A quick nip. Then back to small, questing, gentle rubs. Hot ash and the strangely delicious, breathless, metallic tang of the universe itself. The sense of Calico's celestial being, followed by the grounding grasp of cumin. Burnt charcoal so tantalizing in his nose.

Calico was kissing him back. Eagerly engaged. Awkward. Endearing. Fingers digging into Agustin's shirt. Flooding Agustin's senses again with the aroma of more cumin, and heady, intoxicating smoke and ash.

When it was over, Agustin was surprised and delighted to find his butt had been parked against his desk, wrinkling a contract negotiation. Calico was nicely wedged between his spread legs.

As much as he wanted this to go on, it couldn't. Not if they were to tackle the curse tomorrow. All their energy would be required for it. As if he'd said this aloud, Calico slowly withdrew.

"I-I have made you butterscotch cookies." Calico suddenly announced before ducking his head. "Good night, then, Agu—may I call you Gus instead?"

Gus. The endearment was given, and Calico was his full self. No wandering mind. No troublesome gaps in the measure of his discarded thought-threads. It was a wonderful cushion to his heart.

"I'd be ecstatic."

"Gus, then. I anxiously await your diagnosis tomorrow. Gus." Calico smiled, collected the remains of their meal, and carried out the tray. Stopping briefly and looking back before closing the door behind him.

"Good night, Calico," Agustin finally managed to say to his closed door. Then wondered, hopefully, if there truly were cookies waiting for him in the kitchen.

Chapter 48

Psychic Surgery

THE NEXT MORNING, AGUSTIN only managed to place a single knock to Calico's door before it flung open. Calico had been standing behind it. Waiting. For him. He'd been expected. Agustin reveled in that honor. Calico shyly ducked his head and leaned into him for a long, easy hug.

Agustin wrapped his arms around him in a like manner. They stood there. Quietly taking each other in. Listening to the elevated thump of the other's heartbeat. Offering silent comfort and affection.

He enjoyed Calico's head resting on his chest. The occasional, slow, unstimulating caress, gifted by them both. Taking in each other's company, and providing a gentle good morning.

Even so, Agustin mourned the absence of another fire elemental's body heat. There was only a weak warmth living beneath his fingertips. Not the excepted roar of heat that should be radiating off someone with phoenix blood. Soon, though, Calico would suffer no longer.

When they parted, Calico stood on tiptoe to offer a discreet good morning peck at his cheek. Fresh from a bath, the scent of lavender embraced his shy baker. And sage. A hint of frankincense, too.

As they clasped hands in greeting, Agustin enjoyed the touch of Calico's hands, silky soft with lotions. The fragrance of cumin, a childhood favorite, was also about him, but faint. Scents that had been in the home Calico shared with his brothers, and felt alive.

The combined scents didn't overpower. It was an odd amalgamation that strangely worked. It was as if each herb or spice patiently took its turn to shine, enveloping Calico in its vital essence.

"Gus?" Calico fiddled with his jacket cuffs. "Is something wrong?"

The question brought his head back out of the clouds. "No," he hoped to reassure. "I was admiring how radiant you looked this morning."

Calico's laugh felt nervous. "Thank you. You are looking acute and dapper yourself."

Agustin offered his arm in escort, and Calico took it without hesitation. Once in the dining room, Agustin learned this morning's fare was served family style—covered serving dishes set before them on the dining table. It made for a more cozy gathering, and Agustin suspected that was Etney's doing.

Calico actively engaged in animated conversation—mostly about baking. Or his plan to purchase a delivery truck. His baker sat beside him and sent shy, flirty glances between bites of bacon.

Etney smiled into her oatmeal and also made polite greetings. Agustin prayed she'd hold her tongue. Ramirez and Joe Mist, on the other hand, were a little more rough and rowdy in their welcome, and Calico's high blush remained throughout the meal.

Afterwards, both he and Calico enjoyed the idea of a leisurely stroll in the rose gardens to digest. Agustin thought it would help Calico decompress from Ramirez and Joe's attention. And happily, it was Calico who sought to take his hand, and linger among the floral beauty.

The remainder of the morning, they sought individual privacy. In order to center themselves, and prepare for the daunting task ahead.

At ten to noon, Agustin took a breath and steeled himself. Mentally reviewing the arduous task ahead of him. He knew he had the strength and experience for such a delicate psychic surgery.

The one thing he didn't know was how long it would take, exactly. He calculated spreading the work out to two or three hours a day, depending upon the depth of the task he worked upon.

Then, at noon sharp, with bakery boxes in hand, Agustin climbed the grand stairs. He bypassed the entrances of their shared working suites, and walked down the hall to Calico's personal private bedroom. He knocked.

"Shall we prepare?" Agustin asked when Calico answered.

Calico's enthusiasm brightened Agustin's mood. They breezed into the sunny parlor of their shared work suite; Agustin admired the afternoon rays that cascaded down. That ethereal caress added fuel to Calico's phoenix half, and he wasn't sure if Calico himself was consciously aware of it.

Calico faced him eagerly. "So, may we begin now?"

He had to get him to calm down a little, otherwise it would be too strenuous a start. "We should review our strategy first."

"That is?"

"Depending upon how the situation goes, you may or may not need to rebuild mental blocks and boundaries."

Calico nodded. "The ones I have run deep. The anchors are strong. Great-Grandfather Rupart instructed me on how to lay the foundations."

"Showed you or laid them for you?"

"I had to create them on my own, but he inspected the work for stability and strength, then I had to construct any repairs. He was resolute on self-reliance."

Agustin nodded. "That will make my task easier if I only have to focus on one mental signature. Remove your jacket and relax. Your shoes too, if it makes you more comfortable. The view is serene. Would you care for tea? Confections created by your own hand?" He opened the boxes.

Agustin had hoped the last two days Calico had been in residence would've calmed the baker's nerves. He would've thought Calico would rather supervise the bakery during the day, but he hadn't. Agustin knew Calico was doing his best to calm himself and settle in.

"I-I would rather not eat." Calico made no move to shed his shoes, but he did remove his jacket. "Perhaps tea during a quiescent period—" His gaze brushed the lake, then remained there. "Oh! How lovely..."

The majesty before them had the desired effect Agustin had hoped for. A snowy egret took flight. At the sandy bank, pinpoints of tiny black dots that were quail darted back and forth.

Calico's bright blue eyes drooped, and a gentle smile lit him up even further. He leaned against the wall next to the picture window, and hours lazily passed as they watched the sun sink lower on the horizon, dipping its light into the water.

Quietly, slowly, as if not to break the spell they were both under, Agustin opened the window. The lake lapped at the cattails growing around the banks, and a deer bounded back into the thick cover of the trees.

The lulling symphony of frogs and crickets greeted them. Lazy breezes sweeping off the lake brought in the crisp, refreshing scent of reeds and damp soil.

"Are you comfortable?" Agustin asked just above a whisper.

Calico sank further into the cushions of the window seat. He took in a deep, languid breath; Agustin felt his own heart thump at the expression in those unfocused eyes.

"Yes, I am comfortable. The sounds are wonderfully lulling." Those blue eyes bobbed between open and closed.

Agustin held back a slow chuckle. He wouldn't be the one to tell him that the choruses were mating calls. Settling on an opposite chaise lounge, Agustin relaxed and closed his eyes. Taking a few deep, gentle breaths, he settled in.

Then, quietly, "Are you ready, Calico?"

"I am."

"Then let's begin." He pressed forward with his psychic presence.

Calico suddenly gasped. Agustin snapped open his eyes to be certain all was well.

Calico's eyes were squeezed shut. His calloused fingers dug into the cotton fabric of the window seat, but the man was responding to him, easily, willingly.

The brush of their minds was welcomed, as if Calico had been trapped in the desert with no water.

No, that was the wrong analogy.

Trapped beneath the waves and finally reaching the air that fueled the fire of his soul.

Dear gods. This man was starving. Craving the telepathic touch.

From within their fragile connection, Agustin sensed his baker's heart racing alongside his own. It had to be now, while Calico's mental blocks were at their weakest, and he was inviting.

Calico's mind. So beautiful, so full of light. It was soft edges and rolling green hills with no end in sight. Warmth arrived from the blistering hot sun high above.

Far in the distance, where he could barely make out the silhouettes, there seemed to be a herd of horses running free. Horses. There was something familiar about the concept, other than Calico's last name, buzzing faintly in the back of his mind.

He wanted to give Calico this moment of peace. And perhaps himself as well, for such a vibrant response had left him vulnerable. He wished to savor this, for in the next minute, it would be all work and frustrating pain.

Agustin closed his eyes now. And then he was back within the landscape of Calico's mind, surrounded by millions of images—of himself.

His distorted yet shiny reflection came at him from at all different angles and sizes. As near as he could comprehend, he was surrounded by thousands, if not millions, of reflective soap bubbles.

When Calico had mentioned Mirror Bubbles among the wreckage of the bakery, he hadn't thought the term would be so literal.

He sent a telepathic inquiry. *{Calico, can you hear me?}*

No answer. Nothing but more of the trailing contentment of their first contact.

Agustin braced himself and barreled past the pleasantly numbing sensations, only to again collide with a myriad of his own reflections. And it hurt.

He had gained entry to Calico's inner self, but had not gone far enough to establish the required mental link. He had to pierce these Mirror Bubbles or locate a weak point.

He probed. Applied pressure.

The harmony between them veered sharply. It became uncomfortable. Frustrating.

"Talk to me, Calico," Agustin whispered audibly as sweat built across his brow. "Through our link. Help me."

: ! : Calico's foreign mind-voice arose. Empty, yet full of splitting discord and flashing tangles in the telepathic either.

The cacophony originated on a plane of existence he had never experienced. Agustin braced himself against the unfamiliar onslaught of disruptive pain that was mental and physical.

In the physical world, Agustin hadn't known he'd leaned over and vomited until the episode passed.

The static of their different mindspeaks arrived again to torture him some more. *: ! : :?!:*

Within Agustin's mind, Calico's essence fluttered near, with all the concern of a lover. It was heartfelt. Adorab—another wave of puke simmered in his windpipe. The stress tremored through his physical body.

The volatile disturbance was the sheer, otherworldly nature of Calico's telepathic mind—no. His telepathic being and existence, his core as a god of space-time.

Again, he sensed Calico's worry.

Agustin tried to answer, but the shock of such an exotic offering robbed him of any response. *{...}*

Calico growled, curling his fists into the fabric of the couch when the empty echo reached him.

More emptiness.

More frustration.

"More need," Calico croaked desperately in that voice of gravel and rocks. "Need you. Lost without you. Gusss."

Gus. Agustin couldn't stand it anymore. The intimate endearment launched him into action. He pulled himself off his chaise and wobbled over to where Calico lay. The need to touch was so desperate; his fingers twitched. Physically touching would boost their connection.

Calico startled at the tactility and gasped. His eyes flung open, but they did not see. Agustin stroked his cheek, his chin, overjoyed when the man turned into the caress and mumbled for more.

Their foreheads brushed, ever so gently. Agustin shifted again, his lips grazing the man's shaved temple. There was a faint drawing of breath, from whom he didn't know. With it, Agustin felt a faint mental pinprick.

It was another attempt. Another failure in mindspeak.

The frustration within them both was growing stronger.

This still wasn't working.

Mutual, penetrative sex would easily, instantly create the path they needed, but Calico was not ready for it. *He* wasn't sure if he was, either.

Emotions from them both were running high; they were still getting to know each other. He didn't want to ruin something that could last.

There wasn't enough room for them both on the window seat. Agustin trembled. If he moved them to more comfortable surroundings, would he be able to control himself?

Yes, if he concentrated on what needed to be done.

He stood, drawing Calico into his arms. He carried him across the parlor and used his knee to open the door to one of the bedrooms. The firm mattress welcomed their bodies.

Agustin adjusted his position, wrapping himself around the baker from behind. He nuzzled that shaved head between ragged breaths. *{: . . . r me?:}*

A quick, disruptive psychic pain. Choppy and incoherent. Enough to cause Agustin to spasm.

Calico yelped with excitement, but there was a stressful scowl on his sweet face. *:}:{¡Te oigo, te estoy oyendo!:*

Calico heard him. And responded in Spanish! A connection was forming, yet their mind-voices remained separate and fractured.

Agustin shivered. Calico shivered, then moaned when Agustin renewed the urgency to meld their mind-voice into a single unity.

There was an instant change in their shared mental stage. The edges of the landscape sharpened into fierce clarity. There was indeed a herd of horses on the hill. Watching over the equines was a large, hairy figure, turned away from them. It was a lycanthrope.

Agustin's attention was lured away from the scene by Calico himself. *:This... this is all {so strange,}* the baker thought.

{We've nearly done it.: Agustin responded. *:Opened a path of coherent mind-voice between us. The static between our unique mindspeaks is starting to fade}:*

{Keep working,: Calico urged. *{:It reshapes the more we communicate.}*

:Thank you, for letting me inside your mind. Agustin found his vocal cords worked now when he chuckled. *Ah, it appears the differences in our telepathic languages have finally melded. I was hoping it would do so.*

Calico listened carefully to his own reply as he sent it. *Indeed it has. Now, for the most grueling experience.*

What's that? Agustin asked.

I...am...ashamed. Embarrassed of my weaknesses and failures. That I have been reduced to this frigid ugliness.

A heavy wave of grief eclipsed Agustin's heart. *Calico...please. You are not weak. Don't say that. You have nothing to be ashamed of.*

Then I will show you my shame. There was tearful grief expressed in the reply.

In their shared mind's eye, Agustin felt himself spun around, and for a second, he thought Calico was pushing him away. The Mirror Bubbles shimmered and faded, as did the rolling green hills, the lycanthrope, and the grazing horses.

Ice and frost took their place. Yet the element was not clear and beautiful. It was dingy, coated with the slimy, oozing madness of a celestial curse. As it settled over him, Agustin folded his arms in an attempt to ward off the sharp chill.

Again, his heart ached as this otherworld curse began to pry at his edges, slipping through the cracks of his own defenses. If he stayed here much longer, it would begin to corrupt the core of his powers as well. He could already feel it pressing, pushing against his telepathic safeguards.

Behind them, a colossal network of fleshy cables and knots floated, spanning hundreds, if not thousands, of feet over their heads.

They were dark. Thorny. Jagged. Most were bleeding profusely in several places, and the blood dripped, puddling at his feet.

There were many more shapes and knots, tumultuous and matted in texture. And others encased in iron and steel-like coils of rage and godlike energies.

It was there that Agustin sensed a deeper version of his gentle baker. Calico's true essence lost, hidden. And trapped inside.

Chapter 49

Inside The Curse

Awe and repulsion were his first impressions. Agustin chalked that up to the celestial animosity emanating off this phalanx of writhing and pulsing connections in front of him. He turned back around to inquire how they may proceed.

But Calico was gone.

"Where are you?"

No answer.

"Calico?" he asked, louder this time.

This close, came the faintest of echoes. *Sucked in.*

"Where do I start?" Fists clenched at the urgency, Agustin shouted out into the mental void. "Calico!"

The response was so faint that he could not understand. Agustin reached out but stopped before he ran forward to chase. Where did these connections lead, if anywhere? Where was the primary source? The heart of it all? Running about in a panic would not bring answers.

Looking at what he assumed was left and right, then up and down, he remembered he was in the realm of the mind. Hard directions and literal thinking had no place here. So he mentally focused on the core that was his fussy baker. Permitting himself to be pulled in that direction,

Agustin drifted along, growing more alarmed by the second. The smell of festering, unclean rot grew stronger. So did the ice.

As he reached his target, he was already covering his mouth and dry heaving. Was he also doing so in the real world, he wondered? Perhaps.

Agustin sensed the damage here was much older, powerful. His heart hurt that Calico had had to suffer this for so long. Alone.

The stench was so thick even the cold couldn't mask it. Tendrils lashed out, waving madly. Embedded in those limbs, grief and guilt flailed in aggressive, intense waves. Agustin touched one covered with glistening muck, seeking a weak point.

Blood and diseased pus sprayed across his face. Even though this was all within Calico's psyche, he rushed to spit it out. The curse was the curse, and he couldn't take the chance that he, too, could be infected. Or perhaps he already was.

What was done, was done.

Pressing onward, Agustin made a grab for one of the misshapen tendrils. Once. Twice. Thrice. On the fifth try, he gained purchase and dug his demonic claws in. The spongy tissue gathered grossly under his nails. Another stench arose. This one the rot of damp mold and ice.

Following it was the cloying blanket of hopelessness, rage, destruction. Frost instantly manifested, shooting up the thrashing tendril. It sluiced onto his own limbs in an effort to destroy him; Agustin only tightened his grip. Beneath the curse, Calico's essence engulfed him like a clean, hot summer wind.

I'll not leave you, Calico. Do you hear me? Fight it with me.

Focusing his telepathy and his inner strength into a fixed point on the thrashing tendril, he speared right through it.

The ice intensified, rushing to swallow him whole.

Agustin responded in kind by summoning the demonic element within him. Flames erupted with volcanic force all around him. Somewhere beyond, he sensed Calico's helping hand and renewed his push forward.

The tendrils caught and crumpled to ash. The grasslands reappeared, and they too went up as if it were a trail of gasoline. The imagery of the rolling hills, the lycanthrope, and the grazing horses all burned, and disappeared.

Fetid ice turned to slush, then evaporated over the coil of knots and barriers that was Calico's mind. Fire rioted forward, cleansing the stench, and raced along the next phalanx of tendrils as if it were dry kindling.

Excitement and joy rushed through him. It was working!

Gus!

Agustin's heart skipped. Calico was here. Unseen, but his voice heard strongly this time.

The flames! Calico cried. *Agustin...itfuelsme...too much too soon! The power of you! Of me. Cannot...contain both. Losing control!*

The atmosphere shifted. Calico's thoughts were cut off when Agustin felt the building pressures. Of two like-elemental powers combining, demonic and avian, becoming more than what they once were.

Together.

The flash—the heat was phoenix level—blinding him, ripping at the edges of his own fiery limits.

Burning through the curse, cleansing every trace of it.

Then all was dark. Agustin didn't know if it was his doing, or if all the flame in Calico's mind had extinguished. He carefully moved around in this black void, trying to feel his way.

Something beckoned him before he saw it. In the distance, a flicker of light, no bigger than the head of a matchstick. And he sensed it. This was Calico.

Agustin felt himself running toward it. And like in a dream, he made it no closer. But this flame was calling to him, urging him on. Encouraging his fiery element to burn as it had seconds before. So he permitted his inner fire to breathe and was instantly yanked forward.

There, at his feet, was a human-size bird of glowing milky white. Agustin was awestruck at the breathtaking majesty. His heart thumped faster. His palms went damp, and his stomach twisted in nervous joy.

This was Calico. In his true physical magnificence.

Raising a hand to shield his eyes, Agustin admired the impressive crown of pearly alabaster feathers. The long, slender neck joined a sleek, elongated body that was sprawled and still. So incredibly still.

Casting a telepathic probe, Agustin sensed no curse. No darkness. The fire had cleansed it all. Calico was free. Agustin gasped with joy, but it soon turned to fear.

Calico wasn't moving.

Alarmed, Agustin knelt, searching for signs of life by stroking the shiny, hot feathers that glided like satin past his fingertips. In response, drooping wings with a single blue-and-white feather each, jerked at the touch. It brought tearful relief that Calico had made it through.

And then Agustin was hit with the psychic sense of Calico's full presence again, this time without barriers. Without a curse.

Agustin tittered and laughed. Cried and choked. He fell back on his ass and wheezed as he moaned and giggled. A small part of him realized the madness of the universe against his mind crept closer, ever closer, but he didn't care.

Comfort. Beauty. Without physical or mental limitations. Lovely and horrific chaos in vast fields of nothingness. And more he could not even put into words or begin to comprehend—

It was there Calico halted his quest. Tenderly buffering him from greedily traveling any further. To protect Agustin from going insane at the essence of the fabric of life. Of encountering the core of time and space. By creating a degree of separation from their shared mental being. Agustin knew his journey inside the mind of a god, mostly unscathed, was due in thanks to his angelic nature.

Hands shaking from overstimulation. Through blurry, teared eyes, Agustin gently cupped that slim avian head. Intricate patterns, almost like tattoos, in glowing black and green, streaked over each side of the phoenix's face, the hooked beak, and parts of the feathered body.

"I'm so glad to have found you." Agustin's voice broke, his feelings getting in the way. "Calico, you shine within. So bright—brightly. You're free."

His arrival must have fed the quiet, lazy flames flickering against Calico's avian body, for they roared upwards in a solar flare. The impressive tail train, twice the length of the body, convulsed. The crane-like legs spasmed and scored the ground with razor-sharp talons. With another gentle touch, Agustin coaxed the fire element into obedience, and Calico calmed.

As the phoenix form shifted into human, Calico sighed and his eyes closed. Agustin startled at the change in his friend's appearance. Calico's white-blond hair fully haloed his scalp. He was thinner, paler than usual, and his features haggard.

Green filigree designs decorated the left side of the baker's face, while heavy jet-black shapes similar to parched earth and lightning adorned the right. A raven-hued stripe split these patterns, slashing diagonally from beneath the hairline, across the bridge of his nose, down his neck, under his left arm to his back, where it crept up the opposite shoulder.

His left arm was covered in these lightning marks. An ancient, unknown magic radiated from them, and these birthmarks pulsed and shifted as if they were alive.

But once the thick cover of the fiery white feathers retreated, a shocking sight was revealed.

Three bioluminescent eggs.

Naked, Calico curled in on himself, guarding those eggs.

Agustin stared, fascinated. Then he recalled this was all inside Calico's head. Was this a symbol, perhaps? Yet, he still didn't know what to make of what he was seeing.

Two of the shells radiated a beautiful marbled blue-and-white sheen, each pattern distinct but just as spectacular. The runty one in the center was a bright shade of creamy alabaster. Wisps of weak white smoke arose from this pale egg, and it swayed delicately on its own, as if to say hello.

Agustin caressed Calico's cheek. Those sweet blue eyes opened, and stared blankly. Worried, Agustin sought the quickest avenue of communication.

Calico? How do you feel?

The only reply he got was drooping eyelids.

Why was Agustin starting to panic over this? Because of the emptiness he sensed? He carefully probed around the edges of Calico's mind. The rawness was so overwhelming that he was jolted right out of their shared link.

Back in the physical world, Agustin gasped for breath, his hand digging into his chest, as if begging his heart to stop beating so rapidly. He then noticed two things. The bed sheets and mattress beneath them were charred, flaking away into pieces as he moved. Their clothing, the same.

Tall flames, pale white, surrounded them, snapping and crackling. Reaching out with his own demonic affinity to fire, Agustin tried to contain it. Shape it. Either he was too weak from the cleansing, or it was beyond his abilities. The element reared up in a storm of deep offense, and bit back at him, exploding, sparkling, growing. Agustin could not even cry out.

There was a whoosh. Etney suddenly stood over them, arms spread wide, gathering up the last of the unnatural colored flames eating at the headboard.

The white fire coiled obediently, encircling her in a chaotic twirl. Yet it never touched her directly. It was strangely buffered away from her own scarlet flames, as if an invisible wall separated the two elements.

Soot smudged her face and Infinity Corporation uniform, but the material did not burn due to a magical retardant. Her eye twitched, and her head and body jerked every few seconds.

"You...you all right?" Her voice was high and thin.

Senses returning, he noted half the room had become a tinderbox. Dear gods! She'd saved the lives of his staff, their team, and his estate. And was now containing the energy of not one celestial being, but also a god. The power of the Dasheel forge was truly amazing.

He had to take a deep breath before he could speak. Char and smoke filled his nose and mouth, its texture heady and welcome. No strength left for telepathy. He barely mustered enough to respond in Spanish, instead of his easier, native demonic tongue.

"Es...estoy bien. Gracias."

Etney levitated upward in a churn of red and orange flames before flying full speed out the open window. Seconds later, high in the sky, there was a bright flash, and the whoosh and roar of an explosion as she released the power she had contained.

It took all Agustin had, just to lay his head back on the burnt pillow before he passed out.

Chapter 50

The Loom

WITH HIS PHYSICAL SELF unconscious, Agustin floated within Calico's anoesis; he didn't know for how long; he just existed within this blinding mental bliss. It could have been minutes. It could have been hours. He prayed it was not days.

In this universe of Calico's mind, there was unfettered joy. A lightness of heart and no sense of time itself. Calico's essence was bouncing, vibrating at its freedom.

Agustin called out many times; his inquiries were only absorbed into this strange etheric mist. He felt himself lost, yet at home, and he wondered if these sensations were residual echoes from their telepathic union.

He had to reestablish contact, to bring them both back to the physical world. So he centered himself, and channeled a little more energy into his hail. The second he sent out the call that it was time to return, he was knocked from the pleasant mental surroundings. The numbing elation became deep, gut-wrenching sobs. Calico's sobs.

Instant guilt assaulted him. And shame. He'd shattered the thin embryonic shell that buffered the celestial from the mundane, and was beckoning Calico home. Back to the clumsy and primitive mortal husk that cruelly weighed him down. Yet it had to be done.

Calico, he tried again. *Please. Strive for calm. Reach out to me, let me anchor you. I can help buffer the transition, the intense sensations.*

Dizzying, shivering, echoing cries were the only response.

Agustin braced himself, diving deeper into their psychic connection. He examined the surrounding mindscape.

Chillingly empty and alone.

All of Calico's mental safeguards had burned away with the curse damage. Perhaps he'd made a grave error by permitting their demonic and phoenix flames to merge and burn it all out.

It hadn't just been the great-grandfather's punishments that were obliterated, but also the self-blocks that allowed a god of space and time to function in such a tactile existence.

But...perhaps it was for the best, to start anew. Mental corruption cast by curses and celestial manipulation usually left deep scars that could only be patched and regularly maintained. There were few powerful enough and experienced enough to wipe the entire slate clean, as he had done—with Calico's help. It was best to rebuild with a stable and blank foundation, and it would take both of them to succeed in such a grand task.

Calico's echoing grief became weepy, spent. The man was weakening. If Agustin didn't act quickly, Calico may truly become the god of space and time, and fully lose any grounding of himself, his physical body, and the sense of the physical world. Forever.

Grounding. Anchoring. That was the key, and he wondered why Calico's brothers had not done this in the first place—perhaps because they were unable. Agustin searched around, looking for something he could use. Only the castoffs of rotting mental flesh and pools of slush remained.

There was nothing else but himself to work with. So he stopped where he was. Bracing himself again, he plunged a hand into his own chest and yanked out his heart. Agustin stared at it for a second, watching it pump and jerk.

He hadn't realized what he was doing until now. And that he had done it without a thought. There were only two other people he would ever do such a thing for.

His beloved son.

Diana.

Until Harper had driven her away for good. And he'd stupidly allowed it to happen.

And now Harper was trying to destroy that rare gift of joy and contentment again. He couldn't permit that. Not when Agustin thought that maybe he had some small chance at being truly happy again after so long.

Shaking the distractions out of his mind, Agustin looked back at his heart. Taking the manifested organ between both hands, he pulled at it until there was one whole, perfect heart in each palm. Shoving the ghostly, ethereal copy back into his chest, he studied the original.

It would become his prime template. From that, he would produce the many layered buffers that would permit them to rebuild the foundation of Calico's mental blocks.

Working the heart between his fingers and applying pressure, he transformed this powerful, yet intangible representation into the length of fibers for weaving. These fibers would become the vertical warp threads that would lace his loom and create his project.

Next, he pulled on the ring finger of his left hand until the image of the bone appeared. He had his bobbin.

From one of his angelic wings, he tore a feather with the firmest vane and barbs. He had his shed stick. The shed stick would separate the warp threads and make it easier to weave.

Now he needed to construct a loom. Wielding the hooked thumb of his demon's wing, he stabbed at the space in front of him. Carving out the square frame he needed. He used fingers and claws for the finer work required—digging notches into the top and bottom of the frame, in one-inch intervals.

Reaching into his mouth, he pulled out the ethereal representations of his teeth. He rammed them into the notches to create pegs. The pegs would hold the heart-strings in place.

Picking up his heart-strings, he laced the frame. Then, running his fingers through his long, thick hair, he plucked enough to weave the tapestry-blanket itself.

Throughout all his preparations and work, Calico's lamentations resonated. Ringing out through the heart-strings as he wove. It slowed down Agustin's shaking fingers, but he continued onward.

I'm almost done, mi corazón. Hang on. Por favor.

Once finished weaving, he ran both hands down the length of the fabric.

A blanket appeared, draped at his feet. Agustin picked it up and tossed it into the darkest part of the void swirling around him. A few seconds passed, and the void paled to a dark gray. It took nine iterations of blankets to transform the gray to match the blues and grays of their psychic-celestial landscape.

The crying lessened, then drifted off into faint hiccups of an uneasy rest.

Calico's weariness became his, and he fell into exhaustion.

Something unpleasant jarred Agustin awake. It originated within the foggy depths deep inside his mind, but he wasn't quite sure of its nature. He likened it to when a trout took the fishing line and signaled the fisherman to start reeling. Yet there was a sluggish delay in that action.

The instant he opened his eyes, he realized he was back in the real world, in a room of his precious Demonym estate. Agustin sat up in the scorched bed.

The scorched, empty bed.

The sky was dark. Rain droned on the roof, and he could barely see if the moon was out. Joe Mist was hard at work keeping the weather pouring, and guarding against any more flare-ups that could burn down the estate.

Agustin quickly noted the empty room and stumbled to the bathroom door.

He knocked. "Calico?"

No answer. He glanced at the space between the bottom of the door and the floor, noting the light wasn't on.

"Calico, I'm coming in." He turned the handle and strode across the tile that stretched as far as the bedroom suite itself.

Dark and empty. He checked the bathtub just in case. In his youth, he'd slept off many alcohol-related stupors in such a cast-iron cradle; it kept him from burning down the university dormitory. It was empty. Backtracking, he scanned the bedroom before searching the shared parlor. Agustin headed out into the hall. His pounding heart signaled his panic. Where?

There, he smelled it. Burnt bread. And fresh smoke that didn't originate from the bedroom suite. He quickly grabbed a robe to cover his charred clothing that was about to flake away into nothing.

Sans shoes, he hurried down the stairs and into the kitchen. Etney and several of his household staff, clad in their nighttime attire, huddled against the wall, watching, and whispering.

Calico was baking. Poorly from the sight and scent of it. Still clad in his charred and soot-stained night gown, the man lumbered. His fingers flailed, clumsily grasping at utensils, bowls, or another baking tray. Items crashed to the floor in an ear-splitting clatter. Calico was not even phased by the noise or action.

"I was about to come get you, señor California," his head butler said.

"What time is it?" Agustin asked.

Etney rubbed the sleep out of her eyes, trying to appear coherent when she heard his voice. She didn't look any worse for wear from her earlier save, but she was staring at Calico in a most particular way. A way that made Agustin uncomfortable.

It...wasn't sexual, but it was extremely, deeply intimate. And he felt it was something he would never be able to comprehend or experience with the one he cared about.

"A little before 3 a.m.," Etney said. "Maars says they usually start baking at this godforsaken hour."

Agustin felt guilty she'd been disturbed. She needed her sleep after channeling all that celestial energy and containing the fire. "Gracias. Por favor, uh, please, everyone, go back to bed. I'll take care of it from here."

Minus an audience, Agustin approached. Calico was glassy-eyed and unaware of his presence. His aura was sparking and sputtering, tense and crackling.

"Calico?" he asked in a soothing whisper. "You need your rest. I'll take you back to your room."

Agustin made sure the stove and burners were off, and that a window was cracked open. He placed a gentle hand on Calico's shoulder and was met with a whimper.

The man was *cold*. Wasn't that dangerous for a phoenix? Perhaps he should recall Etney.

"Calico?"

Calico cried out in that harsh, cracking voice. He dropped the pan he was holding; batter oozed over the tile and soaked into burnt socks. He swayed and closed his eyes. Clenched fists rose to clutch his temples, then he twitched as if that, too, was too much to bear.

Agustin bent, and pulled him over his shoulder. Calico whimpered again at the contact.

"Shhh, mi corazón, I've got you."

Climbing the stairs, Agustin noted Calico flinch and whimper more with each step he took and each minute movement. Fingers dug into his lower back, and he felt the nails dig past his human guise and into his fleshy scales. Calico was bawling by the time they reached the second, unburned suite.

Calico's cries echoed down the hallway before Agustin could shut the door. Pulling back the bedspread, he slid Calico onto the mattress and discovered the fan of tears racing down the man's cheeks.

Then, magnified tenfold, Calico's telepathic scream slammed him to the floor. Agustin clutched at his skull, where he writhed around in agony from the blast. Gasping, he tried to roll back in the direction of the bed.

There, Calico was in a frenzied panic, clawing at his own charred clothing. Verbally screaming, hollering, as if that too, brought intense pain.

Scrambling to gather his wits, Agustin summoned another loom-blanket from inside his mind. The instant the last fiber was copied, he flung out his hand to aid his concentration and mentally cast it over his target.

The screaming and thrashing only continued.

So Agustin flung out another. Then another. And another, and another. All the while he knew the screams went on, but his ears were too numb to hear anymore. His mind was too numb to sense anymore.

He'd lost telepathic-count by the time the shrieks ended with Calico passing out.

Chapter 51

Mindless and Empty

DRAGGING HIMSELF FROM THE twisted, sweat-soaked sheets, Agustin massaged the kink out of his neck and pressed his palms against his temples. His brain felt like the decayed matter washed up on the banks of his lake. He grunted and rubbed at his chest. Both of his hearts were too tender, and ached from the stress of telepathic activity.

Sighing, he looked about the room. His interpretation of the physical world was slightly skewed. While he already had the ability to see auras around living things, it now extended to inanimate objects, such as furniture and drapery. However, since they were once-living organisms themselves, the auras were less pronounced. This new experience was an echo left over from viewing reality through Calico's senses.

Agustin looked to the man sleeping in one of his many guest beds, and saw his future radiating as brightly as the sun. Glowing as peacefully as the moon. The realization staggered him; he sank back on the bed and caressed the baker's cheek. Calico was sprawled, paler than normal, and lifeless.

Lifeless.

Agustin sucked in a whimper. Carefully, he put out a telepathic tether to confirm his heart was indeed resting calmly. The dried tracks of hysterical tears still lined Calico's face.

Cotton sheets barely covered the smooth, pale skin of that shapely rump. Agustin's gaze lingered curiously along the sensual, feminine flare of Calico's hips. Then to the masculine bulge beneath that thin sheet. The baker's body wasn't that different from some of the angels he'd dated through the centuries.

Agustin thought again of those strange eggs he'd witnessed within Calico's inner-self.

The stress of the last few days cracked and slammed into him full force. Agustin staggered out to the sitting room, so he would not disturb Calico's rest. His mind felt like the meat scooped out of an avocado skin. He was truly now a part of Calico's world, his essence. And all the deeply celestial sensations that came with it.

Agustin was still drained from repairing the damage. But he was content. They were coming together. Finally reaching an understanding, and he looked forward to their budding intimacy.

Sound reached his overworked brain as his head lolled against the chaise's backrest. Frogs and crickets continued their calls.

Had he fallen asleep here in his chair? He must have. The lakeside chatter was no more. Gathering his strength, he staggered over to a bell rope near the writing desk and pulled it.

A few minutes later, his personal physician arrived. The smaller man saw the connecting bedroom door was wide open, so he quietly closed it to shut out their noise.

"You called for me, my lord?"

"Good morning, Esteban. Or night. I don't know which."

"It's coming on to dawn. It's been two days, going on three this morning."

Surprise was slow to kick in. Agustin was aware of a light shining in his eyes, but he didn't care.

"Pupils are normal. Good sign."

"Of course my eyes aren't normal."

"Pupils, I said, my lord. Not irises."

There was suddenly a hand in front of his face. "How many fingers?"

"Uh. Five."

"My lord," came the stern warning.

"One up, four down. Esteban, as a gentleman, I didn't think you were capable of such gestures."

"You seem coherent enough, but fatigued."

"Thank you for the diagnosis."

"We were concerned. Etney and I 'been camping out in the kitchen, much to chef's objections."

Agustin tried to make sense of that. "Oh...that long? Why the kitchen?"

"To bring you and your guest food." Esteban pointed to a tray left on the writing desk. Dry toast, and two nested bowls, with broth enough to share.

Agustin picked up a piece of bread, still waiting for his question to be answered.

"The bell bank is in the kitchen," his doctor reminded. "We decided to wait there rather than have a servant take the time to find us. Also, to alert you if Mr. Winghorse slipped away to return to his baking." There was an uncomfortable pause. "If I can say, Mr. Harper's left messages, and even sent representatives."

"Nh." Agustin nibbled on the dry toast and already felt full. He didn't care about Harper, or his demands right now.

"Etney showed them the door."

"Things've been handled in my absence, then."

"Well, I'm not sure about that..." Esteban grabbed his wrist to take his pulse. There was a minute of silence as he worked. "Etney had to restrain those brothers, several times."

Agustin managed to lift his head. "Oh?"

"They both arrived not ten minutes after Mr. Winghorse first began his fits."

"What'd she tell them?"

Esteban unwrapped the stethoscope from around his neck and stuffed the ear pieces into his ears. He poked him to lean forward and then pressed the cold metal diaphragm against his chest. "Deep breath. Let it out." Esteban moved the disk. "Again. Again." He did the same against his back.

Esteban pulled the headset from his ears and draped the instrument around his neck. "I'm not liking what I'm hearing."

"The smoke'll clear out. It always does."

"My lord, it takes longer each time you—"

"My question, Esteban?"

The Menehune doctor frowned at him. "She said you had it under control—for now—and you weren't to be disturbed. She put the brothers in the motorcar, drove them home. Even had harsh warnings to her beau to stay out of it. Told them it was Mr. Winghorse's decision, not theirs. She didn't seem comfortable doing that. She was jumpy. Uptight. And, uh..."

Agustin tried to sit up straight. "What is it, Esteban?"

He pulled a fistful of folded telephone memos and six telegrams out of his pocket. "From ICHQ."

From Harper, he meant.

Agustin collected them. "Thank you, Esteban. The meal'll be more than enough for Mr. Winghorse and myself. I'll ring for you again if he needs attention."

The Healer bowed and departed.

Opening his messages, it was as he feared. Harper was incensed. Each inquiry was more hostile than its predecessors. Harper had demanded the return of the contract via telephone calls. Then came the telegrams conveying great offense at Infinity 3 being physically forced off Demonym's grounds. By Etney. By Triptych. And the gathering of his household staff.

He didn't know if he should be surprised or not at Triptych going against IC.

Agustin leaned over and opened the drawer. The aspirin was in his bedroom desk. Downstairs. Too far to go and too much trouble to get. Sitting back, he closed his eyes and tried to relax. His mind followed the weary trail of calm, and he sensed if he took a few moments, he'd be able to recoup a bit of strength to get through the day.

Knuckles rapped at the parlor door; Agustin jerked awake with a cry. "¡Mi corazón!"

He lifted his head off the little desk. The sun's rays had already crept across the room. He'd fallen asleep again. Agustin struggled to orient himself. Calico. He had to check on Calico. He lumbered up from his chair, but that was as far as he got.

The persistent knock arrived a second time, signaling it hadn't been a dream. He had a moment of indecision. As much as he needed to reach the bedroom suite, he wouldn't have been disturbed without good reason. Agustin cinched his robe and bade his visitor inside. The door cracked open only partway.

Etney stood there, looking nervous. She clutched a ribbon-tied bundle of cinnamon sticks in her hand.

Agustin stretched the kinks out of his shoulder and neck. Dear gods, he was tired. He wanted to curl up beside Calico atop that big bed and sleep.

He sat back down in his chair. "Please, come in, Etts. Keep your voice low."

"Sorry to bother you, but the brothers are back—you should see them."

Agustin knew the disfavor reflected on his face. He didn't have time to deal with them. Especially since he hadn't looked in on Calico in the last several hours.

"I sent a motorcar to bring them," she said. "Agustin, they need to be here—Hey! You can't—"

Both brothers pushed past her and strode into the parlor, hovering right over the little writing desk. Agustin pulled himself out of his slump, eyes narrowed and jaw clenched.

It wasn't until he met their gazes that most of his wrath subsided. They were triplets, after all. Psychically connected. He should've known they'd sense Calico's agony. Nevertheless, he couldn't permit the sight of their dark-circled eyes to deter him from challenging this offensive intrusion.

"How dare you," he said, grimly enough, quietly enough to penetrate their aggressive nature. They hesitated, taking a step back.

There was a faint sob from Calico's bedchamber.

Damnation. He was disturbing him through their fragile link. He had to calm down. Ignoring the brothers, he took a deep, cleansing inhale, then exhale. When Agustin opened his eyes again, both men were heading toward that closed door, worry lining their faces.

With a sharp wave of his hand, Agustin sent out his magic; the door shimmered away, leaving nothing but a solid wall. The brothers collided with that barrier, banging their hands against the surface, raising an incredible racket.

"Stop that! You were told not to interfere," Agustin warned.

"You don't understand. He Burned...he needs—" One brother immediately stopped the other from speaking by violently grabbing his arm. Agustin didn't bother examining which sibling did the deed.

"...Is he...all right?" the other brother asked. "Is he talking? Has he said anything?"

"He's resting." Agustin's agitated tone indicated that there would be no further inquiries. "He'll be home when he's home."

"But—" In one hand, each brother held up similar fragrance bundles to those Etney possessed, and in the other, bouquets of lavender.

Among them were items Calico had been hoarding, along with some he hadn't seen at the house.

"Agustin, please," Etney said. "They telephoned me. They felt something was wrong. Calico needs—"

Wood and plaster sizzled, and a faint alabaster glow emerged from where the bedroom door had once been. The scent of char thickened; white flames tore through the timber and paint.

Calico was torching his way out.

Agustin reversed the wall to its original door state and bade it to open. Maars stepped up and tamed the phoenix fire out of existence before it consumed any more of the suite.

Calico stood in the threshold, his blue eyes glazed over and pupil-less. Unseeing. The emptiness instilled tremendous alarm. The brothers gasped at that blank expression; the noise covered Agustin's own sharp dismay.

A full head of scraggly white hair hung past Calico's shoulders. Agustin knew the baker's mind was still trapped deep within the layers of numbness, for the man hadn't sought a robe. His ankle-length nightshirt highlighted his bare feet. He lurched forward, lumbering into the room in a zombie-like state. Calico didn't seek the brothers. He went directly to Agustin without blinking his heavy-lidded eyes. Without pause or sound. As if the brothers were not even present.

The complete detachment, the focus solely on him, terrified Agustin. It was as if the soul was gone. Replaced by an obedient lump of flesh willing to serve his every command.

When Calico wrapped his arms around him and placed his head on his chest, Agustin was there to catch him as he slumped, drifting back into unconsciousness.

The response from the brothers was instantaneous. They crowded them; one sibling tied a potpourri sachet into Calico's tousled hair.

The other brother—Maars—held a bouquet of lavender and summoned his blue-white phoenix flame. Maars drew Calico close, and an inch from his brother's ear, a torrent of rushed words arrived in their native speech.

Agustin startled when Etney yanked him away from Calico. Just in time to avoid a whirling funnel of that azure-alabaster flame. It whipped around the two brothers. Agustin vaguely noted that Frazil fell back, far back behind him and Etney.

The heat was incredible. Tempting. Divine. Repulsive. Dangerous. The sensations were damaging. Alien enough that he, too, finally sought a slow retreat. His emotions surfaced, the same ones that burdened his heart when Etney had stared at Calico in the kitchen. Etney shuffled in front of him now, as if buffering him from both flames and feeling.

The flames blazed brighter. Etney reached out to it with her own; Agustin sensed she was pushing back on the expanding element, keeping it contained, and from burning anything else. And again, there was that strange void that buffered her red from the white.

His eyes teared from the brightness. Seconds ticked by, and Agustin had to turn away or go blind. Then, as suddenly, the fire blew out. Calico and Maars collapsed on the blackened floor. Naked.

The dark coloring of Calico's hair had returned in a full halo of his scalp. The blank look of his gaze, erased. Filled instead with mute exhaustion.

"He's...he's all yours, for now, Ch-chavez lord," Maars mumbled, voice shaky.

"We promise." Frazil draped blankets over both his siblings' shoulders. "Maars and I'll behave from here on out."

Agustin cleared his throat, too choked up and unsure of what had happened, but feeling their intrusive and chaotic actions, however unwelcome, had been vital.

"I appreciate that," Agustin said. "And your loyalty to him."

"Maars, Frazil, please go now." Etney opened the door leading to the hallway. "Ramirez'll drive you home."

"Of course," Maars said. Then to Agustin, "Please tell our brother we're thinking of him."

Agustin shoved aside the need for questions and curiosity. They were all on edge. Worn out. Answers could be presented another time, when nerves were not so raw and bleeding.

"I'll tell him."

Etney shuffled them out in a hurry, closing the door behind her. Agustin knelt, drawing Calico into his arms. The man had watched his brothers go, gaze wanting and grateful.

"Calico?" Agustin asked softly.

Calico said nothing, but radiating from those glossy blue eyes was awareness. Agustin laugh-choked, never feeling so relieved in his life. Following Calico's cognizance was a powerful, newfound respect. *For him.* One cemented in unconditional trust. It made Agustin even more teary eyed. Calico eagerly welcomed him by holding tighter.

Such trust.

The embrace momentarily seized Agustin's lungs and stole the breath right out of him. His chest squeezed as he grappled with intense mixed emotions. He wasn't sure how to handle this incredible gift.

Agustin staggered, guiding them both into the unburned suite. He tucked Calico into bed, huddled beside the one who claimed his heart, and fell into a confused, exhausted sleep.

Chapter 52

Calico Wakes Up

PREPACKAGED CAKE MIXES. CREAMY peanut butter disks dipped in chocolate, wrapped in brightly colored waxy paper. Chocolate chip cookies.

Vacuum cleaners. Television dinners. Music videos.

Men on Mars. Men kissing Maars.

Calico snorted awake.

Birds were singing. A window must be open. The screech of a jay set his teeth on edge, and he clenched his fists; the noise was unbearable. Were his ears bleeding from it?

He forced open gummy eyes when the breeze drifted over him. The heavy weight of his body was unnatural. The prickling of the air and the bed sheet pressing down on his skin felt like he was wrapped in rose thorns.

Chocolate chip cookies. Chocolate chip cheesecake. Such bizarre and wonderful confections that should not exist for many more years, but did. The delicious, gooey granules melting delightfully on his tongue with a glass of milk were one of his favorite treats.

Grunting at swirling memories and yet-to-be memories that floated within the ether of space and time, Calico mentally yanked on all the telepathic blankets Agustin had crafted for him. He wished he had another. Just to further cushion the intensity of all the incredible mental and physical stimulations drowning him.

Past. Future. Scent, hearing, touch. The stale, cotton-like taste in his morning mouth. He swallowed and grimaced. It set him on edge.

Fuzzy visuals.

He briefly squeezed his eyes to try to fix this one malfunction. Even that was too much to handle. *Taste. Smells. The surrounding fibers of the sheets were a mixture of cotton and bleach.*

He listened to his heart beating. He heard the flow of his blood coursing through his physical body.

There, he halted.

Something kept him from reaching out and claiming the celestial part of what he was. It grounded him enough to know that he had to wrestle for stability. Yet, the blockade had vast defects. One firm poke against it and it would shatter and break. He pulled back from it, terrified.

Stronger. He would soon need a more formidable foundation to keep from going mad. He felt his birthmarks itch and sting.

Calico?

Agustin. Gus. His fragile anchor, his balance. His ultimate joy.

...And...and future pain.

Calico shook that away. He was unwilling to delve into a future-something that not yet was, before he could even experience the present.

Trailing behind this fading foreboding was Mr. Triptych's warning about Mr. Harper and Infinity Corporation. He dismissed that, too. Calico could not, would not believe, because the demon lord's automatic gut response to keep the secrets of a phoenix burn secret, proved him worthy of trust.

¿Mi corazón?

The telepathic inquiry was a blessing, further rolled in Agustin's mental tapestries. Calico didn't think he was prepared to listen to the grating cracks of his voice anytime soon. Or chance trying to speak when everything was still turned up to its highest setting.

He rejoiced. Five more telepathically-woven blankets appeared atop the layers he already owned.

Better?

It was. For now. But he would need more. Calico lifted uncoordinated hands and attempted to use sign language without much thought. But his fingers felt thick and heavy. He gave up for the time being and engaged his telepathic talent.

It almost permits me to feel normal again. Thank you.

You're welcome. Calico, what happened?

Calico paused, sensing, knowing. *Yes, I remember. Maars permitted it.*

Alarm bled into that heterochromatic gaze. *Permitted?*

Calico could not help eavesdropping while currently in his empowered state. Agustin found apprehension and distaste in the word. It festered inside the man's mind and grew roots, and his very precious friend wondered over the frightening turn of phrase.

Ah, perhaps 'permitted' is the wrong term. I am still learning English, you see. Calico fidgeted, unsure of how to further deflect Agustin's avenue of thinking.

His beloved was so close to the truth of the phoenix-self, and he did not even realize it. Agustin had witnessed something so secretive, so sacred, he would figure it out sooner or later. Calico did not know if he had the strength to currently deal with the situation.

Why don't I believe that. Calico?

Calico took a moment. Frazil and Maars had talked about it in-depth behind his back. They knew something like this would happen and were thankfully prepared.

Gus, I Burned.

They refused to speak of it, Agustin thought. *Etney refused, too.*

Gus...I do not...even speaking of it with someone who IS phoenix makes me, and my kind, beyond uncomfortable.

Then we shall not.

Thank you, for understanding. And for not revealing what you witnessed, or what you think you witnessed. To anyone. Even to one of us. Or Ms. Dasheel. I know the two of you are good friends.

I promise you, my heart.

I know.

Agustin's thoughts shifted back to the psychic surgery. Calico rushed to head off the self-flagellation.

Gus, please, do not drag yourself through the guilt. You were correct in your belief that it is wiser to start over, with a new foundation. I have full rein of my powers. I will soon have Gigglemug at my side. All without the dark, limiting echoes of my great-grandfather's curse. You have freed me, and I am grateful.

Agustin took his hand. *We did it together.*

The warmth of his touch brought comfort. *I cannot wait for you to meet Ms. Mug. I know she will be eager to greet you. Perhaps you can match wits at chess and teach her Spanish. She adores languages. She was a marvelous help among all kinds of humans as I traveled across Nura in my youth.*

There was a long pause. *She talks?*

Of course she does!

Another pause. *Corazón, you've had a troubled sleep in the last few days. Do you have much strength?*

With the mental blankets locked in place, Calico pulled himself up from his pillow. He was in a nightgown! He squeaked and yanked the bed sheet up to his chin. He panted at the swift, clumsy movements, and grabbed hold of the headboard to combat the mild dizziness. It quickly passed.

Calico?

I—am well. Yes. Sitting up, I feel a little stronger. Ah, um. May I have some clothing? A robe to cover my nakedness? Perhaps a bath to wash away this...perspiration clinging to me.

Of course.

Gus...I—Did I hurt you, or anyone else with phoenix flame?

No. Etney, Joe Mist, and Maars saw to that.

The words were so final, so sure, that Calico didn't feel the need to pursue what had seemed to be the start of a terrible dream—yet Agustin had been there to protect him.

A moment later, his Heart—yes, that designation felt right—draped a thick robe around his shoulders. Calico drew it forward and cinched the belt.

Calico, are you hungry? I sensed your mind surfacing, so I rang for another meal. There's broth waiting.

Calico dragged himself out to the shared parlor and together they sat at the small breakfast table.

Getting stronger with each passing moment, he thought to Agustin. *I think a hot bath will mend things nicely.*

I'll draw one for you when you've had your fill of something to eat.

Calico tried to pick up the spoon with a hand that wouldn't quite obey him. His thick fingers pushed it along the tray as Agustin watched.

Embarrassment, surprise, and warmth pooled in Calico's belly as Agustin slowly nudged it back within his reach. A few seconds went by before Calico mastered it. He flinched at the first bite as mental and physical scurried into their proper places.

Getting easier, he thought to Agustin.

I'm glad.

Gus?

Yes?

Calico waited a few more moments to be sure of his surroundings. The alignment between space and time, matter and pure energy, and the smaller, physical world. *Now that I think upon it, I am feeling good. This may be the best opportunity to use my portal. The energies flowing through me are fresh and vibrant.*

Agustin, sitting across from him, placed palms on the table. *Is that wise?*

I think it wise.

Calico, are you certain of this? *You've only just woken up.*

I want to do this. With this clean slate, there will be no need for lengthy calculations and lengthy planning to slow me down. No errors brought about by physical limitations. I will be able to reach into the exact timeline and landscape required by Infinity Corporation.

Agustin's brows crinkled before he finally nodded. *How long do you think we have? To do all of this?*

Calico thought about that. *Three days—at the very most, but we should not dawdle. We must begin, now, today, before I become fully accustomed to my physical body and can start discarding the blanket blocks—well, I...I would rather not discard them yet, with your permission. And...my physical coordination seems to be shaping up. Ah...*

What Calico wanted was embarrassing. Humiliating. Even with someone he had begun to intimately trust.

Agustin hovered a hand over his. Silently asking permission to offer comfort, and waiting patiently. Hoping. Wanting. And then Agustin conveyed relief and joy when Calico laced their fingers and squeezed.

I...want to use my voice. My first few tries after days of silence will...not be pleasant.

"Then use it," Agustin said aloud. "And the blanket blocks are there for you to keep or dissolve as you see fit."

Calico gulped as Agustin's smooth, cultured accent battered his ears. Sound coming from within himself, and from without, took some adjustment.

His own deep, grating, offensive grunts followed. "We. Need to. Discuss plans." With every instance, he was nesting back into the physical world. "For the portal."

At each word he butchered, Agustin's expression did not break from adoration and encouragement. Calico's heart swelled from it.

"First, must bring it here. From England, anchor it. However. Still searching for a proper hiding spot."

"If you'll trust me, I have the place in mind. It's a mile or so from Cooley Landing," Agustin said. "Accessible but uninhabited, except for the wildlife, of course."

Calico thought it over, gauging the sincerity. He *did* trust this man. *Had* trusted him with his life, with the secrets of a phoenix. Agustin was a local. He knew the area. The idea was sound and wasn't too far from his home territory in Redwood City.

Clasping that warm hand, Calico nodded in acceptance. "I also. Wish to do this before I return home. Before my brothers are aware of my recovery. I will not have them present at the portal aperture. I will not risk them. Even if I am magically stronger with them at my side. Rupart will sense my presence as my portal opens. He will be ready for me."

"But we broke the curse?"

Calico shook his head. "Only *I* have been freed of it. But perhaps how we went about it, will provide future insight of how to free my great-grandfather."

"Once rested and recovered, I might be able to—"

Again, Calico indicated a no. "Rupart is an elemental of ice. It is upon myself and Frazil to secure his freedom. However, I am still not strong enough or experienced enough. But one day." Calico pressed closed fists against his stomach. "Gus?"

"Yes?"

"I must have a chat with you about Rupart. I know you think you can handle him, but I feel we must plan our course of action for his arrival. He *will* come."

"A strategy."

"Yes."

"Tell me more then, about your great-grandfather."

Calico shivered, hugging himself. "The stories Grandfather Acanthus told of what took place before my hatching were enough to make the blood of a fire elemental freeze, for good."

"Mi corazón," Agustin replied gently. "I am much more than a fire elemental."

"I-I understand. But Gus, what you must not do is challenge Rupart telepathically. He is too powerful."

Agustin lowered his eyes. "You don't think I could match him? After what we've just been through together?"

Calico wrung his hands. "I...I do not know. I do not want to cast false hopes. Please do not take such a risk."

"I can't promise, corazón. It sounds like I'll have to think on my feet."

At that declaration, Calico slowly stood, clutching the side table for balance.

Agustin came to him. "I have you." Then tenderly caressed his cheek. "You need a shave."

"I...I am not coordinated enough to wield a blade right now." Calico nervously rubbed his hands together, then pursed his lips as Agustin's fingertips brushed an intimate caress over his mouth. His touch tasted deliciously of salt, smoke and char.

"I would be honored to perform the duty." Agustin's husky murmur caused a lovely riot within Calico's heart. "But after your meal. And perhaps you'll allow me to revive that unusual hairstyle."

A blush heated Calico's cheeks. "I would be most pleased."

Although he'd downed that spoonful of broth to please Agustin, it had been vile and off-putting. His stomach was just as delicate as his current balance of celestial versus physical.

Agustin had excused himself to make urgent telephone calls to Infinity Corporation, brief his Infinity 8 team, and to grant him some privacy. So Calico had taken a quick sponge bath. He had been smart enough to brush his teeth before he dressed; he'd made a mess and mopped up the splatters as best he could. He gave up trying to brush his hair and tied it back into a messy queue.

Wishing to help things along, Calico set out his shaving instruments and stirred up the lather in the small cup. Glancing at the straight blade and leather strop, he decided he'd leave it to Agustin to sharpen the tool. He was still likely to cut himself.

A knock came at the bathroom door. Calico set his shoulders back and glanced at himself in the mirror. He was dismayed at his appearance and adjusted a terribly tied cravat.

"You may enter, Gus."

Agustin stepped inside, his gaze dropping to Calico's stubbled chin, then to the embarrassingly sloppy knot. He glided forward, reworking the bit of fabric without asking. Calico lowered his eyes, as it was all so intimate.

That intimate silence reached all the way down to the tips of Calico's toes. Unsure what to do, he waved his hands a bit nervously. Agustin's fingers joined his, then slowly disengaged to drift across the stubble.

"A striking contrast, this snowy white grit against the black." Agustin reached back to untie the ponytail, drawing the dark hair forward over Calico's shoulders. "I do find it attractive. But from the way you were glaring at yourself in the mirror, I take it it displeases you."

The contrast displeased Calico greatly. He'd never gotten the hang of shifting the color of his whiskers. Just his hair. Only full-blooded Gerin could morph everything.

Instead of allowing his tongue to trip over his mouth, Calico picked up a hairbrush and presented it to his companion. As if encouraging Agustin to proceed, Calico ran a hand over his head. Agustin motioned him to the chair.

A comb replaced the brush. Careful attention created his preferred part. The length on his left side clipped short, and the remaining shaved to the bare skin with a steady hand.

When the blade gently scored his jaw for the first stroke, Calico sunk further into the bliss. Focusing his senses upon Agustin's attention to this task. This willing gift. Of a quiet, intimate moment. Together.

More short, gentle scrapes, going with the grain, and moving slower in the harder to reach spots. The simple pleasure was over much too soon. A towel gently dabbed away the shaving residue. Then there was another comfortable lull.

Agustin's thumb pad reverently feather-kissed his bottom lip, causing Calico to open his eyes.

The urgent knocking at the suite door jarred them. Agustin opened the entrance a slight crack. A note was passed within. The paper crinkled as Agustin read it. The corners of his mouth turned down. It was happening quicker than they anticipated.

"Mi corazón," The endearment was low, gentle. "We have to go now. The oracle's group is moving into position to cross over. Within the hour. Allies won't be able to distract Rupart for long."

Calico made a quick check to assure he was presentable, then they both headed for the exit. But once there, Calico touched his sleeve.

"Gus. Merely think of them. As we make our way to Cooley Landing, I will cast a telepathic aperture across space-time. The three of us will be able to communicate in real time."

In that moment, Agustin cupped Calico's cheek. As if to tell his sweet baker to be careful. As if to convey that there was so much more between them that needed to be said.

In answer, Calico stretched up on unbalanced tiptoes to offer a shy, but quick peck to Agustin's lips. Then, together, they hurried out to the garage.

Chapter 53

The Portal Aperture

STANDING IN COOLEY LANDING's parking allotment, Calico tried to ignore the brisk bay breeze. Agustin encouraged him to consume a few pieces of sliced fruit that Sally's employees passed around on trays. It helped quiet the rumbling in his gut and the trace of dizziness in his skull case.

A large group of women and men milled about. They leaned against passenger motor buses, talking low. Among them were Infinity 3. He recognized two of the men who had trashed his bakery. He was curious to know why they sported black eyes, but he would not inquire. Calico withdrew into himself and tried not to fidget. Infinity 3 avoided trading glances with him.

The crew Agustin had called wore dark blue uniforms that looked far more suited to the soggy landscape than his coat and cravat. Ms. Dasheel was among the crowd, wearing the same uniformed trousers and long-sleeved tunic.

Calico flinched. Her demeanor was radically different from before. The warm sparkle in her eyes had been replaced by commanding daggers, and a slash of flattened lips erased that familiar cheery, easy smile. Calico trembled at it. She was ready to jump into a battle if need be. It made him wonder how old she really was to have such grit in her manner.

Agustin came to his side, his hand lingering on his coat sleeve. Meeting those blue and honey eyes lessened Calico's panic.

"Are you ready?"

Calico nodded.

Agustin turned away from him and lifted a small triangular broach into the air. Twin almond-shaped gems that reminded him of cat eyes gleamed blue, and a portal materialized.

Through this magic-induced tear, Calico witnessed foggier skies and spongy marshlands. The crew gathered immediately and stepped through, single file.

Calico had wondered why they had not driven to the site Agustin had chosen. Now he had his answer. As he crossed over, his boots sank into the quagmire. A motor vehicle would have sunk in the sludge.

Patches of heavy gray clouds muted out the morning sky and played hide and seek with the sun. Mist drifted. As they traversed along the jagged cut of the bay shore, half of the terrain was solid enough that he didn't sink down to his ankles, thank his mother goddess. Trekking the other half, however, found them working their way through the thick, soupy landscape. A few of the younger recruits Agustin had picked up were huffing and puffing with exertion.

Dirt, more sludge, and dew from the sprawling flora left muddy splatters up to his trouser knee. At least he could feel his toes, but for how long? His own shortness of breath was caused by a combination of his anxiety to get there, his recovery, and the walk. He was utterly miserable, cold, and wet for a phoenix-blood, yet he did not complain.

In front of him and walking with Agustin, Ms. Dasheel did not seem bothered by their environment at all. Following immediately behind himself, were Ramirez and Joe Mist. And beyond them, Infinity 3, and the rest of the group Agustin had rounded up.

Calico had not been officially introduced to any of their party. He did not think it an oversight. He was somewhat glad, especially in his delicate condition of being caught between ethereal and physical. Perhaps Agustin felt it would distract him. Perhaps it would have.

Occasionally, mice or rats darted into their path and scurried back into the low brush and grasses. The appearance of rodents caused him to dip his hand into his coat pocket and grip the tiny jewelry case that housed Ms. Mug.

Perhaps not today, or tomorrow, but he would see her again, soon. His fingers shook at the thought of her return, and he did his best to contain his excitement. With her awakening, he would be whole.

Agustin glanced back at him a few more times, concern carved into his brow. Calico realized he needed to begin the required mathematical calculations for space-time. So he turned his mind inward, to draw his portal onto new home soil.

When Agustin stopped and pointed over the gently lapping water, Calico's gaze lingered at that desolate spot. Glancing behind the troops accompanying them to gauge how far they had come, he could see the foggy outline of Cooley Landing in the distance.

Shivering in the morning air, Calico considered the landscape. It was quiet, save for the rustling of waterfowl and other small animals. There was no sign of people-activity, other than themselves. Fog swirled around his feet, but there were pockets of visibility.

"This is an ideal point," Agustin said. "Private, and far enough out so it won't be discovered. Close enough to Cooley Landing that should anything go wrong, you have help. Is it acceptable?"

He liked Agustin's idea of nesting his creation within a cushion of cold water. It was the last place a possible future adversary would look for the secrets of a wizard whose heritage was primarily phoenix.

"There are strong energies here. It is more than satisfactory."

Agustin squeezed his shoulder. "Then, are you ready?"

There was strength in Agustin's voice. Despite it, Calico tucked trembling hands under his armpits.

"I have not opened it since we arrived on Earth. I have let it sleep. And...Great-Grandfather Rupart may be listening on the other side, ready to sense the slightest ripple of my magic. What if the Rupart-creature comes through—? He will. It is my childhood home, after all."

Agustin stepped so close that Calico savored the warmth of his demonic element. Calico leaned in and inhaled the heat through his nose.

"That's why I've brought assistance," Agustin said quietly. "They know what to do, and to stay out of our way. Their purpose is to direct the refugees crossing over and keep them safe if there's an incident."

The indirect mention of the men who tormented him and destroyed his bakery did not bring the comfort Agustin assumed it would. Though it was nothing but suicidal to rebuff aid when it was present.

Especially since he knew the Rupart-creature would come.

"Yet, your team, Infinity 8—"

"Our team," Agustin corrected. "You're one of us now. And despite our team being cast as undesirables and burn outs by the Corporation, we *are* capable of going up against a high priest. We protect our own."

"Your aspiration provides hesitant hope." Calico wiped sweaty palms on his coat.

"Do you need some privacy to prepare?"

Calico shook his head. "As I am, I can do this immediately. We should hurry, though. The ease of viewing the proper window into your oracle's exact space and time is slipping away as we speak."

"Yes." Agustin waved his people into position. "I've been feeling the link I have with her fading. Do you want me with you as you do this?"

"I would appreciate that very much."

"Calico, mi corazón," Agustin looked like he was going to touch him again, but did not. "I won't let Rupart harm you," he promised. Then he nodded at the angels and demons around them. Ms. Dasheel, Ramirez, and Joe Mist stood off to Agustin's side, ready to receive and direct the travelers.

Calico took a deep breath and shuffled his boots at the edge of the bank. It would be much easier throwing off his human-self. Using his phoenix body to awaken the portal by drawing it within his fiery form and spiraling along with it. But exerting that amount of energy now would fell him in his current condition.

With his hands lifted at chest height and fingers spread, his magic coiled forth. Sea-foam green mist curled out over the bay waters. He used this mist to drill into the sediment and transform itself into a low pier that rolled out several yards atop the water. The magic continued to glow and glitter.

Calico flinched and twitched as residue from his spell loitered in his throat. The price of using magic had never been a pleasant one. His craft seized a stronger hold than usual on his vocal cords, as this was powerful wizardry. He wheezed, unused to the sensation after such a long time, but soon found his balance.

His voice would be silenced for three days due to the creation of a walking platform. It would suffer silence for three additional days when he yanked his portal out of England, to plant it here, in America. His divine powers would use the space that was carved out here, to patch the rift left behind in England.

Breathing deep, he walked to the edge of the sea-foam green platform. He sensed Agustin close behind. Calico braced himself. Raising his arms high, he pictured England in his mind, arrowing down the focus to where his pinprick of a portal slept, safe and sound.

Slowly, Calico drew in a breath and languidly exhaled. He was tapping not into his magic now, but into the core of his being that was space and time. Taking another breath betrayed him: it was ragged, terrified, snaking its way through his quivering limbs like lightning.

"I'm here," came the quiet voice directly behind him.

Gus.

Calico felt safer surrounded by the silent power of the man who had welcomed his heart. Agustin's heat warmed him through their clothing, they were that close. The demon lord's strong hands lingered tensely atop his shoulders, ready to spring into action.

Agustin lowered his head, his lips hovering at Calico's ear, nearly distracting him. "We're all here to protect you—your demon lord most of all. If he comes, Rupart will never touch you."

That promise sent a surge of thrilling energy through him. The power gripped his spine, flooding through his veins. Calico lifted his hands higher and pulled, literally hand over hand, at the unseen threads of the universe. As its vessel, it funneled into the shell of his body. Calico patiently waited for it to reach capacity.

Then, drawing in a slow, deep breath, he leaned forward. Lifting a palm beneath his chin to serve as a directional guide, he took his time, exhaling.

A smoky, glittering, black mist left his throat. It crept out onto the bay water, and hovered at the edge of his walking platform. From that mist, the images of three clock faces manifested before them.

The primary mass of whirling energy was as tall as a man. The two flanking it were no greater than a hands-width. Upon all three, tiny numbers emerged from a center point, then followed along the coiling arms of a spiral.

The digits grew larger as they spun toward the outer edges of the circles. There, the numbers fell, where they faded into nothingness, and the cycle continued, unbroken.

Calico studied his work. The transplant had gone much smoother than he had hoped. Briefly, a pang of loss for his familiar's companionship breezed by, but he tucked it away for later. Gigglemug would be awakened soon enough. But she would be displeased with him for missing this grandeur.

He paused for a few seconds, taking a deep breath.

Now to open it and access the world he'd once called home. He knew Frazil and Maars sensed the portal's rebirth through him and were beside themselves with fear. Unable to help, unable to find him, as he had masked his whereabouts through magic. He did not want them harmed.

He frowned, distracted by their welfare and mental well-being.

Courage, comfort, and strength arrived in the form of Agustin, standing closely behind him, the man's thumbs gently brushing his collar.

Calico turned his attention back to business. He placed his hands against the two smaller clock faces. With his left, he spun the face counterclockwise. Then, his right twisted the second circle clockwise, stopping both at the number thirteen.

Just as quickly, he pushed both clock manifestations skyward. The portal's light paused, as if frozen in time, then it seemed to skip and stretch.

Taking another deep breath to settle his nerves, Calico stepped back, with Agustin matching him step for step as easily as if they were coupled for a ballroom dance.

The fabric of space before him split. The burning, celestial scent of space and time rushed into his nostrils, fueling him, embracing him.

And then all was well. No longer did he feel the creeping advance of trivial emotions like anxiety or need. His mind and soul encompassed all, and beyond.

The rip spiraled, and grew larger. Another clock face formed within this primary one; it too, twisted into a hazy black spiral.

This was the other side of his portal. Backwards numbers appeared along these arms—because he was looking at it from behind. The digits originated from the center of the portal, growing bigger as they cascaded, until, finally, they reached the edge of the clock face and fell off, fading into nothingness.

Calico heard many voices raised in awe and excitement. Upon the other side was a crowd of milling shapes. Seconds later, the silhouettes flooded with color and detail.

The veil between worlds had fully split, and he stared, heartsick, at the bright summer sky, and the lush green rolling fields of home.

Home. His chin trembled.

Slowly, Calico lowered his arms and drew his mind-self back into his physical body. Opening the portal after all this time made his bones feel as sound as peanut brittle, but he knew the sensations would pass.

When he blinked to adjust his vision, a woman appeared. The oracle Infinity Corporation wanted returned, Calico guessed. She was tall and lithe. White flowing robes and a hooded green cloak contrasted with her black skin. Long, neat braids wrapped with green and white ribbons framed a youthful face. She wore the colors of his mother goddess, the Goddess of Life. His heart bumped at the emotional pull.

Behind the oracle, the crowd surged forward, dashing through the swirling sea-foam green mist. They spilled out of his portal, and into this realm.

Multiple screams and shouts arose.

Those waiting at the back of this group suddenly broke and ran in several directions. Some dashed through the portal, careening into the oracle; others scrambled away, back into his homeland to hide.

However, the woman was still far enough inside the other world to witness the cause of the unrest. Her tight shoulders and hand to her mouth doubled, nay, tripled the fear seizing Calico's heart. His legs rooted, rendering him unable to run.

A shadow loomed over her.

Spinning back toward them, the oracle looked straight at him—or just above his head, to Agustin. Panic lit up her dark eyes; her shouted warning flew forth in Spanish.

All around them, poised on the bank, the soldiers under Agustin's command readied weapons and ushered their newfound flock away.

Agustin's fingers bit into his shoulders. "Rupart's here."

Calico shivered.

"I'm here, too," Agustin said softly. "Steady. Wait for my order."

Screaming from the other side continued. And then the crowd ducked. A man-sized figure with large wings crafted of ice shot over their heads and rocketed through the portal.

The Rupart-creature flipped back those deity-granted wings of ice. And hovered menacingly. The curse had morphed Rupart even further than Calico remembered.

White hair hanging in strings resembled dirty icicles. His wings were no longer clear and shining bright, but frosted over and jagged all around.

Hands and arms were mostly bones. His face was no better. His beloved great-grandfather had completely succumbed to the death god's revenge, as Calico had long feared.

Calico sensed, felt, when the creature's dark purple eyes found him. There was an echoing shriek of rage, and the fetid scent of death grew thick on the bay breeze.

Rupart circled above, taking in the lay of the land. Examining the Corporation troops. Then those eyes only existed for Agustin. And him. Rupart dove.

At him.

Great-Grandfather laughing with him.

Swinging him up in his arms, making horse noises. Then teaching him how to ride a real one.

Holding him as he cried when Mother and Father left home, left the country... Leaving them, him, behind. Forever.

"Wait," Agustin breathed into his ear. "Just wait."

Calico was already frozen by the guilt. Fear welded him into place. Rupart's skeletal hands reaching for him, coming closer, closer.

I did this to him, Calico thought, his tears gathering. *My fault for just being.*

Then Agustin's telepathic command flashed through his mind. *Down!*

Agustin pushed him to the ground and loomed over him. A shock wave, one originating from Agustin, swept loose soil, rocks, and brush off the landscape. The overpowering smell of sulfur, wood smoke, and roses was at the heart of it.

That same shock wave revealed the stunning grandeur of Agustin's mismatched wings. Just like the ones decorating the gates of Demonym. The hard, leathery skin of iridescent blues and purples on one wing complimented its two counterparts covered in long, celestial ivory feathers.

With another whoosh, those massive appendages arced forward, slamming into Rupart. The powerful blow repelled his great-grandfather across the entire bay.

Calico squirmed around to witness the magnificence of Agustin's true form. A form that never manifested during their telepathic dances.

Nimbus rays of Agustin's angelic heritage emanated from only one side of his head. It was as golden as his one honey-colored eye.

Opposite the nimbus, a single, matured horn curled back off his skull. Just as magnificent as any crown. A second set of two black horns sprang from atop his head. A pointed tail curled restlessly around digitigrade legs and feet.

Patches of bluish-purple scales peppered Agustin's flesh. The most visible one under his golden eye. But it was the additional reveal of that heterochromia that captivated Calico. The blue eye was surrounded by black sclera instead of white.

Such...such unique beauty. Such grand magnificence...

Before Calico knew it, that trinity of mismatched wings shifted and flexed. Agustin launched himself into pursuit. Calico fell back against the sheer magnitude of that lift. Covered his nose and mouth. Struggled to breathe as Rupart met Agustin's challenge.

Calico was vaguely aware of the Infinity teams moving to better vantage points. Ferrying more people through the portal. But the battle above was all Calico wished to see.

It was primal, physical. Skeletal claws pierced flesh and scales. An attack that branded with frostbite and possible death. Agustin erupted into waves of whipping fire.

Calico chewed on his knuckles, spellbound. Fire would only turn Rupart away for mere seconds—his great-grandfather was too intimate with its element, even if he was a vessel of ice.

The Rupart-creature was laughing. A choppy, violent hissing wheeze that filled Calico with terror.

But Agustin was his heart. He could not let the man fight all alone. Calico knew he had to step up. To save himself. To keep Agustin from the harm he himself had brought to this world. And he had to save Rupart, too.

Calico engaged his telekinesis, and sent it forth like a boxer's blow. Deliberately striking his great-grandfather, and foiling a renewed attack. It was a mistake. He'd drawn attention back to himself. The creature hissed at him, abandoning his battle with Agustin.

And charged him.

Calico froze, another heartbreaking memory flashing past. Rupart turning on him and his siblings. The numbing grief rose, for he alone was the cause.

"Calico, the portal!" Agustin shouted. "Keep it open!"

The call jarred him from ancient regrets. The gateway was collapsing. Flashing in and out of existence—because of his fears and doubts. The travelers accessing his gateway were screaming. Trapped between worlds, trapped within space and time. Going mad from the touch of the universe.

Calico clenched his fists and concentrated. The portal stabilized. Even as Rupart closed the distance, coming ever nearer. To him.

In the instant of a blink, his great-grandfather jerked. Screamed. And fell out of the sky, plowing into marsh and mud. Then remained still.

Calico heaved, shaken by the ordeal. He knew Rupart had succumbed to Agustin's psychic attack. His demon lord had taken advantage of his distraction.

"He won't be out long." Agustin was doubled over in pain from his place in the sky. Wings flapping rapidly to keep himself aloft. "Syd!" he cried.

"We're all clear," the oracle shouted back.

"Calico," Agustin commanded. "I'll drag him back through. Be ready to close—"

The crackling slush of ice drowned out Agustin's words. Looking down, Calico soundlessly shrieked. And jumped back. And back again. The swift rush of the frazil ice for which his brother was named, approached with tremendous speed over rocks and dirt. Towards him.

Agustin landed beside him, casting his fire element in an effort to keep it away. Each step Agustin took slammed through the approaching icy barrier, melting it instantly. The demon lord grabbed Rupart's limp form and dragged him roughly toward the portal.

The grotesque malevolence radiating from Rupart's twisted features made Calico hesitate. Yet it was his duty to see this through. So he followed.

Even then, Calico witnessed the surprise attack in slow motion. The Rupart-creature broke free of Agustin's grip with a surprising kick. Turned, and sprang for him as they made eye contact. Panicked, Calico lost his balance and fell into the mud.

In the same instant, Agustin was there. Bleeding into the space between him and the Rupart-creature through his teleportation talent. Bringing with him a fiery wave that reeked of ozone.

Skeletal arms flailed over Agustin's shoulders. Directing the elemental ice toward Calico's boots. To drown him. Torment him as he suffocated under an element that was not his own.

Voice removed, Calico screamed in silence. He tried to crawl away. Yet he felt as if he were weighted with bricks.

"Will...not...permit...you," Agustin snarled through clenched teeth. He clutched at Rupart's skull, his claws digging through rot and flesh.

Both men went limp, falling, sprawling out over the cold ground. The ice halted its advance.

The silence was too sudden. Too jarring. The battle had shifted into the depths of their minds.

Stumbling, Calico crawled forward. He fell atop the heap of flesh, scales, and bone. Cradling them both, his sobbing cries eerily mute.

No! Gus! His fists pounded the demon lord's back. *Gus! No, no! Come back! You can still come back! Do not follow him in there. Too dangerous! Too powerful. Ah, Gus, I cannot lose you. Gus, please! I LOVE YOU!*

There was only telepathic static in reply.

This had not been the plan. Calico had warned him. Advised him not to challenge Rupart in this dangerous manner. He dared not help. Or follow. Despite the psychic progress they had made. Entering a mind while in his agitated state could mean death for whomever he touched, for he had no barriers or safeguards re-built.

The cautious hopes. The plans. The dreams he had foolishly dared to believe were possible. It was all now out of his reach. The man he willingly gifted his heart to was going to die.

Calico crumpled beside their still forms. And mourned without a voice. Minutes did not tick by, but dragged. Every second slowed to torment him. He had hated being the god of space and time only once before today.

He gasped. *Space and Time.* He had wallowed in the curse's despair for so long he had forgotten the true nature of himself. Snapping out of his grief, he sat up straight, held his breath, and focused inward. Then sent out a call for help.

Chapter 54

Telepath vs Telepath

AGUSTIN HADN'T KNOWN THE horrific sight of true fear and terror until now. To see that life-snuffing ice snapping, crackling. Reaching for Calico's boots. To watch as his baker frantically try to kick it away. Too distraught and scared to fight back.

It caused him to snap.

So he'd punched a brutal hole into Rupart's psychic defenses. His target jerked and convulsed. Agustin was appalled at his own savage cruelty. Of forcing himself inside Rupart's mind without a care of how it'd been accomplished. He could still hear the outside echoes. Sense the cerebral discards of Calico's silent cries. But he had to press on. To protect the man who had become his Heart.

Consumed within this mental pitch-black limbo, Agustin suddenly bent over. Gut-wrenching sobs robbed him of breath. Such ferocious, soul-consuming grief. Squeezing. Sucking at his heart, the nexus of his essence.

He didn't realize his own quivering, clawed hands had ripped into his chest until his skin and scales were shredded. Warm blood waterfalled. He was desperate. To reach it, to kill it. Just so it would stop beating. *Stop feeling.*

No. Not me. He healed the damage with a touch to his midsection.

Had this been a psychic attack? Or Rupart's agony? One that the elf relived in a horrific cycle? Agustin hadn't expected such loss and torment. But if he didn't do something, Rupart would fell him with the onslaught of negative psychological power, just as Calico had warned.

With a blink of his eyes, and a tilt of his head, Agustin made the half-nimbus cresting his skull glow brighter. It not only buffered him against the despair, it revealed a disturbing landscape.

The jagged pieces of ice he'd come across within Calico's psyche made sense now, for here was the origin. Spikes jutting from above and below, like the inside of a cavern filled with stalactites and stalagmites. It reminded him of the teeth of a deadly predator. Some of the razor-sharp blades were shiny bright, while others appeared to be dripping with fresh blood.

Agustin maneuvered carefully around these obstacles. As he walked, he recognized the faint outlines of doors within the formations. Some were ajar; many more were firmly shut. Barricaded with great timber beams and ancient wrought-iron locks. Others were wide open. Even more broken barriers hung sadly from a single hinge.

Some of the barred entries burned bright with phoenix energy. Perhaps they were attempts made by Calico's kin to contain parts of the curse. Most of those doors had not held.

Quickly sifting through the tiny bits and pieces he'd picked out of Calico's life, Agustin focused upon his adversary. Bracing himself, he knew two things. His presence had already been detected and he was being tracked, or his opponent was still catatonic from his forced entry.

"Rupart Bright Terra," he called out.

No answer.

Agustin crept forward, on guard. The elf's true psyche had to be somewhere. Drawing abreast of an open door that shone with freshly vivid psychic activity, he carefully looked in.

Among the rolling green hills, Rupart's curse-broken husk stood distracted. Spellbound. Scattered horses of demonic and faerie origin grazed calmly. Rupart seemed to be mourning.

Horses. Winghorse. Agustin now remembered why the name had been so familiar. Winghorse was the designation of soldiers chosen to protect and guard the equines of old and their descendants. Like Pegasus and Sleipnir. But...Calico was not from this world. How was he tied into this—?

Distant thunder rumbled, as if in warning. Then quickly surrounded him with its might. Being inside this elf's mind, Agustin sensed this thundering elemental force was a representation of Rupart's self. Signaling that some part of the man still had the strength to fight back, even if he had fallen to the curse.

Within the swirling backdrop of darkness and ice, of heavy mist, the wraith who had once been Calico's great-grandfather now faced him. Here, Rupart was more tattered and broken than he was in the real world.

Decayed flesh and guts hung in tiny ribbons on gray skeletal bones. Threadbare clothing clung in rotted strips, seemingly the only thing holding the frame and form together. This empty husk hovered for a time, staring with hollowed eye sockets glowing purple.

In that moment, that pause, Agustin again sensed a small kernel of the man within. And there was hope that one day the curse could be broken. But it wasn't now.

Rupart moved so fast, Agustin only felt the devastating blow. He found himself on his back, limbs twitching, and a thin layer of stinging frost spreading quickly. He had to get up. But he'd been struck in the chest. Through blurry vision, Agustin deduced it was some sort of lance or spear. The shaft rose above his torso.

Breathless, and by touch only, he grasped the object, discovering it to be sticky and cold. At that second, it seemed to pulse. Inside his chest, several narrow pinpoints scored his innards. Agustin convulsed, coughed. Tried to breathe. His vision darkened.

A quick scan with his psychic senses revealed it to be an arm bone. A glimpse of the stock-still skeleton confirmed the truth. Rupart's skull tilted sideways, and the jaw opened. To laugh. The dead, mocking sound shook Agustin to his soul.

Another pulse rocked him. The bony digits clawed forward. He cried out in agony. Terror sluiced over him.

For Rupart was going after his heart.

Going after Calico.

Will not let you, Agustin raged. He seized the decayed and fleshless arm with both hands and pulled with all his might. His body jolted again. And bowed as skeletal fingers grasped tissue and organs to hold on. The pain blinded him. Agustin choked. Gasped. He tasted the blood pooling in his mouth. His heart pounded. Ever faster. As if to run from the hand seeking to seize it. Crush it.

Through it all, a wolf's howl flooded his ears and echoed in the distance. This was his nightmare. It had arrived to haunt him. The werewolf. The firebird. The bone-winged wraith.

Fear awarded Agustin the inner strength. Terror that Calico would try to enter this fight in his current condition, and that his Heart would die if he did not act.

Will and purpose renewed, Agustin summoned the angelic light within, melding it with his demonic fire. It had been a long time since he had pushed himself to this level. The maelstrom of it was like that first breath of air after surfacing from a deep ocean dive.

Agustin tore the flailing arm bone from his rib cage; relief arrived when the hand and all five fingers were still attached. But even as he wrenched it from his chest cavity, the spikey digits scrabbled at him, reaching, clawing in their bid to seek his heart.

The howl came again. So close that the evil he held at bay turned away. Ripped from his grasp to chase its true target.

A biting wind scented of cinnamon, rosemary, and the woody smell of juniper cut past. Agustin startled as a bulky white mass sailed over him.

The white lycanthrope.

Within this wolfy shape, were two more shapes. But each incarnation of wolf was layered over the other, and slightly out of alignment. Three sets of sharp, furious teeth met the threat of Rupart's arm.

The crunch. The snarls. The snapping of bones.

The violent struggle stirred up an ethereal mix of frigid mist and white-hot flame. Thick bands of steam drifted. Reassessing the scuffle, Agustin beheld the pale-pelted werewolf. Despite the beast's long, thin limbs and protruding rib cage, its powerful jaws had broken Rupart's arm in several places.

His nightmares.

Heed your dreams, my son, for they have meaning.

The battle. This battle with his Heart's great-grandfather...

This lycanthrope. The alabaster-colored flames.

Calico was here.

Rupart's apparition was nowhere to be seen. That meant...

Agustin dashed forward. *Hurry! He had to hurry.*

Just in time to block Rupart's remaining fingers from slicing into Calico's furry underbelly. The three out-of-phase Calicos yelped. Whined in surprise. Curling and shrinking down in submission, tails between their legs.

Rupart's decaying purple eyes glowed brighter. The dead madness seemed to feed on the terror radiating from Calico's spirit forms.

Making the curse within Rupart stronger.

Agustin refused to let it consume them, again. He reached up and yanked off the half-nimbus shining at his head. As he swung it down on the wraith, the shimmering light in his grip morphed into a gleaming fan of steel. The blade cleaved a deep, gaping slash into the bones. Leaving their foe paralyzed.

Agustin knew it wouldn't be for long. Arcing his triple wings, the blasting force pushed his adversary back. Then, thumping his fist to his chest, Agustin manifested even more light. From it, he drew a spear capped with three sharp prongs. It crackled with lightning.

Rupart rushed them again.

Agustin launched his forked weapon, hitting his target square in the chest. The wraith crumpled. Twitched. Bones clicked and ground together as it tried to free itself. To pull out what pinned it down.

"Calico." Agustin touched the shaking bundle of beasts at his feet. "Hurry. We have to go."

The three Calicos turned up their muzzle and whined again before their wolf forms faded from view. Agustin followed behind, opening his eyes in the real world.

"Hurry..." Agustin mumbled. "He's trapped. But not much time."

Calico was there, back in his human-self, helping Agustin to his feet. Together, with other members of I-8, they dragged Rupart's unconscious body toward the portal.

Kneeling at his great-grandfather's side, Calico reached out to the twisted husk, but hesitated. Fists clenched, and chin wobbling, he turned away.

Gus, Calico called. *The momentum of a gentle push will sail him home.*

With Etney and Ramirez's help, Agustin lifted the unconscious elf and permitted him to drift back through the curling ether of the portal.

"He's made it," Agustin said. "I can see him resting on the grass—Oh! A white phoenix comes! Is that—?"

Calico raised a hand, then waved sharply. The portal view on the other side froze. Then through it, a dizzying blur of motion. Crossing mountains and shoreline, flashing even faster across choppy ocean waters. The portal on the other side came to rest on an island shore, one with bright sun and sandy beaches. Waves crashed. Then, the portal in their realm popped out of existence like a soap bubble.

Startled, Agustin wondered at the abrupt dismissal, then realized it was for the best. It would do no good to dwell on the sorrow or leave the gateway in Rupart's back yard. It was done. He turned his attention to Calico.

His Heart rewarded him with a weary, relieved smile. All Agustin wanted to do was stride across the short distance that separated them. To berate Calico for his foolishness of entering the battle and putting himself at risk. Then embrace him, kiss him, hug the stuffing out of him now that he was safe.

Instead, here Agustin stood on weak legs. Trying to regain his equilibrium, and chase the numb chaos of a stranger out of his mind.

Calico blinked. At him. The shaken, exhausted gaze communicating that he accepted the reprimand. Agustin staggered forward, one foot in front of the other, giving in to his desires.

Their embrace was feeble, both using the other as a crutch. Gentle, clumsy kisses punctuated heavy breathing. Kisses that peppered across cheeks, bumping over noses, and along chins before the journey came to an end with a tender wrestle of lips. Frantic hands rubbing across shoulders, brushing back tangled hair.

"Mi corazón," Agustin cried softly. "Why? Why did you risk yourself? You had no psychic safeguards. What you did could've been the end of you."

I called for help.

"Help? From who?"

Calico smiled. *From myselves. From the future, and across dimensions. They lent just enough grounding, just enough balance and foundation to protect me. Guide me.*

Agustin sobbed and laughed and drew Calico closer. "I thank them, and you, corazón."

A crowd of bodies and footfalls rushed past, disrupting their reunion. It was the soldiers he'd gathered. Reminding Agustin they weren't alone. The operatives swarmed and surrounded. Jostling them on accident. Frantic of their own accord. Rushing, guiding scattered travelers away from the echoes of a violent battle.

As much as Agustin wanted to hold onto Calico, the real world was intruding. He sensed what was coming. For the discarded thought-threads told him so.

Chapter 55

The Aftermath

CALICO PULLED AWAY FROM Agustin. Anxious and confused. The citizens of his homeworld had witnessed behavior meant for closed doors. His shame and embarrassment roiled.

The telepathic blankets Agustin provided were tearing at the weight of his unfettered and ungrounded psychic abilities. Calico could hear the whispers. The disgust. The rage and deep offense. *The judgment.* His eyes filled with tears. Was he starting to hyperventilate?

"Corazón." Agustin reached out to comfort, but his hands drop to his sides. *"I'm sorry.* I didn't mean..."

Calico shook his head and dug around in his pockets for a handkerchief to blot at his grief. He sniffed and dabbed at his nose before tucking it away. He motioned along in sign language as he continued their private conversation. *Gus. I will...be all right. I am...mortified. The shock will pass. I take responsibility for my own actions. I do not regret showing you my affections, especially under the circumstances we just endured. The terror and pain you endured. For me.*

"Corazón..." Agustin stood there, dejected.

It made Calico feel worse.

More soldiers arrived, disrupting their melancholy. Agustin waved off those who crowded around them. Calico tuned out Agustin's verbal interactions with his troops.

As if the conclusion of their mission had signaled a change in weather, the rolling fog quickly burned off. The sky became bluer, and the hard chill that gripped Calico's bones retreated.

His lycanthrope senses alerted him to the loud splash. Three more splashes followed. Calico turned, studying the bay waters. Multiple ripples from four points undulated vigorously. He sniffed the air. Nothing but damp, muck, mildew, aquatic fowl, and rodents.

Calico gripped Agustin's sleeve. Now that his magic had robbed him of his voice, he furiously used his sign language and sent the mental message at the same time. *Did...did you hear that?*

Agustin looked up from his conversation with Ms. Dasheel and Ramirez. "Hear what?"

Calico glanced back to the bay, feeling strangely worried. Was he still coming down off a deity high? Was it his imagination? Or had their robust skirmish disturbed the numerous waterfowl? He dragged his attention away from the shore.

Ms. Dasheel and Ramirez glanced at each other, then Agustin. "We didn't hear anything," came their disjointed chorus.

Ah, never mind, then, Calico sent as mindspeak but continued to use Sign. It was too much of a habit due to his magic use.

Calico turned back to the water. Why was this bothering him? There was a thread of...something he could detect, but his ethereal senses had waned. He'd fully assimilated back into his body once he'd closed the portal. The only task left was to rebuild the foundational blocks of his psychic powers.

Agustin's commanding voice sounded far away as Calico continued to watch the ripples. "Etney, Ramirez, Joe. Please help escort the travelers to Cooley Landing and get them boarded onto the buses. Calico and I will follow shortly."

A presence close beside him snapped Calico's attention off the water. It was Agustin. Decision made, Calico melted into his embrace.

Agustin tensed. "I thought..."

Calico clung tighter. *Hugs are risqué, and barely tolerated. And I apologize for my reaction. It hurt me to see you caught between ideals.*

"We'll work through this, my Heart," Agustin replied with quiet warmth. "So I repeat that answer to you. I want you to set our pace."

Calico's fists clenched against Agustin's back before they relaxed. *No. We will deem how we carry out our relationship. Not the Earth citizens. Not the people of my homeworld. You, and I. Together.*

Agustin's arms came around him willingly. All Calico wanted to do was hide in that suite that they had shared and burrow under the blankets. Just as he was still hiding under the psychic ones Agustin so thoughtfully nested him beneath. For the sake of his sanity.

Handling the portal had sapped his strength. The phoenix Burn had reset all he had worked for. He dreaded relearning control, the rebuilding of all that was torn away. But there was now hope, and someone to support him as he picked himself up and moved forward.

Calico tried to summon a smile, but he was too spent. He toyed with the ends of Agustin's silky hair, laden in moss and sweat. Just wanting to lean into the strong frame that protected and loved him.

"My Heart, about your great-grandfather."

Agustin was circumventing his attempt to put family and the incident out of his mind. The pain was too fresh. Calico turned to study the water that continued to unnerve him.

A roughened palm gently cupped his cheek. Calico glanced up.

"Rupart may be cursed, but you'd be proud to know how much he's fought against it. Every step of the way." Agustin's hands rested atop Calico's shoulders. The weight brought comfort.

Calico stared at the ground now as his fingers made the signs. *Gus...thank you.* Then he clutched at Agustin's broad chest. *I...I wish to kiss you again,* Calico only thought, as he was not brave enough to put it into physical words. Lest someone read his Signed words. *But...but...*

"Give yourself time to be brave. Be kind."

His resolve and courage failing, Calico beheld the retreating group. These were people who had crossed over from his world. His homeland, his culture.

Would his life continue as it was, or would it become more complicated as they joined him in this new society? Maars's advice of a simple show of affection did not seem so easy now. But he refused to let anyone dictate how he was to love.

It's all right. Agustin lazily brushed at the marshland residue soaked into Calico's cravat. *We have the time, and the privacy of Demonym, for when you are ready.*

Calico sighed soundlessly and stepped away from their embrace. For he wanted to do more than hug.

¿Mi corazón?

Calico looked up into Agustin's eyes. Agustin took his time, permitting the beat to weigh between them, further coalescing their private moment. The question came through mindspeak as Agustin took his hands and caressed his fingers.

Will you teach me to sign?

This time, Calico's smile lingered. For dramatic effect, he slowly finger-spelled his answer so Agustin could follow along. *Y-e-s.*

Agustin's deep chuckle flooded through him, bringing peace. They turned, as one, their arms locked together. And staggered through the marshlands, back through Agustin's magically summoned portal. Back to Cooley Landing.

Chapter 56

Agustin vs Harper Round 3

AGUSTIN WALKED DOWN THE cold, desolate Infinity Corporation hallway, his heart pounding in his chest. Up here, on the top floor, the angels passing by didn't even deign to greet him, much less acknowledge his existence. They were of the old guard, the ones who'd arrived on Earth along with Harper.

He hung on to the fact that he had at least gotten smiles and hellos as he worked his way up the stairs to Harper's office lair. The younger generations accepted him, and were willing to give him a chance to prove himself. He had to keep reminding himself of that.

He *had* proven himself. One of the most critical missions had been a success. He'd secured a stable avenue to move their people back and forth between worlds. He'd also made a most dear friend and lover along the way.

The oracle, Syd, was back. Ready to help guide the Corporation after years of training and honing her gifts. Ready to assist in protecting Earth from the Amaranth Empire. And Calico was home, safe in his bed, ready to head out to his bakery in the morning.

Now to deal with the hardest part. Facing Harper with a long over-
due report—at least in Harper's opinion—and without a prearranged
appointment. He knocked on the door.

"Enter, Agustin."

That Harper knew he was here didn't surprise him.

The head of IC was alone. He stood tall in his crisp white suit, with
his hands loosely clasped behind his back. Standing at the large picture
window, Harper looked down on Market Street below. The faint roar of
motorcars and trolleys vibrated through the glass. The fading sun cast
rays that enhanced and magnified the full nimbus at Harper's temples.
The man was relaxed, amicable. That was not a good sign.

Agustin hung his hat on the coat tree next to the door. "Syd and the
others are getting settled among nym populations based in Fremont and
San Jose, with a few handfuls in Redwood City and Palo Alto."

Harper turned around with a leisurely twist. "I'm aware of the attack
during the transfer. A transfer you took upon yourself to manage, and
not inform me was taking place."

Spies were everywhere. It was nothing new.

Harper continued. "It concerns me when I receive reports from lesser
operatives. Why is that, Agustin? I should be hearing this from you."

Because he'd been too caught up in Calico's needs. "I admit my error
in not contacting you regarding the portal opening. We were working
within a tight window. There wasn't time to confer with you." Because
Harper would only talk to him if he scheduled an appointment.

"Yet you had a chance to rouse members of Infinity 1, 3, and 7."

"They were already at Cooley Landing, lounging at Sally's. Luck was
with me. I wasn't certain any of the teams would be there."

"So you would have gone on this mission alone? Risking yourself,
Winghorse, the portal, *and* Ms. Badweather? Irresponsible!"

"I had Infinity 8," he reminded Harper. "And I would've used the general corporation troopers also visiting Sally's, if I'd had to."

"Infinity 8! A phoenix and two humans who have burned out from seeing too much action in the field! That is not a team. My patience is wearing thin, Agustin. You've begun to take chances I do not approve of. I'm debating the risk of keeping you on active duty. You've been moved to a new office. You should be using it."

"Sir," Agustin rushed, "I would prefer to remain where I am. I don't want to be trapped behind a desk."

"You will be trapped behind a desk when you take my place. Is this hesitation because of Winghorse?"

"Not only because of him," Agustin verified. "My place is leading my team. They trust me. We've established more than a working rapport. We're a family."

"*I* am your family," Harper huffed. The jealousy didn't last long. He sat at his desk and drummed his fingers for a moment. "I have a meeting scheduled with Syd and the other team leaders this Thursday evening. You will attend too, of course—as befits the future head of IC. Bring your files, and Winghorse's signed contract.

"It's also your official coronation of sorts. And a trial run to see how well you perform for my upper support staff. It's also a working dinner party. Fancy dress."

And there it was. The gauntlet was down. He'd begun his descent into the rabbit hole.

"I've heard rumors you've fallen hard for Winghorse. Groping and manhandling him in front of everyone after the mission."

It was a jarring accusation. Agustin narrowed his eyes. "You villainize an innocent embrace."

"Pawing at your lovers in public is unacceptable. This corporation has a reputation to maintain. Decorum and dignity, Agustin. Morality."

Agustin clenched his jaw and did not answer.

"My retirement is planned," Harper went on. "As my successor, you're now required to be at my side to learn how to run things. And don't think I've forgotten. I'm still reviewing the suitability of your marriage prospect."

Agustin's gut tightened. He'd find a way to negate his arranged marriage. He continued to wonder how the angels of Harper's generation would feel about a half-breed leading them. A half-breed who favored his demonic heritage instead of his angelic.

Harper wasn't finished bellowing. "Your mother expected heirs to continue her noble California legacy. I expect the same courtesy. You will marry."

"I already have an heir. For California. For you. Ganymede—"

"A bastard is unacceptable."

Agustin clenched his jaw. *Do not call my son that again.*"

"This is not about family," Harper snapped. "It's about business."

Agustin hissed. "You and your snotty angelic pride and—"

Harper slammed a fist on his desk. "How dare you speak to me this way? I respected the mothers of my children by marrying them."

"You think me that much of a blackguard?" Agustin shot back. "I honored Isabella and offered marriage before I got her pregnant. She didn't want to be tied down."

"Agustin, you chased Isabella away with your roving eye."

"No. You chased her away because, as always, you deem any choice I make unacceptable."

Harper continued without acknowledging the protest. "While our kind do have places to go and be ourselves, this is still a human world, and we live in human cities. Thus, we largely live by human custom and expectations.

"Your Diana and Isabella preferred human society. As does Winghorse. In associating with him, it will draw the humans' attention to our kind. And to IC."

Agustin grunted, motioning helplessly. It was something that burdened him, too. He was careful. Humans already knew he labeled himself a demon lord. They respected and avoided the crazy rich bastard on his high-hilled estate.

Gathering his thoughts, Agustin tried to reason. "I know a relationship with someone who has deep ties into human society will be risky. I will risk it. Calico already risks it by living in a human world."

"You still don't understand. A risk not just to IC, but to our nym community."

Agustin flinched. "That's the core of your offense, isn't it? Having to lower yourself and deal with other races. I know you've tried. But you're much too old and set in your ways. Perhaps if you'd been born here like the rest of us."

"You are my heir, Agustin, so start getting used to making the hard decisions and sacrifices. You enjoy work, so work."

Burying himself in work was what got him this assignment in the first place. And a demotion.

Harper tossed a folder at him, bulging with paper. "Your schedule of meetings and reports to read. With the first meeting starting in," he glanced at the wall clock, "two hours. That's two hours to read the material and prepare. You're dismissed."

Chapter 57

Triptych Protests

HARPER IGNORED THE SIDE door that opened after Agustin stormed out the main one. He was too focused on pulling out a file from his drawer cabinet. He spread it across the worn walnut surface, then looked up. Triptych worried and clutched at the veiled hat pressed to his chest.

"So you're actually going through with it?" the regional liaison asked.

Harper met that stormy, heterochromatic glare of blue and gold. Eyes framed by short, ivory-white curls. Eyes that even sported one white sclera, and one black, just like Agustin.

To one with paranormal vision, the godrays kissed Triptych's too-pale skin. Fed those wispy, tiny swirls of white smoke that floated among those curls. The longer Triptych lingered in the light, the more the element slowly morphed into white flame. Harper squinted a little, permitting his old eyes to adjust as Triptych glided over and perched on the edge of his desk.

Harper took offense to the accusation. "Don't take that tone with me, young man. He'll thank me for this later." Harper reached for a pen as he spread out the pages of the portal contract. The header glittered with Infinity Corporation's official seal, the seal that signaled the primary, rewritable contract.

Triptych crossed his arms. "Sir, you're creating nothing but grief and heartache. You'll only have yourself to blame."

Harper ignored him and set about erasing phrases and rearranging the edited passages.

"I will not be a part of this," Triptych pressed.

"Pascalico," Harper warned, banging his fist on the desk. "Bastard grandson or not, I think your shenanigans have interfered with the time-line quite enough. I am genuinely considering what you have shared, and believe it as truth, but I will listen to no more of your origin story. My original plans continue to stand. This is business."

Triptych responded with a frustrated, wolf-like snarl. He shoved his veiled hat on his head, and departed. Slamming the door shut behind him.

Chapter 58

Missing You Greatly

THE BELL ABOVE THE shop door jingled. With his back facing the entrance, Calico glanced up, meeting Ms. Dasheel's gaze in the decorative wraparound mirror. She gasped softly, her attention leveled on his wan face and tired eyes. Calico searched past Ms. Dasheel's reflection, scanning for the demon lord.

She was alone.

He felt gutted.

After the successful use of his portal, and escaping harm from his great-grandfather, he and Gus had returned to Cooley Landing via the same transport spell that had funneled them out onto the marshlands.

The boisterous and disoriented newcomers had separated him from his companion as they jostled toward the motor buses. What hurt and puzzled Calico the most was the approach of a stranger. Agustin had arranged for someone else to drive him home.

Home. Not back to Demonym. But the home Calico shared with his brothers. He had not even been permitted to retrieve his belongings from the estate. Which meant he was sharing clothing with his brothers.

That had been two weeks ago. And not a telegram delivered or telephone call returned. So he'd hooked Dot up to the pony cart and visited the estate. The gatekeeper had turned him away, reporting that the demon lord had not been in residence since the newcomer influx.

Calico worried. Maars had worried as well, for he'd had not heard from Ms. Dasheel either. Until now.

Upon some level, he understood. Agustin was a leader, and his people needed him to lead. But after Agustin had swept him away and freely given his heart, in more ways than one, the loneliness stung deeper. The severe colors and emotions of that loneliness sharpened in contrast. Tortured. Poked at the tender ribbons of their connection.

"Etney!" Maars hurried out from the kitchen.

His brother welcomed her with a most graphic, passionate hug and kiss while, er, groping her, uh, bottom. Calico blushed, busying himself with switching out pastry trays, and thankful there were no customers to witness the explicit act.

"I apologize, firebug," she said to Maars. "It's been a headache getting everyone settled. Then there were the debriefings and orientations! So many, one after the other. If I had a penny for every time I had to explain what a train or motorcar was, I'd be richer than Agustin."

Frazil exited the kitchen, stacked baskets of bread in hand. He dropped them on the counter and joined the conversation. "Cal told us all about the mission and of moving his portal here—after the fact," he said with a sour tone.

Calico's attention drifted from the conversation. He was thoroughly disheartened. Agustin hadn't accompanied Ms. Dasheel, or even sent a note. Wandering over to the window, he stared out.

People bustled up and down the sidewalk, carrying their afternoon packages. It was too much visual stimulation for his troubled thoughts, so he focused on Ms. Dasheel's Daimler Phoenix motorcar. She'd parked it right in front of his shop. Its bright red paint was a fitting match for its driver.

He was in love with Gus. The renewed admission popped into his head, refusing to be pushed aside. Calico knew he should be with Agustin. Supporting him. Was he not also a member of Infinity 8?

But here he still stood at the window. Customers came and went. Calico barely nodded at them, including the regulars, and they, in turn, only nodded back. He was certain they noted his swollen eyes and dejected nature.

"I haven't seen him so depressed since we settled in England." Maars's tone went low when the shop was once again empty.

"Is he ill?" Ms. Dasheel asked.

An illness of the heart, Calico thought. He had finally encountered someone who made the cold exile from all he held dear, a bearable one. And now he felt Agustin's loss greatly.

Maars shook his head. "Lovesick. He was so happy in the last few weeks. But after he anchored and opened his portal, he's been...different. And I feel it's not just the skirmish with Great-Grandfather Rupart. We...haven't heard from Lord California."

"Agustin's been as moody," Ms. Dasheel noted. "He misses Calico too."

Calico perked up at Agustin's name, but did not turn around.

"The Demonym gatekeeper said he hasn't been home," Frazil said.

Ms. Dasheel nodded. "Agustin's been working himself and I-8 into the ground. He's been living in the ICHQ apartment wing. He didn't even come home for any of his clothes, just had HQ personnel go buy him what he needed. I swear, it's a repeat of our life before you three came into it."

"Was that normal?" Maars asked.

"Yes, but this time, Harper has something to do with it. I think Agustin's trying to make a career decision."

"What's that?"

"I'm not sure. Agustin's been juggling three jobs," Ms. Dasheel said. "Being Lord California, leading Infinity 8, and preparing to become the head of Infinity Corporation when Harper retires. It's finally taking a toll."

She sighed. "I think he's really going to give up California. When I visit him at ICHQ, he barely has time for me. He's been trading telephone calls back and forth with the Demon Queen of Mexico, probably setting up an interim leader. We've even hosted her ambassador at Demonym.

"Agustin won't talk to me, or Ramirez about anything. Really, I wish I knew. All the conversations are in a demon tongue, so I couldn't eavesdrop. And Agustin's servants refuse to take a bribe to do so."

"Ms. Dasheel," Calico said kindly. "You cannot eavesdrop upon a telepath. His employees know that."

She sighed again, helpless. "I know, I know. But he's gone back to working himself to death. We have to do something. When he did come home for a few days, the household even tried banding together to kick him out again. Oh, the dark, pulsing rage those eyes shot us. The maids started sobbing. The footman even threw up."

Calico put his palm over his chest, realizing what the numb ache in his heart had been. Agustin had been shielding him from the stress, bottling it all and eating the grief to protect him.

"Oh. We didn't know," Maars said.

"What Agustin needs is a reprieve." Ms. Dasheel's voice was a bit louder now, perhaps to catch his attention.

Calico focused back on her reflection in the window as she continued.

"But today seemed to be a better day," Ms. Dasheel announced. "Ramirez, Joe, and I've bullied him into a single night off to visit a nym-based theater so he can relax. We promised we'd stop harassing him if he went, and he relented. I've got the tickets right here in my handbag."

Calico pivoted and set his attention upon Ms. Dasheel.

"Ah," she cried, looking into the bakery case. "Brownies! Maybe I can use them to help tame the lord beast, at least for a few hours."

Maars grinned. "You're in luck. This is the last batch of the week. Yesterday's ended up in the day-old bins."

"Oooooh," Etney breathed. "More for Agustin, then."

Chocolate and butterscotch were Agustin's favorites. Decision made, Calico spoke up. "Frazil, please package up both the day-olds and the fresh-baked. *I* shall bring them to Gus."

His brothers wrapped up the confections—even bound the container with a blue ribbon. Calico received the box with eager, nervous hands, wondering if Ms. Dasheel would drive him to the estate. There he would wait until Gus came home. A motorcar would be much quicker than hitching Dot up to the pony cart.

Ms. Dasheel fidgeted with her handbag. "I need to tell you: Harper's pressuring Agustin to take over the Corporation, and he's pressuring him to marry for an heir."

Calico felt bad for his dear friend. His knowledge of arranged marriages consisted of awkward introductions, and equally uncomfortable social gatherings.

"Gus has an heir," Calico said. "Surely you have met his son, Ganymede."

"A legitimate heir." Ms. Dasheel rolled her eyes. "Ganymede apparently isn't legitimate enough. It's ridiculous. That poor kid's going to come home from university thinking he'll have a nice birthday and walk into a mess. We need to act. To get Agustin's mind back to where it belongs. On the heart, and family."

"What do you suggest?" Calico pressed. "I will help."

"We need to remind our lord he has something to live for beyond his duties." She unfolded a copy of the Paranormal Gazette tucked under her arm and presented the advertisement. "How would you like to take your overworked beau to tonight's play? There's a party for the cast afterward. For the sponsors only, and, ha-ha, Agustin happened to make a sizable contribution just this morning. Via me, of course. I have tickets to both events."

Calico witnessed the wiggle of her eyebrows—in his direction. He sputtered, his cheeks heating in embarrassment.

She pulled a small envelope out of her handbag. Then, spinning dramatically, she held it out to him. "Here are the tickets. I can drive you home now to dress." She looked at his brothers, her voice no nonsense. "He's leaving work early."

"Not a problem," Frazil said.

Maars grinned and waved. "Have a wonderful time, Cal."

Revitalized, Calico discarded his apron, tossing it to Maars. "That I will. An opera sounds most exciting! Especially if I attend with Gus." He hurried into his hat and coat.

Ms. Dasheel nodded. "Thank you all for helping out." She looked at Calico now, pointedly. "Oh, full disclosure? Agustin thinks I'm his escort."

Chapter 59

Officially A Couple

AGUSTIN CONTINUED TO PACE as he checked the grandfather clock in the grand foyer. He compared the time against the wristwatch Ganymede sent him. Etney was late. At least she'd chosen a venue where he didn't have to put on a show just to enjoy one.

Harper was correct about playing human all day. It was exhausting. Always keeping oneself in check, never slipping with his self-concealment magic spells. Glancing at his watch once more, he could see the steam coming out of his nose.

The bell rang, indicating the curtain would rise in thirty minutes. His foot tapped as the crowd of nyms around him surged into the theater to take their seats. Excited chatter in demonic tongues and old-world fae was a refreshing change of pace.

But he was still waiting on Etney. Hell and fireworks. Where was that infuriating woman?

"My lord, my lord!"

It was Ramirez who made his way through the throng of the nym elite. He was waving a note. Agustin sighed. So help her, if Etney was ditching him at an outing she'd nagged him to go to, to play kissy-face with the eldest Winghorse triplet, he was going to dock her pay for standing him up.

Agustin unfolded the message:

Hey boss,

I'm sorry I can't make our date. Something important came up, and no, it wasn't me eloping with Maars—though that is an interesting and quite archaic idea. I know you hate wasting money, so I'm sending a proxy to fill my balcony seat. And no, my proxy isn't Ramirez, but still precious family.

Hugs and kisses and all that, and your right arm, you'd be lost without me,

Etts

Agustin slid the note into his pocket. The evening might be salvageable.

"Where's Syd?"

Ramirez scratched nervously at his ear, then shoved a ticket into his hand.

Agustin glanced at the seat number, eyebrows raised. A balcony box with a private sitting room. Etney was crazy to spend so much money. What did they need a fainting suite for?

Well, maybe it was for the best. Syd had been showing signs of fatigue over the last few days, too busy getting her people settled and getting used to Earthen society again. She might want to rest during intermission instead of loitering in the halls, socializing.

"She must've come earlier to people-watch," Ramirez babbled in Spanish. "A new culture to take in, and all that after being gone so long. Gotta go, see you at home."

His man left like the building was going to collapse. Agustin shrugged, then headed to stand in line to punch his ticket. Then he took to the stairs, searching the numbers above the closed doors. Finding the one printed on his ticket, he entered the private suite.

He frowned. Next to the leather lounge sofa, a bottle of champagne chilled in a bucket. Silver platters of cheeses and meats were arranged on a heavy oak side table. Beside that was a washbasin full of fresh water and several rolled towels. Hanging from the washbasin was a jar of personal lubricant. And a condom pouch. He recoiled.

What in hells was going on?

Striding across the room, he almost shoved the curtain aside, but composed himself at the last second. Quietly poking the heavy brocade fabric aside a few inches, he looked into the small balcony nook. And felt the wind knocked out of him.

Syd wasn't his companion for the evening. It was Calico.

Agustin hung his head, and his shoulders slumped. Dammit. Etney knew him better than he knew himself. He should have known the instant he read her note.

Calico watched the crowd below. The excitement and wonder on his face lit him up. He wasn't quite leaning over the balcony, but damn near close to it.

He was dressed in his Sunday best. A black silk scarf concealed his half-shaved head. Agustin figured its purpose was twofold: first, to avoid stares from the mundanes on the way over. And second, to dress for the social activity.

But the scarf looked awkward when paired with his cravat. After a moment, Agustin decided it was definitely all Calico. It only made the man—no, the phoenix he loved more endearing.

That was when his heart flooded with love and hope.

Calico sat back in the seat and turned around. His infatuated smile went brighter. It speared Agustin directly through the chest, making him think the heartstrings that joined them vibrated out a sappy melody. Maybe it had. He beheld the orchestra warming up and tuning their instruments.

"Gus," Calico greeted in that husky, grating voice. "I hope this is a pleasant surprise." The baker choked and laughed. His fingers slightly drumming against the bakery box balanced on his knees. "When Ms. Dasheel informed us of her ruse, I pushed my way into it. I hope that is acceptable behavior."

Etney. Etney had left the condoms.

It was a little hard for Agustin to catch his breath. So he outstretched his arms in welcome. And answered despite the emotion clogging his throat. "Mi corazón. More than acceptable."

Calico sprang out of his chair. The bakery box barely made it to the small service shelf set into the balcony railing.

This hug was questing, a little desperate. The heat Agustin had been missing from Calico now rose with vigor. In a smooth dance, they spun, back behind the heavy brocade curtain that concealed them from public view. Agustin wasn't even sure who orchestrated the move. Maybe it had been them both, guided by the heartstrings that bound them.

Their kiss was passionate and full-mouthed. No inch of their lips were safe. It was a tidal wave of greeting, of yearning. One accompanied by wandering hands that brought satisfaction. And wrung an eager moan out of Agustin.

To think he'd willingly drowned himself in Harper's never-ending meetings and schedules. No. Harper had nothing to do with it. He'd lost his way. Again. It had been his own doing, denying himself a second chance. With a dearer friend than he'd ever known.

"I've missed you," Agustin mumbled between heated kisses.

"I have missed you back." Calico's reply was immediate; his soft lips curled into a toothy smile. The high joy was infectious, and their teeth bumped. They laughed together and parted, but lingered close.

Calico caressed Agustin's arms, then eagerly collected the bakery box. He held it out. "A gift. For you."

Agustin kept his heavy-lidded gaze on Calico as he placed his nose to the package. "Mm, chocolate. We should save these for later." And suddenly, he wasn't so shocked and offended at his discoveries in the fainting room.

He enjoyed the way Calico's eyes went big and the flush that spread across his cheeks. Through the curtain parted by Calico's quest for the baked goods, Agustin surveyed the crowd below, reminding himself they were among nyms. They were safe. He leaned forward and boldly touched that precious cheek.

The music began to crest. The lights dimmed further, and the stage curtain rose. A hush settled over the crowd. The opening song echoed.

Calico eagerly drew him to find their seats, his attention fully centered upon the performers. Agustin was a little slower to settle in. He was still too enamored, drunk on love.

A moment later, Agustin was aware of a faint disturbance against his cuff links. Could it be?

Slowly, Agustin shifted to the side, crossing his legs, and permitting his arm to dangle down between the chairs. He propped his free elbow on the opposite armrest and settled his chin in his palm.

Calloused fingers tentatively bumped against his own. It brought a bigger smile to Agustin's lips. He sensed the warmth radiating from this man sitting beside him.

A few seconds passed before there was another shy attempt. Those calloused fingers entwined with his own roughened ones.

Agustin offered a brief squeeze, acknowledging the gift. His heart skipped several beats as the gesture was reciprocated.

Gus?

It wasn't Calico's telepathy, but a discarded thought-thread. Calico was still healing, still needing to rebuild those psychic safeguards. He needed a little help.

I am listening, mi corazón.

Calico's gaze remained upon the stage, but all his attention was focused on him. That thrilled Agustin. Excited him. It allowed an air of mystery. A serious kind of playful mischief. Gentle humor filled their mind-connection before the mood turned serious enough that Agustin held his breath.

Gus, I am eager to explore our pledge. Further.

The request was full of confidence. And love. Agustin felt fingertips stroke and explore his palm.

"Maybe...tonight?" Calico asked aloud, but in a whisper meant just for them. "After the opera?"

Agustin's euphoria soared. He had to swallow the joyous shout. There were still the questions of beds, and the meaning of marriage they needed to figure out. Although working that into the conversation could be as meaningful and intimate.

Sí, mi corazón. I will whisk you away to our lake view suite. Together we can watch the fiery sunrise, and bask in its warmth.

Calico's giddy gasp anchored itself into his heart. Those eyes remained turned away from him, which strangely made everything even more intense. Their fingers continued to caress and entwine.

Agustin watched the actors below, the stupid smile blooming wider on his lips. Who would have thought he would've ever felt joy again?

Here he was, now, holding hands with someone he was willing and eager and hopeful to share his future with, and it was truly happening. He was—*they were*—living for something very precious. Not just existing.

It was happiness truly worth fighting for. And he would fight for it with his last breath.

The Demon and the Phoenix Glossary

Acanthus Yale Breese

Calico's maternal grandfather. The white phoenix god. Rupart's husband.

Agustin Chavez de la Cruz

The Demon Lord of California and hereditary heir to Infinity Corporation. Loves chocolate and butterscotch. Uses magic to conceal his true form.

Amaranth Empire

An empire originating from Calico's homeworld. They have been stealing people off Earth for thousands of years.

Breese Forge

The family group of the white phoenix. The white phoenix forge is on the brink of extinction due to the hereditary defect of being unable to consume or generate enough fire energy to survive.

They wield white flame and take a form similar to the Secretary birds on Earth, but with much longer flowing tails, and head crests. Their feathers are brilliant shades and combinations of white, alabaster, and/or cream colors.

Cadence (Kay-dense)

Agustin's former ward. A member of Infinity 3, former member of Infinity 8. Telepathic abilities. Orphaned. Origin unknown.

Calico Acanthus Winghorse

Baker, wizard, God of Space and Time. Loves cupcakes. Hatched in a phoenix body, his human form is just as natural. Of the Breese phoenix forge.

Charade Winghorse (Sh*uh*-reyd NOT Sh*uh*-rahd)

Calico's paternal biological grandfather. Charade is lycanthrope and demon. Rupart's ex-lover. Chilsaneene's husband. Biological father to Kane Winghorse. Charade is the origin of the curse lineage.

Chilsaneene Pegasus (Chill-san-neen)

Wife of Charade and Myles. Daughter of Rupart. Biological mother to Kane Winghorse. Calico's paternal biological grandmother.

Curse, the

A horrific punishment brought down upon Charade and Rupart for leaving the service of Nolth, Nura's death god.

It keeps the two lovers apart by inflicting Rupart with rot and decay, and the desire to kill Charade (or Charade's bloodline) when they are nearby.

Curtain, the

A magical spell used by Infinity Corporation to keep their activities secret from the mundane human population.

Dasheel Forge

The family group of the red phoenix. They wield flames primarily of red, with, or without highlights of yellows and oranges. Their phoenix body type is similar to eagles with a longer tail train.

They are extremely powerful, able to absorb much more energy and fire than they need, or can handle. This naturally makes them a perfect and harmonic (mutualistic symbiosis) match with the Breese forge.

Demon Lord of California, the

Agustin's noble title.

Demonym (De-mon-nim)

Agustin's estate home. The name is a play on words from the word demonym (pronounced dem-uh-nim). Demonym definition: the designation for people who live in a particular area, country, or state.

Diana Luna

Agustin's ex-lover and ex-fiancé. Co-founder of Infinity 8. She is half angel, and half fairy.

Dot

Calico's pony lives in a barn behind Scrivens Bakery.

Etney Dasheel (Et-knee/Ette-knee)

Second in command of Infinity 8. (I-8). Of the Dasheel phoenix forge. Agustin's best friend.

Frazil Winghorse (Frey-zil, Fraz-*uhl*)

Calico's middle brother of his triplet set. He likes to tailor and sew. Smokes to deal with stress. Wears his hair short and neat. Hatched in a human-like form. Of the Breese forge, but does not have a phoenix form.

Ganymede Chavez (Gan-uh-meed)

Agustin's son. Currently away at university on the East Coast.

Gardenwood

Of noble blood. A lord. One of Agustin's ex-lovers, and Agustin's first serious relationship.

Gerin (Gur-in)

One of several races of Calico's homeworld. They are human in appearance, live far longer than humans, and can shapeshift.

Gigglemug (Also known as Ms. Mug)

Calico's wizard's familiar. A kangaroo rat who appears as a small pewter barrette while in her 'at rest' or stasis form. In this form, her long tail serves as a wrap for Calico's pony tail.

Goddess Triad

The triplet deity sisters from Calico's homeworld. Rattani is the oldest, Ysannee is the middle sister, and Staritti is the youngest.

Harper

An angel originating from Heaven. Founder and head of Infinity Corporation. Father to Agustin and Molly.

Infinity 3 (I-3)

One of the elite groups of angels that patrol the warded boundaries of Earth to keep the Amaranth out.

Infinity 8 (I-8)

A group co-founded by Agustin and Diana to help Infinity Corporation troops who have burned out from seeing or experiencing too much combat. Membership is voluntary but they must prove they are fit to return to active service.

Infinity Corporation (IC)

A gathering of angels and other paranormal beings dedicated to keep the Amaranth Empire from harvesting and kidnapping Earth's citizens.

Isabella

Mother to Agustin's son, Ganymede. Agustin's childhood friend.

Joe Mist

A member of Infinity 8 and Agustin's found family. Joe Mist is a human who is a water/rain elemental.

Kane Winghorse

Calico's father. Kane is the biological son of Myles, Charade, and Chilsaneene. (This minor plotline originates from *The Seasons of the Phoenix* gritty epic fantasy saga.)

Lady California

Agustin's mother. A teleporter with very accurate Future Sight through dreams. Harper's wife. She passed away when Agustin was attending university.

Maars Winghorse (Mars)

Calico's oldest sibling of his triplet set, and often the one sought for final family decisions. Wears his hair shaggy and a bit long. Hatched in a phoenix body, his human form is just as natural.

Mirror Bubble

Calico's signature magic. It surrounds or covers its caster or an object, rendering it hidden and protected from harm. From the outside, it looks exactly like a mirror, or can blend into the environment. When in contact with the ground, it appears as a half-circle.

Molly

Half angel, half sea-dragon. The five-year-old daughter of Harper, and a sea dragon goddess. Agustin's half-sister.

Mundanes, the

Humans without powers. Mundanes are not aware of the paranormal world or its paranormal citizens.

Mutualism/mutualistic symbiosis

A relationship between two organisms/species where both benefit from each other

Myles Starling

Calico's paternal and biological grandfather. Chilsaneene's husband.

Nolth

The God of Death on Calico's homeworld. Priests serving Nolth can manifest wings of creaking bones.

Nura

Calico's homeland country across the dimensions.

Nym (nim)

A (positive) slang term for paranormal. Nyms are beings with extra senses or powers. They can be human, or a paranormal being.

Phoenix

Celestial avian beings that can control, eat, sleep, bathe in, or become fire itself. Each phoenix forge commands a different color of flame. Phoenix is both singular and plural. There are other species of phoenix that favor different elements.

Portal / inter-dimensional gateway

Calico's pathway between worlds. Created out of his essence, and the multi-verses as the God of Space and Time.

Ramirez

A member of Infinity 8 and Agustin's found family. Ramirez is human with no powers, but is still considered a nym due to hereditary ties.

Rattani (Rat-tan-knee or Rat-tany)

The eldest of the goddess triad. Staritti's sister. Calico's aunt.

Rupart Bright Terra

Calico's paternal great grandfather. Lord of Bright Terra, former elf king of the country Nura. Acanthus Breese's husband. Charade's ex-lover.

Sclera (skleer-uh)

The dense, white fibrous membrane that forms the outer covering of the eyeball. Or, as in the case of the Dasheel forge, the sclera is black. Agustin has one white sclera, and one black in his true form. Plural=sclerae.

Star Lands, the

A tropical island archipelago west of the mainland country of Nura, settled by Staritti and her followers.

Staritti (Star-itty)

The Goddess of Life on Calico's homeworld. The youngest sister of the goddess triad. Mother to Calico/the Winghorse triplets.

Syd (Sydney) Badweather (Sid)

An oracle employed by Infinity Corporation. Agustin's former ward. As a child, she was sent to Calico's homeworld because there were better teachers there to hone her powers.

Temple Prime

The home of the Staritti goddess, located in the Star Lands.

Triptych (Trip-tick)

Mentor, benefactor, and guardian to the Winghorse triplets. Infinity Corporation's new regional manager/liaison for the San Francisco Bay Area, which was formerly one of Agustin's positions.

Warrior Priests

Those who serve the various gods of Calico's homeworld. Each deity grants their servant a specific set of wings that reflects the deity's nature.

Winghorse

Calico's family name. Members can choose the surname of either Winghorse, or Pegasus. Generally, the men prefer Winghorse, while the women prefer Pegasus. Also, it is the name of an Earth-based group that protects the steeds of old like Pegasus and Sleipnir.

Winghorse Triplets

Maars, Frazil, and Calico are the Winghorse triplets.

Wolthwatt

A tinkerer and inventor god from Calico's homeworld of Nura.

Ysannee (Yuh san-knee or Is-sanny)

The middle sister of the goddess triad. Staritti's sister, and Calico's aunt. Ysannee has heterochromia like Agustin. She has one orange eye and one blue eye, and hair of white, black, and green.

Also by Bennu Bright

Romantic Fantasy

The Demon Lord of California: The Demon and the Phoenix, book 1

Fantasy Romance

Compass To My Heart: Compass-Born Trilogy, book 1

Short Stories

A Phoenix Halloween Fantasy Ball (Romance)

Gritty Epic Fantasy Rising from the Ashes by 2027 (formerly published under Jeanne Marcella)

Through Rain and Missing Mantaurs
The Phoenix Embryo

About the Author

GREETINGS, MY FORGES! I'M Bennu Bright. It's been my passion to tell stories that entertain. Larger than life characters and adventures are the foundations of my work.

Born and raised in the San Francisco Bay Area, I spend my days nose to the keyboard, or attempting to revive an ancient interest for the arts.

Sign up for my newsletter at *www.BennuBright.com* and receive updates on upcoming novels.

Follow me on socials at *https://linktr.ee/bennubright*or use the handy QR code below.